Forbidden Highlander

by

Donna Fletcher

This is a work of fiction. Names, characters, places, and incidents are either the product of the author's imagination or are used fictitiously, and any resemblance to actual persons, living or dead, business establishments, events or locales is entirely coincidental.

Cover art
Marc Fletcher

Visit Donna's Web site
www.donnafletcher.com
http://www.facebook.com/donna.fletcher.author

Table of Contents

Chapter 1
Chapter 2
Chapter 3
Chapter 4
Chapter 5
Chapter 6
Chapter 7
Chapter 8
Chapter 9
Chapter 10
Chapter 11
Chapter 12
Chapter 13
Chapter 14
Chapter 15
Chapter 16
Chapter 17
Chapter 18
Chapter 19
Chapter 20
Chapter 21
Chapter 22
Chapter 23
Chapter 24
Chapter 25
Chapter 26
Chapter 27
Chapter 28
Chapter 29
Chapter 30
Chapter 31
Chapter 32

Chapter 33
Chapter 34
Chapter 35
Chapter 36
Titles by Donna Fletcher
About the Author

Chapter One

Dawn listened to the tolling bell with a sinking heart. Cree's future bride would soon be entering the village. There had been a flurry of activities in preparation of her arrival the past week. And a light snow that had fallen a few days ago had some worrying that she would be delayed.

The villagers were probably gathering now, lining up along the entrance to the Village Dowell just as they had done when Cree had been captured and strutted before the village a couple of months ago, though he had not been greeted with joy, but rather fear and trepidation.

While Dawn had been as eager as the other villagers to get a look at the infamous warrior Cree, she was not as anxious to see his intended. And if she heard one more whisper of sympathy for her plight she would scream... if only she could.

There were so many times she wished that she had a voice. That she hadn't been born unable to make a sound. She would love to laugh as others did, even cry, though most of all she'd love to scream out in pure pleasure when Cree made her climax over and over.

She shook the sorrowful thoughts away. She would never have a voice so why dwell on the impossible. What mattered now was that she carried Cree's child and he knew nothing about the babe. She had managed to avoid him this past week by feigning illness after having learned that he was to marry, though she hadn't been able to avoid Elsa. Cree had insisted that Elsa tend her, and she had been relieved when the woman claimed that she suffered from a sour stomach and suggested a light fare and rest for a few days.

How long she could keep Cree at a distance when their appetites for each other were ravenous, she didn't know. She missed him already, but then she had foolishly fallen in love with the mighty warrior... a mistake. One, however, she had no control over. She could not stop loving him no matter how hard she tried. And he had told her that he would never let her go. That she belonged to him and always would.

She wondered if he would feel the same when he discovered she carried his child.

A knock sounded just before the door opened, and she prayed it wasn't Cree. She didn't want to see him now even though she missed him terribly.

Old Mary shuffled into the cottage, a light dusting of snow covering her hooded cloak. "The snow will be heavy by nightfall. It is good the bride arrives soon."

Dawn nodded, though didn't smile and motioned Old Mary to join her at the table, filling a tankard with hot cider for her.

The old woman sat, her gnarled hands eagerly seeking the warmth of the tankard. "Tongues are wagging so fast about the pending arrival of Lucerne Gerwan that it makes my head hurt. I hear tell that her father and mother will be arriving soon as well. I have also heard that Lucerne is beautiful and thought you might want to have a peek for yourself."

Dawn raised a brow.

"Don't tell me you don't want to see what she looks like?" Old Mary whispered conspiratorially. "How could you not want to see the woman who will wed the man you love?"

Dawn's eyes turned wide. She had not dared tell anyone how she felt about Cree. It had been her secret or so she thought. Was it that obvious that she loved him?

Old Mary nodded, as if answering her silent question. "Anyone would have to be a fool not to see how much you love him." She reached out and patted Dawn's hand. "But then I see more than most."

Dawn shook her head and circled her finger over and over again at her temple.

"You most certainly are not crazy for falling in love with him. Love is the crazy one. I sometimes think that love is a prankster that enjoys playing tricks on people until finally love stops its antics and brings two people happily ever after together."

There would be no happily ever after for Dawn, though she had to agree with Old Mary... love was certainly a prankster.

"You should go take a peek at the woman who thinks to steal Cree from you."

How could the woman steal what rightfully belonged to her? An arrangement had been made and Cree would honor it. She had been irrational to think that she would be anymore to Cree than what she was... a kept woman.

"Go see for yourself that you have more to offer him than she ever would," Old Mary encouraged.

Even if she wanted to, and there was a part of her that did, everyone thought her ill and resting. Lila had stopped to see how she was doing and had told her that many villagers inquired as to her well-being.

Dorrie had even delivered her meal one evening and had fussed over her as had Flanna. And then there was the warrior who stood guard outside the cottage door. If she dared step foot outside, Cree would be informed of it immediately.

Old Mary eased her bony frame out of the chair and slipped off her cloak to hand it to Dawn. "Pull up the hood and hunch yourself over and no one will be the wiser. Go observe from the covering of the big pine by your old cottage. No one pays me heed so you will be ignored. Have your peek and satisfy your curiosity."

A gleam sparked in Dawn's eyes. She was tempted. She had been secluded in this cottage too many days and while she had savored the solitude, it would be good to get out and feel the crisp bite of the cold and hear the snow crunch beneath her feet.

"Go see, and then hurry back and I will take my leave and no one will ever know."

Why did Dawn doubt that? Cree seemed to know everything that went on in the village, though with the arrival of his bride Dawn doubted he would be thinking of her today. And the thought annoyed her. She wished his mind was as burdened with thoughts of her as her mind was burdened with thoughts of him.

She stood, suddenly eager to sneak out, and draped Old Mary's cloak around herself, tucking the hood down so that it concealed her face. She hunched over and shuffled to the door. She turned and smiled at the old woman, then walked out.

Dawn bobbed her drooping head at Neil standing stoically beside the door and wasn't surprised that he didn't acknowledge the nod. Old Mary was right; people simply ignored her as if she wasn't there.

Flurries fell with considerable enthusiasm and children chased them, their small hands reaching up to get them as they hurried with their parents toward the entrance to the village. Villagers were lined up two rows deep, and there was a joy in the air and on people's faces that had long been absent from the village.

Flanna had talked about how busy she had been getting the bride's bedchamber ready and how Turbett had his hands full preparing for her arrival celebration. There would be food and drink aplenty, music and merriment, and the whole village was looking forward to the festivities.

All except Dawn, she hadn't been invited, but that hadn't surprised her and besides she had no want to take part of the celebration.

She made her way slowly to the small cottage she had once called home and concealed herself under the snow-covered branches of the large pine that nearly hugged the side of the house. It gave her a good view of the procession that would pass, yet kept her hidden enough so as not to be noticed.

A cheer went up and Dawn tensed. The procession approached the village, though from where she stood she could not see it. Cree no doubt had ridden out to meet his intended so that they could enter the village together. It would not be long before they passed in front of her and her stomach churned at the thought of seeing Cree with another woman.

Her heart pounded in her chest as she waited anxiously. Part of her was curious to have a look and another part of her kept urging herself to run... run as far as she could and not look back. Curiosity won out. She kept her feet firmly planted on the ground, though her legs turned weak when she caught sight of the couple who would soon wed.

Cree was strikingly handsome as always and intimidating attired in all black. He sat his stallion tall and proud, though he wore a scowl, not unusual for him. And as expected the sight of him flared her passion. It never failed. All she had to do was lay eyes on him and she grew wet with the want of him. It was sinful how much she ached for him. Never in her wildest dreams had she imagined she would enjoy coupling so much, though never could she imagine making love with anyone other than Cree.

She finally turned her attention on the woman who rode beside him, and Dawn felt a catch in her heart that stole the breath right from her. The woman was beautiful. She had long luxurious dark hair that fell in generous waves around her flawless face and down over ample breasts. And she had the most startling blue eyes even at this distance. Never had Dawn seen such beauty.

Dawn gave one last look to Cree before she would turn and hurry back to the cottage, her heart heavy with the thought that he would no longer find her appealing. His scowl had deepened and his eyes searched the crowd anxiously, and she wondered why.

Her eyes widened. Could he possibly sense that she watched? His head turned her way and she hastily moved to conceal herself behind thicker pine branches. It didn't stop him from focusing his attention there and when his dark eyes narrowed and remained steady on her hiding spot, she felt as if she'd been caught.

Dawn didn't wait. She rushed off even though her movements caused the branches to rustle. He knew. He knew she'd been hiding there and she knew him well enough to know that he would confirm for himself what he suspected. And that meant he would go to her cottage.

She hurried behind the cottages and wished she could continue that way, but she would have to approach her cottage from the front as Old Mary or she would be caught. She didn't have much time before the procession reached the spot on the path she would need to cross to get to her cottage. She approached the area with caution. It was clear, though villagers had already started to gather there as they followed ahead of Cree and his bride.

Dawn gave a quick glance and saw that Cree had turned to speak with Lucerne. She bobbed her head, and then he took hold of his reins to guide his stallion away. Could he be coming to see if she was in her cottage? She didn't wait. She hunched over and walked a bit faster than Old Mary would usually do. When she reached the cottage she kept her shoulders and head stooped and entered without knocking.

Old Mary took one look at her and paled. "He knows?"

Dawn nodded and slipped the cloak over Old Mary and shooed her to the door.

Old Mary shook her head though kept the cloak on and pointed to her snow covered boots. "Put your boots by the fire so the snow will melt, and then sit and warm your chilled hands on the tankard. I will stand by the hearth so that it appears as if I have just entered."

Dawn hurried to do as Old Mary said amazed by her quick, sharp wit in judging the situation.

Just as they took their positions, the cottage door flew open.

Chapter Two

Cree stood in the open doorway, glaring at the two women. He couldn't explain it, but he knew that Dawn had been watching as he rode through the village with Lucerne, yet here she sat, her feet bare. And Old Mary, her cloak with traces of snow, warmed herself by the fire.

He closed the door and looked from one woman to the other.

"M'lord," Old Mary acknowledged him respectfully and bobbed her head.

"Leave us."

Old Mary bobbed her head again and did as ordered, leaving without further comment.

"You are feeling well?" he asked approaching the table and grew annoyed when he watched as Dawn slowly drew her body back away from him.

As well as can be expected after I discovered that you will wed and bed another woman. It was good that she could not speak for she would have blurted out how she truly felt. Instead she turned her hand from side to side.

"Yes and no?"

She nodded and grew wary when he slowly rounded the table.

"Elsa says that a few more days of rest and you will be fine."

Dawn froze when he stopped to stand directly behind her, then placed his chest against her back and planted his hands, palms down on the table to either side of her, in a sense, imprisoning her.

"Do you agree?" He leaned down and with a husky whisper in her ear said, "I want to feel your answers."

A tingle shot through her so strong and hard that she thought she would climax. It had been a week since they had last made love and with his body nearly wrapped around hers and the warmth of his breath against her cheek, her body was bound to respond.

She swallowed hard and was relieved that he could not see her reaction and answered him with a light tap to his arm.

"I am glad to know that you agree." He pressed his lips to her temple for a moment then said, "No fever and yet I taste heat."

Damn, why did she always have to burn for him.

"Do you feel the heat, Dawn?"

She wanted to deny it, but how did she deny what he could taste, touch, and see for himself. She tapped his arm harder than she intended.

"Are you angry with me?" he asked pressing his cheek to hers.

She was angry, though she wasn't sure who to be angry with. Was it her station in life that placed her out of his reach or was it herself for dreaming the impossible? Was it him for not caring and not loving her even more than she loved him? She had no answer, so it was easy for her to tap his arm twice for no.

"Have you missed me?"

With all my heart, she thought, but kept her answer to a single tap.

He grabbed her chin and turned her face as he brought his down. "Do you want me to kiss you?"

She turned his question on him by poking him in the chest and then poking herself.

He scowled. "I've ached to kiss you all week."

He had missed kissing her, which meant he had missed her. Everything drifted away at that moment. There was simply the two of them, and a need that burned deep in them both.

She pressed her fingers to his lips then to hers.

"I'm glad you want me to kiss you, for I want desperately to kiss you."

And he did, his lips settling over hers with a rough hunger that Dawn understood since it gnawed at her as well. Neither could get enough of the other. They were starved for the taste of each other and so they feed off the kiss.

Cree ended it abruptly, placing his brow against hers and giving himself a chance to recover his breath before he spoke. "I have to go... but I will return later tonight."

He was returning to her. The thought was like a slap in the face. This would be the way it was from now on, he returning to the woman who would be his wife while she was left alone. Her stomach turned at the thought or perhaps it was the babe. That reminder had her paling, for there would come a time she would have to tell Cree that she carried his child.

"You're not feeling well," he said anxiously.

She pressed her hand to her cheek and closed her eyes. It wasn't a lie that she needed rest. She had found that the babe depleted her of strength now and again, but a good rest always restored it.

"Yes, you should rest," he agreed and kissed her lips lightly, lingering as if reluctant to stop.

The strange ache that constantly took hold of her whenever he took his leave grasped at her now, though more tightly than ever before. Did she worry that he would not return to her now that his future bride was here? And then she thought of the babe she carried and the revelation that it would bring, and she worried over her future.

He ran a tender finger down her cheek. "You grow paler. You will rest that is an order."

Before she could confirm with a nod, he scooped her up in his arms out of the chair and carried her into the other room to place her gently on the bed. He grabbed the blanket at the bottom of the bed, though before he pulled it up over her, he took hold of one bare foot, raised it and glared at her. "You will wear stockings. The weather grows colder."

She yawned and he quickly covered her, tucking the blanket tightly around her. He gave her a quick kiss, and then went to the hearth and added more logs. He stopped before leaving the room and turned a scowl on her.

"I cannot prove it, but I know without a doubt that you left this cottage today without protection. And if I was not in a generous mood, I would not only punish you, but I would see Old Mary suffer for her part in it. Do such a foolish thing again and you'll taste my wrath."

Dawn did not take a breath until she heard the door close. He was much too aware of all things going on in the village, and she feared that it wouldn't be long before he realized that she carried his child. What then? The question haunted her and too often turned her fearful of the future.

She yawned again and turned on her side and drifted off to sleep as soon as she closed her eyes.

~~~

Cree would have preferred to crawl in bed with Dawn rather than take part in this farce of a celebration, but then she would get no rest if he did. And he had his duty to keep to his men and now the villagers.

He entered the keep reluctantly, yet anxious for the day to be over so that he could return to Dawn and crawl in bed with her. He ached to make love to her, but the way she had paled worried him and he would not tax her strength, though he would wrap himself around her and seek the sleep he had been lacking for the last week.

He had slept well enough, broken as it was, before Dawn had entered his life. He now slept a much more solid sleep curled around her. And he missed waking beside her in the morning and making love. It was a good way to start the day.

A scowl crossed his face as soon as he caught sight of Lucerne warming herself by the large hearth. She was of fair height and slender shape, and the midnight blue gown she wore hugged her narrow waist. And she held herself with a regal bearing that only one born of nobility could. He had never seen a woman as strikingly beautiful as she was; delicate features that caught the breath and eyes so blue the summer sky would be jealous. And yet surprisingly, he was not attracted to her. His groin did not tighten in anticipation and his lack of reaction puzzled him.

"My lord," she said with a gracious bob of her head when he stopped only a few feet from her.

"We will speak in my solar," Cree ordered, the Great Hall busy with a flurry of servants making sure all was ready for tonight's celebration.

"As you wish, my lord."

Beautiful and obedient, he could have done worse. At least she would not be difficult to handle. He turned to Sloan with a brief nod, and then extended his arm to Lucerne. She placed her hand lightly on it and they walked to the solar in silence.

He no soon as seated her in a chair by the hearth when Sloan entered with Flanna and two servant lassies and within minutes food and drink covered the table between the chairs. Flanna filled two goblets of wine, shooed the two servants out and gave a respectful bob before leaving. Sloan remained by the door his arms behind his back looking as if he stood guard.

Cree handed a goblet of wine to Lucerne.

"I am impressed with the efficiency of your servants. The head servant woman, I believe she is called Flanna, took my two servants in hand immediately and directed them to my quarters. And she spoke not a word to me as a good servant should do."

"Flanna does her chore well," Cree said, "but then I expect all in Dowell to do their chores well."

"As they should. Laziness is the devil's way and should not be tolerated. With your permission I will take charge of Flanna and, of course, the cook and see that things continue to run as they should."

Cree heard Sloan cough, and he knew exactly what he was thinking. "You may speak with Flanna, but Flanna will deal with Turbett the cook."

"As you wish, my lord, I am here to serve you as a good wife should."

"That is good to hear for I expect obedience from my wife. Pay heed to my word and speak no lies to me and we will do well together."

"I am sure we will, my lord. I look forward to our union."

They shared the food and drink as they spoke.

"Your fortuitous acquiring of my father's land and holdings has been fortunate for him," Lucerne said.

"Does your father agree with your opinion?" Cree asked, curious that she chose to bring the matter up for discussion.

"Not at first, but after careful consideration he realized that with his advancing age it was for the best. You will not only protect his lands far better than he could, you will no doubt expand his holdings."

"My land; my holdings," Cree clarified.

"Of course," Lucerne said with a smile. "You must forgive me. My family has held the title of Earl of Carrick and the land that goes with it for many years, which is why I am ever so grateful to wed you and have my family continue to be part of it. And God willing, I will give you a son who will carry the title for years to come."

"I would like many sons and daughters as well." Cree caught how her smile faltered. Was she the type of woman who when she once bore a son felt her duty was done and thought to bear no more children? He hoped not, for he wanted many children. He recalled how his younger sister had filled the home with such joy when she was little, and he wanted to know that joy once again.

"I heard that there is a celebration tonight?" she asked. "And I saw how the servants were busy preparing the Great Hall."

"It is for you. The villagers have been looking forward to your arrival."

"The villagers will take part of the festivities in the Great Hall?" she asked.

Was that annoyance he saw on her face? Cree nodded. "Yes, the villagers will be welcomed into the hall for the celebration and to meet you... the lady of the keep."

Lucerne stood. "In that case, my lord, I should like to go rest before the evening's festivities. My journey has tired me."

Cree waved a hand to Sloan and in seconds a servant appeared to take Lucerne to her bedchamber. After she left, Sloan and Cree sat before the hearth each with a tankard of ale in hand.

"What do you think?" Cree asked.

"She is beautiful."

"That's obvious. What else do you see?"

"Obedience."

"Anything else?" Cree asked.

"She's hungry for power, which could be good or bad. I would say she needs watching, though..."

"Spit it out."

"She doesn't strike me as the type of woman who would tolerate her husband having a mistress."

Cree glowered at him. "It is no concern of hers."

"She might think differently. No wife wants the other woman flaunted in her face. You may want to consider moving Dawn to a more secluded—"

"No," Cree snapped. "She stays where she is. Is all ready for the celebration?"

"Changing the subject won't change the situation. And remember keeping one woman content is difficult enough... you now have two." Sloan bit back his laughter.

Cree glowered at him again. "Don't you have duties to attend to?"

"They have been seen to," Sloan said and stood. "The only thing left to do is to go enjoy the celebration." He raised his tankard and downed what was left. "Come, let's go make merry before you must deal with your future bride again."

"That's the first wise thing you've said today," Cree said and downed what was left of his ale before both men took their leave.

~~~

Dawn woke with the sound of the door opening. She wondered how long she had slept. Then she heard Lila call out, "Dawn."

She smiled, hurried into her boots and using her fingers as a comb worked them through her soft hair while hurrying into the other room.

Lila smiled and greeted Dawn with a tight hug, which had her suspicious. It wasn't that her friend rarely hugged her; it was the degree of the hug. Lila had always hugged her tightly when she was concerned for Dawn. And the hug was extremely tight.

Lila shed her cloak, draping it over the back of the chair closest to the heat of the hearth. "It's snowing heavily. There should be a generous accumulation by morning and possibly more if it doesn't stop."

There was fresh food and a fresh pitcher of cider on the table, which meant that Dawn had slept through the evening meal. She placed her hand against the pitcher. It was cold. That meant it was *well* past the evening meal. She moved it to the hearth to heat.

Lila sat. "The celebration continues," —she shook her head— "so much food. Everyone cannot believe Cree's generosity, and though his future bride is beautiful, she doesn't appear to tolerate the villagers well."

Dawn wrinkled her nose and tossed her chin up.

Lila laughed. "You are right. She is nobility and we are lowly peasants she must tolerate." She lowered her voice. "The women already worry that she will change things around here and not for the better."

Dawn shook her head, then scowled and puffed out her chest.

Lila laughed again. "You look so funny when you imitate Cree. So you don't think Cree would allow it?"

Dawn shook her head slowly.

"He does rule with a tight fist, though a fair one." Lila stretched her hand out to Dawn.

Dawn smiled and squeezed her friend's hand, then pointed to Lila, then herself, and then her mouth.

"I should realize that I can't keep anything from you. I do have something to say. While the lady of the keep smiles, it is a forced one. I do not trust her and my worry for you grows. Cree still keeps a guard at your door, so therefore it must mean that you are still in danger and now this, and" —Lila pointed to Dawn— "what has gotten into you of late? You seem" —she paused as if unsure of her next word— "fearless. I should say more fearless than I've known you to be. I fear that one day soon Cree will have you beaten for your defiance."

Dawn did not think of herself as fearless or defiant, quite the opposite, though she supposed climbing out the window, which was now boarded, twice could be defined as defiant.

"He will lose his temper one of these days, and you will suffer for it. Cree was furious when you went missing. He had Thomas taken from me while we spoke and I feared that he wouldn't return him."

Dawn felt her heart catch and she squeezed Lila's hand. She patted her chest profusely and shook her head.

"I know you're sorry, so am I. I cannot imagine what it is like for you being Cree's kept woman. I love my husband and he loves me and we will share our lives together. I had always wanted the same for you, to find a good man and share your life with him. Now..." She lowered her head with a brief shake. "You must be careful, especially now with his intended here." She raised her head. "I fear Lucerne's arrival does not bode well for the village, and I fear she will not tolerate her husband having a mistress a short walk from the keep."

Dawn did her best to reassure her that all would be well and soon talk turned to other things until Lila left, needing to get home to feed baby Thomas.

The food on the table had lost its appeal, and she didn't even favor a tankard of the now heated cider. And it wasn't due to the babe nestled in her stomach. It was worry that wore at her gut. She had wished for a love like Lila and Paul's and a husband to share her life with.

Now look at her, she was nothing more than a kept woman who could be discarded at Cree's whim. And yet the fool that she was, she loved him. How could that be?

She didn't know how long she sat at the table, but she was quickly snapped out of her musings when the door flew open and snow rushed in along with Cree.

He shook the snow from his hair and wiped off his cloak to drop on the chair, but stopped in mid-stride when his eyes met Dawn's. "What's wrong? Are you feeling ill? I'll send for Elsa." He dropped his cloak and hurried to her side scooping her up and carrying her to the other room.

She rested her head to his chest. She knew why she loved this man. His silent heart had learned to speak through gestures and actions rather than words. He cared more than he would admit. Could he be holding love as silent as he had his heart? And though it would take time, it was a question that she intended to have answered.

Cree placed her on the bed and hunched down in front of her. "I will have the guard fetch Elsa while I settle you in your nightdress."

He was removing her blouse as he spoke and she did not stop him, but she didn't need Elsa—she needed him.

After disrobing her, he turned to go for her nightdress when her hand went to the ties of his leather tunic. She helped him slip it off, and then pulled his shirt off and pressed her bare breasts to his chest, rested her head on his shoulder, and wrapped her arms around his waist.

"You are not well, you need to rest," he said trying to convince himself so that he would stop growing hard.

Dawn had had no intentions of making love with him this night, and yet when he walked in the door and immediately realized her distress and didn't hesitate to see to her care, her heart went out to him. It seemed that they had been apart for years rather than a week, and the separation had been far too long. She missed him whether she wanted to or not. When would she accept that he had stolen her heart? When would she accept that she belonged to him and he belonged to her, though had yet to realize it?

Fearless. That was what Lila had called her, and she would need to remain fearless if she did not want to lose him. She didn't know what the future would hold for them and at the moment it didn't matter. What mattered was that he had returned to her, cared for her, and...

She slipped her hand down over his growing arousal and squeezed.

"Dawn," he said with a sharp intake of breath. "You play with danger."

She looked up at him, smiled, and squeezed him harder.

Chapter Three

Cree shed his leggings, grabbed Dawn around the waist and went down on the bed with her landing on top of her.

"It has been too long since I have been inside you," he said with growl and nipped at her nipples. He raised his head and glowered at her. "Are you certain you are well enough—"

She grabbed the length of him and rubbed him against her sensitive bud.

His brow shot up and he grinned. "I think this will be quick... we have been apart too long."

He had referenced their time away from each other twice. Had it troubled him as much as it had troubled her?

His mouth found her neck and he kissed and nipped at the soft flesh as he worked his way gently inside her. That he was considerate of her warmed her heart and heated her passion. And when he was fully sheathed in her, she sighed inwardly with pleasure.

She had missed him. Lord, how she had missed him.

She welcomed him, her legs going around him, drawing him deeper, wanting, and needing him as close as she could possibly get him. He took his time, going slow, driving her mad with the want of him, and yet she enjoyed the torture, every plunge and withdrawal fed her pleasure, her need, and built to a climax that was certain to have her screaming... if only she could.

Cree saw the desire building in her eyes, felt it in the way her body moved frantically against his and it fueled his already soaring passion. Lord, how he had missed her and though he wanted to burst with pleasure, he also selfishly wanted the passion to linger. He wanted to feel her grind against him, feel her finger tap, tap, tap against his arm and watch her eyes burn with desire for him and revel in the way she tightened around him with each thrust, driving him to the brink of a climax that he was eager to taste, but not yet wanting to surrender to.

It had been too long though, his body too needy.

"Come with me," he urged and plunged into her like a thirsty man in need of quenching... once, twice... he exploded with passion like never before, and if he was a praying man he would have thought himself blessed not only for such a powerful, never-ending climax, but for the fact that Dawn had burst right along with him.

He wrapped her in his arms a short time later, after their breathing had calmed, their hearts had stopped racing, their bodies had cooled, and he had covered them with the soft wool blankets.

They snuggled together more content than ever. "You feel well?"

She tapped his arm once.

He kissed her temple again. "I am glad, for I have missed you greatly."

Her heart fluttered at his admission, though a soft voice warned, *be careful he can give you no more.* But another voice countered with, *let his heart speak for itself.*

He snuggled himself more firmly around her, keeping her tight against him, and they both drifted off into a contented slumber.

~~~

Cree woke Dawn the next morning with soft kisses and gentle lovemaking and, afterwards, he reluctantly left her to sleep and returned to the keep.

Lucerne was seated at the dais with Sloan when he entered the Great Hall.

"Good morning, my lord," she said with a bow of her head. "I hope you slept well."

"Exceptionally so," he said joining her at the long table, though normally Sloan and he took their meals at a table close to the large hearth. The dais always seemed too removed to Cree.

"Does the snow still fall," she asked.

"Yes, though lightly." He sat beside her famished and eager to enjoy the morning meal.

A large warrior tramped into the Great Hall, snow falling from his cloak and boots. He stopped before the dais with a bow. "Sorry to disturb you, my lord, but tracks have been spotted in the woods."

"Alert the guard at her house and take more men and see what you can find," Cree ordered. The man bowed his head and took his leave.

"Someone is in danger and needs guarding?" Lucerne asked.

"It is nothing that concerns you," Cree said.

"Everything that concerns you concerns me. I am to be your wife, and I will stand by your side and defend you no matter the circumstances."

"I would expect no less from you; it is your duty." If she had hoped to impress him with that declaration she had failed. As his wife that was her duty plain and simple, and he didn't want to have to remind her of it.

Dawn wasn't his wife, but she had suffered a beating because of him and had still retained her courage and also her foolishness. He looked to Sloan. "The window has been boarded?"

"It is most secured," Sloan said with a nod.

"Perhaps I should leave you two alone to discuss matters," Lucerne said with a bit of sarcasm.

"A wise choice," Cree said.

Lucerne stood with a scowl that would rival Cree's and left the Great Hall.

Sloan turned to Cree. "She is a formidable woman."

"Who will learn her place," Cree said as if decreeing it. "As soon as I'm done fortifying myself for the morn we'll go see what the trackers have learned. I don't care for the fact that someone has been spotted. Who would dare travel in this weather?"

"Those who are up to no good," Sloan answered.

"Rem's warning troubles me," Cree said. "To think that men will keep coming after Dawn until one of them succeeds in taking her life makes no sense. The only way to stop them is to discover who hired them."

"Not an easy task"

"But not impossible," Cree said. "Also, it's time to bring my sister home. As soon as the snow stops, send a troop of men for her."

"Having two women to deal with aren't enough for you? You're going to add your sister to the lot?" Sloan chuckled.

"We had once been close,"—Cree's brow knitted as if recalling troubled memories— "circumstances forced us apart and it's time for us to be a family again. It's time she had a home. Send a sizeable troop to the Abbey to bring her here."

"I will—"

A piercing scream had both men jumping out of their seats as Lucerne rushed into the Great Hall. Her face was flushed, her cheeks cherry red, and her chest heaved as she stopped in front of the dais.

"The insolent man insulted me. Punish him, he deserves a whipping," she all but screamed at Cree.

Sloan turned and sent Cree a pleading look. They both knew what this was about and Sloan, as usual, worried about losing Turbett.

Cree leaned over the table, slapping his hands down on it. "You come screaming in here like a harpy, demanding that I pay heed to your command, and you are yet my wife. Is this rude manner of yours what I am to expect from you when we wed?"

"I may not be your wife yet, but I see no reason why I should be abused by that insufferable man when all I'm trying to do is learn the workings of your keep so that when we do wed I have my duties firm in hand."

"Did I not tell you that Flanna would deal with Turbett?"

"See," Lucerne said with a shake of her finger. "You know who I speak of without me having mentioned his name. Therefore, he must be a difficult servant to deal with. I know well how to handle an insubordinate servant. I will have him obeying me in no time and, besides, it's my duty."

"We have yet to exchange vows. Until we do you are not to dictate to any of the servants. If you have a problem with any of them, you will report it to Flanna and she will deal with it as she sees fit. And you are not to disturb Turbett again—"

Lucerne went to interrupt and Cree cut her off.

"*Never* interrupt me when I am speaking and *never* make me repeat myself. My word is law, understand that and obey me or suffer for your insolence."

Lucerne's blue eyes stormed with anger, her chin went up, and her shoulders back. "I understand perfectly, my lord." Her chin went up higher. "Though I must inquire as to what you expect me to do all day if I am not to see to the running of the keep."

"You will be busy tending our children."

Her eyes turned wide. "That is a servant's chore."

Cree stood straight, his shoulders wide, his chest impressive in its muscled girth. "It is a mother's caring love I want my children to know."

Lucerne looked ready to argue, then seemed to think better of it and calmed. "Of course a mother loves her children, but their care is left to the servants. It is the way of things."

"It is not *my* way."

Lucerne said no more on it, though it was obvious that the matter was yet settled. "Will you at least reprimand your cook for speaking to me and treating me like a lowly servant?"

"I will tell him that you will not disturb him again."

"You sound as if you apologize for me."

"You disobeyed me, therefore, you leave me no choice," Cree said.

Lucerne seemed at a loss and could do nothing but stare at him. Cree had the feeling that she was accustomed to having her way. And since her brief tirade didn't have the results she was used to, she did not know what to do.

It didn't surprise him when she pressed her fingers to her temple and said, "My head pains me. I believe I will rest."

"Would you like me to send the healer to see you?" Cree asked, though doubted that she needed the woman, the headache nothing more than an excuse to take her leave and be left undisturbed.

"It is not necessary, my lord," she said and bowed before turning to walk away, though after a few short steps she stopped and turned. "Is this healer skillful?"

"She is extremely knowledgeable," Cree assured her.

"Then perhaps she could help me. I will await her in my chambers." She left the room, her servant scurrying out of the shadows to follow behind her.

"Summon Flanna," Cree said to Sloan.

"I am here, my lord, Flanna said, stepping out of the shadows and bobbing her head.

Cree scowled. "This room needs more light. It seems that the shadows harbor eyes and ears that I am not aware of."

"I may hear and see things, my lord, but I speak not of them."

"Then why were you lurking in the dark corner?" Cree asked.

"I waited so that I could defend Turbett if necessary."

"You witnessed the exchange between my future wife and Turbett?"

"I did."

"Tell me about it," Cree ordered.

"Turbett and I were discussing the meals for the next few days when my lady entered the kitchen demanding to speak with the cook. Turbett, of course, proudly stepped forward. My lady then proceeded to tell him that his meals were too flavorful and that she would instruct him on how the food was to be prepared."

"Too flavorful?" Sloan said stunned. "She prefers bland?"

"My lady says that spices are expensive and that Turbett was not to be generous with them."

Cree's brow furrowed as his eyes darkened. "Turbett's response?"

"He told my lady that there was only one master that he answered to and that was... Cree. Then he told her to leave his kitchen and never return."

Lucerne hadn't been here one full day and Cree wished he could tell her to leave and never return. "Turbett is correct. Lucerne is never to return to the kitchen, not even after we wed. You will notify me if she should attempt to disturb Turbett again. And you have my permission, if it proves necessary, to remind Lucerne that she is not permitted in the kitchen"

Flanna smiled. "As you wish, my lord."

"Send one of the servants for Elsa and inform her that my lady has requested her help in healing a headache."

Flanna bobbed her head and waited to be dismissed.

"One other thing," Cree said lowering his voice. "Keep me abreast of any incidents concerning my future wife. That is all."

Once Flanna left the hall Sloan asked, "I take it that means I should keep a careful eye on m'lady too."

Cree nodded. "She arrived like a whirlwind that has yet to settle."

"A whirlwind has a way of scooping things up in its wake and depositing them God knows where."

"Her whirlwind way will settle or else," Cree warned.

"Not that I think you can't do it, for I have seen you do many things I thought impossible—but—how can a whirlwind possibly be controlled?"

Chapter Four

Cree had just finished speaking with Taggart, the miller, in regards to the few repairs that the mill required when one of his warriors approached and informed him that the snow had made it impossible to follow the tracks. However, they were able to determine that there were two separate tracks and therefore two men. The search continued, though it didn't look promising.

As Cree finished giving orders that he was to be made aware of any strangers seeking shelter for the winter, he spotted Dawn leaving her cottage. He wondered what she was doing out in the cold, she should be resting, regaining her strength, especially after he had robbed her of some last night and this morning. He almost smiled at the memory of her naked in his arms, though caught himself and scowled. It wouldn't do for the infamous Cree to be smiling for no reason, and yet there was a reason... there was Dawn. He had been smiling more often around Dawn. She brought a joy out in him that had been buried for as long as he could recall. It reminded him of the time he was loved so unconditionally. And that kind of love was worth everything.

He finished issuing further precautions that were to be taken, then left Sloan to see to it, and then caught up with Dawn and her guard a few steps from her cottage. With a nod to his warrior Neil, the man drifted off, though kept them in view as they walked side by side.

"You are feeling well enough to be out?" Cree asked worried that she would worsen and hoping she had recovered. He missed her greatly and grew annoyed at himself for the constant thought of having missed her.

She nodded and breathed deeply.

"It's fresh air you are hungering."

She smiled happy that he understood her and happy to see him. While his absence had been her doing, she had realized last night how very much she had missed him beside her in bed, not that she hadn't missed his lovemaking more. It was just that she found peacefulness when he rested beside her all night and woke to his loving touches in the morning. She was glad she was already smiling, for she would have burst with a foolish grin at the remembrance of how tender he had been when making love to her. It was almost as if she could feel how much he cared... possibly loved her.

She chased the maddening thought away. It had only served to cause her heartache, and she had suffered enough of that when she had learned he would wed. The reminder wiped the smile off her face.

"Are you all right?' he asked anxiously, her smile vanishing much too fast and her face paling a bit.

She nodded and smiled again, though it lacked zest.

"Perhaps a visit with Elsa would prove wise," Cree said and offered his arm to her.

Dawn knew it wasn't a suggestion and had no choice but to take his arm and do as he commanded.

At least she would not be deprived of the walk she had been eager to take.

"You slept well?"

Dawn's smile grew when she caught just the hint of Cree's lips turning up in what she suspected would be a wide grin if he let it. She gestured with her one hand, pointing to her left and slowly drawing it in front her and pointing down.

He nodded and couldn't help but let a smile slip out, but only for a moment. "Better than you have slept in a while."

She nodded, her eyes lighting bright along with her smile.

Good lord, but her smile could steal his heart. He leaned down and whispered, "Me too."

"MY LORD!"

The screech startled them both and had them turning around. Dawn didn't realize that her hand grasped more tightly to Cree's arm as she watched Lucerne hurry toward them.

She stopped in front of Cree, ignoring Dawn as if she was not there or was too insignificant to acknowledge. "You have a miraculous healer. My headache is gone, and I thought that perhaps you now have free time to show me around the village."

It was hard not to notice that villagers were lingering around them, and Dawn was certain that they were curious as to how the notorious Cree would handle the delicate situation. Dawn wondered herself, so she waited, her eyes on Cree.

Lucerne gave a haughty lift of her chin and spoke before allowing Cree to answer. "Is this poor peasant in need of help that she dares to keep hold of your arm?"

Fear of punishment would have had Dawn removing her hand immediately, but she had no fear of retribution from Cree and for some reason—she found surprising—Lucerne did not intimidate her. What had surprised her was Cree's reaction. He had placed his hand over hers. Was he warning her to remain as she was or was he making it known to Lucerne that Dawn belonged to him?

Cree finally spoke. "I have matters to see to." He gave Neil a nod and the warrior walked over to them. "Neil will escort you back to the keep."

Lucerne's blue eyes turned stormy and she appeared ready to protest when suddenly she turned a brilliant smile on Cree. "Another time, my lord, though could I be so bold as to ask for an introduction to the woman who obviously takes you away from me."

Dawn waited. It would be rude of Cree to ignore her request, so sweetly asked, though laced with sarcasm and with so many villagers watching curiously. Though if there was one thing that she had learned about Cree, it was that he did not care what people thought of him or if he was mannerly.

"You will meet everyone in good time," Cree said.

Lucerne stiffened and looked to Dawn. "I'm sure the peasant wouldn't mind telling me her name."

"Another time," Cree commanded so sternly that Lucerne took a step back. He nodded to Neil, and then turned forcing Dawn along with him since his hand rested even more firmly over her hand.

A shiver ran through Dawn and her stomach churned, for she realized at that moment Cree had made a difficult situation worse. Once Lucerne found out that she was Cree's mistress, there would be no telling what she would do. Cree's wrath was one thing. It was there for all to see and fear. Whereas a woman's wrath could be secreted away until she decided to let it loose and still one might not see it coming until too late.

Dawn wanted to glance back and see if Lucerne watched them, but she dared not give the woman the satisfaction to think that she had been disturbed by the exchange. And, furthermore, she intended to find out what she could about Lucerne, and the one person who could help her do that was Flanna.

She wished she could speak to Cree about his forthcoming marriage. But when he had told her that he was to wed, the arrangement having been made, he also decreed that they would speak of it no more. It had been settled. He would wed and she'd remain his mistress.

Her churning stomach grew worse, possibly because of her growing concerns or perhaps it was the babe protesting the bit of food she had eaten before leaving the cottage. It seemed that he did not like particular food or perhaps he was just as contrary as his da. She thought to tug on Cree's arm and have him stop a moment, but they weren't that far from Elsa's cottage where she could sit and, hopefully, calm her protesting stomach.

They were a few steps from the cottage when Dawn realized that she could not keep her stomach from heaving. She let go of Cree's arm and ran around the side of the cottage to the edge of the woods to let her stomach relieve itself.

She hadn't expected him to follow or have his arm go around her waist or his hand to pull her hair away from her face as she retched. And when she was done, he scooped up a bit of clean snow and wiped it gently across her mouth. After tossing it aside he lifted her into his arms and shoved Elsa's door open with his shoulder and carried her inside.

Elsa pointed to the bed in the corner. "What is she doing out in the cold?"

Cree scowled at Dawn after placing her on the bed. "I should not have listened to nonsense of fresh air."

The door flew open and Sloan rushed in. "An issue that needs your immediate attention, my lord."

Elsa shooed Cree to the door while assuaging his concerns. "Go and see to your duty. I will see to Dawn and not let her leave until her guard arrives to see her home."

Relief flooded him and, knowing that Elsa would keep her word, he left Dawn in the healer's care.

No soon as the door closed, then Elsa was at Dawn's side. "I know you carry Cree's babe and he is not an ignorant man and will surmise, for himself, soon enough." Elsa pulled the folded blanket at the bottom of the bed up and over Dawn to tuck around her. "Do not wait too long to tell him. Now rest, the babe tires you."

Dawn didn't need reminding that Cree was no fool. She knew he'd realize soon enough that she was with child, but she wasn't ready yet to tell him, and she wasn't tired. She wanted to go back outside and let the cold air sting her cheeks, watch the children at play, and the villagers busy at their tasks. She wanted to talk with her friend, visit Old Mary and not be a prisoner anymore.

She turned on her side, wishing there was some way she could escape and freely roam the village a bit before returning home. The heavens must have heard her. A young warrior hurried into the cottage demanding Elsa go with him. His wife was having their baby right now and he wouldn't be surprised if the babe hadn't arrived already.

Elsa was quick to calm the frantic man who no doubt had gone into battle with less fear than he was experiencing now and just as quickly gathered her things to leave. Dawn waited a moment after they left and was glad she did since Elsa popped her head back in a few moments later, as if checking to see that Dawn still slept. After she heard the door close again, she waited to make certain Elsa hadn't planned another surprise return and when several silent minutes followed, she got out of bed, grabbed her cloak from the peg, and peeked outside.

Neil stood there smiling, and she grinned and nodded at the warrior who guarded her throughout the day. She should have known that Elsa was too faithful to Cree to leave Dawn alone at the cottage. It also gave her pause to think that Elsa might not keep her secret about the babe from Cree much longer.

She walked through the village with Neil now eager to get home, eager for solitude once more. When they were only a few feet from the cottage, Neil suddenly jumped in front of her letting out a roar similar to the one she had heard Cree cry out, though Neil's was not as ferocious. Then he pushed her to the ground, shielding her with his body.

They were surrounded by warriors in minutes. Neil issued orders for some of the warriors to search the woods in the back of the cottage, and then he yanked her up off the ground and quickly shoved her into the safety of her cottage. It was only then that she noticed he had an arrow sticking through his arm. He had taken the arrow meant for her.

"Are you hurt?" Neil asked.

Her eyes turned wide and she frantically pointed at the arrow sticking through the muscle in his upper arm.

"That's a wee bit of a bother, nothing more," he assured her after glancing at it. "You're not hurt?"

The man stood with an arrow in his arm more worried about her than his own injury. She shook her head and shooed him to the door with one hand while pointing to the arrow with the other.

"I'll have Elsa tend it as soon as Cree arrives and I finish telling him about the incident."

She shook her head furiously, stomped her foot, and pointed to the door.

"No use in arguing with me. I take my orders from Cree."

Dawn was never more relieved to see the door open and Cree enter along with Sloan and Elsa. Cree walked over to her while Elsa went directly to Neil.

She had been asked enough if she was all right, so she stopped Cree before he could repeat it and patted her chest and held up her hand assuring him that she was fine. She then pointed to Neil and demonstrated how he threw himself in front of her and knocked her to the ground shielding her.

Cree ran his hand along her face, as if ascertaining for himself that she spoke the truth. That she was unharmed. The gentle gesture was her undoing. She swayed and pressed her brow to his chest. His arms went protectively around her and he drew her tightly against him.

"You're safe," Cree whispered and then looked to Neil. "Tell me what happened."

While Elsa examined the wound, Neil explained. "I saw movement in the woods to the side of the cottage and I didn't wait, I stepped in front of Dawn and took her to the ground. I wish I could report that I saw the culprit, but it was movement that stirred me into action."

Elsa interrupted. "I need to get this arrow out and the wound cleansed and bound. And he needs to remain at my cottage for the night so that I can make sure that the wound shows no signs of rotting and he no signs of fever."

"Go on with you," Neil teased. "You just want my hulking body in your bed."

"Dreams do come true, Neil, that they do," Elsa teased right back.

"Take good care of him, Elsa," Cree said. "He is to be rewarded for what he has done here this day."

"I have my reward, my lord... a home after years of constant battle."

Dawn felt her chest swell, seeing the tear that lingered at the corner of Neil's one eye. The man would do anything for Cree and all because Cree had made certain that his men had been provided with a home. And at what cost?

"You will be rewarded, Neil, and I'll hear no more about it," Cree ordered. "Now go with Elsa, and you will not return to your duties until Elsa says you are well enough."

Neil looked ready to protest; a look from Cree stilled his objection.

Elsa hustled him out the door, the two arguing like an old married couple.

Cree turned to Sloan. "You know what to do. I will join you in a moment."

Dawn couldn't hide her disappointment that he would be leaving her. She didn't want him to leave. She wanted him to stay there with her and hold her tight and let the whole world disappear for the rest of the day. But that would not be, no matter how much she wanted it.

He lifted her chin, Dawn not realizing it had drooped. He brushed his lips over hers and then kissed her ever so gently, as if he was afraid she'd break. It sent a shiver of passion through her, and she wished again that he would stay.

"I must see to this," he said and this time kissed her, not with a fiery passion, but with a taste of temptation, almost as if he purposely teased her. "I will return later, after supper."

She placed her hand over his heart.

He smiled and stole a quick kiss. "I promise. Nothing will keep me from you this night."

She nodded and forced a smile, praying that it was true and he would return to her this evening.

"You will not leave this cottage the rest of today," Cree ordered.

She crossed her heart.

"You promise me?" he asked as if shocked. "You know I will hold you to it."

She nodded and crossed her heart again, then narrowed her eyes and pointed her finger at him.

"Is that a *but* I hear?"

She grinned and nodded. He would never know how very much he pleased her when he spoke with her, as if he could actually hear her.

"I'm listening," he said, pushing a stray strand of her hair behind her ear and giving her a playful kiss.

He was not taking her seriously and this was important to her. She frowned and scolded with a shake of her finger.

"It is important."

She pressed her finger once against his arm, confirming that it was.

"You have my attention," he said, his dark eyes steady on hers.

She pointed to him, then to herself, and then tapped her mouth.

"We need to talk. About what?"

Dawn pointed around the room and then held her wrists together as if shackled.

"You are no prisoner," he said adamantly.

She pointed to him, and then to her and tapped her mouth again, and waved her hand.

"You want to discuss this later, but I tell you now that you are no prisoner."

She titled her head and placed her hands on her hips.

"You're going to be stubborn about this aren't you?"

She nodded, her expression softened and her hand reached out to rest against this chest.

"If it is that important to you we will talk."

Dawn nodded and tapped his chest, thanking him.

"I will see you later," he said and gave her a brief kiss before heading out the door.

Dawn slipped off her cloak and after hanging it on the peg, she went and retrieved the comb she had hidden behind the baskets the first day she had entered the cottage. She unwrapped the cloth she kept it in and admired the intricate design carved along the top of the bone comb. It had been her mum's and she had kept it hidden these many years. Her mum had warned her that if she showed it to anyone that someone would accuse her of stealing it, for a peasant should not own such a fine item. But her mum had assured her that it had not been stolen that it had been given to her by a generous person who felt that a mother should have something to pass onto her daughter.

Dawn took it out to look upon every time she felt the need to feel her mum near. Her mum had taught her to be strong and brave even against great odds. She supposed that was why she had held onto the possibility that Cree would someday love her enough to wed her.

However, she had spent enough time on dreams. Her life was in danger and it made no sense as to why. She was a peasant—an insignificant lass. Why would anyone want her dead?

She needed to find out for herself what was going on, and she knew where to start and who could help her.

A knock sounded at the door and it opened. Dawn smiled as the person she was thinking about walked in.

Chapter Five

Flanna placed a fresh pitcher of cider and a basket covered with a cloth on the table, then reached out to take Dawn's hand. "Are you all right?'

Dawn smiled, nodded, and gave Flanna's hand a reassuring squeeze. It wasn't only this incident today that had people wondering over how she faired. She had hid herself away, feeling sorry for her circumstances instead of staying strong like her mum had taught her. She did not know what fate she would face once it was known that she carried Cree's babe, but she intended to keep her courage, no matter the outcome.

She was suddenly hungry and eagerly snatched the cloth off the basket.

"I will do that," Flanna said chasing her hands away. "You sit and rest yourself."

No more rest, Dawn thought. She had had enough of it.

Flanna placed bread and cheese on the table in front of Dawn and filled a tankard with cider as she talked. "Cree is furious that more men have been sent to do you harm. He worries greatly over your well-being and well he should. There is talk—" Flanna stopped and shook her head as if silently scolding herself.

Dawn was pleased that Flanna spoke freely in front of her and curious why she suddenly stopped.

She patted Flanna's arm, shrugged, and wrinkled her brow in question.

"I do not wish to add to your ailing. You have enough to concern yourself with."

Flanna worried about her as did others. And it pleased Dawn to know that people cared for her, though she wanted no one feeling sorry for her. Dawn thumped her chest and grinned as she threw her arms wide.

Flanna laughed. "You feel better."

Dawn threw her hands up and around as if forming a big ball.

"Much better," Flanna corrected and Dawn confirmed with a nod.

Dawn pointed to the chair across from her, tapped her mouth, and then waved her hand and Flanna understood that she wanted her to sit and tell her more, and she obliged.

"There is talk that Rem, the culprit who saved your life, had told Cree that the attempts on your life would not stop until you were dead. And it puzzles him, as it does many, as to why someone wants you dead."

Dawn tapped her chest.

"Of course it puzzles you as well since it makes no sense at all. No one wishes you ill will, except..." Flanna frowned and shook her head. "The soon-to-be lady of the keep is one to watch out for, a nasty one she is. Barely a day here and she has already raised her hand to her one servant several times. And such a lovely lass Bree is, with bright curly red hair and a pleasant smile for all. I feel sorry for her other servant Magda. The poor woman's hands are gnarled from years of stitching and must certainly pain her, yet Lucerne has her busy stitching away day and night.

The woman has enough garments to last her forever. The servants worry that she will do the same to them, work them until they're gnarled with pain, once she weds Cree and takes over the running of the keep." She smiled. "Though there was an incident between Turbett and Lucerne and Cree has forbidden Lucerne to enter the kitchen, and he has given me orders to remind her if necessary. He also told me to report any problems concerning Lucerne to him."

She shook her head again. "I digress. We were discussing the attacks, which started before Lucerne arrived and she has yet to learn," —Flanna paused— "your status in the village. And she won't be hearing it from any of my servants, I can tell you that. I warned every one of them that they'd answer to me if their tongues wagged. "

Dawn placed a hand to her chest and nodded her thanks, then tapped her finger to her temple.

"You have a thought," Flanna confirmed.

She gestured with her hands, as if two mouths talked and then tapped her brow.

"We can learn from wagging tongues."

Dawn nodded, patted her chest, and tapped her brow.

Flanna leaned closer. "You want to learn what's going on."

Dawn nodded, pointed to Flanna and then to herself.

"Of course, I'll help you. If it wasn't for you I would still be putting up with that bear of a man, Turbett." She smiled. "Once I became his equal and he could no longer dictate to me in the kitchen, he changed." She sighed. "Or perhaps I changed and realized that his constant badgering had been his inability to show that he favored me."

Dawn patted her chest rapidly and smiled.

"You are happy for me." Flanna sniffled back a tear. "I am grateful to you. You have been a good friend and I will help you all I can."

Dawn pointed to her ear.

"You want me to listen," Flanna nodded. "A good tactic since most nobility think servants hear nothing, though Cree is more cautious, lowering his voice when a servant drifts near. I have noticed that recently Cree and Sloan often seek the privacy of his solar, and it makes me wonder if plans are being made."

A questioning gesture from Dawn had Flanna responding.

"Plans for what I don't know, though I will do my best to find out."

Dawn pointed to her and back to herself, and then locked her hands tight.

"I will tell no one about what we've discussed. It will be our secret."

For a moment Dawn wondered if she was being fair to Flanna. If Cree discovered that the woman helped her, she would certainly suffer for it.

"I see the worry in your eyes, but what is it that I truly do?" Flanna said with a shrug. "I listen and gossip. It is what everyone does."

Dawn smiled and nodded. Flanna would prove a good ally and not only for this matter. Already she had learned from Flanna, without asking, that Lucerne had the habit of striking her servant, which told Dawn that the woman cared little for those beneath her.

"I have to go and tend to my duties," Flanna said standing. "I will see what I can learn and return with your evening meal and, hopefully, some useful information."

Dawn pressed her hand to her chest.

"No need to thank me. I look forward to the challenge." Flanna smiled and hurried out the door.

Dawn decided to busy herself with adjusting one of the gowns in the chest. It required only a few tucks here and there and she would leave it loose so that it would eventually hide her rounding stomach. And with her hands busy, her mind would idle. She could use the rest from the constant worry of late.

She gathered what she needed and sat on a chair by the fire to spend the afternoon stitching and waiting for night and Cree to visit and for them to talk.

~~~

The hour grew late and Dawn was brought no meal, and she wondered what was amiss. Flanna had said she'd return and if for some reason she wasn't able to, she would have made certain that someone brought her meal. She could very well cook herself, but after having a taste of Turbett's delicious fare, she much preferred it to her own.

Dawn had given Cree her word that she would not leave the cottage or she would have walked to the kitchen to see if there had been a problem and fetched the food herself. She would have also liked to see how Neil was doing. She understood that Cree worried for her safety, but she could not remain confined. She needed to be free.

There was a stirring outside the cottage door, then a rap upon it before it swung open to admit Dorrie, a basket on her arm.

"I am sorry that your meal is late, but there has been a terrible mishap at the keep," Dorrie said, hurrying to spread out the food on the table. "Cree took ill during the meal and took to his bed chamber. Elsa is with him now. Lucerne carried on endlessly that it was the cook's fault and that the fool had poisoned Cree."

Dawn's heart hammered in her chest. She grabbed Dorrie's arm, needing to know how Cree was, yet her hands trembled so much that she feared Dorrie would not understand her gestures.

Dorrie patted her hand. "Cree is doing well. From what I hear, Elsa purged his stomach and he is now resting, though not before he spoke to Turbett. I don't know what was discussed, though I do know that when Turbett returned to the kitchen he got busy preparing a special meal for you. He would not let anyone touch the food and chose me to bring it here since Flanna was busy."

Dawn wanted desperately to run to Cree's side and see for herself that he was all right, but she couldn't. And it angered her. She should be there for him as he was for her this morning when she had retched.

"I have to hurry," Dorrie said. "Turbett has us busy discarding the old meal and preparing a new one." She turned to go, then stopped, and lowered her voice. "I thought you should know that they caught another warrior who meant you harm. Talk is that he died before telling them anything. A brave one he must have been to suffer such torture and not confess."

Dawn paced the room after Dorrie left. Worry and anger churned in her. She did not know how she would be able to live this way, being part of Cree's life, yet not being part of it. She so badly wanted to be by his side, be there for him whenever he needed tending or caring.

She would get no rest this night. She would worry until he came to her, and she could see for herself that he was all right. This would not do, not do at all. If Dorrie hadn't brought her meal, she would not have known that Cree had taken ill. And then there was Neil. She had yet to hear if he was doing well.

Anger spewed up inside her and she wanted to scream with frustration, but she couldn't even do that. This day had taught her one thing and given her more determination than ever... she would be a prisoner no more. She did not care if someone was out to harm her. She would not hide away. Tomorrow she would visit with Elsa and see what she could learn about Cree. She would visit Lila and then Flanna and she would stop at the kitchen and thank Turbett for the meals he sends her. She would make her presence known in the village and to hell with the consequences.

She dropped down in the chair; her anger suddenly spent and worries consuming her. A tear spilled form her eye and she wiped it away. Elsa would take good care of Cree. He would be fine. He would return to her soon and she would see for herself.

Dawn got up and paced again and that was how she spent the next few hours pacing, sitting, and thinking, and pacing again. Her worry would surge, then be replaced by anger, and then she'd shed a tear or two in frustration.

No one came to take the food away, which worried her all the more. Could Cree have worsened?

Or perhaps the kitchen servants were being punished. But why? What had caused Cree to take ill? And why were others not ill as well if it was the food? And why had Turbett prepared a fresh meal for her after speaking with Cree? Did he fear someone might try and poison her? So many questions and not a single answer.

Finally, after endless hours Dawn collapsed on the chair to pace no more. Anxiety and anger had exhausted her, though it was feeling so helpless that brought her the most concern. She could do nothing to help Cree and that was something she found the most difficult to deal with.

When the door opened slowly, she jumped up hoping Flanna had managed to get away and let her know what was happening. Her eyes rounded when Cree stepped into the cottage. He looked pale and tired, though his stance was as imposing as ever.

She flew to his side and threw her arms around him. He hugged her tightly and rested his cheek to hers. She felt his exhaustion and was quick to react. She kept an arm around his waist and walked him to the other room where she quickly began to undress him.

"I am not feeling too well," he said.

She nodded and gestured that he needed to rest.

He reached out to run his hand gently down the side of her face. "I'll get no rest unless you're in my arms."

He had come to her in need, wanting her in his arms so that he could rest, for it seemed he could not do so without her. Her heart soared, for surely it was a sign that he loved her.

"You will not leave my side."

It was meant as an order, yet it sounded more like a plea to Dawn and she tapped his arm once. She then finished undressing him and pulled the blankets back for him to climb into bed.

He stopped her from covering him. "I want you beside."

She nodded and pointed to her garments to let him know as soon as she undressed, she would join him.

Still he would not let her cover him. "Hurry, for I will not seek any warmth until you are beside me."

Stubborn, she thought, though it did please her to know how much he wanted her in bed with him. She rushed out of her clothes and slipped into bed curling herself around him. Only then did he pull the covers over them.

His arms went around her, drawing her tightly against him and draping his one leg over hers. "This is what I've needed. Now I will heal."

My love will heal you; it will always heal you, Dawn thought and wished with all her heart that she could speak those words to him. She let him know the only way she could that she loved him. She squeezed her hand between their chests, pressed it to her heart and then to his.

Cree was already half asleep when he whispered, "You belong to me."

Dawn nestled her head against his bare chest wondering if that was the only way he could let her know that he loved her.

Chapter Six

Dawn woke early the next morning with Cree still wrapped around her. His breathing was steady and his body warm, though thankfully not feverish. It was good he still slept, rest would help heal him. And she intended to see that no one disturbed him. She would chase away anyone who came searching for him, no matter who it was.

Cree didn't budge when she eased herself out of his arms and out of bed. She slipped on a wool skirt and linen blouse and used the plain bone comb Paul had made for her years ago to get the tangles out of her hair, then she used a slim strip of leather to tie her long dark red hair back. Her hair was straight, not a curl or wave to it, though it was soft and had the loveliest shine to it.

She quietly left the room and being it was so early, and not knowing if food would be sent to her this morning, she decided to make sure she had food for her and Cree when he woke. She grabbed a bucket and went to the door.

Elwin, the warrior who first guarded her, stepped in front of the door as soon as she opened it. "You're not to be going anywhere," he said. "And Cree ordered that no one was to enter until he permitted it."

That brought a smile to her face and she held the empty bucket up.

Elwin smiled and nodded, filled the bucket from the rain barrel, and returned it to Dawn. She was pleased to learn that Cree thought the same as she did and had ordered that no one was to disturb them. She had him all to herself, if only for a while.

She got busy setting leaves to brewing for a tasty drink she and her mum used to enjoy on cold days. She also had enough oats and barley to make porridge and to make bread, though it would not be as tasty as Turbett's. It would however fill them.

It felt good to prepare her own meal again and this time it was not for her alone, which made the task that more pleasant.

She had just taken the last of the bread loaves, she had made, off the hearth stone when she heard...

"Dawn?"

She hurried into the other room to find Cree, blanket pushed back and ready to come find her. And ready for much more since he was as hard as stone. She rushed over to him and pushed him down on the bed, pulling the covers over him to his waist with her eyes focused above his hard chest... *hard*... damn but he was hard for her.

"You left me," he said upset.

She shook her head and sat on the bed beside him. She pushed her eyes wide, and then gestured holding a bowl and stirring and pointed to him and then herself.

He smiled. "You're cooking for us."

She nodded, then patted her stomach and pointed to him.

"I'm feeling better, though I'd feel much better if you crawled in beside me and kept me warm."

Dawn was ever so tempted, but he needed his rest, though she was curious as to what happened that had caused him to fall ill. She pointed at him, shrugged, and narrowed her eyes.

"A bit of bad food I suppose," he said and stretched his hand out to her.

She shook her head, not believing him.

"Do not worry about it; I am fine. Now get in this bed."

She shook her head adamantly and placed her hands on her hips.

"You're going to be stubborn about this, aren't you?"

She gave a sharp nod.

"My stomach soured, there is nothing more to it," he insisted. "Now come over here."

She crossed her arms over her chest and narrowed her eyes.

"You're going to make me come get you?" he asked with a grin that warned and tempted.

She pointed at him, her stomach, the bed, and then stepped back.

"I am well enough. I don't require anymore rest and did you just back away from me?"

She wanted nothing more than to crawl in bed with him and make love. The sight of his naked chest thick with muscles and the size of his organ thick and hard had made her wet and turned her legs limp, not to mention what it did to her resolve to see that he rested.

She had to remain strong and see that he healed, so with her chin set firm, she took another step back.

"Oh, my love, you're going to pay for that." He grinned and jumped out of bed.

She was so shocked that he called her *my love* that she failed to react and she was even more shocked that he had loosened her skirt and pushed it to the ground. Her mouth dropped open.

He pressed a finger to it. "Not a word."

He startled her again by speaking to her as if she had a voice, though she should be used to it by now, he had done it so often. And again he distracted her so that her blouse was dismissed without a thought.

His grin grew wicked when he grabbed her shoulders and walked her backward to the bed, giving her a shove when the back of her legs touched the edge. As she fell back, he took hold of her legs and yanked off her boots. Then he came down on top of her, nesting his hardness between her legs.

"Now that's where I want to be." He kissed her softly. "Do you want me there, love?"

Love. The word turned her into a simpering fool, but what did she care. She wanted him snug inside her just as much—perhaps more—than he wanted to bury himself in her.

She wrapped her arms around his neck and kissed him with a fervor that had stirred in her from when she had first entered the room and saw him naked and hard.

He responded in kind, his kiss deep and hungry. His arm went around her waist, lifting her to move her further along the bed so that their legs did not hang off the edge. Then he nestled over her raining kisses down along her neck until he reached her breasts, and then he nipped playfully at her nipples that budded tightly like a flower before full bloom.

She ran her fingers through his glorious soft hair, digging into his scalp, holding him against her, wanting him never to stop. But he did, not that she complained since he moved slowly down her body worshiping it with gently nips and tender kisses.

He raised his head for a moment and said, "Damn, but I love the taste of you."

He worked his way slowly down her body and before he could settle his face between her legs, she tugged at his arm. He looked up and she shook her head and gestured for him to enter her and relieve her torment.

With a wicked grin he shook his head. "I am going to make you come over and over until you're so spent you can do nothing but collapse in my arms... where you belong."

Belong. Yes, she belonged in his arms, belonged here in bed with him and belonged in his heart. His love was silent like her voice, but she heard it as clearly as he heard her. Her heart swelled along with her passion as his tongue pleased her in ways she never thought possible. He did make her come over and over until finally, he could no longer stand it himself. He entered her quick and fast, though he did not climax that way. He took his time pleasuring her as well as himself with deep, penetrating thrusts. And she locked her legs around him taking him deeper and deeper, locking tightly around him until neither one of them could contain themselves any longer. In unison they exploded in a climax that sent them hurdling, surging, and erupting over and over until Cree collapsed, spent on top of her.

After a moment, when sanity returned, Cree felt Dawn's body shake with laughter. He looked at her and saw that she wore a wide grin and that her body still rumbled against him with laughter.

"You find our love making funny?" he asked teasingly, knowing her too well to think their love making anything but satisfying.

She shook her head and continued smiling as she tapped his chest, sighed soundlessly, though heavily, her shoulders drooping and then wrapped her arms as far as they would go around his back.

He laughed. "I'm spent and in your arms."

She nodded, patted her chest and hugged him.

"You love me in your arms."

There was that word again. *Love*. And he was right. She loved him in her arms and all others ways too, though for now she nodded and smiled and hugged him tighter.

"I love being in your arms," he whispered and brushed her lips with his. "And I love being inside you."

She wiggled against him.

"You like it too."

She nodded, pressed a finger to his mouth, then to hers and patted her chest.

He scrunched his brow for a moment. "You like the way we talk?"

She pressed once against his arm.

He brushed his lips over hers once again and slipped off her, settling her in his arms to rest against him and pulled the blanket over them. "I have found it easy and pleasing to talk with you ever since we first met."

Dawn raised a brow.

"You communicate much better than you think, although when you get angry it is a bit more difficult to understand you. In time, I'm sure that won't matter. I'll understand you perfectly."

In time. They had time and it would seem much of it and that pleased her, though feeling a prisoner didn't. Now, however, was not the time to burden him with such a discussion. He was still healing, though she could attest to the return of his stamina.

"I'm hungry," he announced with a hug.

She scrambled over him, and he teasingly wrapped his arm around her waist and his hand went to her buttocks, giving it a firm squeeze. "We spend the day in bed, you and me. I have left instructions that no one was permitted to disturb me until I allowed it. So we have the day and the night, for I need the time to heal and I need—you."

She pointed to herself and then to him.

"I know you need me as well. We are one, you and I, and we always will be."

His hand went to the back of her neck, and he forced her head down so that her mouth met his. He kissed her with a fiery fury that let her know in no uncertain terms that he meant it.

She rested her brow to his for a moment to catch her breath. Her hands cupped her face and he brushed his lips over hers. "I have never known such tasty kisses until I kissed you."

Her heart soared. She smiled, patted her chest, shook her head and tapped his chest.

He laughed. "You have no one to compare my kisses to."

Her smile faded. She tapped his lips, tapped her lips, and shook her head.

"You want only my kisses?"

She nodded.

"That is good, for my kisses are the only ones you will ever taste, the only ones you will ever need."

She smiled again and nodded enthusiastically.

He smiled and laughed and kissed her soundly. "You make me laugh and smile. Things I have not done often enough." He slapped her bottom playfully "And now it is time to feed me, woman, for I have an insatiable lover and I must keep up my stamina to please her."

She laughed soundlessly and tapped his chest.

"I'm insatiable?" Cree huffed.

Dawn grinned and crossed her arms over her chest, hugging herself.

"You love that I am."

Her eyes went wide, her brow went up, and she nodded slowly.

Cree laughed again and hugged her tightly rocking them back and forth. "Damn, woman, but I'm glad your mine."

She gave a pat to her chest to let him know she felt the same about him as she scrambled off him. Cree reluctantly released her.

Dawn leaned over to pick up her clothes.

"Don't dare dress. I want you naked. We will stay naked all day and stay in bed all day. We will eat, talk, sleep, and make love throughout the entire day."

That sounded perfect to Dawn and she hoped it would be so. She hurried to gather the food she had made and they were soon feasting on porridge and bread.

"I have sent for my sister to come live here," Cree said tearing a piece of bread off the flat loaf.

Dawn's eyes turned wide, and she didn't need to gesture for Cree to understand.

"Yes, I have a sister. I let no one know about her for fear my enemies would harm her," he said. "I have not seen her in a few years. She is a woman grown now, ten and nine years. I hope to make a fine match for her, a man of substance, one who will look after her and treat her well."

Dawn wondered how is sister would feel about having a husband chosen for her. But then being of nobility, his sister had little choice. She would have to obey her brother's edict whether it pleased her or not.

"Wintra is like you," he said with a tweak to the tip of her nose, "getting herself into all sorts of things she shouldn't. You two will get along well."

Dawn looked forward to meeting her, though she wondered how friendly they could become. She was after all a lowly peasant. It was Cree's wife his sister would befriend.

He rested a hand on his stomach, and Dawn was quick to place her hand over his, his eyes having taken on a pained expression.

"I am fine. My stomach but sours slightly. Elsa had told me it was to be expected and that I should rest a day or two and eat lightly. But my body calls for sustenance and I have never lain abed all day." He smiled. "But then I never had reason to. Now I have you." His smile faded as a heavy yawn hit him and he dropped his head back.

She hurried to clean away the food. When she went to tuck the blanket around him, he stopped her.

"Not until you are in this bed with me."

She nodded and quickly added more logs to the fire before slipping into bed beside him and tucking the blanket around them both. She snuggled against him, and his arms went around her.

"You will not leave me," he said. "I want to wake with you in my arms."

She nodded and rested her head on his chest. She did not know if she would sleep, but it did not matter. She was content to have him here beside her. She would enjoy this time she had with him even if it meant lying there in his arms while he slept, for she did not know when she would have him to herself for a whole day again.

She woke with a start, not knowing if she had slept a few moments or several hours. When she realized that the room had taken on a chill, she cast an eye at the hearth and saw the flames had burned low. She knew then that they had slept hours. Cree still slept, and she did not want him to wake to a cold room so she eased herself out of his arms, though she didn't get far.

"I am not awake yet, and you are to be in my arms when I wake.'

She poked him playfully, and then pretended to shiver.

"The room has chilled. You stay, I'll tend the fire," he said opening his eyes.

She shook her head and wiggled out of his arms.

"Dawn," he warned, but she was out of bed and at the hearth before he stretched himself awake.

She added three logs, some kindling, and stoked the embers until the wood caught and the hearth was ablaze, and then she added another log. She held her hands out in front of the fire for a moment before hurrying back to bed.

Cree held the blanket back for her, and she climbed in beside him. He shivered when she pressed her chilled, naked body against his.

"I'm going to have to warm you," he said hugging her tight.

She agreed with an eager nod.

"This lying abed all day is not bad at all," he said and nibbled at her neck.

She scrunched her shoulders, against the tickling sensations running throughout her body.

"I think we'll take this love making slower than before."

She grew wet at the thought, thinking that they certainly hadn't hurried the last time. And wanting to give him as much pleasure as he gave her, she slipped her hand down to take hold of his hard organ and relished its silky feel.

"Hmmm that feels good," Cree whispered in her ear and then nibbled at her earlobe.

Not sure what to do, Dawn let instinct take hold. She found herself stroking him, up and down, harder, softer, harder again. Then she suddenly got the urge to taste him as he had done to her. She wiggled her way down and when she gave a tentative taste, she discovered that she liked the flavor.

She gave no thought to anything but enjoying herself. She licked and tasted, fueled by her passion. When he moaned loudly, she realized she had fueled his as well and liked that she held such power over him. So she set to work, though it was no work at all but rather pure pleasure, driving him mad.

After several minutes Cree groaned, "Good God, woman."

She grinned before taking him deeper into her mouth and that's when the pounding on the door interrupted them.

"Cree! Cree! I insist that you open this door now."

Dawn jumped off the bed upon hearing Lucerne's screeching voice.

Cree let several oaths fly, lunged out of bed and, stark naked, walked into the other room and flung open the door.

Chapter Seven

"You go against my command!" Cree screamed at Lucerne.

For a moment Lucerne stood speechless staring at him, her eyes growing rounder as she took all of him in.

Dawn had slipped on Cree's shirt and had positioned herself at the bedroom doorway to peek beyond the curtain that separated the two rooms and catch a glimpse of what was going on. A draft swirled in from the open door and along the floor to nip at her bare feet, and she worried that Cree, in his naked splendor, would catch a chill. She also could not believe that Lucerne questioned Cree. She had barely arrived and wasn't yet his wife, yet acted as if she was.

Lucerne finally moved to step into the cottage, but Cree blocked her entrance with his arm.

"Why are you here and not in the keep in your bed chambers?" she more demanded than asked. "And why are you naked?"

"Neither is any concern of yours. Return to the keep *now*."

Lucerne went to respond.

Cree leaned forward, planting his face an inch from hers. "Disobey me and I'll see you secluded in your quarters until your parents arrive. Elwin," he roared and the guard stepped forward, "see that my lady returns safely to the keep."

"Aye, my lord," Elwin said with a bob of his head and as Cree stepped back Elwin stepped between them and ushered Lucerne away.

As soon as Cree slammed the door shut and bolted the latch, Dawn hurried out of his shirt and jumped back in bed.

Cree entered the room shivering, and this time Dawn pulled the blanket back to welcome him in bed. He slipped in, and she shivered when he hugged her close, his body chilled. She grew concerned and started rubbing warmth back into his flesh.

"You'll warm me much faster if you finish what you had started."

She smiled and moved down along his body heating it with kisses as she went. Then she once again settled her mouth over him and proceeded to finish what she had started. She was pleased with herself when she heated him to a feverish pitch, and he moaned with agonizing pleasure. Her own body squirmed with need, aching to climax and just when she thought he would come, he reached down and grabbed her waist. With one swift motion, he had her under him and with another swift motion, he buried himself deep inside her with a single thrust.

He pressed his cheek to hers and whispered in her ear, "We climax together."

She pressed her finger against his arm over and over and over as he drove into her again and again and again.

"Come with me now," he demanded and she obeyed and they both burst in blinding passion.

They lay silent in each other's arms after Cree rolled off her. After a few minutes, he pulled the blanket over them and hugged Dawn close. She rested replete against him. The silence remained, but it did not hang heavy as it would with most. It was peaceful silence, for they were content and needed no words between them.

The fire in the hearth crackled and popped, Cree stroking her arm until finally he said, "I am famished. Are you?"

She was hungrier than she had been of late, and so she nodded rigorously.

"I will remedy our situation. Stay in bed," he ordered and got out, slipped on his shirt, and walked into the other room.

She heard the door open, but since this time there was no shouting, she could not hear what he was saying. He returned fast enough, discarding his shirt, and once again joined her in bed.

"We will have a feast in no time," he said with a grin.

She patted his stomach, rock hard, against her hand.

"My stomach is well. The sleep did me good as did our lovemaking."

Dawn smiled at him and draped her leg over his to lock herself more closely around him. She relished this rare time with him and wished that it didn't have to be so rare.

They talked, ate, and slept well into the next day, and Dawn was pleased that he was not in a hurry to leave. And she believed he would have remained the entire day with her if the village bell hadn't tolled, alerting all to an approaching troop of warriors.

Cree dressed quickly. "You stay in the cottage —"

She shook her head before he could finish and hurried into her clothes.

"I have no time to argue with you." He grabbed her chin. "You will do as I say."

She tapped her chest, shook her finger, and stamped her foot to demonstrate her displeasure.

"A tantrum won't work," he said with a laugh.

She shook her head, letting him know that it was no tantrum but rather annoyance at being kept prisoner, and so she raised her arms and crossed her wrists as if shackled.

"Damn, woman, you're not a prisoner," he said with an angry growl and brushed her wrists apart, then gave her a gentle shove into the other room. He grabbed her fur-lined cloak from the peg and tossed it at her. "You'll make sure to stay close to Elwin or he'll be dragging you back here and locking you in."

She patted her chest in promise.

Cree swung open the door and Elwin stepped forward. "A small troop of warriors approach at a slow pace. Sloan has taken a troop out to meet them."

Cree nodded and yanked Dawn in front of him. "She is not to be far from your side or leave your sight. If she gives you any trouble, return her here and don't let her leave."

Elwin bobbed his head. "Aye, my lord."

Cree gave Dawn a quick kiss. "Take no chances, behave, and stay out of trouble. I will see you later." He hurried off, though stopped after a few steps, turned and with a grin said, "Elwin, if she does not obey, you have my permission to do whatever is necessary to get her back to the cottage. And I suggest throwing her over your shoulder would be the best approach."

Elwin couldn't help but smile upon seeing Cree's grin. It was a rare sight, and he nodded and said once again, "Aye, my lord."

Dawn tilted her head and produced a sweet smile and hooked her arm around Elwin's to the big man's surprise.

Cree's grin vanished in an instant, and he stomped through the few inches of snow that carpeted the ground to stop barely an inch from her. Elwin had wisely moved aside, giving the couple privacy.

Cree lowered his face and whispered harshly in her ear, "I warned you once that you touch no man but me. Do not make me warn you again." He was startled when she responded by resting a gentle hand to his cheek, then patted her chest and then his. "That's right you belong to me and only me." He kissed her possessively, and then stomped away.

Dawn stared after him and her lips crept up in a smile. She turned to Elwin.

He stepped forward. "It is good to see him smile. He deserves to be happy for all he has done for us."

She purposely set a slow pace, hoping that Elwin would keep talking about Cree, and she wasn't disappointed.

"He saved many of us from suffering terrible fates and gave us a chance for a good life. And he didn't ask anything of any of his men that he wouldn't ask of himself. He fought and suffered along with every one of us, reminding us all that we worked for a common cause... a permanent home and a better life. And he gave us just that."

Elwin stopped a minute and gazed up at the gray sky. "More snow today. That's probably why that troop of warriors are here. They seek shelter." He smiled. "I have a cottage, and now a good woman to share it with thanks to you."

Dawn turned a wide grin on him.

Elwin actually blushed. "If you hadn't rescued Dorrie from the stocks and I hadn't been sent to guard her, she would have never looked twice at me, though your unselfish actions certainly did much to change her selfish ways."

Dawn's eyes widened.

Elwin laughed. "I'm not a fool. Dorrie was selfish and cared for no one but herself, though not anymore. She's different or maybe she just needed to be shown a different way, much like what Cree did with the men he gathered."

Dawn had no time to consider Elwin's words. He stopped and nodded. "They approach."

She and Elwin stood off to the side, not far from her cottage, to watch the troop that followed Sloan and his men stop at the keep. Cree waited at the top of the steps, the breadth and width of him all in black sending a shiver through her and no doubt intimidating the small troop of ten men that stared at him.

Cree didn't descend the few steps to greet them. He waited for them to come to him, and Dawn wondered how one man could exude such power and confidence. She recalled the first time she had seen him being brought into the village, a captive, his wrists shackled. Even though a prisoner, he exuded the same power and confidence.

The warrior in the lead dismounted while the other warriors remained astride their horses. He was fairly tall, broad-chested, and had long hair as white as freshly fallen snow. He ascended the steps quickly and after what Dawn thought could be construed as a tense exchange both men smiled, and the stranger called out to his men to dismount. They all filed into the keep, and Dawn wished that she could be privy to what was going on. Not wanting to wallow in disappointment, she decided to begin a routine for herself. So that once again she was part of village life. She had already tasked herself with the chore of finding out who would want her harmed, but she would also like to find something that would keep her hands busy as well as help settle her overburdened thoughts.

She decided to visit with Lila. She would be happy, though more relieved to see that Dawn was feeling better and had finally gotten herself out of the cottage. She recalled Lila telling her that Cree had placed her in charge of weaving plaids for the villagers and had assigned her not only women to help, but a separate cottage where the work could be done.

Dawn made a motion of using a spindle and distaff and shrugged her shoulders in question.

Elwin nodded. "You want to know where your friend Lila carries out her daily chore." He smiled. "She weaves a fine cloth."

Dawn agreed with a quick nod and followed next to Elwin. They came upon a good-sized cottage not far from the healer's place.

Elwin gave a glance skyward and shivered. "A storm brews and a good one at that."

Dawn shivered herself, though she didn't know if it was from the impending storm or something else that brewed. But something was coming, she felt it in her bones, as Old Mary would say.

She entered the cottage and Lila beamed with delight, quickly handing a smiling Thomas to her. Dawn eagerly took the babe in her arms, hugging him tight, and he gurgled and rubbed his face against her chest.

"That babe loves you dearly," one of the four women working the wool said.

Dawn felt a flutter in her heart. She loved Thomas just as dearly and the thought that she would have her own babe to cuddle and love thrilled her. Lila was quick to show off the weave of red, black, and a touch of yellow that would become the new plaid for the Clan Carrick. The women talked, and Dawn joined in now and again, Lila interpreting for her, though a couple of times it wasn't necessary. The women understood her and that pleased Dawn.

Thomas fell asleep in Dawn's arms and Lila had her place him in the cradle next to another cradle holding a sleeping babe. She told the women she'd be only a moment as she grabbed her cloak from the peg and walked with Dawn to the door. They told her not to rush and bid Dawn a good day. She smiled, nodded, and extended her hand and wished them the same.

Elwin walked several steps away when the two women stepped out of the cottage, affording them privacy.

"I'm so relieved to see that you are feeling well again. I have missed you," Lila said, her eyes a bit teary.

Dawn patted her chest and grinned to confirm she was feeling mighty fit.

Lila lowered her voice. "I heard that Neil saved you from being harmed. Gossip is that Cree was furious that the two captured men succumbed to endless hours of torture. I am glad you have Cree to protect you, so do not do anything foolish."

Dawn gestured her lone window being boarded.

Lila laughed. "You have created a stir in the village with your courage, and tongues wag as to how an angel tames the devil."

Dawn's eyes rounded surprised that people should think that, though she was more surprised by how wide Lila's eyes suddenly turned. She followed Lila's startled gaze and stopped herself from appearing as alarmed as her friend, staring at the warrior sitting astride his horse that slowed when it neared them. She would not do to another what often had been done to her...stare in pity and discomfort.

Elwin stepped protectively closer to Dawn and kept his eyes on the warrior, especially since the man seemed focused intently on Dawn. And she could not help but hold his gaze, for she had never seen a facial wound so vicious. It ran from above his left eye down along his cheek to end at his chin. It was still healing, red and raw, and appeared ever so painful.

Villagers looked on, whispering among themselves for without the scar the stranger would be a handsome man with dark hair and piercing blue eyes. He sat his mare with confidence that mirrored Cree's, and though he was not possessed of the breadth and width of Cree, his lean hard frame and broad shoulders warned that he was a man of strength and not to be dismissed without thought.

Dawn wondered why he stared at her as if puzzled, and she knew that Elwin would not fail to report the incident to Cree. Since he wore the same colored plaid as the troop that had just ridden into the village, it seemed reasonable to assume that he was part of them. She didn't want an unnecessary problem arising because of her, and so she decided to handle the situation here and now.

She grabbed Lila's arm and dragged her along with her as she hurried around Elwin, who was so surprised by her action that it took him a moment to rush after her. By that time, the warrior had stopped, and she and Lila stood beside his horse.

Dawn gestured and Lila instinctively interpreted. "Dawn cannot speak. She has no voice, but she wishes to know if she is familiar to you somehow since you stare at her?"

"Forgive my rudeness, I meant no disrespect," the warrior said with a bow of his head to Dawn. "You resemble someone I knew."

Dawn found his response curious and wanted to know more, Elwin thought differently. He stepped in front of her. "Be gone with you; join your troop at the keep."

The warrior gave Elwin a brief nod and without another word moved on.

Elwin turned on Dawn. "Are you a fool, lassie? You don't go speaking to strangers, especially when your life is in danger. And he appears a mean one. You don't get a scar like that in just any fight. Now be minding yourself and behave."

It was Lila's turn to reprimand her. "Elwin's right. That man does not appear afraid of anything." She shivered. "I cannot imagine how he will fair with Cree when he learns of the stranger's rudeness to you."

Dawn wanted to shake her head and plead with them not to tell Cree. What good would it do? Nothing had happened. She simply resembled someone the warrior had known, nothing more. Damn if she didn't feel like a prisoner again.

"Time to be getting back to your cottage," Elwin ordered.

Dawn shook her head and gestured rapidly.

Lila explained. "She wants to go to the kitchen and gather some items she needs."

"That's good," Elwin said with a nod more to himself than the two women. "You can keep yourself busy cooking.

Dawn held up her hand and gestured again.

Elwin looked to Lila. "She wants to stop at the healer's cottage first and see how Neil is doing."

"He's having a fine time of it with Elsa fussing over him," Elwin said with a grin.

Dawn tapped her chest several times and narrowed her eyes. Her gesture needed no interpretation.

"All right, you can see for yourself," Elwin said.

With a quick hug to Lila, Dawn walked off with Elwin, their pace brisk as snow flurries began to fall.

Her stop at Elsa's proved brief. Neil was sleeping, though Elsa assured Dawn that he was doing fine. Rest and a healing hand were all he required. She wondered if perhaps Elsa could lend a healing hand to the scarred warrior. Though he was a stranger, he had spoken kindly to her and had not been appalled or disturbed by her not being able to speak. She would approach Elsa about it another time. With a smile and a nod, Dawn bid Elsa good-bye.

The flurries were turning quickly to a heavy snow that had the villagers hurrying inside their warm cottages. Dawn intended to do the same as soon as she collected a few items from the kitchen.

A snowy wind rushed her into the kitchen when Elwin opened the door for her, and he was quick to close it behind them. Turbett was shouting orders as usual and the workers were jumping to his commands.

He rolled his eyes when he spotted Dawn. "Dorrie see to whatever Dawn wants."

Dorrie smiled broadly and hurried over to stand close to Elwin and gave Dawn a nod. "What can I get you?"

Dawn turned and grabbed an empty basket by the door. She tapped her chest and pointed around, letting Dorrie know she could fetch what she needed herself. She had barely taken a step when Flanna entered the room, her eyes turning wide when she spotted Dawn.

She hurried over to Dawn, grabbed her arm and whispered, "We must talk."

Chapter Eight

Flanna ushered Dawn into the small storage room off the kitchen and kept her voice low, not that it mattered. There was so much commotion in the kitchen that no one would hear Flanna.

"Lady Lucerne ranted like a banshee last night after being escorted back to the keep from your cottage. Sloan was in the Great Hall having returned from one of his nightly trysts just in time to stop her from delivering a hard blow to her servant's sweet face, though there was a bad bruise on Bree's wrist this morning, so she took her anger out on the poor lass anyway. She knows Cree seeks your bed and she doesn't like it. Be careful, she's an evil and untrustworthy woman."

Dawn nodded, having surmised the same herself from what she had seen of Lucerne thus far. There was no doubt she would be a problem, and Dawn was concerned that in her position she could truly be helpless against the woman. Lucerne would be the lady of the keep and, therefore, Dawn would be bound to obey if such an occasion ever arose. The thought troubled her, and her hand went protectively to her stomach, pressing flat against it, suddenly worried about the babe.

"The servants listen and hear, I will learn more," Flanna said. "Go get food to keep you for a few days. The storm that blows in will keep us close to our hearths. It is the reason the troop stopped in the village and requested shelter. They were returning home when the storm forced them to turn around, and it kept close on their heels all the way here."

Dawn shrugged in question wondering about the troop.

"Laird Kirk McClusky and his son Torr," Flanna said. "Their land borders Carrick land and are neighbors to Kirk Gerwan , though Lucerne barely acknowledges them. One of the servants heard her refer to them as a fighting brood of poor stock. When she had been informed that there would be guests, she fancied herself up and entered the Great Hall as if she were a regal queen. When she saw the boisterous men, her hand went to her head, and I knew she was about to feign one of her frequent headaches. Then she caught sight of Torr and her nose wrinkled in disgust and she fled the room. He bears a bad facial scar and a shame it is, since he'd be as handsome as Cree without it."

Dawn shook her head and smiled.

Flanna grinned. "You're right. No one is as handsome as the devil."

Dawn scolded playfully with a shake of her finger and, though meant in jest, there was some truth to her admonishment. Cree was no devil; he was a good man.

"He's a quiet one though, sits there and stares with those stark blue eyes of his. I've never seen eyes such a vibrant blue. They can cause you to shiver or send tingles over the flesh." And Flanna shivered just thinking about them. "I have to get back. We're busy with the unexpected arrival of the troop, and you need to get home and stay put."

Dawn nodded and took Flanna's hand squeezing it, letting her know how appreciative she was for the news.

"I have my eyes and ears open. There'll be more to tell for sure. Now fill your basket with dried apples to brew cider, so it appears that's why I dragged you in here. Don't want to give gossiping tongues more fodder."

Flanna joined Dorrie in gathering more food staples for Dawn. When Turbett saw what they were up to, he praised Flanna for being sensible in providing Dawn with enough food to see her through the storm so that the servants did not have to brave the horrid weather.

Dawn had to smile. Turbett had eyes only for Flanna when he talked and Flanna actually appeared to soften as he spoke. They made an odd pair; Turbett so large and Flanna small in stature, though not in nature. It pleased Dawn to see that Flanna had finally found someone who cared for her rather than someone who simply used her for his own pleasure.

Turbett turned away, shouting orders once again. "There'll be no rest today. We have hungry warriors to feed."

The kitchen bustled like never before, though the workers did seem a happy lot. Flanna had mentioned once that Turbett fed them well and allowed them to take some food staples home to their families. Many had gotten to realize that while Turbett blustered and brandished a wooden spoon, he had never harmed anyone. And it was obvious that he enjoyed cooking and took great care in preparing tasty meals.

Dawn and Elwin were soon on their way, though the snow had worsened and slowed their pace. Visibility was poor and the wind snapped at them like icy whips. Dawn was never so happy to enter the cottage. She tugged Elwin in with her and when he tried to protest, she stepped in front of the closed door, hands on hips, shaking her head.

He attempted to argue with her, but it did little good. When she finally got him to understand what she was trying to tell him, that no one could possibly be out and about in such horrid weather so there was no need for worry, he nodded.

"Only a fool would risk venturing out in this," Elwin said finally realizing it himself.

The door burst open then and Sloan rushed in the cottage. "Is Old Mary here?"

"No," Elwin said. "We haven't seen her."

Dawn grabbed Sloan's arm and looked at him anxiously.

"Someone saw her go into the woods earlier and now she is nowhere to be found," Sloan explained, then looked to Elwin. "Cree orders your return to the keep to help search the village and her old cottage. But we must hurry the storm worsens by the minute."

Dawn had wandered over to the hearth, her worry for Old Mary growing rapidly. The old woman had been good to her ever since they had first met. And the thought that she could be out there in the freezing snow alone, chilled Dawn to the bone and angered her. Both men knew as well as she did that if Old Mary was without shelter for long, she would not survive the storm. But with visibility so bad, any attempt at searching for her would surely prove futile and dangerous to those who searched, for they too could get lost and succumb to the blinding storm.

"Dawn."

She turned to Sloan. "You are to remain here. You will latch the door when we leave, and you are *not* to open it to anyone except me, Elwin, or Cree. Do you understand?"

Dawn nodded and removed her cloak. She did as Sloan ordered; she latched the door once they left. She looked at the baskets of food and told herself to get busy fixing a meal for later, but she had no want to do so. She could think of nothing but Old Mary.

Why would the old woman go into the woods when she knew a snowstorm drew near? And she certainly could not feign ignorance of the approaching storm, for Old Mary—more than anyone in the village—was the most accurate in predicting the weather. What could possibly be of such importance that she challenged a storm to go into the woods?

Dawn paced thinking about it. Old Mary knew the woods well, especially since her old cottage had sat a bit of a distance from the village. A sudden thought stopped her pacing. There was another spot Old Mary frequented not far from her cottage. It was the remnants of an old shed. Dawn never understood why she puttered around the place, though lovely wildflowers did grow there in spring and summer. It made no sense though for her to go there now when a snowstorm brewed.

But what if she did go there? The warriors didn't know that area well and in the storm they certainly wouldn't be able to find it. Her thoughts continued to ramble and she continued to pace. The knock on the door startled her, and she wasn't sure if it had been minutes or hours since the men had left.

"It's Elwin. Open up."

Dawn anxiously lifted the latch, eager to find out if they had found Old Mary.

Elwin stepped in, his cloak covered with snow and his cheeks stung red. "We've had no success in finding her and the whipping snow blinds so badly that you can't see your way through it. You'll not need a guard tonight. No one can brave that weather and survive." Elwin cringed realizing what his words meant. Old Mary would die if she was stuck without shelter from this storm. "Latch the door and thank the heavens you are safe."

She should be grateful for her good fortune while her friend could possibly be dying? She latched the door after Elwin left, her decision having been made as soon as Elwin had informed her that they would search no more today.

It didn't take her long to slip her stockings on and to wrap her hands with strips of cloth. She then wrapped her shawl around her head so that it would cover her nose and mouth and slipped on her wool cloak and placed her fur-lined cloak over that. She took a wool blanket and wrapped it around her. She was not only set to tackle the storm, but to keep Mary warm once she found her.

She hoped that she was right as to where Old Mary had gone. If Dawn was lucky, she would find her there and they could both wait out the storm at the old woman's cottage. If not, then she hoped she would at least find Old Mary somewhere along the way. Whatever the case, she intended to find her friend and see her safe.

As soon as she stepped into the harsh swirling snow, she knew her task would be far more difficult than she had imagined, but that only spurred her on. Time was of the essence if she was to find Old Mary, and so with her head down and her determination strong, she pressed forward battling the raging snow and howling wind.

~~~

Cree was not comfortable with the decision to suspend the search for Old Mary, but he had little choice. Visibility was so poor that his men could go in circles for hours and not realize it. Whatever possessed the old woman to go off on her own when the weather had obviously bore signs of a snowstorm puzzled him. Her careless decision could not have come at a worse time.

With the arrival of the McClusky troop he was needed at the keep and so were several of his warriors. The McCluskys were known as fierce fighters, had strong opinions, and known to brawl for little reason or perhaps that had to do with their steadfast opinions. They were also honorable warriors and true to those they called friend and being their land bordered Cree's, he intended for them to be friends.

He had heard tales of Kirk McClusky's son, Torr, and his fighting abilities. Gossip had it that ten men could not take him down and his prowess with a sword was legendary. So Cree could not help but wonder who had scarred the mighty warrior, and if the culprit still lived. It would be rude to ask him and being the man was not one to speak about his exploits and silenced others—who dared to try—with a threatening look, Cree would not know the tale.

The scarred warrior sat at the dais with them, though was not at all present. He did little but grunt when a question was directed at him until finally no one bothered him. He was left alone, while talk and laughter went on around him as if he did not exist.

Cree politely excused himself for a moment when Elwin entered the Great Hall and went to speak with the man.

"My lord," Elwin said with a brief nod. "The snowstorm has turned brutal and we had no luck in finding Old Mary. Sloan is seeing to a warrior who was injured in a fall during the search. He will be here shortly. I told Dawn she was to remain in her cottage with the door latched and to answer it to no one but me, Sloan, or you. She conceded without protest and latched the door behind me."

"You are to check on her from time to time until I join her later," Cree ordered. "Now go and get yourself warm and eat."

With a bob of his head, Elwin went off to join some of his fellow warriors at a table close to the hearth while Cree returned to the dais. He would have preferred to go and see for himself that Dawn was safe, but he could not spare the time at the moment.

Cree no sooner got involved in an interesting conversation with Kirk McClusky regarding their adjoining land when he saw Lucerne's servant Bree meekly approach the dais.

She was a petite lass with bright curly red hair and a pretty face. More often than not she appeared skittish like an animal that had been whipped too many times, and Cree was fairly certain that Lucerne took a heavy hand to the lass. It was an issue he would have to address soon.

She stood silent before the dais waiting for him to acknowledge her, but Sloan caught Cree's attention as he entered the room and hurried to the table.

"The storm rages like an angry woman," Sloan said and everyone at the table, except Torr, laughed. He was about to make another remark when he caught sight of the servant, her head bent, waiting. "I interrupted the lovely lass. Please forgive my rudeness."

Bree's cheeks turned red and she shook her head. "Forgive the intrusion, but Lady Lucerne has requested the healer."

"Is it another headache?" Cree asked without an ounce of concern.

"Yes, my lord," Bree said.

"I will not have the healer wade through a raging snowstorm to the keep for nothing more than a headache." Bree went to say something and Cree raised his hand. "There is nothing more to say. Go."

Bree turned and fled.

"She's a pretty thing," Sloan said filling his tankard with ale.

"Too timid."

"You never know, those quiet ones can prove not at all docile."

"Is that all you think about is bedding women?" Cree snapped.

"What else is there?" Sloan said with a laugh.

"Love," Kirk McClusky said raising his tankard.

Sloan shook his head. "No thank you. I've seen the consequences of falling in love and I prefer not to suffer them."

Kirk let loose with a boisterous laugh. "What makes you think you'll have a choice? Once love hits, you're done for, you're finished. She has your heart and there isn't anything you wouldn't do for her."

"Never," Sloan protested.

"You just sealed your fate, lad," Kirk said, hoisting his tankard high once again. "Now love will get you good."

The teasing continued, Cree laughing along with the others as Kirk and Sloan voiced their strong opinions on the subject of love. His thoughts however wandered to Dawn and how he felt about her. There wasn't anything he wouldn't do for her, but there were also things he couldn't do. He had a duty that love could not even amend. And why was he even thinking of love? Was it because he detested being separated from Dawn? He missed her badly even when they were separated for only a few hours. He loved the feel of her in his arms, the way she molded herself around him when they slept and how she forever responded so eagerly to his every kiss and touch.

"The timid one returns," Sloan whispered and Cree could almost hear him smile, though when he looked to Sloan, he saw that his smile was fading and his jaw turned tight in anger.

Cree knew he wasn't going to like what he was about to see. He turned his eyes on Bree once again standing timidly in front of the dais and had to stop himself from pounding the table in anger, for his actions no doubt would frighten the already fearful lass. Her right eye was bruised and swollen and there was a fresh welt on her cheek from a hit that had to have been delivered with brutal force.

"Who did this to you?" Cree demanded.

"I spoke out of turn, my lord. It was my fault," Bree said.

Cree was aware that she wasn't defending Lucerne, but rather protecting herself, for if she spoke against the lady she would suffer for it and that angered him even more.

"Lady Lucerne insists that the healer be brought to her and that I am not to return without the woman," Bree said with bravery spurred by fear.

Cree stood and turned to Sloan. He had helped treat many a wounded warrior on the battle field so Cree felt confident in leaving Bree in Sloan's care. "See to her while I speak with Lucerne."

Bree's eyes turned wide. "No, my lord, please I beg you. My lady will be furious if you arrive unannounced at her bed chamber door."

"*My lady* doesn't set the rules here—*I do*." And with that said Cree walked out of the Great Hall and made his way up the stone staircase, his temper mounting with each step he climbed.

Lucerne deserved a good thrashing, but he would not raise his hand to a woman. His memories were too vivid of what had been done to his mother, and he would not cause a woman to suffer such abuse.

Cree didn't bother to knock on her door. This was his keep and it was time she realized that. He walked right in slamming the door behind him.

Lucerne was so shocked she could do nothing but stare at him for a moment, and then she let loose with her temper. "How dare you enter my bed chamber without so much as a knock. You will apologize, my lord, for your rude and barbaric behavior."

He walked over to the bed where she sat ensconced like a queen, bolstered by numerous pillows and wearing a dark green velvet robe, a soft green wool nightdress beneath. He reached down, grabbed her wrist, and yanked her out of bed.

She stumbled, gasped, and looked ready to kill him. "How dare—"

Cree took hold of both her wrists and yanked her hard against him. "I dare to do anything I wish in my home. You seem to forget that you are yet my wife and when you are you will not issues orders like a tyrant and you will *never, never* raise your hand to any servant or peasant again."

Her eyes turned wide and tears rushed to fill them. Cree wasn't surprised to see them, he had actually expected them. She was the type of woman who would use tears to her advantage and to control.

"Forgive me, my lord, but my head pains me so." She sighed dramatically and let her body go limp against his.

Cree hated the fact that he would have to marry this lying, manipulative woman. He would never be able to trust her, and the thought that she would bear him children unnerved him. He shoved her down on the bed.

"Since your head hurts you shall stay abed for the remainder of the day with no one to disturb you. I will have one of the servants bring your supper."

"Bree will—"

"Remain in the Great Hall and have her wounds tended," —he pointed a finger at her—"and if I see another bruise or wound on the lass you will be confined to your quarters for a week."

He didn't wait for a reply, didn't want to hear one. He left the room without looking back at her and returned to the Great Hall grateful to be away from her. He no soon as sat at the table, joining the other men then he got the overwhelming urge to see that Dawn was all right. He looked to Elwin who was already slipping on his cloak and Cree wondered if the man got the same uneasy feeling, for he nodded to Cree to let him know he was going to check on Dawn.

Cree grew more uneasy as he waited for Elwin to return and when the man rushed into the Great Hall, Cree sprang out of his chair.

"She's not in her cottage, my lord."

Chapter Nine

Cree's heart slammed against his chest and his stomach roiled. What in God's name had she gone and done now?

He was surprised when Torr jumped up and said, "Are you speaking about the voiceless one?"

Kirk McClusky stood as well. "What voiceless one?"

"Later, Father," Torr said.

"What do you know of Dawn?" Cree demanded.

"I met her briefly upon entering the village."

Cree turned to Elwin and the warrior nodded his head toward Torr. "He stared at her as if he knew her. Naturally, Dawn had to find out why, so she approached him and they spoke briefly. Lila interpreted, before I sent him on his way."

Cree turned to Torr with a fury in his eyes that had Torr drawing his shoulders back and clenching his fists. "Dawn is my woman and you'll keep your distance."

"We can stand here and argue or we can go find her," Torr said.

"Unless you wish to die, stay away from her," Cree said and then turned to Sloan. "Gather the men."

"We'll help you," Kirk offered.

"It's not necessary," Cree snapped.

"Perhaps, but it is what friends do for each other."

Kirk was extending his hand in friendship and Cree would be a fool not to accept it, so he said, "You're help would be appreciated."

"Wise move," Sloan whispered when Cree turned to him.

"I hope I don't regret it." Cree didn't know why he said that, perhaps it was because he wanted to beat the hell out of Torr for even speaking to Dawn as foolish as that was. And he wondered if it would eventually come down to that since Torr had not acknowledged his warning about staying away from Dawn.

It wasn't long before the men were gathered and Cree issued orders for the entire village to be searched. If she wasn't found, they would move beyond to the woods, though as soon as he stepped outside the keep and into the snowstorm, he knew this would not be an easy task.

•   ~~~

Dawn knew the woods well, especially the path to Old Mary's cottage. Her mother and she had visited the old woman often, and so the trail was instinctive to her. Then there were the markers her mother had pointed out to her so that if she wandered off in play she could find her way back. It was why, when she spotted the large gnarled tree through the falling snow, she knew she wasn't far from the cottage.

What she hadn't realized, or prepared for, was the fact that the cottage hadn't been tended to since Old Mary moved out of it and to the village. She stood blinking away the falling snow that tickled her eyes and stared at the gaping hole where the door should be. The shutters were gone from the lone window and there was a large hole in the thatched roof.

This meant that she had no choice but to return to the village and with night not far off she would need to hurry. She made her way around the cottage and was barely a few feet down the path when she noticed movement in the snow. It was low to the ground and could be an animal burrowed in a hole against the cold or...

She didn't have time to weigh her actions. She hurried over to where she had seen the movement and dropped down beside the mound, brushing the snow off to reveal Old Mary curled in a ball. She shook the woman awake, her eyes fluttering open, and then she helped her to sit up and wrapped the blanket around her.

The old woman trembled and hugged the blanket around her. "I knew you would come for me. You have the kindest and most unselfish heart, just like your mother."

It pleased Dawn to know she was like her mother, but there was not time to dwell or waste, they had to get moving. Dawn helped Old Mary to stand and, after adjusting the blanket around the woman, she slipped off her fur-lined cloak and placed that on top of the blanket. Old Mary tried to protest, but Dawn showed her that she had another cloak on and though not fur-lined, it would do.

Dawn wrapped an arm around the woman and held her close as she led them on the path back to the village. It didn't take long for Dawn to realize that Old Mary was already exhausted from her ordeal and she feared that she would not be able to make it far. If she could get her close to the edge of the woods that boarded the village, she could then go for help.

After a few more feet, Dawn slipped her shoulder under Old Mary's arm and practically carried the woman along. She kept a steady pace and as the old woman grew weaker Dawn took more of the woman's weight on her.

Dawn felt hot and cold all at the same time and her arms and legs hurt, though she barely felt her feet, and she knew that was not good. She had to keep going, no matter what she could not stop, if she did she might not get moving again.

Old Mary's body suddenly went completely limp and Dawn wrapped her arm tightly around the woman's waist while continuing to support her with her shoulder and lifted her slightly so that her feet lightly dragged along in the snow. Her own limbs screamed from the added burden and the cold, but she was determined to get them both back to the village and into the safety and warmth of Old Mary's cottage. And so she pushed on against the raging wind and snow.

~~~

"Dawn's not in the village," Sloan said.

At that moment, Cree felt completely helpless and it infuriated him. He stood outside Lila's cottage having just finished speaking with her and trying to calm her down once she found out that Dawn was missing. Paul had immediately donned a cloak and went out to join the search as did many other village men when they learned of the news.

"Do you think someone could have abducted her?" Sloan asked.

"Why would someone do that?" Torr asked joining them, his father at his side.

"I haven't the time to explain," Cree said, "but there have been attempts on Dawn's life."

"Why?" Kirk asked anxiously.

"We haven't been able to determine that yet," Cree said. "But I don't believe that is what happened here. Old Mary is a good friend of Dawn's and she would worry over the old woman."

"She would brave a snowstorm to help a friend in need, even if it meant risking your wrath," Torr said as if he understood Dawn's kind nature. "So where else might she search for her friend?"

Cree didn't get a chance to respond, shouts from behind the cottage drew their attention. And not one of them hesitated, they all ran. Cree spotted Dawn through the swirling snow, Old Mary weighed on her and Paul about to take hold of the old woman. Cree was at her side and scooped her up in his arms after Paul freed her of Old Mary.

"See to recalling the men and the old woman's care," Cree shouted to Sloan and tucked Dawn tightly against him. He could feel her body shiver and he hurried to her cottage.

Cree latched the door behind him and went directly to the other room. He sat her on the bed for a moment with strict orders not to move. He then added extra logs to the dwindling fire, so that the small room would blaze with heat.

He returned to Dawn, took her by the shoulders, brought her to her feet, and slipped her cloak off tossing it on the chest at the foot of the bed. He ran his hands up and down her arms, alarmed at how cold she felt. And when he spotted her hands wrapped in rags, he nearly roared with rage.

He meet her eyes ready to admonish her for being so foolish, and the words died on his lips. Her face was pale and her eyes were heavy with exhaustion, and she looked as if she was ready to collapse. He chided himself for even thinking of scolding her and gently sat her on the bed. Then he carefully unwrapped the strips of cloth that were meant to keep her hands warm, though had failed. He took one hand gently in his and as he began to unwrap the cloth, she shivered.

Mumbling several oaths, he once again scooped her up and carried her over to the hearth. He went down holding her, and then he braced her between his legs so that she could rest her back against his chest. He then proceeded to gently unwind the cloth on one hand. As he did he noticed that her boots were wet and he worried that her feet had suffered badly in the snowstorm.

He pressed his cheek next to hers as he massaged warmth into her hand. "Can you feel your feet?"

Her finger pressed his massaging hand twice.

He swore several times, hoping that her feet had not suffered badly in the snowstorm. He concentrated on rubbing her hands warm and let the fire chase her shivers. Then he would stripe her and see to the rest of her.

Cree wanted to ask her why she had done such a foolish thing, but he didn't think she had the strength to gesture. Besides, he already knew the answer. Old Mary's life was in danger and Dawn could not sit by and see her friend die. She had a generous heart and a caring soul, and he wished to the heavens that he could make her his wife.

She shivered against him, and he quickly snatched her up in his arms and carried her to the bed to stand next to it. He wanted to warm her as quickly as possible and the one way to do that was... he hastily shed his clothes. Then he rid her of her garments and as if she realized his intentions she draped her arms around his neck and rested her head to his naked chest. He ran his hand down along her body, savoring every familiar line and curve that excited him each time he touched her. Her skin was still chilled, but it had lost that icy coldness, except for her feet. But by the time he got done with her, he expected them to be greatly improved.

She pressed against him, though not with her usual eagerness, and he slipped his hand between her legs and wasn't surprised to find her moist with desire. He hadn't doubted that it wasn't passion she lacked, but rather strength. And the thought that even though she was exhausted, she wanted him, had his blood simmering all the more and his already engorged member thickening.

With a swift scoop he picked her up and deposited her in bed, and then he straddled her.

"You are to do nothing," he ordered and dropped down over her, his hands on either side of her head as he brought his mouth close to hers, "but enjoy and get warm."

Dawn managed a smile and her body shivered, though she wasn't quite sure if it was from feeling chilled or the anticipation of what Cree intended to do to her.

He kissed her ever so gently almost as if he was afraid she'd break, and then he straightened up and his hands reached out and began to caress her, starting along her neck and working his way down over her shoulders. His hands were warm, his touch full of strength. He took his time, his hands moving down along one arm, digging his fingers into her flesh and then caressing it, until she felt the chill fade and warmth spread throw her limb. He gave the same attention to her other arm and then he focused on her chest.

As soon as his large hands took hold of her breasts and kneaded them, she couldn't stop herself from lifting her body so that the thick, hard length of him rested perfectly between her legs, teasing her senseless.

He bent over her, his mouth capturing one nipple at a time and suckling it like a man who couldn't get enough.

He raised his head for a moment to say, "Damn, but you taste good."

He moved off her then and she frowned with disappointment, but then his hands went to work on her legs and she sighed inwardly with pleasure. Her limbs had burned with the pain of trying to trudge through the snow with her extra burden. She closed her eyes and relished the way his strong fingers dug into her legs forcing the pain away. When he took hold of her foot, she startled. But he paid her reaction no heed. He held her foot firmly, his thumbs pressing hard along the soles. And she thought she'd die from the pleasure.

She was shocked when he turned her over, straddled her again, and went to work on her back.

He leaned down and whispered, "I'm going to have you more than once tonight and I'm going to make you come over and over and over. And you, my love, will be helpless to do anything about it." He bit playfully at her ear and chuckled.

He was right; she was helpless right now, much too tired to defend herself, and she didn't want to. He could have his way with her and she would enjoy every moment of it, for it certainly had its benefits.

He kneaded her buttocks and followed that with kisses and light bites that sent gooseflesh running over her. But when he slipped two fingers in and out of her, she thought she'd come in an instant, and only minutes later, she did.

Cree knew as soon as she moved into the throes of a climax, her body bucked and tightened and when he thought she was almost finished, he turned her over, spread her legs and slipping his hands under each of her legs, he pulled her up against him so that he could slip easily into her.

He wanted to come then and there, but he wasn't done warming her or making her climax.

Dawn felt the heat down to the tips of her toes, and he certainly had kept his word about making her come, but if he thought she was helpless... he was wrong.

She reached down as he drove into her and ran her fingers faintly across his sizeable sac and then cupped it in her hand and squeezed ever so slightly, sending him over the edge.

"Damn it, woman," he groaned and she tightened around him as he exploded in a blinding climax that seemed to go on forever.

When Cree's senses finally returned, he rolled off her and she was the one to pull the covers over them and cuddle against him. His arm wrapped around her and held her close, demonstrating what his labored breathing won't allow him to say, but what she deserved to hear... how very much he loved her?

Chapter Ten

Cree had guests to tend to, but he didn't want to leave Dawn. She slept comfortably against him as she always did, and he felt at peace with her there beside him. And the thought that he loved her filled him with joy and fear. He had no idea how this plain, voiceless woman had worked her way into his heart, but she had, and now his heart belonged to her and always would.

He was angry that she had gone off on her own to find Old Mary, and he would let her know that she was never to do such a foolish thing again, though he doubted that would stop her. Dawn had courage that could not be contained. She was, in a way, like a warrior ready to take up arms and defend. Only her weapon was her courage, and he admired her for it.

She stirred and cuddled closer, as if she couldn't get close enough and he hugged her tighter, slipping his leg over hers and tucking it between his legs. His groin stirred against her warm skin, though couldn't do much more since he had come so hard only a short time ago.

He had never climaxed so hard and long in his life and he damn well looked forward to doing it again with Dawn. He could easily spend the rest of the evening here with her in bed, but that wasn't possible. His guests were probably already wondering where he was, though they no doubt knew what he was up to and that bothered him. He didn't want anyone thinking any less of Dawn. But how did he stop that when he himself had made her his mistress?

Damn if things hadn't gotten complicated.

He reluctantly climbed out of bed, tucking the blanket around Dawn, pleased that her body was now nice and warm, and she was ensconced safely in bed. He hoped she would remain asleep until he returned. Then she would be well rested and they could make love again and again.

He smiled at the thought, leaned down, and lightly kissed her cheek and whispered, "Until later, my love."

It took him only a short time to dress, though longer to walk the short distance to the keep, the snow still falling furiously. He entered the keep, stomping to remove the snow from his boots and swinging off his cloak and walked into the Great Hall to see Kirk and his son Torr deep in conversation. Their warriors were congregated at one table; eating, drinking, and talking. Some of Cree's warriors were spread out across several tables and while they appeared engaged in much the same as the McClusky warriors, he knew they kept a watchful eye on their guests.

Cree didn't expect trouble from the McClusky's, but he had taught his men to be prepared for the unexpected so that they would never be caught unaware, and the advice had saved them many a time.

As Cree approached the dais, Kirk turned away from his son and asked, "Is the voiceless one all right?"

"Dawn is fine," Cree said. He sat and filled a tankard with ale.

"How odd that the woman has no voice at all," Kirk said, refilling his own tankard. "She makes not even the smallest sound?"

Cree wondered over the man's curiosity. What should it matter to him? Why was he interested in Dawn?

"No sound," Cree confirmed.

"Though she does communicate well enough for one who cannot speak," Torr said.

It sounded as if Torr praised Dawn, and Cree grew annoyed. Didn't the fool recall that he had warned him that Dawn was his woman? Would he need to plant his fist in Torr's face to make him realize he was to stay away from her?

"Torr told me that though a woman interpreted for Dawn, he had had no trouble understanding her gestures," Kirk said.

"Dawn communicates better than most would expect," Cree said with pride that was not lost on the two men.

Their attentions were diverted when Sloan entered the hall with Bree tucked close to his side. He saw her to an empty table and sent Cree a nod as he filled a tankard with hot cider.

Cree was about to call for fresh drink and food for the McCluskys when Flanna appeared with several servants. They got busy replacing the food on the table with fresh dishes and full pitchers of ale replaced the empty ones.

He stood. "I'll be a moment. Enjoy the food and drink."

"We are grateful for your generosity," Kirk said and Cree noticed that as soon as he left the dais father and son were once again deep in whispered conversation.

"How is Old Mary?" Cree asked as he approached the table.

"She does well," Sloan assured him. "Elsa says she is no worse off for her ordeal and simply needs rest."

Cree turned to the Bree who kept her head lowered out of respect or fear, he wasn't certain. "What were you doing outside the keep, Bree?"

Bree's head shot up and anger burned in Cree's gut. The bruise she had suffered had turned worse and the spot where the welt had been was now darkening.

"Please, my lord, I have no choice but to obey my mistress or suffer the consequences."

Sloan slipped onto the bench beside her and took her hand. "I've told you that Cree is a fair man and not the monster you think he is, no matter what your mistress has told you."

Cree was surprised by how gently Sloan spoke to the young lass and how he kept her hand clasped in his, as if he offered her protection against the infamous Cree. Sloan appeared genuinely concerned about her and Cree had to hold back a grin. Could the carefree Sloan actually be attracted to the meek lass?

"Lucerne sent you to fetch the healer?" Cree asked.

Bree shook her head. "To bring back a potion for her headache."

"Tell your lord the rest," Sloan said continuing to hold her hand.

Bree paled so badly that Cree thought she would parish.

"I will not let anyone hurt you. You have my word."

Cree sat shocked by the way Sloan was protecting the lass and that he still hadn't let go of her hand. Again he kept a grin locked away, but later when they were alone...

Bree cheeks suddenly grew so red Cree thought she would burst into flames. First she pales and then she turns scarlet, whatever was going on?

"One of you tell me now before I lose my temper," Cree ordered sternly.

Sloan lowered his voice and leaned across the table as if he were about to share a secret. "When I went to fetch Elsa, Bree was there waiting for the potion to finish." His hand tightened around Bree's. "When Bree saw me she blushed and Elsa smiled and said that we would make a perfect pair since we both favored a variety of partners. Bree burst into tears and I was surprised myself by Elsa's careless remark until she explained what had precipitated it.

"It seemed that Lucerne had requested a potion that prevented pregnancy for her servant, who enjoyed rutting with various men. She feared the lass's wanton ways would leave her pregnant and Lucerne did not want that."

Cree raised his hand before Sloan could go on. "Bree, you will finish telling me."

Bree sighed and shook her head. "My mistress will make me suffer when she learns of this and she will learn of it for she has a way of finding things out."

Sloan went to speak, but Cree's command stopped him. "Tell me."

"My mistress wants the potion for herself. She does not want a babe as soon as she weds and once she does have one, she wants no more." Her cheeks grew pink and she pulled her hand free from Sloan's and dropped her head into her hands. "My mistress will kill me when she finds out what I have told you."

"That will not happen." Sloan sounded as if he decreed it.

"Bree need not worry about her mistress, but she does need to worry about me," Cree said with a voice of authority that had Bree staring at him with tears in her eyes. "You went to the healer in a blinding snowstorm when I specifically told you that was the very reason I did not want the healer fetched. For disobeying me you will serve me until I command differently."

Sloan smiled, Bree didn't.

"My mistress will have her way; she always does," Bree said, as if resigned to her fate.

"We will see about that," Cree said. "Your chore will be to tend Old Mary. Sloan, take her to the old woman's cottage and see that she is settled there and tell Old Mary that Bree is to remain with her until I say otherwise."

"Aye, my lord," Sloan said with a smile and a nod.

Cree longed for a bit of solitude to think over what Bree had just told him, but again his guests made that impossible. To him such news would be reason enough to break the marriage agreement that had been made, but the King had made it clear that in exchange for Gerwan's land he had to wed the daughter. It would have been difficult, but he would have tolerated Lucerne if it hadn't been for the news that she intended to only give him one child. He did not doubt that if she found herself with child again, she would abort his babe. The thought that she would do that to one of his babes fired his anger and made him determined to find a way to break the marriage agreement.

Cree no soon as sat in his chair at the dais than Lucerne's other servant an older woman he believed called Magda entered the hall inquiring if Bree had been seen.

"Bree is being punished for disobeying me and has been given duties elsewhere. Your mistress will have to do without her until I decide otherwise," Cree said with a sharp tongue.

"Aye, my lord," Magda said, bobbed her head and hurried out of the hall.

Cree half expected Lucerne to come charging into the hall demanding her servant, but perhaps her outburst in the bedroom earlier had taught her to hold her tongue. He doubted that would last long, by the morn he would hear about it.

A couple of hours later found many of the McClusky warriors bedding down for the night and Kirk and his son soon joined them.

Cree was happy to see this day come to an end and returned to Dawn's cottage to find her still sound asleep. He stared down at her lying on her side wrapped snugly in the blankets, a few strands of her dark red hair spilling across her cheek. He reached out to brush them away and realized that his hands were cold. He went to the hearth and stretched his hands out to the fire to warm them.

He had grown hard seeing her sleeping there, knowing she was naked beneath the blankets and all he had to do was...

He shook his head and rubbed his hands harder. He couldn't disturb her, though he wanted to, it wouldn't be right. She had been through an ordeal and he had probably fatigued her even more when he had made love to her. And damn if he didn't want to make love to her again.

He braced his hand on the roughhewn mantel trying to force his thoughts in a different direction. It didn't work, his mind filled with images of their last lovemaking only hours ago and he grew harder and harder.

It was best if he left or he would wake her when she needed to rest. His hand went to his groin. Damn, if he wasn't as hard as a rock. If he didn't leave now he was either going to jump in bed and jump her or he was going to stand here and relieve himself of the endless throbbing ache.

He warned himself to leave, not turn and look at her, just get out now and let her sleep peacefully. He didn't listen to himself, and he was glad he didn't.

Dawn was sitting up in bed, the blanket gathered at her waist, her long hair tickling her bare breasts and hard nipples, and her hand stretched out to him. He didn't hesitate; he shed his garments and went to her.

An hour later they fell asleep in each other's arms and woke at dawn only to make love again and it was with reluctance that Cree left her. The snow had stopped falling and on his walk back to the keep he thought about all the battles he a fought, the hardships he had endured, and the marriage agreement he had made to make certain his men would have a home. And through it all he had made a name for himself that people feared and well they should, for he swore he would not live by any rule that forced him to go against what he believed was right and for the good of his people.

Marriage to Lucerne was a mistake and was certainly not good of his people. So as he trudged through the deep snow, he was more determined than ever to find a way to make Dawn his wife, for wedding her would be for the good of all.

~~~

Dawn bounced out of bed feeling remarkably well. The babe no longer troubled her in the morning and her appetite had turned hardy. She was happy to see that Flanna brought her morning meal and urged her to sit and visit for a moment.

"I cannot stay long," Flanna said, taking a seat at the table and pouring them both hot cider. "There is much to do with the McCluskys here." She rolled her eyes. "And then there's the soon-to-be mistress of the keep who is making it known how displeased she is with Cree's decision to punish her servant Bree."

Dawn scrunched her brow and shrugged.

"The servants have been talking and they agree that Cree punished Bree to keep her safe from her mistress." Flanna shook her head. "A day never went by that she didn't have a bruise on her. Cree ordered her to tend Old Mary until he says otherwise. I tell you, that Lucerne is a mean one."

Dawn smiled. Cree would do something like that, and she now was even more eager to visit with Old Mary.

"The lassies' tongues are wagging over Torr. Even with that scar he's a handsome one, though he keeps to himself. He could have had a choice of some fine women last night, but he paid no heed to a one of them. He was concerned for your safety and glad when you were found. He seems a quiet one." Flanna popped up out of her seat. "I have to get back to the keep. I or another will bring you the noon meal."

Dawn pointed to the food she had taken from the kitchen yesterday and shook her head, letting her friend know that she had food aplenty and that no one needed to bring her anything.

"You may have enough food, but the order comes directly from Cree. Your food is to be brought to you today since you will be resting."

Dawn smiled and Flanna grinned.

"I had a feeling that you might have different plans, especially since there's no guard at your door."

Dawn's eyes turned wide along with her smile.

Flanna laughed and the two women hugged. "Be careful, I don't trust Lucerne and while the McCluskys seem nice enough, they've asked a lot of questions about the mute lass."

Dawn didn't give the McCluskys much thought, perhaps they were simply curious. She hurried through breakfast eager to see how Old Mary was and meet Bree.

The snowstorm had dumped a good amount of snow, though paths had been made so that daily chores could be seen to. She made a quick stop at Lila's, knowing her friend would be worried about her.

"You shouldn't take such foolish chances," Lila scolded her after hugging her tightly. "One of these days you'll find yourself in a situation you can't get out of."

She already was in one of those now that she carried Cree's child.

They chatted while Lila tried to get a fussing Thomas ready to take along to her daily chore. Dawn scooped the babe out of Lila's arm and he instantly settled when she hugged him against her.

"I swear that babe loves you more than anyone," Lila complained, though with a smile.

Dawn gestured with her one hand and Lila easily understood.

"Aye, take him for a while. It will give me rare time to myself before I'm off to tend to my daily chore."

Dawn layered clothing on the babe, and then wrapped him in a warm wool plaid. Out they went with a smile and a wave to Lila. Thomas was fascinated by the snow and squealed with delight when Dawn cupped some in his hands to feel, and then she tossed some in the air.

She smiled wide and he laughed.

They soon were at Old Mary's door, and it was a young lass with curly red hair that opened the door and, of course, she could not help but smile at a red-cheeked Thomas and bid them to enter.

"Dawn," Old Mary cried out in delight from the bed. "Bree, you must meet this courageous woman who so bravely saved my life. She is valiant beyond words, for she has no voice and would never be able to call out for help and still she didn't hesitate to help an old, foolish woman."

Dawn waved her praise off as if it were unnecessary and unwrapped Thomas, removing some of his garments since the small cottage was toasty warm. She removed her own cloak as well and sat on a chair that Bree had moved by the bed.

"Give me that little lovey," Old Mary said, reaching out for Thomas who went willing into the old woman's arms.

"It is pleased I am to meet you," Bree said with a bob of her head. "Old Mary has told me much about you and I envy your courage."

Dawn gestured and Old Mary interpreted, not many knowing how well she understood Dawn.

"She says that you must have great courage of your own to suffer the bruises to your face."

"It is no more than the lot of the servant to be at the whim of her mistress," Bree said with a resignation that Dawn and all peasants understood.

Dawn learned much about the young lass as they talked and while Thomas enjoyed the attention of all three. And she came to like the Bree, realizing that she was trying to survive a difficult situation. What troubled Dawn was that Bree seemed to have no way out. She belonged to a mean-spirited mistress, and it would be her lot until she dismissed her or she died.

The door swung open with force and Bree jumped out of her chair when she saw that Lucerne stood in the doorway.

"You will return to the keep with me now," Lucerne ordered.

"Cree has rescinded my punishment?" Bree asked.

Lucerne stepped further into the cottage. "You dare to question me. I'll have your tongue for that."

That and a whimper from Thomas, who no doubt grew upset from Lucerne's angry voice was all Dawn needed to hear to have her react. She walked over to Lucerne, her gesture clear. She stretched her arm out, her finger pointing to the door.

"How dare you command me to leave, you dumb harlot," Lucerne screeched.

Bree moved as if prepared to do as Lucerne demanded, thereby settling the matter, but Dawn blocked her path with her arm and shook her head.

"Who do you—" Lucerne never got to finish, Dawn advanced on her so fast that Lucerne stumbled backwards right out the door and into Cree.

Chapter Eleven

Lucerne turned with a fury as if ready to berate the person who dared get in her way, but when she saw who it was, she collapsed against Cree, though his arm did not go around her.

"This peasant dared to threaten me," she cried, "punish her for her insolence."

"What are you doing here," Cree demanded of Lucerne.

She backed away from him, her hand flying to her chest. "What does that matter? This woman," — she pointed to Dawn— "threatened your intended. She must be punished."

Cree took a step toward her and looked ever so intimidating dressed all in black, his black fur-lined cloak making his already broad shoulder appear broader. "Answer me."

Lucerne stiffened and crossed her arms protectively over her chest. "I came to collect my servant."

"Did I not make it perfectly clear to you that your servant was being punished and that you were not to interfere with her punishment or you would suffer the consequences?"

"It is barbaric to force me to do without my servant. And her punishment should be left to me not you. I can promise you that she will never disobey you again." Lucerne turned. "Bree come here at once."

Bree hurried to the door, not bothering to fetch her cloak.

"Stay where you are, lass," Cree ordered and Bree stopped abruptly.

Lucerne turned to him. "Bree is my servant. Until we are wed you cannot dictate to her. Besides, this land does not officially belong to you until you wed me, so it is I who rule here not you."

Cree's scowl turned so menacing that Lucerne stepped away from him and Bree hurried over by Old Mary. Dawn was the only one not affected by his ominous expression and remained as she was.

"Let's see whose land this is and who rules here," Cree said calmly and with a simple raise of his hand Sloan seemed to appear out of nowhere. "Sloan escort Lucerne to the keep and to her bedchamber. Post a guard at her door with instructions that she is not permitted to leave her chambers."

"You cannot be serious?" Lucerne said paling.

"I warned you there would be consequences if you disobeyed me. The fault is yours."

Lucerne sent Cree a murderous look. "You will regret this."

"I already do."

Lucerne stepped back, as if she had been slapped. "I should have known, once a peasant always a peasant."

Cree waved his hand and Sloan stepped forward and took Lucerne's arm.

Lucerne yanked it out of his grasp. "My father will hear about this and he will not be pleased." With that she turned and with her chin held high, she walked off with Sloan close on her heels.

Cree stepped up to the open door just as Thomas let out a wail. Dawn turned and hurried to take him from Old Mary and the babe stopped crying instantly. He had to be hungry since Dawn had not expected to have been gone this long.

As Dawn finished wrapping Thomas for the cold, Old Mary called out, "Don't forget your fur-lined cloak. You'll need it soon."

Bree hurried to snatch it off the peg, but it was Cree who stepped in the cottage and took it from her to place over the cloak Dawn already had on. He then turned to Bree. "I will see about finding you a cottage and chores that will suit you. You are no longer Lucerne's servant. You are part of my clan now."

Bree looked surprised and a bit skeptical, but bobbed her head and said, "Thank you, my lord."

Cree followed Dawn out of the cottage and watched as she scooped up snow and let it fall in front of the babe who laughed. She gestured to him that she needed to return Thomas to Lila and while they walked, her one hand entertained the babe as if she were singing him a tune and the babe smiled and cuddled against her. She had no voice and yet here she talked with the babe.

She would make a good mother. The thought pleased and irritated him and made him all the more determined to find a way for them to wed. He could not abide the thought of Lucerne as his wife and he doubted that she could abide him for a husband. They would want to kill each other once they wed, and she just might attempt it.

Cree waited outside the cottage while Dawn turned Thomas over to Lila and when she came out and they walked only a few feet she stopped and frowned, pointed to him and then to herself.

"Why should I be angry with you?" he asked with a smile.

She playfully counted off on her fingers.

"You're right. There could be a number of reasons why."

She laughed silently, and he never thought she looked more beautiful. Her creamy cheeks were tinged red from the cold and her dark eyes sparkled with joy. It startled him that she appeared so happy. He had not made her lot an easy one, and yet here she stood smiling and laughing with him.

She turned in a flourish and he thought she meant to dash off and was about to run after her when she turned around and a snowball hit his chest. He was stunned and made the mistake of not seeking retribution immediately since a second snowball hit him in the shoulder.

He saw that she was laughing as she made another snowball and it spurred him into action, though not before another one caught him again in the shoulder as he turned to scoop up snow.

To his surprise, he missed her twice while she pelted him three times. She ducked and twisted and moved so fast that he kept missing her and she appeared to laugh harder with each of his misses.

A couple of young lads came upon them and stood watching, their eyes wide and their mouths hanging open, shocked to see Cree engaged in playful antics.

He turned a half scowl, half smile on them and they froze. "What are you waiting for? Help me defeat her."

The lads didn't hesitate. They joined in the fight. Snowballs flew and not a one of them hit Dawn, but she landed every one of hers on one of them.

"That's it," Cree yelled and the lads stepped back. "I'm going in to get her, protect me, lads."

The two lads nodded vigorously and hurried to make several snowballs.

Cree turned ready to charge and caught a snowball in the chin. The two lads gasped and froze. Not Dawn, she was laughing so hard that she held her stomach.

"That's it, you're finished," Cree warned, pointing at her and stomped toward her. He took two snowballs to the chest, one to the leg, one to the arm, and three to the back, courtesy of his young warriors behind him before he reached her, scooped her up, and flung her over his shoulder.

He turned to the lads. "In battle you always make certain you hit the enemy and not your leader."

The two lads gulped simultaneously, fear filling their rounded eyes.

"She was a worthy opponent and you both did a worthy job. Go collect yourself a treat from the kitchen. "Tell Turbett that you helped me win a snowball fight and I said you are to be rewarded."

The two lads bobbed their heads and profusely thanked their lord before running off smiling.

Cree swatted Dawn's backside. "Now for your punishment."

He only got a few steps when Sloan approached and Cree could tell by his expression that there was a problem so he eased Dawn to her feet. "I have to go. Get back to the cottage and stay warm." He leaned down to give her a kiss, and then whispered in her ear. "I look forward to giving you the punishment you deserve."

Dawn smiled sweetly and crossed her heart.

Cree growled low and grew aroused by her response. "It certainly is a promise." He no longer whispered when he said, "Now get to the cottage and keep warm as I commanded."

"I'd be happy to escort the lassie home."

Cree turned to see Kirk McClusky standing nearby. He appeared to have been out for a walk. His cheeks were red, his smile broad, his eyes alert, and his sword strapped to his side.

He didn't wait for Cree to give permission. He stepped forward and held out his arm. "Kirk McClusky at your service, lassie." He turned to Cree. "I'll make certain she gets home safely."

It would have been rude of Cree to refuse the man's polite offer, and he had no doubt that Kirk would see to her safety. It did, however, please him that Dawn waited for him to give his permission, and it was for that reason that he gave it.

"Your offer is appreciated, thank you, Kirk." Cree turned to Dawn and with a smile said, "Behave."

Dawn bobbed her head respectfully, though he didn't trust her smile. It was much too sweet.

Dawn accepted Kirk's arm as Cree walked off, Sloan leaning in close to whisper to him. Something was amiss and she wondered what. Kirk seemed a pleasant sort, with fine features and a strong voice.

"You were certainly brave going in search of your friend in a snowstorm," he said as they wound their way through the paths that had been dug out of the snow.

She shook her head and patted her chest.

"Yes, yes, you are brave. Do not be shy about your courage. Old Mary must be a dear, old friend for you to take such a risk."

Dawn nodded and placed her hand low in front of her.

"Since you were young, but you are still young," Kirk said with a smile.

Her grin grew and she spread her ten fingers and then took one away."

"Nineteen," Kirk confirmed with a nod. "And you have lived here all those years?"

Dawn spread ten fingers again.

"Ten year you've been here." Kirk nodded. "Your parents brought you here?"

Their conversation continued the whole way to the cottage with Kirk asking many question and when they finally got to the door, Dawn released his arm and turned to stand in front of him, her smile gone.

She gestured quickly, as if annoyed, having realized after a short time that he had easily understood her motions. That was odd since it took most people time to decipher. So to confirm what she had suspected, she gestured as if talking to Lila.

"You want to know how I can so easily understand you," he said.

She nodded.

"I knew someone voiceless just like you. She could not make a sound, yet she spoke clearly with her hands and expressions. She was a beautiful young woman and brave as well, much like yourself."

Dawn was too stunned to respond. She would love to meet the woman he spoke about, but he talked of her as if she had passed, so she was hesitant to ask him since she saw sadness in his eyes when he spoke about her.

"You both would have gotten along well. I'm sure of it, probably would have spent hours chatting." A tear pooled in the corner of Kirk's eye. "She's gone now and is missed much."

Dawn extended her sympathy to the man and wondered if the woman had been related since he appeared so very saddened by her death. Before Dawn could ask any more about her, Flanna appeared with the noon meal. Dawn wanted to ask him more, but she also wanted to know if Flanna knew if anything was amiss at the keep, besides Lucerne being confined to her quarters.

The decision was taken from her when Kirk wished her a tasty meal, claiming he had to return to the keep. She invited him to visit with her, hoping to speak to him some more before he left. He promised he would and off he went.

Flanna latched the door behind her. "I have little time to talk but something goes on at the keep. It seems that the secret entrance to the keep that Cree had boarded up was torn apart and it is feared that someone has entered the keep. The whole place is being searched as well as the surrounding area. Cree is furious that his home has been invaded and wants the man found or else. And then there's Lucerne," Flanna said rolling her eyes. "She's carrying on like a harping banshee and not a soul wants to go near her. Even the old servant of hers that does all her stitching is spending more time in the servant's quarters."

Dawn made gestures of little holes and cubbies, and then shook her head.

"You'd be surprised at how many places one could hide in that keep. I even wonder if there are more secret entrances and exits that no one knows about, though no doubt they'll be found now. Cree's warriors are searching the place from top to bottom. If he's there, they'll find him.

"I can't stay. The servants are busy cleaning up behind the warriors since their search is leaving a mess, besides finding nooks and crannies that could do with a bit more attention. I know you took food for yourself yesterday, but braving the storm to find Old Mary wouldn't have left you with much time to cook for yourself and it gave me the excuse to bring the news to you."

Dawn smiled her appreciation.

"That was a brave thing you did going to find Old Mary. You are truly a good friend." Flanna grabbed Dawn and hugged her. "I owe you so much." With that the woman rushed out of the cottage, wiping tears from her eyes.

A minute or two passed when a knock sounded at the door, and Dawn smiled wondering what Flanna had forgotten. But when she opened the door, it wasn't Flanna standing there.

~~~

"It was a blinding snowstorm. So tell me how someone could have found their way to that boarded up door, and damn the wind for not drifting the snow in front of it," Cree said, though it sounded more like an irate growl.

"You know the answer to that," Sloan said, filling a tankard with ale and shoving it at Cree to force him to stop pacing in front of the hearth in the solar.

Cree grabbed the tankard. "I do and I don't like it. It means that the person knew where that secret entrance was located. Old Mary told me that only Goddard and Colum knew of its existence and their both dead, so that would mean that one of them told someone."

"And what else does that person know? Something is amiss in this place, I can feel it. It chills to the bone and sends the shivers through you. And it has grown worse since the McCluskys have arrived. Father and son whisper much too often with each other."

"You think they plot?" Cree shook his head as soon as he asked the question. "I feel no ill will from them and they would have more to lose than gain if they should take as an enemy."

"They don't seek to be our foes. It is something else, though I do not know what and that irritates me. Now they will be here until the snow clears enough for them to continue on. Here I was looking forward to a quiet winter with different lassies warming my bed, and we have a keep full of problems."

"Problems that need solving sooner than later," Cree said. "Let's go see how the men are doing and I have another chore for you. I need you to find Bree a chore and a cottage of her own. She is one of ours now."

Sloan broke out in a huge grin. "Finally, a task that has some promise."

The two men raised their tankards in a toast and downed the remaining ale before leaving the solar.

~~~

Dawn stared at Torr, his lean frame filling the doorway.

"I would like to speak with you. You have nothing to worry about from me, nothing improper. I just want to talk."

Dawn felt no fear toward this man. Actually, she felt the opposite. She felt safe with him. Cree, however, would probably not be happy with it, but she did want to learn more about this woman who had no voice and if Kirk knew her than his son must have known her as well. Her curiosity won out and she bid him to enter with a nod and closed the door behind him. She pointed to the table and gestured eating.

Torr smiled. "I would love to join you for the meal."

He was a handsome man, though like Cree there was a sense of danger around him. He was a man you did not cross for the consequences could prove fatal, and yet she sensed a caring heart.

Dawn pointed to one of the chairs and then slipped off both her cloaks. Something spilled out from one and Torr leaned down having seen it and scooped it up. He stood staring at the object in his hand until he finally turned slowly and stretched his hand out.

"Where did you get this?"

His tone was taut and curt and fear prickled her skin as it once had when she had met Cree and he had spoken to her in much the same way. She was hesitant about approaching him and when she didn't move, he stepped toward her so that she could easily see what he held.

There in his hand was her mother's comb. The one she kept hidden away.

Chapter Twelve

Dawn could not believe that Torr held her mother's comb in his hand. She had hid it the day she had settled into this cottage and hadn't touched it since. So how had it gotten there?

It had flown out of her cloak—she shook her head—but that wasn't possible. She hurried to the hiding spot buried behind the stack of baskets beneath the narrow table against the wall and was surprised when her hand found the cloth she kept the comb wrapped in. And she could feel that the comb was still there.

She stood and carefully unwound the cloth and seeing it laying there in her palm, an identical match to the other one, made her wonder if the comb had ever belonged to her mother. She reluctantly held it out to show Torr.

He stepped forward and snatched it out of her hand, pairing it with its mate. He touched it gently, almost reverently, and then he looked over at her. "These belonged to my mother."

Oh, good Lord, had her mum stolen the comb? That couldn't be, her mom had been a good woman. She never would have done such a thing.

"Where did you get it?"

Once again Torr used that commanding tone and her skin ran with gooseflesh. She didn't know if she was in trouble, but the only thing she could do was tell the truth, and so she did. She gestured, assuming that Torr would understand her and he did.

"Your mother gave you this comb," he said, confirming her explanation.

She nodded.

"These combs are a set that my father gave to my mother many years ago. I remember my mum wearing them. How could your mum have gotten one and where did the other comb come from?"

Dawn pointed to her fur-lined cloak.

"How did this other comb get in your cloak?"

There was only one person who could have put it there—Old Mary. Dawn did not want to implicate her, but then she didn't have to.

"You lent your cloak to Old Mary, didn't you?"

Dawn nodded reluctantly.

"My father needs to know of this right away," Torr said and wrapped both combs in the cloth and reached to take Dawn's hand gently in his. "There is much you need to know as well."

The door opened and Cree filled the doorway. He took in the scene in front of him and a murderous scowl suddenly filled his face. "What did I tell you about leaving my woman alone?"

"I have no designs on your woman, but I do need to know why she is in possession of combs that belonged to my mother. I think it is time Dawn accompanies us to the keep and we talk."

Cree didn't like what he was hearing. Had he been wrong about Torr? Was he not as trustworthy as he first believed? Was this a plot or a plan? Could he be responsible for the items found in Dawn's possession? But why? Too many questions and doubts that he intended to put to rest immediately, but first...

"Take your hand off her," Cree ordered with what sounded like a feral growl, and Torr dropped his hand and stepped away from Dawn.

Cree held his hand out to her and she reached for it. He pulled her against him, hugging her tight. "Where you in possession of these items?"

Dawn held up one finger.

"One comb was yours?" Cree confirmed.

She nodded.

"She says her mum gave it to her," Torr explained and then told Cree how the matching mate was found. "My father could help settle this matter, perhaps he had given the combs away to someone or perhaps to two different people and I didn't know about it."

Dawn could tell by his tone that he didn't believe that for a moment, but it was a good enough excuse to get them all to go to the keep. But why was he so intent on getting her to the keep? His father could come to her cottage to discuss the matter.

And that is exactly what Cree proposed. "Bring your father here. It will be discussed in private."

Torr seemed annoyed with the decision, but didn't argue. He left the cottage to fetch his father.

As soon as the door shut, Cree turned and lowered his mouth to hers in a kiss that turned her knees weak. He finished with tiny nips across her bottom lip that sent a quiver through her and turned her wet.

"I thought I told you to behave," he whispered and nibbled along her ear.

Her limbs appeared to melt and her body slumped against his. He held her as if he'd never let her go and kissed her again almost as if it was their last kiss and he wanted to always remember it. The thought frightened her, and she shivered.

He grabbed her chin and forced her eyes to meet his. "You have nothing to fear. You are mine and no one will take you from me."

A rap at the door had her pulling away from him, but he refused to let her go. He kept her tucked close against him as he called out, "Enter."

Kirk entered with a smile and Torr with a scowl that rivaled Cree's. The four of them were soon seated at the table in front of the hearth. Dawn saw to filling tankards with cider and cupped her hands around hers to stop them from trembling.

Kirk placed the two combs on the table in front of him and got teary-eyed. "I gave these to my wife many years ago and a couple of years after she died I gave them to a woman I fell in love with. She was kind and loving and I would have wed her, but circumstances didn't allow for it. I wanted her to have something that would always remind her how much I loved her."

"There is something else you need to know," Torr said. "Tell them, Da. It could explain why Dawn had one comb."

Kirk looked to Dawn. "There was a reason I asked you so many questions during our brief chat today. And why I told you of a woman I knew that was voiceless just like you. You see that loving brave woman was my daughter. It seems that several of the women in my family have suffered from this strange voiceless affliction throughout many generations."

Cree reached out and took hold of Dawn's hand and he wasn't surprised to feel her fingers close tightly around his. Kirk had frightened her and that did not sit well with him.

"Are you saying what I think your saying?" Cree said.

Kirk nodded. "There is a chance that Dawn could be my daughter and that her mother, the woman I loved gave her the comb."

Dawn tightened her grip on Cree and his fingers did the same to hers, letting her know that she was not to worry.

"It is the reason I stared so rudely when I first saw you," Torr said. "I thought I was seeing my dead sister. You look so much like Teressa."

"My son is right. You bear a remarkable resemblance to her and as I told you earlier, you two are much alike."

"There is no proof of this," Cree said growing concerned, for if Dawn did turn out to be Kirk's daughter he could demand that she return home with him. Of course, Cree would never let her go, which could start a war between the clans, and if Kirk chose to bring it to the attention of the King, no doubt the King would side with Kirk since Cree was to wed Lucerne.

"Not yet," Torr said, "but perhaps Old Mary could shed some light on the problem since she was the one who was in possession of the other comb. And I have no doubt that she had been a midwife at one time, the reason for her gnarled fingers. Many of the midwives have such a condition after years of helping mother's with difficult births."

You will need it soon. A chill ran through Dawn as she recalled Old Mary's words when the old woman reminded her to take her cloak. She did not like the implications of what was being inferred, and she needed to clarify who her mother was.

Dawn gestured clearly so that they would all understand that her mum was a simple peasant woman who loved her dearly.

"I have no doubt she was a good mother and no doubt she did love you dearly, my dear. You can see what a wonderful job she did in raising you," Kirk said with a tender smile, "but she may not have been the mother who gave birth to you."

Dawn could not believe what he was suggesting. She had only one mother and always would. No one could take her place. She thought about her own babe growing safely in her stomach. And the thought of giving him away tore at her heart. She could never do that... *never*.

"I know that look well," Kirk said. "Teressa wore it when her thoughts challenged her, and I daresay you probably wonder why your true mum would give you away. I imagine it was to protect you."

Dawn seemed even more confused and it showed.

"The woman you loved was married, wasn't she?" Cree said. "And if she birthed a voiceless babe her husband would have questions and might even have had the babe done away with."

Dawn paled at the thought. If that was so, then her true mother must have been terribly courageous to do such a thing to save her child. She doubted that she could be that brave.

Kirk nodded. "The rarity of Dawn's condition is common place in my family and accepted without sorrow or disappointment. It is rare that a woman in my family is born *with* a voice."

Dawn felt her stomach roll. She had hoped to spare any of her children the horror of being born voiceless, and yet here she learned that if she had a daughter she would most certainly bear the burden of having no voice. If she was Kirk's daughter and that certainly seemed probable, her own daughter's destiny was sealed.

"We should speak with Old Mary posthaste and see this matter settled," Torr said anxiously. "If Dawn is family then we can make ready to take her home with us."

That had Dawn jumping out of her chair, shaking her hand back and forth vigorously, and shaking her head vehemently.

Cree got right to his feet and went to stand in front of Dawn. "She's not going anywhere. She belongs to me and I won't warn you again about this... and if it's a war you want, I'll give it to you."

Dawn couldn't believe his threat. He'd go to war to keep her?

Torr jumped up. "It isn't your choice or her choice. It is my father's choice, and if necessary we can always petition the King."

Dawn had no qualms that she was merely a possession and had no freedom of choice, but since being with Cree, she had grown—to a point—independent in thought, word, and lately, in action. So she didn't hesitate to step around Cree and have her say.

She tapped her chest and her hands flew, letting them know she did not like being treated like chattel and that her wishes should at least be considered, but mostly the decision should be hers to make and no one else's.

"Slow down, we can't understand you," Torr said a bit apologetically.

"You riled her," Cree said with a smile. "There's no slowing her down when she's riled."

Kirk appeared upset. "I never knew what to do when Teressa got like this. How do you deal with her when you can't understand her?"

"I get her best friend Lila to interpret for me," Cree said.

"Could we do that now?" Kirk asked. "I would truly like to hear all she has to say."

"Talk to her directly, not around her," Cree said.

Dawn turned and smiled at him for being considerate of her, but then he had made that same mistake himself, though not often.

"My apologies," Kirk said and Dawn stared at him realizing for the first time how truly difficult this must be for him. Here she was thinking how she felt when he too had only found out that she could possibly be his daughter. And Torr was concerned for his sister. They were doing what they thought best—protecting her. This was quite a mess.

Dawn had had enough. She didn't want to talk to anyone about anything, anymore. She wanted to be left alone. She stepped aside and pointed at the door, looking to each one of them.

"I didn't mean to upset you," Kirk said and stood. "You should have some time to yourself to consider what you have learned and what might be. We will talk later." He motioned for Torr to stand, and he did so hesitantly.

Dawn kept her arm straight, her finger pointed at the door, and her expression stern.

Torr shot Cree a look. "She means you too."

"I don't take orders from my woman."

Torr went to lunge at him, but Kirk's arm shot out stopping him. "Since Dawn may be my daughter, I ask that you respect the possibility."

"*May* be your daughter," Cree said. "Until it can be proven, she is still my woman and even then it doesn't change the fact that she is my woman and will remain so."

"You are to wed another—"

Cree cut Torr off. "That doesn't concern you. Now take your—"

Dawn stepped between the two squabbling men and shook her finger at the door, her face red with anger.

Kirk gave his son a shove to the door. "This will be settled soon," —he looked to Cree— "and if it becomes necessary, I will petition the King." He turned to Dawn. "I do not wish you harm. I do what I do to protect my daughter."

Dawn kept her finger pointed at the door after the two men left and her head turned away from Cree. She wanted him to leave. She didn't want him to see the tears filling her eyes. She wanted to be alone, not to think this through, but to go see Old Mary and see if she could discover the truth."

She silently gasped when his arms went around her waist and he turned her to face him, though she kept her head down.

He grabbed her chin, forcing it up. "Do you honestly think that I would leave you alone after what you have just learned?"

Her tears began to fall then, for he had stayed to comfort her, and she couldn't help but think that he would only do that if he truly loved her.

His hands went to cup her face and his thumbs wiped away each tear that fell. "You belong to me and you always will. I will not let anyone take you from me."

Every time she heard him say those words she imagined it was his way of telling her that he loved her and did not want to live without her. And she felt the same. She did not want to leave him. Her heart would break if she did.

She pressed her hand to her chest, then to his and shook her head.

He smiled and wiped away more tears. "I never thought for a moment that you wanted to leave me. We do well together."

She smiled and nodded and he kissed her again, a lingering kiss that tempted and teased.

His hand slipped down to cup her buttocks and he pushed her close against him He wanted her to feel how hard he was and how much he wanted her. He already thought about scooping her up, tossing her down on the bed, lifting her skirt, and driving into her with fast hard thrusts that—

The rap at the door had him cursing as he unwillingly tore his mouth away from hers. "I'm going to kill whoever that is."

Dawn nodded adamantly, agreeing with him.

Cree walked over to the door hoping that Torr stood on the other side so that he could do what he'd been aching to do—punch him square in the face. He was disappointed to find Elwin standing there.

"You're needed at the keep, my lord."

"It can't wait?" Cree all but growled.

Elwin took a step back and let Cree judge for himself. "A messenger arrived half frozen. It seems that Roland Gerwan decided to journey here sooner than expected and got caught in the snowstorm. The messenger was sent to get help. It seems he and his entourage are stuck at an empty croft and demand that you send help immediately."

Cree shook his head. Didn't he have enough to contend with? Now he had to deal with Lucerne's parents? He turned to Dawn. "I will return later. Stay put and stay out of trouble."

She nodded and smiled, and Cree shook his head again as he walked out the door.

Dawn dropped down into one of the chairs at the table and refilled her tankard with hot cider and tore a piece of bread off the flat loaf to munch on. She barely swallowed the piece when there was another rap at the door.

She hesitated to answer, preferring to be alone, but another quick rap made her realize that she had no choice but to answer the persistent person. She opened the door and was surprised to see Bree standing there. And was even more surprised by what she said.

"Old Mary needs to speak with you right away."

Chapter Thirteen

Dawn didn't hesitate. She slipped her fur-lined cloak over her shoulders and hurried out of the cottage to be greeted by Elwin. Her guard was back, but then she couldn't blame Cree. With what they had just learned, he had no way of knowing what the McCluskys might do. So she was relieved rather than perturbed to see Elwin, and she greeted him with a smile.

Bree was so polite in her explanation that Elwin couldn't say no. "We'd like to go to Old Mary's, if that is permitted?"

"I'll be right behind you, lassies," Elwin said and followed.

Once inside the cottage, Old Mary was quick to request that Bree take two tankards of hot cider and a loaf of bread out to Elwin and keep him company while she spoke with Dawn. Bree did her bidding and was soon out the door.

Dawn was grateful for the privacy. There were things she needed to ask Old Mary that were better left between the two of them. And then there were— she hoped—things that Old Mary intended to tell her. Dawn moved a chair from the table to the side of the bed where Old Mary rested. She looked worn-out, her eyes heavy, and her shoulders sagging.

Dawn immediately gestured asking if she was feeling all right.

"Tired, age, the cold, take your pick," she replied with a wave of her hand as if it didn't matter. "You found the comb."

Dawn nodded, confirming what the old women already knew.

"And others know as well."

This time Dawn didn't bother to confirm. It amazed and, at times, frightened Dawn how Old Mary knew things. There were those who whispered that she was a witch, others thought her crazy, but Dawn knew she was neither, though she did harbor secrets.

Old Mary sighed and reached for Dawn's hand and Dawn took hold. "I knew it was time that you had the mate to the comb you already possessed." She smiled. "Unfortunately, I didn't count on the snowstorm, and I couldn't wait any longer to get the comb to you. I should have brought it with me when Cree had me moved from my cottage, but I hadn't wanted to take a chance of someone seeing it, so I left it to return and collect another day. As usual the days slip past faster than we expect and suddenly the time was upon me." Old Mary gripped Dawn's hand tighter. "The most important thing for you to remember is that your mother gave you those combs. They belong to you. She wanted you to have something of hers. She wanted you to know how much she loved you."

Dawn felt a catch in her stomach and she didn't think it was the babe. It was finally settling in that perhaps what had been implied could very well be true and if that was so, then who was her mother? She was afraid to ask, but she had to know. She gestured rocking a babe in her arms and pointed to herself.

"Who is your mother?"

Dawn nodded vigorously, eager yet fearful to hear the answer.

Old Mary's eyes shot to the door and Dawn looked to see what had her worried, but no knock came. Then suddenly raised voices were heard just beyond the door before it flew open.

Torr strode in, shutting the door behind him, though not before Dawn caught a glimpse of Elwin on the ground holding his jaw. She jumped to her feet and pointed to the door, letting him know he was not welcome here.

"I'm not going anywhere without answers from the old woman." He took a step forward and Dawn did the same, her shoulders back, her hands hugging her hips, and her chin tilted up daring him to get past her.

"It's all right," Old Mary said and Dawn turned to her. She smiled at Dawn and waved her hand for her to move aside, though she only moved so far. She had no intentions of letting Torr get too close to Old Mary.

Torr advanced only one step. "I mean no disrespect, but I want answers. If Dawn is my sister, I will protect her with my life."

Dawn looked at him perplexed. She had always wished that she had had siblings, though Lila and Paul were like a sister and brother to her. Here, however, was standing a man who could be her true sibling. And she had to admit that when she had first met him, she thought him a good man, and she still did.

"Please tell me what you know of the combs," Torr said.

"The combs belonged to Dawn's mother."

"And you know who that woman is?" Torr asked anxiously and Dawn waited just as anxiously.

Old Mary sighed and tears sprang up in her eyes. "You are a man of your word, Torr?"

"That I am," Torr said proudly.

"Then you will understand and respect what I have to say." A tear ran down her wrinkled cheek. "I made a promise many years ago. I gave my word, and I will not break it."

Torr appeared as exasperated as Dawn felt. Old Mary had the answer, she could settle this whole ordeal with a few words and yet—a promise was a promise, and Dawn understood why the woman refused to speak of it.

"What I can tell you," Old Mary said and had Dawn and Torr listening closely, "is that you will have answers soon, but the matter itself will not be so easily resolved."

"Is there—"

"There is nothing you can do to persuade me to go back on my word," Old Mary said before Torr could finish. "I am tired and need to rest, though first I will speak to Dawn alone."

Torr looked to Dawn. "I will wait outside for you."

Dawn nodded, knowing it mattered not if she wanted him to wait, he intended to.

As soon as the door shut, Old Mary reached out and grabbed Dawn's hand, tugging her closer.

Dawn bent down to listen.

"You must not yet tell Cree that you carry his babe."

Dawn's eyes popped wide, the old woman surprising her again with her knowing. She nodded, though her advice wasn't necessary. She hadn't planned on telling Cree about the babe yet. She actually didn't know when she would tell him, though no doubt a time would present itself.

"It took a strong heart and much love to do what your mother did that night you were born. Remember that." Old Mary released her hand and closed her eyes, and Dawn knew she would say no more.

When she reached the door, her hand stilled before grabbing the latch and she turned to stare at the old woman who looked to be sleeping peacefully.

That night you were born.

Old Mary had been there at her birth. Had her true mother given her to Old Mary to see that she was kept safe? The old woman knew much, and Dawn intended to find out just how much.

Elwin waited outside for her, rubbing his bruising jaw and keeping his distance from Torr. Dawn didn't see Bree anywhere and assumed that Elwin sent her to tell Cree what had happened, which meant he would be here soon. And there was no telling what would happen then.

Torr offered her his arm, but Dawn shook her head. It wouldn't be wise to have Cree see them walking arm in arm.

"At least let me escort you back to your cottage," Torr said.

And since Dawn knew he would do so whether she agreed or not, she nodded.

"My father is thrilled with the possibility that you may be his daughter, as am I thrilled with the idea that you may be my sister. I know you may not feel the same way, after all, your life has been here in Dowell. I can, however, assure you—"

Dawn waved her hands back and forth in front of her and shook her head, forcing Torr silent. She kept her gestures tempered so that he could understand her, though her heart beat wildly and her stomach roiled at the thought of leaving her home and the people she loved. She could not imagine not sitting and chatting endlessly with Lila or watching as baby Thomas grew and seeing how Flanna faired with Turbett or how Dorrie and Elwin did. But most of all she could never leave Cree. That was one thing she didn't gesture to Torr.

"I understand you have friends here, but you would have something with father and me that is so much more precious—you would have your freedom."

The thought stunned her and Torr saw that it did, so he continued.

"You would be a peasant no more and able to make choices."

"She's made her choice."

Dawn and Torr stopped and turned to see Cree only a few steps behind them, wearing a murderous scowl. And then without thought or provocation, Cree charged forward and landed a blow to Torr's jaw that sent him flying backwards to land in a snowdrift.

He stood over the fallen man and shook his fist at him. "Next time I'll drive a sword through your heart if you see Dawn again without my permission. Now get up so I can finish beating the shit out of you."

"That won't be necessary," Kirk said, joining them and going directly to his son to extend him a hand. "Torr will abide by your wishes, but again let me warn you that if it is proven that Dawn is my daughter, it will be you who is made to stay away from her."

Torr got to his feet and didn't say a word. He and his father walked away, leaving their threat hanging heavy in the air.

Cree took hold of Dawn's arm and all but propelled her to her cottage. She felt as if she skipped along the ground, he had her moving so fast. He slammed the door behind them after they entered the cottage, then he whirled her around in front of him, his grip still firm on her arm.

Before he could say a word her hands started moving, explaining how Old Mary asked to see her and how Torr simply showed up there. She finished with what she hoped would abate his anger that Old Mary was there at Dawn's birth.

Cree released her arm. "I can't fault her for having an honorable nature and staying true to her word, though it doesn't help us. Though this news may very well shed light on why someone is trying to kill you. The most plausible reason would be that someone doesn't want your true heritage known."

Dawn had never given that possibility thought. She had been too caught up in the consequences of what it meant to be Kirk's daughter to think of anything else. But what Cree said made sense.

"This information will help in tracking the culprit." His hands moved to hug her waist. "There is much going on and now with Gerwan and his wife showing up..." He let his words drift off, his eyes having settled on her lips that were red from the cold, and he decided to warm them.

His kiss sent a jolt through her, not that it was unexpected. She had seen the way he had stared hungrily at them. The jolt was to her passion, shocking it so suddenly that it rippled repeatedly through her body as if building toward a climax and all he had done was kiss her.

She had grown tired of berating herself for being wicked and wanting him so much. She loved him and making love with him was one way of expressing it, and she so much wanted to express herself right now. And she did. Her hand drifted between his legs and she wasn't surprised to find that he was hard. She stroked him until he grew even harder, and then she pushed him to sit on a chair. She straddled him giving herself enough space to fumble with the ties of his leggings.

She wasn't quite fast enough for him. He throbbed unmercifully and needed to be inside of her as fast as possible, and so he pushed her hands away, freed himself and grabbed her around the waist to plant her on top of him in one swift thrust.

He couldn't hear her gasp, but he saw it in her startled expression and her wide open mouth, which he instantly claimed, his tongue delving in deeply. Damn if she didn't feel good and taste good and he lingered in the pleasure. After a few minutes, he reluctantly tore his mouth off hers and brought her up and down on him harder and harder.

She dropped her head back and though her cries of pleasure were silent, he felt each and every one of them as her finger tapped his arm harder and harder.

He slowed her pace for a moment and she brought her brow to rest against his, and then she pushed his hands off her waist, lifted her head and grabbed the chair posts on either side of Cree's head and began to bounce up and down on him.

Damn if he wasn't ready to spill inside her with each forceful bounce. And when she stopped and grinded against him in slow circles, he thought he'd burst, and damn if he didn't when she switched to bouncing again.

He dropped his head back and let out a moan that probably reverberated right through the cottage walls and surrounding area. What made it all the more pleasurable was that Dawn climaxed right along with him.

When she collapsed against him, his arms went around her and he held her close. He didn't want her getting off him anyway. He knew that with a bit of shifting, she could very well come again since she always had multiple climaxes. And he smiled when she shifted once, twice, and grabbed his arm as she came again.

Damn, but he loved this woman and the thought that she could be taken away from him filled him with a helpless fear he hadn't experienced in a long time. He couldn't lose her. Life would be worthless without her.

A knock had Cree cursing, though not nearly as badly as he would have if he had been interrupted a bit earlier.

"You're needed, my lord," Elwin called out.

"A moment," Cree yelled back.

Dawn went to lift herself off him, but he stayed her with his hands at her waist. He brushed his lips over hers and whispered, "You are mine."

The last time that she told Cree that she loved him did not go well and he warned her not to love him, but that was not possible. And she wanted him to know once again how she felt.

She pressed her hand to her heart and then pressed it to his heart and leaving it there she kissed him gently.

He sighed and shook his head. "You shouldn't love me."

She pressed her hand to her heart again and then to his.

He swiftly lifted her off him, stood, and went to the door. Before he lifted the latch, he turned to her. "You shouldn't love me, but I'm so very glad you do."

The door closed with a click behind him, and Dawn smiled. At least this time he hadn't gotten angry with her and that gave her hope. She would tell him that she loved him more often and perhaps, just perhaps, one day he would tell her the same.

Chapter Fourteen

"The men have been dispatched with extra supplies and one of the women Elsa has been training as a healer has gone along in case anyone needs tending," Sloan said, joining Cree at the dais the next morning. "It should be two or more days before they return."

"Good, it gives us time to prepare for them," Cree said. "I've spoken to the men who continue to hunt for the intruder. They have searched the entire keep three times and have found no one."

Sloan scratched his head. "Why would the person purposely break through the boarded door? He would alert everyone to his presence. It makes no sense."

"Perhaps that was his intention, to let us know that he is among us and yet undetectable." The idea did not sit well with Cree. He worried that it might have something to do with those who meant Dawn harm.

Sloan lowered his voice. "Here comes your intended looking penitent, if you can believe it."

Cree looked to see Lucerne approaching the dais, her head bowed and her hands clasped together and pressed firmly against her stomach. She was a strikingly beautiful woman and the deep red velvet dress she wore paid homage to her creamy skin. It was a shame that her callous nature did not match her fine features.

She stopped close to the table and bowed her head. "My lord, I wish to thank you for releasing me from my punishment so that I may see to the preparations for my parents' arrival."

"Don't make me regret it," Cree said, "or reinforce it."

"I realize that you are lord and master and that I must obey you as a dutiful wife should. It is my hope that you will come to recognize my strengths and allow me to ease some of your burdens."

"Time will tell." And Cree hoped time would help in finding a way of getting out of this marriage to her. He abhorred the thought of having her as his wife, though perhaps it was more that he hated the thought of marrying anyone other than Dawn.

"Now if you will excuse me, my lord, I will see to having quarters prepared for my parents."

"Flanna already has the servants working on the task," Cree said and saw Lucerne bristle. "Tell her what more you need and she will see it done."

"My father also likes his food prepared a certain way. I would like to discuss his preferences with the cook if you will permit it."

"Discuss it with Flanna and she will relay your suggestions to Turbett." Cree could see that she wasn't pleased, though she had little choice in the matter.

"As you wish, my lord," she said. "I assume the McCluskys will be gone before my parents arrive?"

"They will be staying on for a while yet."

Lucerne's eyes went wide. "Why?"

"That doesn't concern you."

She bristled again and her eyes narrowed. "It is imperative that Bree be returned to me right away. I require her assistance in preparing my mother's quarters."

"You have enough servants at your disposal. You don't need Bree, and besides, Bree is part of my clan now and obeys me."

Red splotches popped out along Lucerne's neck and up over her cheeks. "Bree belongs to me. You cannot do this."

"I already have. Now go and see to your duties."

Cree had dismissed her and Lucerne could do nothing but to take her leave. She turned and walked off not in a flourish, but with strong, determined strides.

"That woman is going to be a problem," Sloan said.

Cree turned to him. "Do you forget how often you have warned me that it is my duty to wed her?"

"That was before I learned what a manipulative, lying, and malicious bitch she is. And the more I learn about her, the more it makes me wonder if she had put something in your food that night you took ill."

Cree's brow scrunched in thought.

"Don't you recall that your meal was different than the rest of ours? I teased you and asked if there was something special about that day since you always ate what we all ate."

"I hadn't given it thought."

"I did, especially after Bree told us about Lucerne wanting something from the healer to prevent pregnancy. She evidently knows about potions and such stuff, though I've wondered her reason behind it. What had she hoped to gain by making you ill?"

Cree had a thought he didn't care for and he voiced his concern. "Perhaps it wasn't intended for me. Talk with Bree and see if she knows if her mistress is acquainted with poisons. Have you found Bree a suitable daily chore and cottage yet?"

"I'm not sure she wants to be on her own right now. She still worries that she will be returned to Lucerne. And she is taking good care of Old Mary."

"Let her stay with Old Mary and look after her for now. I'd rather the old woman not be alone."

"You know there is talk?"

"I expected no less. And no doubt the McCluskys started it, hoping to garner support if it proves true that Dawn is his daughter," Cree said ready to kick the McCluskys off his land.

"A wise maneuver, though McClusky doesn't realize how faithful your warriors are and how they would go to battle without question for you."

"It's the villagers Kirk is looking to stir, thinking perhaps they would somehow help is cause if necessary." Cree stood. "Old Mary claims this will be settled soon and it cannot be soon enough for me. Right now, though, we have Roland Gerwan and his people to worry about, and I wonder who Lucerne favors, her mother or father."

"Whichever one it is, I plan on avoiding that one in particular," Sloan said with a laugh.

"See what Bree has to say and let me know right away."

Sloan headed out of the keep while Cree walked down the stone passageway that connected with the kitchen. When he entered all talk and action stopped.

"A word, Turbett," Cree said to the cook and stepped aside away from prying eyes and ears.

"All is well with your meals, my lord?" Turbett asked anxiously. While many feared Turbett's brusque nature and the size of him, there was one person Turbett feared, and that was Cree. He had witnessed Cree in battle and there was no warrior fiercer, more determined, or more fearless of death than him.

"As always the food satisfies like none I've ever tasted."

That was another thing about Cree. He gave praise when it was due.

"I'm curious about the night I took ill. Do you recall why I was served a different meal from the others?"

Turbett paled. "I would never serve you bad food, my lord."

"No, you never have, but why the different meal that night?

Turbett tapped his chin as he gave it thought, relieved that he wasn't being accused of anything. His eyes suddenly brighten. "Yes, I recall. The trencher was meant for Dawn, then I discovered that Flanna had taken her a lighter fare since she hadn't felt well. I didn't want to see the food wasted and since it was a favorite meal of yours I had it served to you."

"Everyone in the kitchen knew the meal was meant for Dawn?"

Turbett nodded. "Yes, my lord."

"Was anyone in the kitchen that day that usually wasn't there?" Cree asked, knowing that Turbett ruled his kitchen with an iron hand and did not appreciate visitors.

"Yes, the young lass that serves my lady. She came to fetch a brew for her mistress."

"Make certain that no one handles Dawn's food but you, and no one is allowed in the kitchen but your workers and Flanna."

Turbett bobbed his head. "Aye, my lord, I will see to it."

Cree returned to the Great Hall, grabbed his cloak, and walked out of the keep. His mind was overrun with different possibilities. He had no doubt that Lucerne had directed Bree to plant the poison, but now he wondered if Lucerne had also arranged it so that Bree was placed in a situation where the servant could gather information for her. And was Bree more of a willing participant in the plan than she made it seem? And what of the poison? Would the amount have caused Dawn to take ill as it had done to him or would it have killed her? And if it was meant to kill, then could it in anyway be connected with the warriors sent to kill Dawn?

He had a strong feeling that it all had to do with Dawn's true heritage and the sooner he could resolve that, the sooner he could resolve this whole dilemma.

His men were busy plowing a path, with the help of a couple of horses and two sizeable logs, through the village for when Gerwan and his troop arrived. He hurried along, a fierce look of determination on his face that had villagers scurrying out of his way and a few brave souls bidding him a good morning.

He had briefly considered stopping to see Dawn, but he knew that would be a mistake. They had enjoyed each other last night and had fallen asleep exhausted, not just from their lovemaking but from the trying day. He had itched to have her again this morning but she had been deep in slumber and he hadn't had the heart to wake her.

Now, however, she would be awake, her body warm and the scent of their lovemaking still on her. Damn, he was getting aroused just thinking about it. He pushed the thought away. It would wait until later when he was finished with all the things that needed his attention. Then there would be nothing to interfere with their time together. And he'd leave his scent on her again.

He turned past a large snow pile and stopped when he saw Sloan speaking with Bree. He was smiling at her like a love-struck fool and her cheeks were blushed pink as she smiled sweetly at him.

Damn, Sloan was going to be useless to him were this was concerned. Unless they learned that it was all a ruse, then Sloan would be livid. He hated deception in women, which was why he always made it clear that he was only interested in one thing from them—coupling.

He seemed to be different with Bree and Cree wondered yet again if love had struck his friend. He only hoped that Bree was who she appeared to be or God help her if Sloan found out differently.

He walked over to them and looked to Sloan. "Bring Bree to my solar."

Sloan went to say something, but the look Cree shot him warned him against it, and so Sloan nodded his head and took Bree's arm and started walking toward the keep.

"Have I done something wrong?" Cree heard Bree say nervously and that was exactly what he intended to find out.

~~~

Dawn was disappointed when she woke to find Cree gone this morning. If she were his wife, she would be able to go and find him and no one would think anything of it. She warned herself against thinking such foolish thoughts, though she couldn't help it. Life would be good with Cree as her husband, but then she would need a miracle for that to happen.

Deciding against feeling sorry for herself and her circumstances, new and old, she chose instead to keep herself busy and free of worry if only for a while. She donned her fur-lined cloak and scooped the black leather gloves off the table to slip on. She sniffed the leather before sliding them on and her senses prickled with images of Cree. He had insisted on leaving his gloves for her to use. He had made it clear that he could not abide having her hands wrapped with strips of cloth to keep them warm.

The gloves were soft and supple, the complete opposite of Cree, and she smiled hugging them to her chest. She opened the door and greeted Elwin with a smile.

He returned it in kind and asked, "Where to today?"

She gestured how she wanted to collect some pine branches so that she could place a few along the mantel and allow the pine scent to permeate her cottage.

Elwin nodded. "Dorrie did the same to mine. You know I've been meaning to thank you for rescuing Dorrie from the stockades that night. If you hadn't, I would have never been assigned to guard her, and we would have never gotten to know each other." He laughed. "A pretty thing like her wouldn't have looked twice at me. And I had to see for myself that Dorrie is a good soul. She was just misguided until you paid her that act of kindness. That changed everything for her."

Dawn was happy that the two had found each other, in a way it gave her hope that miracles did happen.

The pines were the best behind her old cottage. Branches always fell off in a snowstorm and she would collect a few to enjoy their rich scent. She stopped to see how Old Mary was doing first.

Dawn was glad to see her sitting by the hearth, sipping a steaming brew. She gestured that she was happy to see her looking well.

"Feeling my *old* self," Old Mary laughed. "How about collecting a few extra pine branches to share with me?"

Dawn smiled and nodded, though her smile faded as Old Mary's did and the old woman urged her closer with a crook of her finger. "Remember what I told you, trust no one, secrets abound."

A shiver ran through Dawn and she nodded again, then Old Mary shooed her out the door.

Dawn didn't want to think about secrets and what they could mean just now. She simply wanted a few hours without strife or worry.

Elwin stayed close, his eyes alert to their surroundings as soon as they passed beyond the edge of the woods. It was quiet and the snow a bit difficult to maneuver. Dawn didn't care. She loved the woods after a snowstorm. It was a world of pristine white with icicles glistening here and there. It was also quiet, no sound was heard, the animals were safely nestled in their lairs, and the birds tucked in their nests. The forest was at peace and it was lovely to be part of it.

Elwin stood guard as Dawn enjoyed foraging for pine branches. He helped her once or twice to break a couple of large branches into smaller pieces all the while keeping an eye on everything around them. Dawn didn't worry. With the snow, it would be difficult for anyone to approach without hearing them.

They finished much too fast to Dawn's liking, though she was pleased that she would spend some time with Old Mary before returning home. She wasn't, however, prepared to see that Old Mary had another visitor when she entered.

Torr sat by the hearth, sipping a hot brew.

Dawn had no intentions of staying, though Old Mary put a stop to that.

"I have a hot brew all ready for you," the old woman said and nodded to Torr who picked up the tankard being kept hot by the hearth.

Dawn wanted to decline the offer, not wanting to hear any more of what Torr had to say about her being his half-sister. But it would be rude of her, and so she decided to stay at least for a few minutes and then take her leave. She did however bid Elwin to join them, insisting it was too cold for him to wait outside and though the man usually refused, when he saw that Torr was there, he accepted the offer.

It was over an hour later that Dawn took her leave, surprisingly having enjoyed the visit. Torr hadn't once commented on the possibility of her being his half-sister. He simply talked about his home and clan. From his descriptions, his home sounded appealing and she was certain that had been his intentions, for her to see that his home was warm and welcoming. But she already had a home, a home that she didn't want to leave. He and Elwin had also entertained them with some funny stories, and she had been glad that she had lingered longer than she had intended.

Once she arrived at her cottage, Elwin helped her clean the branches of snow as best as possible and helped break them into more suitable sizes. He then carried them inside for her and bid her good day since a guard had come to replace him for the afternoon.

Dawn decided to work on the bed chamber first so that the fresh pine would have time to fill the room before Cree returned for the evening. It didn't take long to fan a few branches across the mantel and, once finished, she stepped back to admire her work when she heard voices.

They were barely distinguishable, and she scrunched her brow wondering where they were coming from. She closed her eyes and listened more intently and realized that the voices came from just beyond the boarded window. She slipped off her boots and hurried to climb up on the bed and press her ear to the roughhewn boards.

"It's dangerous to meet here. Someone may see us," the woman said her voice trembling.

"No one is here right now," the man said. "I saw her leave with the guard and no one else lurks about. Besides, this boarded window may be an asset to us if need be. It is something to keep in mind in case other efforts fail."

"But the person who enters here would never make it out alive."

"As long as her life is ended what difference does it make?" the man said and Dawn shivered at the indifference in his voice.

"How many are there to help?"

"There are enough. Of course, it would have been an easier task if she hadn't taken up with the devil." He laughed. "He thinks he's invincible, but wait there are plans for him and his time will come."

That was all Dawn needed to hear. Her life being in danger was one thing, but the thought that Cree was in danger as well spurred her into action. She hurried into her boots and out the door not bothering to collect her cloak. The guard was quick on her heels as she rounded her cottage.

No one was there, so she hurried further around the cottage and was disappointed when she didn't find anyone. She returned to the spot by the window to see if perhaps there were distinguishable footprints but a large swatch of area had been wiped clean and there were no tracks to follow.

Had they heard her scurrying inside to get her boots on and hurried off? She grew annoyed with herself for wasting precious time in discovering the culprits' identities. She did not, however, intend to waste another minute in letting Cree know about this.

With determined strides and a guard on her heels, she headed to the keep.

Chapter Fifteen

Cree and Sloan sat in the solar talking.

"Do you believe Bree?" Cree asked.

"Evidently, you're not sure or you wouldn't have asked me that."

"Women can be a deceiving lot."

"I'll drink to that," Sloan said and raised his tankard and took a swig. "Bree seemed terrified when she spoke about Lucerne and how she manipulates, threatens, and hurts people to get what she wants. She threatened to have Bree drawn and quartered on a fake charge of theft if she didn't put the poison in Dawn's meal that night. The poor lass was in tears, fearing not only Lucerne, but you."

"Or she could be putting on a good act."

"And what? Be in cahoots with Lucerne? Whatever for? What would it get her?"

"I don't know," Cree admitted, "but I'd prefer not to trust either woman until we can determine who is telling the truth."

"You heard Bree yourself. Lucerne knows about potions and poisons and has seen with her very own eyes that she has used them on people before. The lass has a right to worry. The damn woman could poison her at any time."

"It's obvious that Lucerne has been spoiled and pampered her entire life. She is accustomed to having her way, accustomed to servants jumping at her every command. And she has enough power to do away with anyone who displeases her. Why resort to poison?"

Sloan shrugged. "No one can make sense of what these nobles do. And you have always defended the downtrodden."

"I've defended the truth, whether downtrodden or noble."

"True enough, for I have seen you do it many times. Bree did say that Lucerne rages with anger over your mistress. That she cannot understand how you can rut with a voiceless woman."

Creel scowled and his eyes narrowed.

Sloan held up his hands. "Lucerne's words not mine. I say the woman is crazy. You heard tell yourself what Bree had to say about Lucerne's odd behavior. And we've seen for ourselves the way she carries on, loses her temper badly, and demands things. Then there are the bruises on Bree. She certainly didn't put them there herself."

"No, some of those bruises would be impossible for her to have inflicted on herself," Cree agreed.

"But still you doubt even when it seems logical?"

"I have learned that logic doesn't always equate with truth."

Sloan smiled and raised his tankard. "That is why you lead and I follow. You are much wiser."

Cree laughed. "You, my friend, are allowing a young lass to turn your head. Something I have never seen you do."

"I have to admit that I fancy her and I feel she needs protecting."

"That needs to be determined and until it does, you need to be careful not to lose your heart."

Sloan grabbed his chest, feeling around as if he'd lost something. "Wait, how can I lose what I don't have? I'll not be finding love. It's not for me."

Cree shook his head and stood. "I need to talk with Old Mary and see that the old woman holds her tongue around Bree." He stopped. "Though perhaps she can tell me what she thinks of Bree since the old woman has a knowing about her."

Sloan stood after downing the remainder of his ale. "That's a good idea. I'd like to hear what she has to say myself."

They entered the great hall to see Lucerne slipping off her cloak and Dawn rushing in without a cloak.

"How dare you enter this keep, you harlot," Lucerne screeched and advanced on Dawn.

Cree was between the two women in a flash, his hand catching Lucerne's by the wrist as she swung at Dawn. He yanked her hard against him and whispered harshly for her ears alone. "Harm her and you will die."

Lucerne gasped and paled, Cree's warning made all the more potent by his murderous scowl.

Dawn stepped around Cree so that both he and Lucerne was forced to look at her. She pointed to her lips and to his over and over, informing them that they most talk now.

Cree nodded, cast a hard glare on Lucerne, and shoved her away from him. "If you cannot be civil then take yourself to your quarters and remain there until you can."

Lucerne tossed her chin up. "*Me* be civil? You are a barbarian who does not know the first thing about civility."

"And you would do well to remember that."

Lucerne flushed with anger, her skin blotching red. "I would give anything to prevent this marriage."

"My thoughts exactly," Cree said.

"Then you'll be free to rut endlessly with your—"

"Demean Dawn again and I will see you put in the stocks. It will make a welcoming site for your parents' arrival."

"You wouldn't."

"Do you wish to find out?"

Lucerne clamped her mouth shut and ran from the room.

Cree turned to Dawn. "What are you doing here and why aren't you wearing a cloak?"

Dawn waved her hand as if dismissing his questions, then grabbed his hand, and dragged him toward his solar.

As they passed Sloan, he said, "This looks interesting may I come along?"

If looks could harm, Sloan would be dead from the lethal glance Cree shot him.

"I will wait right here," Sloan said backing away.

Once they stepped into the solar, Dawn's hands started flying and Cree knew that he would never understand her. She was much too agitated and he grew worried.

"Wait," he ordered and opened the door to yell, "Sloan."

Sloan appeared in an instant.

"Go get Lila."

Dawn shook her head and stormed past the two men. Her actions caught Cree by surprise and it took a moment for him and Sloan to catch up with her. By now Torr and Kirk had entered the Great Hall and seeing Dawn marching across the wide plank floor in determined strides had their eyes popping wide.

Torr stepped forward ready to protect Dawn, but she brushed him away with a wave of her hand.

"What's wrong?" Torr demanded as Cree nearly caught up with her.

"Nothing that concerns you," Cree said and kept walking.

Kirk came up alongside him. "I disagree. Anything that has to do with Dawn concerns us."

Cree ignored the man and his son and grabbed his cloak from the peg as he hurried out the wide wooden door. He caught Dawn as she reached the last step and draped his cloak over her shoulders, then took hold of her hand to walk alongside her.

"This must be important," he said.

She nodded vigorously.

Villagers hurried out of their way while some stopped to whisper, but Dawn ignored them all and kept a quick pace. When they reached the cottage where Lila worked on the wool with the other women, Cree was quick to order the other women outside. They rushed into their cloaks and huddled a bit of a distance from the cottage to wait. He ordered Sloan to stand guard in front of the door and barred Torr and Kirk from joining them.

The two men could do little but protest, which Cree ignored.

When Cree closed the door, Dawn's hands started flying. Lila talked as Dawn gestured. "She heard voices outside the boarded window and climbed on the bed to listen." Lila was speechless for a moment as Dawn related the conversation she had heard.

"Tell me," Cree ordered none too gently.

Lila told him about the exchange between the man and woman outside the window, and Cree grew angrier with every word he heard.

Dawn stopped abruptly and shook her head, her hand going to her chest.

Cree was at her side immediately. "Are you all right?"

She shook her head.

"I'll get Elsa," he said with worry.

Dawn shook her head again and placed her hand to his chest, and then she gestured slowly. She explained to him that the man and woman intended to see him dead as well and she told him that she did not want to think of life without him.

Her slow gestures and her expression allowed him to easily understand her. He rested his brow to hers. "That is not going to happen. I will always be in your life. We are one you and I and nothing can tear us apart."

His loving words sent a joyful tingle through her, and she smiled.

He kissed her, a light teasing kiss and whispered, "I want you."

It wasn't a joyful shiver that ran through her this time. It was a shot of full blown passion and she shuddered from the strength of it.

Baby Thomas started crying then and they both turned to see a red-faced Lila scooping him up.

"You will say nothing of what was discussed here or what you saw," Cree ordered.

Dawn responded before Lila could, her gestures slow enough for Cree to understand.

He smiled. "I agree. Lila is a dear friend you completely trust and who would never betray you."

"I concur, my lord," Lila said with a smile to Dawn.

Cree took Dawn's hand, then turned to Lila. "We will disturb you no more."

Once outside the cottage, Cree gave the women permission to return inside. They hurried past him bobbing their heads.

Kirk stepped forward. "Anything we can help with?"

"Not at the moment, but I would appreciate it if you stand ready to help if necessary."

"We are at your disposal," Kirk said with a nod. He then turned to Dawn. "I hope we can talk again soon."

She smiled and nodded, and Kirk and Torr wisely took their leave.

"Well done," Sloan said, "Am I to be dismissed with bullshit so easily."

"As if I ever could," Cree said with a slight grin. "We have an important matter to discuss."

Sloan nodded and walked along with them to Dawn's cottage. Not a word was spoken until they were inside, then Cree reiterated what Dawn had told him.

"I can have one of our trackers see if they can pick up any trail," Sloan said.

"Also post more guards, but where they can't be seen and tell the men not to speak of it to anyone."

"You're letting the McCluskys think you trust them and would count on them for help, but you have no such intentions of doing so, do you?" Sloan asked.

Cree shook his head. "I do not know if it is a coincidence that someone breaks into the keep around the same time the McCluskys arrive or if their intentions are far different than they have led me to believe."

"You must recall that Lucerne had just returned from outside when we entered the Great Hall. She was still wearing her cloak. And she certainly made it known that she didn't want Dawn around and doing away with you after you're wed and taking a potion to prevent you from getting her with child would make certain that you have no heir, leaving her to wed again. And perhaps she already has someone more to her liking in mind. Maybe it's her lover who broke in the keep and hid in her room. She's conniving enough for such a scheme."

"Wasn't her room checked?"

"I believe so, but I cannot say for certain since I was not there. Perhaps she refused the men entrance, claiming that she would never do anything as improper as allowing a man in her bed chamber and they like fools believed her."

"And what of Bree?" Cree asked. "Couldn't it just as well be her? After all, she did poison food intended for Dawn."

"Only because Lucerne threatened her."

Dawn listened to the exchange between the two men with interest and concern. Much of it confirmed what Flanna or Dorrie had told her, though this news about Bree was new. Old Mary had cautioned her well about trusting no one and now she saw why. Bree could be involved in this, though Lucerne did seem like the most likely person. Though they both were forgetting one important thing, and she intended to remind them.

She gestured as if shooting a bow and pointed to Cree and demonstrated how he had flung her to the ground shielding her with his body.

Cree nodded. "Yes, I did—" He shook his head. "You're reminding me that the threats on your life started before anyone had arrived here. Lucerne and Bree had only learned of your existence when they arrived here."

"You think that a woman in the village may be involved in this?" Sloan asked shaking his head. "But who?"

"The one thing that will solve this mystery is to find out why someone wants Dawn dead. Once we do that I think other questions will be more easily answered," Cree said.

Dawn reminded, with a gesture, that she was unimportant.

"Evidently, you're important to someone, though I'd say it appears that you're more a threat to someone," Sloan said.

"Sloan's right," Cree agreed. "And since the person wants you dead, it would seem that the threat is of great importance." He turned to Sloan. "Go see that the extra guards are posted immediately and get the trackers on that trail. I'll be with you shortly."

Sloan nodded and looked to Dawn before he turned to leave. "Do not worry. You are well protected."

Dawn smiled, nodded, and patted her chest in thanks.

"You're easier and easier to understand each day." Sloan grinned. "When you go slow that is."

Dawn's smiled widened, though it faded after the door closed behind Sloan, and she turned to face Cree. His face was set in a scowl that warned he was about to chastise her. And thinking back on her actions, she could see that she had been foolish for entering the keep. She could have had the guard fetch

Cree for her, but fear for his life had taken precedence over comportment. And she had no intentions of being reprimanded for trying to protect the man she loved.

Her hands went to her hips, she cocked a brow, and she titled her chin up, daring him to admonish her.

A brief smile touched his lips, though it disappeared fast enough and he stepped toward her so fast that he startled her, and she stumbled. He reached out and grabbed her around the waist to tug her up snug against him. And damn if she didn't feel that he was hard for her.

"Your courage and defiance sets my passion boiling."

She smiled sweetly.

He laughed. "Don't think I'm going to let you get away with your antics. Storming into the keep the way you did was not wise. And taking command as if you were in charge and pulling me to my solar, then charging out so that I had no choice but to follow?" Cree shook his head. "Extremely unwise." He kept shaking his head. "And yet I admire your brave— though foolish action—which is why I'd like nothing better than to toss you over my shoulder, carry you to our bed, and spend the next couple of hours making love to you."

Dawn nodded in agreement, already feeling herself ready for him.

He brushed his lips across hers and groaned. "We can't. I must tend to this matter first. I will return later and we will—"

That he left it unsaid caused countless images to flick through her mind, and she shivered at the endless possibilities.

He kissed her quick and laughed. "I love that you're always willing and ready to make love." He tugged her closer. "You are mine, always remember that."

She nodded, tapped his chest, and then her chest.

"Are you telling me that I am yours and that I should always remember that?"

She gave him one firm nod before kissing him.

They lingered enjoying each other for a moment, and then Cree stepped away with a growl and mumbled an oath as he headed to the door. He stopped, his hand on the latch, and turned his head to Dawn. "Lila knows all your secrets?"

She scrunched her brow wondering why he would ask her such a thing.

"I want you to feel as safe confiding in me as you do to Lila."

She patted her chest and nodded, letting him know that she did.

"That doesn't answer my question. "Does Lila know all your secrets?"

Dawn gripped the sides of her skirt to prevent her hands from going protectively to her stomach where the babe nestled safely inside. She answered truthfully and shook her head.

"But you do harbor a secret or why else would you clench your skirt so tightly?"

She did not confirm or deny his question. She stood staring at him, her hands still gripping the sides of her skirt.

"Later," Cree said with a nod, "you will tell me this secret that makes you clench your hands in worry."

Dawn collapsed in a chair as soon as the door closed and wondered how she would keep her secret.

Chapter Sixteen

Cree walked through the village with Sloan on their way to Old Mary's. He also wanted to make certain that the guards had been posted strategically. He was pleased to see that they had been and that they were also unnoticeable. No one would be the wiser that more sentinels than usual were about.

"So far the tracker has had no luck," Sloan said. "Whoever it was covered their tracks well, but he hasn't given up yet. Henry is determined."

"He usually is." Cree scowled at Torr headed his way.

"He's a determined one too," Sloan said with a nod in Torr's direction.

"An observant one too. His glance drifts as he walks and his pace slows when he notices something out of the ordinary. His eyes and senses are sharp. He's a skilled, seasoned, and cunning warrior."

"You admire him," Sloan said.

"He may be an annoying thorn in my side that I want to pluck out and be rid of, but he is also the type of warrior you would rather have beside you in battle rather than across from you."

Cree stopped a few feet from Torr, making him close the distance between them.

"You post extra guards and make them inconspicuous, leaving father and I in the dark. Not a place a warrior wants to be," Torr said and crossed his arms over his wide chest.

"And tell me, Torr, how you and your father would react if I arrived at your home and suddenly things went awry. Would you be so welcoming and trusting?"

Torr smiled. "I see your point, though I give you my solemn word that we mean harm to none here."

"While I believe that, I also must protect what is mine and until the situation is made clear, I will take precautions."

"As would I," Torr admitted, "though please know that I would defend Dawn with my life."

"I have no doubt of it and I greatly appreciate it."

"Then you will grant me permission to visit with her now?" Torr asked maintaining his smile.

"No," Cree said bluntly. "She has had a trying day and rests, perhaps tomorrow."

"Tomorrow then," Torr said as if confirming it and walked off before Cree could respond.

"He is similar to you in many ways," Sloan said watching Torr walk off.

"I don't need another thorn in my other side." Cree continued walking.

Sloan laughed following alongside. "It's thorn I am now? Well at least that's better than some things you have called me."

They turned up the path to Old Mary's door and knocked before entering. The old woman was filling three tankards with ale as they walked in.

"I've been expecting you, sit, and join me," she said, pointing to the fare on the table. "Dorrie brought me fresh bread and some fine cheese."

Sloan didn't hesitate, knowing Turbett had made it.

Cree looked around.

"Bree claimed she needed a walk. She was upset after returning from the keep," she said, as if knowing his thoughts.

Cree sat. "And what do you think of that?"

"I think that many who have arrived here in Dowell recently are not what they seem to be. And you would be wise not to trust any newcomers."

"They can't all be bad," Sloan said.

"But they all, in their own way, play a part in it," Old Mary said with a nod.

"A part in what?" Sloan asked.

Old Mary pressed her lips together and laid a gnarled finger against them, looked around, and then moved her hand away and whispered, "In the secret."

Sloan shivered and reached for his tankard.

Old Mary grinned. "You do know that the woman you will fall in love with, your future wife, is now here."

Sloan choked, the ale spewing out of his mouth.

Cree laughed. "And do you know who she is?"

Old Mary's smile disappeared in a flash, and it was with a distinct voice neither man recognized that she said, "She is the one who will grant your wish."

A chill ran through Cree, though he did not shiver. He remained stoic. Sloan, however, openly shivered again.

Cree knew enough of Old Mary that the woman would say only so much and no amount of prodding or threats would budge her, though Sloan certainly tried.

"At least tell me something about this future wife of mine."

"She is sweet and loving."

Sloan grinned at Cree. "That says it all."

"She will give you sons and daughters."

Sloan's brow shot up.

"And one son will wed Cree's only daughter."

Cree looked to the old woman.

"You will be blessed with many sons."

He had to ask. "What of Dawn?"

Old Mary shrugged. "She is not here so I cannot say."

"If I command you?" Cree said irritated.

"I cannot tell what is not in front of me." She yawned. "You must forgive me. I grow tired and must rest."

Cree was beginning to realize that when the old woman didn't want to say anymore she used fatigue as an excuse to get rid of her visitors. But there was not much he could do, for he knew she would not utter another word.

He and Sloan bid her good day and left, both men remaining silent as they walked.

Sloan stopped abruptly. "It can't be that simple; it never is. What are we missing?"

"I don't know, but keep a vigilant eye on everyone that has recently arrived."

~~~

Dawn had no appetite, though the food Flanna had left looked appealing. She had no desire to eat. She had hoped Flanna would have more news, but the only thing she had to tell her was that the keep was abuzz with how Dawn had marched in and took command of the devil.

That was not good. Add to that Cree wanting to know any secrets she kept and her stomach soured even more. She sighed silently, and then a thought struck her. If he found her asleep, he surely wouldn't bother her, though he might tease her awake for them to make love, but at least he would not wake her to talk.

It was too early to seek sleep now. The Great Hall would be having the evening meal and with guests present, Cree would not leave until the meal was done. She would give herself a quick wash and then bury herself beneath the warm blankets and go to sleep.

She was pleased with her plan and the guard at her door gave her several buckets of snow that she filled in the pot that hung over the flames. She then quickly washed herself with the heated water, keeping close to the hearth to stay warm.

When she ran the cloth over her stomach, she stopped and gave thought to the babe nestled inside her. She would do anything to protect her child. Her mother had felt the same from what Old Mary had told her, and her mum had made the ultimate sacrifice to do just that... she gave her daughter away to protect her.

It was difficult for Dawn to think of anyone other than the woman who raised her, as her mum. Her mum had been so good, loving, and patient with her and had taught her so very much. And yet she was curious about the woman who had given her birth and loved her enough to have sent her away.

A chill ran through her and she hurried to finish and slip on the soft wool shift she had draped over the chair near the fireplace. Its warmth chased away her chill and, not wanting to lose the comforting pleasure, she rushed into the other room and crawled beneath the covers. This time she sighed with contentment and snuggled her face into Cree's pillow, inhaling his enticing scent.

Damn, but she missed him. She wished that he was there with her, his arms wrapped around her, holding her close, his fingers exploring her naked flesh, his lips tickling her ear with sinful whispers of what he intended to do to her. How he would make her come over and over. And how he loved the way she moved against him, as if she couldn't get enough of him, always wanting more and more.

She turned, flopping on her back exasperated. If he was here right now, she would climb on top of him, ease herself down on him since when enlarged he was quite a size, a size that brought her endless pleasure. Then she would ride him until she—

What was she thinking? She abruptly stopped from touching herself, having realized what she was about to do. She didn't need to feel herself to know that she was wet and throbbing for Cree to fill her. Whatever was the matter with her thinking such sinful thoughts? She should be ashamed of herself, but she wasn't.

She loved how Cree made her feel, loved the way her body surrendered to his every touch, loved when he slipped inside her and took her hard and fast or slow and easy. Then there were the times that he had her begging for mercy, tapping his arm harder and harder until he finally drove into her with such hard thrusts that she burst in two quick climaxes.

Lord forgive her, she loved making love with the devil.

She squirmed in bed suddenly feeling heated, her skin breaking out in a light sweat. It was then she realized that her hand had betrayed her and had drifted between her legs, and she was touching herself. And it felt good.

She kicked the covers off, discarded her night shift, and slipped her hand once again between her legs, though stopped when her palm grazed her tight little nub and sent a shiver through her. Dear lord that felt good, though it didn't compare with how it felt when Cree touched her there and the thought sent the nub throbbing mercilessly. She ached to feel more, but should she dare? Was it allowed? But then who would stop her? Who would know? She would ease her ache and drift off into a peaceful sleep and forget her burdensome day.

She spread her legs and began to explore.

~~~

Cree had enough of everyone. There was only one person he wanted to be with right now and that was Dawn. He bid everyone good night and left the keep, his strides swift and determined. He had been thinking about her for most of the night and while he wanted to talk with her, he wanted to make love more.

He intended for them to do just that—make love. Talking would wait until tomorrow. He wanted her, needed her, and damn well ached for her. He had grown hard thinking about her until he couldn't stand it anymore. He would not last long. It would be a quick joining at first, perhaps they wouldn't even make it to the bed chamber. He would bend her over the table and...

Damn, he was ready to burst just thinking about making love to her, though taking her that fast was more like rutting. Damn, if the thought didn't grow him even harder.

When Cree arrived at the cottage, he dismissed the guard. There was no need for one at night. He kept the door latched tight and his sword close by. And the added guards throughout the village would keep a watchful eye from a distance.

He entered and seeing the room empty, he feared her asleep. He walked over to the table and saw that the food had not been touched. Did she not feel well? Then he spotted the bucket and cloths and smiled. She had washed. She was ready and waiting for him. He slipped out of his garments as he walked to the other room and entered stark naked.

Chapter Seventeen

Cree stopped, startled by what he saw. He shook his head briefly wondering if it was a mirage and he wasn't truly seeing what he was seeing. Then when he realized the sight before him was real, his eyes grew ever wider and he grew even harder.

Dawn's naked body moved in a sensual rhythm as she pleasured herself. Her body bowed now and then as she responded to her own teasing touch. Her eyes were closed, how mouth open and damn if he couldn't imagine hearing her silent sensuous moans. He had never seen anything more beautiful or anything more inviting.

Her eyes suddenly sprang open and turned wide when she caught sight of him. Her flushed cheeks deepened in color. She was embarrassed for him to find her this way, and yet he was enthralled with how he had found her and wanted her to know that.

Before he could take a step, she surprised him even further... she smiled and held her hand out to him.

She was inviting him to join her and damn if he didn't feel like he'd come right there and then. He hurried to the bed, stretching out alongside her, and she took his hand and slipped it between her legs so that he could join her in the pleasure.

He slipped his finger, along with hers, inside her and moaned. Then he turned to nibble along her ear and whisper, "You are the most beautiful, gorgeous, sexy, loving, generous woman I have ever met and I'll kill anyone who dares to take you from me."

Dawn's smile grew, his words touching her heart and tingling her already heightened senses. And then there was the way he had looked at her from the doorway, so hungry with want, and all her embarrassment had faded away and all she wanted was him inside her.

They were both so wound with passion that it didn't take long for Cree to growl in her ear, "I cannot wait."

She agreed with repeated taps to his arm and he hurried over and into her with a forceful thrust that had her tossing her head back and lifting her hips to meet his welcoming and potent rhythm.

It didn't take long for them to climax and what climaxes they were. Dawn's silent screams echoed in her head like never before and she tapped his arm repeatedly and so hard that she feared she'd leave him bruised. Cree let out a roar that had her smiling since she was sure it reverberated throughout the village. And it pleased her to know that she had been the cause for his outcry of pleasure.

When finally the last ripples of release faded, Cree fell off her to lie beside her spent and unable to do anything but wait for his labored breathing to subside. Though their hands did find each other's and locked tightly together, as if by holding on they could never be separated.

There was so much he wanted to say to Dawn, so much for them to discuss, but for the moment he simply wanted to lie beside her and linger in the aftermath of their lovemaking.

Dawn couldn't stop from smiling. She felt different, though she didn't know why. Perhaps it was because she hadn't waited for someone to tell her what to do or if what she chose to do was right. She had made her own decision, had taken charge and, in a sense, it had made her feel free for the first time in her life. And she very much liked the feeling.

It also gave her the courage to know that when the time came to tell Cree of the babe that no matter what happened she would do well. She would make sure of it. Not that she wanted to lose Cree. She wanted him in her life forever. Besides, it was because of him that she was able to gain a bit of independence. Without realizing it, he had given her two precious gifts... a child and freedom.

She turned ready to talk and found Cree sound asleep. She laid there staring at him. It was almost sinful at how handsome he was. How one man should have such find features surely had to be a miracle?

You are the most beautiful...

Cree thought her beautiful and he had meant it. She had heard the sincerity in his voice, and oddly enough at that moment she had felt beautiful and never, ever in her life had she thought herself beautiful. Cree had given her the courage to feel that way about herself, another gift she was grateful for.

She did not know what would happen between them, but she did know that she would never stop loving this man. She pulled the soft wool blanket over them and cuddled against him. Even in his sleep he sought her out, his muscled arm wrapping gently around her and tucking her close.

Dawn fell asleep more content than she had in a long time.

A pounding at the front door woke them both the next morning and had Cree mumbling several oaths as he slipped into his leggings before he yanked open the door.

Sloan grinned. "Sorry to disturb, but a messenger arrived and there seems to be a problem with getting Gerwan and his party here, and I think it is advisable that you see to this one yourself."

Cree agreed reluctantly. "I'll be right there."

He returned to Dawn who had donned her shift and was adding wood to the dwindling fire. Cree eased her aside and tended the fire until it blazed heating the small room. He then scooped her up and carried her back to bed, tucking her beneath the warm covers.

"I must go, though reluctantly. I would much prefer to climb in bed beside you and spend the morning making love, but duty calls."

She gestured that she would see him later.

He leaned down and kissed her briefly before whispering, "You can count on it." He turned to leave, and then stopped, his hand going out and running down the side of her face, along her neck, continuing over her breast, her stomach, and slipping beneath her shift to stop between her legs. "I love the way you greeted me yesterday and, hear me well, for it is the truth when I tell you that you are the most beautiful woman in the world."

He leaned down and kissed her again, as his fingers slipped inside her.

She grabbed hold of his massive shoulders and arched against his playful teasing, though when he pulled away from her and stood, she frowned and shook her head at him.

"I want you ready and waiting for me when I return later."

She shook her finger admonishing him.

He laughed. "I will see you later."

The pillow struck him in the back of the head when he reached the curtain that separated the two rooms. He turned with a playful scowl. "You dare strike your lord and master?"

Another pillow hit in square in the face.

He ran at her, and she scrambled across the bed to get away from him but wasn't fast enough. He had her pinned beneath him in no time, and she smiled inwardly for that was exactly where she wanted to be.

Needless to say Cree did not leave as soon as he had planned, though he left the cottage a much satisfied man.

Dawn did not know what to do with herself. She wished she had parchment and charcoal for she would spend her time drawing. She hoped when William returned in the spring that he brought drawing materials with him as promised. She could spend many hours drawing and never grow tired of it.

After glancing outside and seeing the gray skies that possibly promised more snow, she decided to spend the day stitching the few garments in the chest that required alterations for the clothes to fit her properly.

Flanna arrived with breakfast and Dawn was glad that her friend sat to chat for a while.

"You watch out," Flanna warned. "That Lucerne is an evil bitch and intends harm and with Cree gone there is no telling what she will do."

A chill ran through Dawn and she gestured, asking if Sloan went with Cree.

Flanna shook her head. "No, he remains here, though Bree seems to have caught his attention, too much of it if you ask me."

Dawn frowned.

"There's nothing like a besotted fool who fancies himself in love and Sloan does not know the first thing about love."

Dawn smiled and nodded, agreeing with Flanna. The man had had his share of women but when it came to love he was a neophyte.

"The villagers talk," Flanna said. "They wonder what will happen if it should prove true that you are Kirk McClusky's daughter. You will no longer be a peasant and you will have a father and brother to protect you from—the devil."

Dawn smiled, hugged herself, patted her heart, and stuck two fingers up from her head.

Flanna laughed. "You love the devil."

Dawn nodded and hugged herself tight.

"Very much," Flanna confirmed. "And it is easy to see that the devil loves you just as much. That has the villagers talking, for they do not see the devil surrendering you to your new family and they worry it will be the cause of a war between the clans. And with life having turned good in Dowell many do not wish to see that happen."

Dawn shook her head trying to reassure Flanna, though truthfully she could not say what Cree would do. He often told her that he would let no one take her from him. But would he truly go to war over her? It had taken years and many battles for him to finally achieve a home and some modicum of peace for his warriors. Would he risk all that for her? And would she let him?

"Lucerne is no longer locked away in her bed chamber, so be careful, there is no telling what that mad woman will do," Flanna cautioned.

Dawn thanked her and enjoyed the meal, her appetite having returned. She cleared the table, leaving the remnants of the meal in a basket by the door and scrubbed the table with some fresh, clean snow. She then gathered the dark red velvet gown that she favored and was set to stitch when a knock sounded at the door.

Lila entered before she opened it.

Her best friend hugged her tight. "I wanted to make certain you were all right and to find out if it is true that you are not a peasant but a nobleman's daughter."

Dawn dismissed her claim with a brief wave, as if it was nonsense.

"You should not make light of it," Lila said as both women took seats at the table. "Perhaps it could afford you a good marriage."

Dawn shook her head, gesturing that Cree was already promised to Lucerne and that would not likely change.

Lila reached out and took hold of Dawn's hand. "I don't mean Cree."

Dawn shook her head adamantly. Was Lila crazy? She would not wed another."

"I knew you would dismiss this claim without giving it thought and without realizing that you may not have a choice."

Dawn shook her head even more vehemently.

"Do you truly think you would have a choice if it is proven that Kirk McClusky is your father? Do you think the man would allow your liaison with Cree to continue?"

Dawn waved her remark away as if not wanting to hear it. Then she gestured quite adamantly that she loved Cree and always would.

"I know that," Lila said with tears in her eyes. "And surprisingly it is obvious how much Cree loves you, but he is promised to another. I worry what will become of you. I want to see you happily wed like Paul and I. And Thomas loves you dearly. You would make a wonderful mother and should be able to have children of your own."

Dawn stiffened for a moment. She didn't mean to, but she couldn't help it, and it was enough for Lila to take note.

Her eyes turned wide, "Oh dear Lord, you're already with child. You carry Cree's babe."

Dawn tapped her fingers to her mouth warning Lila that she must not tell anyone about it.

"He doesn't know?"

Dawn shook her head.

"When?"

Dawn gestured the sun high in the sky and fanned herself to demonstrate heat.

"Summer," Lila confirmed and smiled. "I will pray for a miracle, for I could not abide you moving away. While I want what is best for you, what will make you happy, I am selfish and want you to remain here so that Thomas and your child can grow up together and become the best of friends just like we are."

Dawn smiled and nodded and patted her chest and gestured that staying in Dowell was what she wanted.

Lila got up and rushed around the table to hug Dawn, then the two women talked about what birth is like and how they best get started on stitching clothes for the babe. Until finally, Lila realized that she had to leave and with a quick hug and kiss, and a promise that she would not say a word, she left.

Dawn was glad Lila knew about the babe. She had wanted to share the news with her but feared doing so, not wanting to place her friend in a difficult situation with Cree. But time was drawing near when she would have to tell him, so she wasn't as fearful as sharing the news with her friend as she once had been. And Lila was right, clothes would need stitching and there were a few items in the chest that she would not make use of for herself, but would serve well to turn into several garments for the baby.

She returned to work on the red velvet dress when she heard a commotion outside her cottage door. She opened it to find Elwin blocking the doorway and Bree standing a few feet away in tears.

"I just wanted you to know that I mean you no harm, Dawn," Bree said.

"And now that you've told her, take your leave," Elwin commanded.

Bree wiped at her falling tears. "I am sorry for all the problems I have caused."

"Nonsense," Sloan said approaching and slipping his arm around Bree's waist when he came alongside her. "You have caused no problems."

Elwin crossed his arms over his chest. "Cree ordered that Bree be kept a distance from Dawn, and so it shall be. Besides, she's said what she came to say and now she can be on her way."

Sloan looked past Elwin to Dawn. "Have you anything to say about this?"

Dawn felt for the lass, but she also worried for the babe she carried. Lucerne very well could have forced Bree to put poison in Dawn's food, but what if Bree had done it of her own accord? And what if she tried again? There would be a chance that Dawn could lose the babe and that was a chance she would not take.

Dawn shook her head, turned, and went inside, closing the door behind her. She felt terrible for hurting the lass, but she was more concerned with the safety of her unborn child and, therefore, couldn't take a chance.

She got only a few stitches done when Dorrie showed up with the noon meal. The scent of the delicious food had Dawn realizing that more time had passed than she had realized, and she was hungry. With all her unexpected visitors this morning, she had lost track of time.

Dorrie smiled as she unloaded the basket full of food. "You have become much admired by the villagers. They believe you bring good luck to them, though they also fear that war will be waged in your honor. I tell them it will never come to that. That you would never permit it and would do what must be done to keep peace and the village protected just as you did when Cree arrived here." She grabbed the breakfast basket as she went to leave. "One thing everyone agrees on is that you are a brave soul. You have more courage than the fiercest warrior, for you have commanded the devil."

Dorrie disappeared out the door and into Elwin's arms.

Dawn's status in the village certainly had changed and continued to change, not that she minded. Going from mostly being ignored to being acknowledged and now praised was nice, though she could have done without the praise. She had done what she had to do. She had no choice, though she supposed it did take courage to do things that you feared or didn't want to do. But it wasn't until later that you realize that you had courage after all.

The day turned quiet and as night settled in, Dawn began to miss Cree more and more. It was rare that he didn't spend the night with her. Missing him, she crawled into bed earlier that night, not bothering to wait for supper to be delivered. If she woke later, she could eat. She found the bed much too empty. She tried reassuring herself that he would return in a day or two and soon be back in her bed. But all the reassuring in the world didn't help chase the loneliness or fill the empty spot beside her or ease the ache in her heart.

Hours passed with her twisting and turning so much that she became entangled in the blankets. Finally, exhaustion claimed her and her eyes drifted shut. Hours later, though perhaps it had been minutes that had passed, Dawn woke disoriented. She had to focus a moment to see what had jostled her from her sleep. She bolted up when she heard pounding at her door and a voice shouting her name.

She hurried into a skirt, blouse, and boots and grabbed her fur-lined cloak from the peg as she rushed to open the front door.

Elwin stood there, his face solemn. "A messenger just arrived. There's been an attack on Cree and the Gerwan troop."

Dawn felt as if her heart slammed against her chest.

"The news sounds bad, though we can't be sure if anyone has been killed or injured. Sloan gathers men now to ride."

"Go with them, I will see that Dawn is kept safe," Torr said, stepping out of the night shadows. "I give you my word. I'll see no harm comes to her."

Dawn could see how badly Elwin wanted to join the warriors who would go to help Cree. And so she also urged him to go, stepping out of the cottage to shoo him away with her hands, and then pointing to Torr and nodding that she would be fine. With only a bit more of coaxing, Elwin left, though not before telling Torr that he would cut his heart out if anything happened to Dawn.

"We can watch them leave if you'd like," Torr offered.

Dawn nodded, and Torr shut the cottage door before they turned and walked to the keep. Torches flickered in the dark night as the warriors mounted their horses. Sloan vaulted down the keep steps and hurried to his horse, waiting in the lead.

He stopped before mounting when he caught sight of Dawn and Torr and walked over to them. "If you let anything happen to her Cree will kill you, and it won't be a slow death."

"I understand," Torr said, "and I've already given my word that I'll see that no harm comes to her. Now go and help your fearless lord."

Dawn grabbed Sloan's arm before he could leave and hoping he'd understand, slowly gestured for him to bring Cree home safe and unharmed.

Sloan patted her arm. "Cree is a heartless soul; he can't die."

Tears sprang to Dawn's eyes as she watched Sloan hurry off and mount his horse. His remark was meant to ease her concerns, but it only made her worry more. Cree was no heartless soul. He had a generous and loving heart that was as silent as her voice.

Soon the troop disappeared into the night and when she turned to return to her cottage, Kirk was standing there.

"I am so sorry we have to do this, Dawn, but I have no choice. I know that you're my daughter and I must protect you."

Dawn didn't have a chance to react. Torr scooped her up, tossed her over his shoulder and hurried off into the night.

Chapter Eighteen

Dawn was angry. It wasn't until several hours later when the sun was barely on the horizon that they finally stopped at a deserted croft, and she was able to let her anger loose. Her hands flew wildly around her in gestures and though Kirk and Torr probably didn't understand a word of it, they certainly could see how upset she was.

She repeated her last gesture several times, patting her chest and pointing to the door.

Kirk shook his head. "I am sorry. I can't take you back to Dowell."

Her hands started flying again, and then slowed as she realized that the cottage had a blazing fire in the hearth, food on the table, and three narrow beds across one wall. They hadn't randomly chosen this place to stop—they had planned on stopping here. They had planned on abducting her.

Dawn ceased all gestures and looked from Kirk to Torr, shrugged and scrunched her brow asking why.

Kirk pulled out a chair at the table. "Please sit and we'll talk."

Dawn sat, wanting to hear what he had to say, but also wondering over her options. She wanted to go home, but they had traveled a good distance and with the snow she would be foolish to try to escape and make it home on foot. Besides Cree had told her often enough that she belonged to him and he would not let anyone take her away from him. Once he found out about the abduction, he would come after her, though that could take time considering Cree's own predicament. That gave her a thought and she began to gesture again, though slowly.

"I told you she'd figure it out quickly," Torr said to his father, smiling with pride.

Kirk nodded, his own pride obvious. "You are correct. There has been no attack on Cree. We needed his warriors to believe that to give us time to get you safely away. Our tracker is rarely visible, so it was easy for him to pose as one of Gerwan's men and deliver the false message. He played his part well. Appearing exhausted from his rush to get help, Sloan insisted that he remain behind. Our tracker provided Sloan with precise direction, giving us plenty of time to carry out our plan."

The news that Cree was all right filled Dawn with such relief that she sighed silently. Cree was safe and when he discovered her gone, he would come for her. For now, she would listen to what Kirk had to say. With that thought in mind, she gestured that they should talk.

"I ask that you listen to all I have to say," Kirk said. "Lives depend on the decision you will make, including yours."

Dawn pointed at him, then to her temple, then gestured as if she was shooting an arrow and then pointed to herself.

Kirk nodded. "I think I know who has been trying to kill you, though I have no proof, but it makes the most sense."

Dawn waited eager to hear more.

●   ~~~

It was just passed sunrise when Sloan realized that it had been a ruse and he feared the worst, though truthfully the worst wouldn't be Dawn being abducted. It would be what happened when Cree found out about it.

He alerted the men who had already surmised the same and saw fear in their eyes. They too did not want to face Cree. They had seen him angry and it was not a sight one wanted to ever see again.

Sloan had them keep a fast pace, wanting to return home and see if his fears were founded, though he had no doubt they were, but he could hope. Unfortunately, all hope was dashed as an hour later they converged with Cree and Gerwan's troop.

One sight of Sloan had Cree halting the caravan and riding to meet him and his men.

"Tell me Dawn is safe," Cree demanded as the two men reached each other. His stallion pranced and snorted, seeming to sense his master's agitation.

Sloan hesitated and fiery anger sparked in Cree's eyes. Sloan drew back, as if scorched by their heat and spoke quickly. "A messenger arrived several hours before sunrise to inform us that you had been attacked and needed help. I gathered the men and left Dawn in—" Sloan shook his head. "My concern was for you and I did not see it for the ruse it was. Torr swore he would see no harm came to Dawn."

"Of course he wouldn't you fool," Cree spat. "He believes that she is his sister. He would not hurt her, but he would abduct her given the chance, which you gave him."

Sloan was wise enough to remain silent.

Cree looked past Sloan to Elwin. "I trusted you to put Dawn's safety above all else."

Elwin hung his head. "I am sorry, my lord, I was foolish."

"You and Sloan both," Cree snapped. "Wait here, and when I return be prepared to ride fast and hard."

Both men nodded as Cree turned and headed back to the caravan.

Roland Gerwan had stepped out of the wagon that he rode in alone, his wife traveling a distance behind him in a much smaller wagon than his. Cree had not liked the man on first sight. He was a pompous, uncaring fool. He stood barely four inches over five feet, but acted as if he were a giant amongst men. He was lean with fine features, pure white hair, and blue eyes similar to is daughter's, though there was a coldness to them that Lucerne's eyes lacked.

Cree brought his stallion to a stop in front of Roland, the beast prancing uneasy, as if he was as anxious as Cree to take his leave. "My men will see you safely the remainder of the way."

"You cannot mean to leave us to your warriors. That is an insult," Roland snapped as if chastising Cree like a child.

Cree turned such a harsh stare on the man that he took several hasty steps back nearly tripping over his own feet. "What is an insult is that your men are so poorly provided for that they care not a whit of what happens to you."

"How dare you—"

"Watch your tongue," Cree warned. "You are addressing the Earl of Carrick."

Roland drew back, as if he had been slapped hard across the face. He quickly gathered himself together and sputtered, "The title becomes yours when you wed my daughter."

"A mere formality since the King has already decreed me Earl of Carrick." Cree turned and rode off not wanting to exchange another word with the man. His concern was for Dawn, though not that she would be harmed. He knew that Kirk or Torr would never hurt her. What concerned him more was getting her back. And another concern was why Kirk had chosen now to abduct her. What had forced his hand?

Sloan fell in behind Cree as he rode past and several of his warriors followed. Their pace was fast, though the more heavily snow-covered areas slowed them down. It wasn't until mid-afternoon that they arrived at Dowell. With the time it had taken them, Cree judged that the Gerwan caravan wouldn't arrive until sometime tomorrow.

Lucerne stood on the keep steps looking anxiously passed him, no doubt eager to see her parents. The smile she wore faded as she realized they did not follow.

"Where are my parents?" she demanded when Cree dismounted his horse, handing the reins to a young lad who immediately saw to the animal's care.

"They should arrive tomorrow," Cree informed her and turned away eager to get to Dawn's cottage.

"You leave my parents' safety to others so that you can return to your peasant wh—"

Cree turned back around in a flash. "Watch what you say, Lucerne, for you will not like the consequences."

Lucerne bit her lip as if fighting to keep from speaking, and he supposed she feared losing the battle, for she turned in a huff and hurried inside the keep.

Sloan approached Cree cautiously as he continued on to Dawn's cottage.

"Go see if any of the sentries saw anything," Cree ordered. "See that men stand ready and see if Henry can find any tracks."

Sloan nodded and slipped away to see it done.

Cree entered the cottage and stood taking in the room in one sweeping glance. The fire had died down and he quickly added more logs. He did not want Dawn to return to a chilled cottage. He hurried into the other room and did the same to the dwindling fire. He then went to the bed and stared at the rumpled bedding.

He reached down and swiped her pillow, bringing it to his face and inhaling her familiar scent, heather and pine. Damn, but he missed her and he wanted her home here in this bed where they made love, laughed, talked, and slept naked in each other's arms.

He tossed the pillow back on the bed and examined the remainder of the room. He cursed when he saw her stockings lying rumpled on the chest, though was relieved when he saw that her fur-lined cloak was gone. His gloves, however, had been left behind, and so more oaths spewed from his mouth.

The stillness suddenly bothered him and he cast a quick glance around the room. There were no remnants of a meal. Had no food been brought to Dawn? Had no one realized she was missing? He swore again and marched out of the cottage and straight for the kitchen. Meals had to have been delivered to her. Hadn't anyone questioned why she hadn't been in her cottage?

Every villager that caught sight of Cree hurried to bless themselves and move out of his way. If their suspicions of him being the devil were ever proven true it would be at this moment. His expression was pure evil, as if he had just emerged from the depths of hell and was intent on claiming souls.

He stormed into the kitchen and all movement ceased, even Turbett blanched at the sight of him.

"Was no meal taken to Dawn today?" Cree demanded.

Flanna took a cautious step forward. "All but supper. We were informed that she would tend to that herself today."

"Who told you that?" Cree snapped and Flanna jumped.

Flanna hurried to tell him as she took a step back. "Old Mary."

Cree was out the door so fast that it took everyone a moment to realize he was gone and, mumbling amongst themselves, they returned to their work.

With heavy footfalls Cree made his way to Old Mary's cottage. Could the old woman have helped Kirk and Torr? He stopped abruptly when he saw Lucerne arguing with Elsa outside her cottage. He didn't want to waste time on the matter and he was sure that Elsa could handle it, but he could not ignore the chaotic scene, especially with villagers lingering about in curiosity.

"What goes on here?" Cree demanded as he approached the two women.

Lucerne turned on him, her eyes framed with tears ready to fall. "My head throbs mercilessly. I need more potions for the pain." Lucerne grabbed hold of Cree's arm, her grip tight. "Please."

Her plea shocked him. It wasn't like her to plead, though she made herself heard, she had never pleaded with him—she had always demanded. The desperation in her voice was also something unfamiliar to him. He turned to Elsa to order her to give Lucerne what she needed, but the healer shook her head.

"Something is not right that she suffers so with these headaches. The potions should have at least eased them, if not gotten rid of them, but the pain should not have escalated. There are questions I need to ask so that I may better help her, but she refuses to talk with me."

Sloan approached then and Cree took Lucerne's hand and placed it on the startled man's arm. "You will stay with Lucerne while Elsa speaks with her, and then you will see her safely back to her bedchamber so that she may rest."

"I need the potion," Lucerne begged.

Elsa took Lucerne's other hand. "I will give it to you, and then we will talk."

Sloan looked to Cree with pleading eyes. To sit with the nagging, demanding woman while she talked with Elsa was a harsh punishment to suffer, though he supposed it could have been worse. He almost shook his head, for nothing could be worse than what he was about to suffer.

Cree shot him a fiery look and Sloan felt its sting. He nodded, complying with the command and accompanied the two women into the cottage, Lucerne's fingers biting into his arm.

Cree had already turned away and had nearly reached Old Mary's cottage when the old woman stepped out of nowhere startling him.

"A good time for a walk, my lord," Old Mary said with a wrinkled grin.

Cree held out his arm, leaned down, and whispered, "And a talk." He directed her away from curious faces to a more secluded spot where he dusted snow off a bench for her to sit. He stood towering over her, his broad back blocking anyone from seeing her.

He didn't hesitate in asking her, "Why did you tell Flanna that Dawn was preparing her own meals today?"

"Dawn is where she needs to be at the moment."

"I don't care for riddles. I want answers."

"Then go find Dawn, for by now she has them."

Chapter Nineteen

"Ten and nine years ago I fell in love for the second time in my life," Kirk said. "Some men would think her plain," — Kirk smiled— "but to me she was beautiful, and she had the most generous heart. Unfortunately for us both, she was already wed, though it was a loveless marriage. However, that didn't stop us from loving each other. Then one day she told me that she feared that her husband had grown suspicious and she feared not only for her own life, but mine as well. I would have battled the devil himself to make her mine, but she felt compelled to honor her marriage agreement. So I reluctantly let her go."

Dawn felt a catch to her heart. She was familiar with the pain he suffered, for she could never truly be with Cree, never be his wife. At least, though, she could stay with him. She did not know if she could bear the pain of being separated from him forever. Just the thought sent a sense of loss so strong through her that she shuddered.

"I found out months later that she had given birth to a daughter and I wondered if the child was mine. When I learned that the lass could speak and had her father's blue eyes I knew the child was not mine." Kirk choked back tears that pooled in his eyes.

Torr spoke while his father composed himself. "I was ten at the time and oblivious to my father's suffering, though my sister Teressa who was barely six seemed to understand that something was wrong."

"She tried to ease my sorrow," Kirk said. "She was such a loving child. I didn't know true pain until I lost my Teressa. She died two years ago from a sudden illness. There is nothing as painful as being helpless to save your child." This time Kirk couldn't prevent his tears from falling.

"Not long ago," Torr said, "an old friend of my father's, who we hadn't seen in years, passed through our land and stopped to visit. He had known my sister and was heartbroken to hear she had died. He then told us of a young woman who he had seen that had suffered the same affliction as Teressa. Neither Father nor I thought much of it since there were other people who could not speak, though they could make a minimal of sound. This fellow had insisted that the lass he had seen had been exactly like Teressa."

"It was when I learned that the lass lived on the Earl of Carrick's land that I became more curious," Kirk said. "You see the woman I fell I love with was Ann Gerwan, the Earl of Carrick's wife."

Dawn stared at Kirk, her eyes wide.

"I decided it was time to see this lass for myself, so Torr and I journeyed here with the sole purpose of finding you. The snowstorm was God-sent, landing us right where we needed to be. You look much like my daughter Teressa, but then my wife and Ann had similar features."

Dawn continued to stare at the man who could very well be her father, still too shocked to make a gesture.

"I was stunned when I first saw the similarities and upset that you had been forced to become Cree's—"

Dawn's hand shot up, stopping Kirk from going any further and shook her head adamantly, wanting him to understand that Cree had not forced her. She had joined willingly with him. The doubtful look in his eyes troubled her, so she made it clear how she felt about Cree.

With slow, precise gestures, she let the two men know that she loved Cree.

Neither man smiled. It was Torr who finally said, "But does he love you enough to let you go?"

Dawn's brow scrunched in confusion and she shook her head.

"The reason someone wants you dead is because they have discovered your true identity," Kirk said. "One of two people could possibly be responsible, Gerwan and Lucerne. Naturally, if Lucerne found out, she loses everything if the truth is revealed. If Gerwan knows, then he fears that he has no bargaining power to retain his lands, no daughter to wed Cree."

Dawn felt a seed of excitement start and smiled as she gestured—

Kirk raised his hand to stop her. "I know what you're thinking that if you are my daughter, no longer a peasant, then there is a possibility that you and Cree could wed."

She nodded slowly, desperately hoping it was possible, though a thought poked at her... would Cree want to wed her?

Kirk hesitated. "You are not my legitimate child, therefor the King could refuse to recognize you and with Cree gaining a title and power, having a bastard wife might not be to his liking."

A pang to Dawn's heart had her fighting the suggested rejection. Though Cree's love was silent, she didn't doubt that he loved her. But was that love strong enough for him to accept a bastard as his wife?

"There is something else we must consider— your true mother," Kirk said. "Her life could be in danger. She is the one person who could verify that you are Gerwan's daughter, and I fear for her life."

Dawn felt a sense of protection toward the woman who gave her birth. Perhaps it was because she carried Cree's child and understood the motherly instinct to protect. And there was part of her who would like to meet the brave woman who had so unselfishly saved her life.

"I thought by removing you as a threat, it could save your life and Ann's as well," Kirk said sounding as if he searched for a miracle. "But to completely remove the threat," —he paused and took a breath— "you would need to wed right away. Your marriage would eliminate you as a threat and protect Ann. I have a good man in mind for you. He will treat you well and you would have a good life with him."

Dawn stood so fast that her chair flew back and fell to the floor. She waved her hands back and forth adamantly and shook her head just as furiously.

"It's the only way," Kirk said as if he wished differently.

She gestured repeatedly for him to take her home.

"You are home, Dawn," Kirk said. "And your safe and so is Ann. It is the way things must be."

Dawn shook her head and gestured slowly and clearly enough for Kirk to understand that she did not recognize him as her father, for a father would not cause his daughter such pain. He obviously understood her since he recoiled, as if slapped in the face.

"I am your father and as a father who loves his child I do what is best for you whether you believe it or not. I'm offering you a chance for a good life, please think about it."

Dawn refused to resign herself to Kirk's plan, and she let him know it. And she let him know that Cree would come for her and take her home.

Kirk stood. "By then you will be wed and there will be nothing he can do about it. Get some rest we leave in a few hours."

Dawn wished she had a voice, for at that moment she had never wanted to scream so much in her life. How dare Kirk McClusky walk into her life, claim that he is her father, and force her to wed a stranger for her own good. She was exhausted and furious at being dictated to, her life decided for her.

She turned her back on the two men, not able to look upon them without growing angrier. She wanted nothing to do with either of them. She wanted to go home to Cree and tell him all she had learned and see if they could find a solution to this ever growing dilemma together.

With the ruse Kirk had played on Cree, she feared he wouldn't reach her until it was too late. Could she somehow delay their departure? She was relieved when she turned to see that both men were gone. She had been so engrossed in her thoughts that she had not heard them leave.

The bed beckoned, but she shook her fatigue away. She couldn't waste time on sleep. She had to remain alert and ready in case she had a chance to escape. Her stomach suddenly protested, and she realized that though she didn't feel hungry, the babe thought differently and needed nourishment, and so she grabbed a chunk of bread and cheese.

She had just washed it down with hot cider when the door flew open and Torr stormed in.

"We're leaving now," he snapped and grabbed her cloak and tossed it to her.

The sudden departure could only mean one thing—Cree was on the way. She slipped on her cloak and hid her smile as she preceded Torr out the door.

She once again was planted in front of Torr on his horse, eliminating any chance of escape. They kept a relatively fast pace considering the snow on the ground, and she worried that Cree would not be able to find them. She thought of possible ways to slow them down, feigning feeling ill the most obvious, but quickly discounted it. She doubted anyone would believe her.

Thoughts of the babe suddenly filled her head. He would be a bastard like her. Would she need to worry for his life as Kirk did for her? Would there be those who would want him dead? Lucerne would certainly feel him a threat.

More importantly what of Cree? He had told her to take the potion Elsa had given her to prevent her from getting with child. Was it because he did not want a bastard child? If that proved true, would she be better off accepting Kirk's offer and wedding his friend? Her son would then be safe and well protected.

The thought of never seeing Cree again was like a knife to her heart, and she couldn't help but think that her mother must have felt the same when she bid a final farewell to Kirk. But could she be as strong as her mother had been?

Tears stung her eyes. She loved Cree with all her heart, but she also loved his babe that she carried. She never had a choice before. There had never been any place for her to go. Now she had another option, one where she and her babe would be safe. She didn't want to have to choose, but she might not have a choice.

The horse was suddenly drawn to a stop, and she glanced up and couldn't help but smile. There a few feet away in the clearing sat Cree on his stallion and spread out behind him was a sizeable troop of his warriors.

She noticed that a few of the McClusky warriors blessed themselves, and she could understand why. Cree was all in black and wore the most evil look, as if he were ready to kill each and every one of them singlehandedly. His jaw was set tight, his nostrils flared, and his dark eyes appeared filled with venom. He was beyond angry.

Kirk rode up next to Torr and looked to Dawn. "Think on what your future would be with him against what I offer you."

"It will not matter," Torr said surprising his father, though not Dawn. She understood what he referred to. "Cree will not let her go, and we do not have enough warriors to battle him."

Cree guided his horse forward while his men waited where they were. When he got a few feet in front of Torr, he stopped and glared at the man. "You have something that belongs to me. And let me warn you that if you should decide to start a war over this, I will massacre every last one of you, and then claim your land as mine."

"I want no war with you, Cree," Kirk said, "though I do want what is best for my daughter."

"Dawn has what is best for her—me."

"Do you love Dawn?" Kirk asked.

Dawn felt her breath catch. Cree had never told her he loved her, though she never doubted he did. He showed his love in many different ways and each time he had told her that she belonged to him, it seemed as if he was saying I love you. But it would be wonderful to actually hear him say it. She almost laughed at the ironic thought, after all, he would never actually hear her say the words.

"That's between Dawn and me," Cree snapped.

"When a man loves a woman he has no problem admitting it."

"I will not discuss this here and now," Cree said sternly. "Return what is mine and I will let you live."

"And what if she doesn't want to go with you?" Kirk asked.

Cree shot Kirk such a lethal look that Dawn half expected to see him fall off the horse dead.

"She doesn't have a choice," Cree said, as if it were a decree.

"But she does," Kirk insisted. "I have provided her with one. I will openly accept her as my daughter, and I will provide well for her. I know someone who would wed her. It would be a lucrative marriage for her."

Cree appeared ready to lunge at the man. His dark eyes cut into him like sharp daggers as he said, "Listen well, McClusky, Dawn is mine and always will be mine. And I will let no one, and I mean no one—not even the King himself—take her away from me. So you would do well to release her, for I long to run a sword through you and my patience wears thin."

Dawn felt Torr's arm tighten around her waist, though it was for only a moment. He did not like that Cree threatened his father, which was understandable.

And if something wasn't done fast, she feared there would be much bloodshed.

She took matters in hand to settle the volatile situation and began gesturing over and over that she wanted to go with Cree. It wasn't a permanent choice, for she still had the babe to consider, but it was a choice to end this standoff without blood being spilled. And it wasn't a lie, at this moment she wanted to be with Cree.

"Your daughter has spoken," Cree said and brought his horse next to Torr's.

Dawn pushed Torr's arm off her and reached out to Cree. He leaned over, slipped his arm around her waist and in one powerful lift he scooped her away from Torr and sat her in front of him on his stallion.

She could have sworn she felt a sigh of relief low in his chest as she rested against him.

"Are you all right?" he whispered.

She nodded and her hand gripped his arm, as if letting him know that she was relieved to finally be returned to him.

Cree turned to Kirk and Torr. "You are no longer welcome on my land."

Dawn squeezed his arm. She certainly had not agreed with Kirk's plan, but it had made her realize that he had done it out of love. And besides Cree had to be made aware of what Kirk had told her.

Cree raised a questioning brow when he looked at her. And she pointed to Kirk, then to her and then repeatedly patted her lips.

Cree looked to Kirk. "You have told her things that I should hear?"

"I have and it would be beneficial for you to know as well."

"Follow me back to the village," Cree instructed.

"I do not think that is a good idea," Kirk said. "When you hear what I have to say, you will understand my concern. There is a cottage where we can stop and talk, if that is agreeable to you."

Cree nodded and before he turned his horse away, he looked to both men. "Know this, if you dare try to take Dawn from me again, I will kill you on the spot."

Dawn shivered as they rode off, for she knew he meant it.

He wrapped his cloak more tightly around her and hugged her close. She snuggled against him, drinking in and relishing his familiar scent. She was surprised that he remained quiet. She thought that he might question her about what had happened, but he said nothing, though his hand squeezed at her waist now and then as if making sure she was really there with him.

After riding only a short distance, the lull of the horse's steady gait felt much like the rhythm of a cradle and Cree's warmth was like being wrapped in a soft wool blanket. And no matter how hard she tried, she couldn't keep her eyes open. But then she hadn't gotten much sleep and before she realized it, sleep claimed her.

Cree felt the moment Dawn dozed off, her body going limp against his. He was glad she slept. He had worried upon seeing her, thinking she looked tired and pale. He wanted to get her home, tuck her in bed, and circle the cottage with guards, so that no one could get near her ever again.

He was still trying to contain his rage upon hearing that Kirk intended to arrange a marriage for her. He had felt like lunging off his horse at the man and strangling the life from him. It took all his willpower to remain in control and not succumb to the overwhelming desire to hurt the man who had caused him such anguish.

But Kirk had answers, and he was grateful that Dawn had made him aware of that. He wanted to know everything, for somewhere in it all, he intended to find a way to make Dawn his wife.

Chapter Twenty

"Lucerne isn't Gerwan's daughter?" Cree asked wanting to make certain he had heard Kirk correctly, for it could be the very thing he needed to negate the marriage agreement.

They had no soon as entered the cottage when Kirk had begun to explain everything. Cree had listened intently as the tale unfolded and with it the knowledge that there might be way out of this dilemma. He had kept a firm arm around Dawn the whole time, tucking her close against his side. And the more he had listened, the more he had liked what he heard.

"That's correct. Gerwan has no heirs," Kirk confirmed.

"Whose daughter is Lucerne?"

Kirk shrugged. "I wouldn't know."

"Ann Gerwan would."

Kirk glared at Cree. "I'll not have Ann placed in harm's way."

"That is why you don't want to return to the keep. You don't want to be there when Gerwan arrives."

Kirk nodded. "It could be a problem not only for Ann, seeing me after all these years, but also seeing the daughter she had given away. I'm assuming that she doesn't know that Dawn is here."

"Regardless, she is the one person who could shed the most light on the situation."

"And in the process condemn herself," Kirk said shaking his head. "There is no telling what that bastard of a husband would do to her if he found out that he has no legitimate heirs and that he could very well be stripped of his title and lands."

"I'm not a fool, Kirk, this all can be handled quietly until we know exactly what we're dealing with. Ann Gerwan may be more prone to confiding in you, if you approach her confidentially and ask for the truth. And don't tell me that you don't want to see her again. It's obvious that you still love her."

"He has a point, Da," Torr said. "It might be wise to do as he suggests."

"But don't the villagers think I abducted her?" Kirk asked. "How do we explain that?"

"That's easily explained," Cree said. "You were worried for Dawn's safety and decided to take her away from the village until my return. I met your courier on route to find Dawn and I was appreciative of you protecting her and we returned to the village together."

"What of everyone in the village knowing that I claimed that Dawn is my daughter?"

"Long lost daughter," Cree corrected, "which could work well for us. With so much attention called to her it just might be more difficult for those who wish her harm to get near her."

"There is another problem that must be addressed," Kirk said seriously. "As Dawn's father, I could not allow your liaison with her to blatantly continue."

Dawn pressed closer to Cree, and his arm tightened around her. She had listened to the exchange with interest, but once again she felt left out of it, as if these men alone would determine her fate.

The thought did not sit well with her, nor did the thought that Cree and she would be kept apart.

"That's not your choice," Cree said.

"Yes, it is my choice and you are fully aware of it," Kirk said calmly. "What type of father would I be if I stood by and did nothing? You, yourself, would have no respect for me."

"Dawn and I will not be parted," Cree said vehemently.

Dawn had listened to enough. They discussed her fate right in front of her and yet never bothered to ask what she wanted. Colum had forced her on Cree to begin with and now the man claiming to be her father insisted on taking her away from Cree. But no one ever gave her thought.

She stepped out of Cree's arms and moved away from him. He went to reach for her, and she brushed his hand away. A deep scowl warned he wasn't pleased with her action and she sent him a scowl back, letting him know that she wasn't pleased as well. His brow shot up as if he could not believe her reaction.

Dawn pointed to each one of them, and then tapped her chest hard, then her ear and once again pointed at them, letting them know that they better listen to her. The three men stared at her shocked or compliant it didn't matter. She intended to have her say.

With tempered gestures so that they could understand her, she began, though it didn't take long for those gestures to turn adamant and become obvious to all that she was angry. She let them know that she was tired of being dictated to and that she would be making her own decisions from this moment one. And if any of them didn't like it, she didn't care. She would do whatever she had to do to take care of herself. She had been doing so before they had come along and she would do so again.

Kirk was the first to speak when her hands turned silent. "I am proud that you are so courageous and have such an independent nature, but you are in danger and in need of protection."

"Father's right," Torr joined in. "If someone wasn't out to harm you I would agree with you and so would have Teressa. Her nature was much like yours. But you are in danger and must keep that in mind."

Dawn felt a twinge of sorrow for never having gotten to know her sister. It would have been nice to have spent time with someone just like herself. They no doubt would have understood each other better than anyone could have.

"We cannot waste any more time here discussing this," Cree said. "I want Dawn safely back home before Gerwan arrives. We can settle this there."

Kirk and Torr agreed and before Dawn knew what was happening, they mounted their horses and were on their way home.

Dawn knew Cree well and she could tell that he was annoyed. While his scowl was not as deep, a slight scrunch between his brows had remained. And when she rested her hand on his arm that wrapped snugly around her waist, she felt the muscles there bunched tightly. She waited, knowing any moment he would have something to say to her.

Sure enough, he leaned down and whispered, "Nice little speech, but it changes nothing. You are mine and will remain mine."

It wasn't that she didn't like being his, after all, she did love him, but annoyance stirred in her at being dismissed so easily. Didn't he even give thought to what she had said? Did he not care what she wanted? Were his wants his only concern?

Agitated, she felt the need for a bit of distance from him and moved away from where she leaned against his chest and without realizing it removed her hand off his arm.

Cree yanked her back against him and rested his face next to hers as he whispered, "Do not pull away from me. I do what I do to keep you safe. If you are angry with me for that then so be it, but that will not change... not now, not ever."

How could she stay mad at him for wanting to keep her safe? His actions continued to prove how much he cared for her, though she wished he would pay more heed to her wants. Perhaps she hadn't been clear enough.

She tapped his chest and turned to look at him.

"Don't bother to argue with me. You won't win."

His words angered her. It sounded as if he delivered a final edict. She cocked a brow and jabbed him in the chest.

"Not here, not now," he said with a snarl.

She gestured adamantly, jabbing the space between them and shrugging, wanting to know if not here and now, when?

"Later when we are alone, though there is little that you can say that will make a difference."

Perhaps he was right. His word was law, though that didn't mean she could not have her say, make herself heard and, at least, feel that she finally spoke up for herself. Not that it mattered all that much since little she said would probably be given any consideration, but she strongly felt the need to do so. She might not have a voice, but that didn't mean she couldn't make herself heard.

They arrived home late in the evening. Cree took her to her cottage and told her that he would return later. She did not argue with him and she did not care that the men might talk without her. In the end, she would have her say.

She did not gesture a word to Cree, she simply turned and walked away from him and entered her cottage without looking back. She collapsed back against the door as soon as she closed it. She was exhausted. She had had little sleep and little food since this ordeal had begun. And there was no doubt that the dilemma would grow more difficult.

All she wanted to do was drop down on her bed and sleep and forget all her problems for a while. She had barely moved away from the door and dropped her cloak on a chair, when there was a knock. It couldn't have been Cree returning so quickly, since he never announced his entrance.

Dawn opened the door reluctantly, not wanting to bother with anyone at the moment.

Old Mary stood there. "Lila needs you; baby Thomas is sick."

Dawn didn't bother to grab her cloak. She was out of the cottage in a flash, only to be stopped by a guard she was not familiar with.

"Cree has left strict orders that you are not to go anywhere."

Old Mary explained the situation, but still the guard refused to let her pass.

"I have orders," he said. "Back in your cottage, you go."

That was it. Dawn could not take another minute of being told what to do and her anger finally exploded, not at all as she would expect. She made a fist and swung at the guard with all her strength and

sent him stumbling to fall into a snow drift. It gave
her enough time to run.

It was late and no one was about. Her booted feet
flew across the snow-covered path. She feared for
Lila and baby Thomas. Too often she had seen babes
die before they reached their first year, and she
prayed that wouldn't be the babe's fate.

She was a few feet from Lila's cottage when she
suddenly and violently got hit from the side. The
initial shock stunned her and tumbled her to the
ground, but when she saw the dirk poised in the air
ready to strike, all she could think about was
protecting the babe inside her. Her mounting anger
turned to pure rage, and she fought like only a mother
could to protect her child.

Her reaction caught her attacker off guard and
she grabbed for the man's wrist to keep the dirk at
bay. They struggled and Dawn soon realized that his
strength far surpassed hers, and she wasn't sure how
long she could keep him from doing her harm. And
with it being the evening hour, there was no one
about so she only had herself to rely on. With that
thought, she turned into a wildcat, bucking and
kicking as she fought to stop him from jabbing her
with the dirk. She managed to dislodge him and
scrambled to her feet and ran when she suddenly felt
a jab to her side. Her hand pressed against the pain,
and she felt sticky warmth and knew she had been
wounded.

She knew another blow could prove fatal, so she
turned and stepped to the side abruptly. The culprit
startled and stopped much too suddenly and trying to
stop himself from falling proved unwise. He twisted
in an attempt to save himself and fell on his own dirk,

though scrambled to his feet and ran off faster than she thought his wound allowed.

The pain in her side was now minor, but when she looked down she was shocked to see blood covering her hand, her blouse, and the upper portion of her skirt was also soaked with it. Her first thought was of the babe. She could not lose Cree's child; *their* babe. She couldn't.

The savage roar seemed to tremble the ground at her feet and when she looked up, she saw Cree running toward her. He appeared almost a wild beast on the rampage and, for a moment, she thought to step back away from him.

Then her mind cleared and she silently cried with relief. He would help her and their child. He would save their babe—he had to. She stretched her bloody hand out to him and took only a couple of steps when her legs turned too weak to hold her up. She went down, bracing for the hit to the hard ground, but it never came. Cree caught her, his arms going around her, holding her firm as he easily scooped her up in his arms and held her close.

He didn't say a word to her. He rushed to her cottage, his shouts filling the cold air. People ran at his commands as he went. She heard him shout for Elsa and for his warriors to find the bastard who did this to her.

She felt his anger reverberate in his chest with ever command he bellowed and oddly enough it felt soothing. She was in his arms and safe and that was what mattered. She thought she heard Sloan's anxious voice and Elwin's as well. And was that Lila she heard? It couldn't be, Thomas was ill and she would be with him. And that thought had her wondering how Thomas was doing. He was so small and vulnerable. Surely, Elsa had helped him as she would the babe that grew inside Dawn.

Dawn heard Cree kick her cottage door open and she hoped he hadn't broken it. She was beginning to favor the cottage. After all, it was where their babe was conceived.

The babe.

She had to tell Cree about their babe.

She was gently deposited on her bed and her only thought was to tell Cree that he would be a father come summer. Though the worried look in his eyes when he glanced at her wound made her think that perhaps it was too late to save her and the babe.

Dawn shook her head. She couldn't die. She would fight for herself and her child. Besides, Cree would never let her go. She belonged to him. He would never permit it. She stretched her hand out to him, needing to let him know.

Cree grabbed hold of it. "Elsa will be here any moment and all will—"

She shook her head and pressed his hand to her stomach while she raised her other hand and pointed to herself and then to him, and then pressed his hand against her stomach.

Cree already wore a scowl and it deepened, and she worried that he didn't understand her, and then his eyes turned wide, as if it had finally dawned on him.

"You carry our babe?"

She nodded and fought to stay conscious, but the darkness was closing in fast around her. She heard him shout her name, but it was as if she was falling down a deep dark tunnel, further and further away from his pleas for her to stay with him, until darkness completely engulfed her.

Chapter Twenty-one

"Do something, she carries my babe," Cree shouted when Elsa entered the room. He hunched down beside the bed, his hand still resting on her stomach and his other hand stroking her forehead. "I cannot lose her." He shook his head and repeated. "I cannot lose her." He turned a threatening eye on Elsa. "They will be hell to pay if she dies."

"Threatening me will not help her or your child," Elsa said calmly. "Now please step aside and let me see to her wound."

Cree reluctantly did as she asked, knowing that Elsa was the only one capable of saving her. And knowing that if it was possible, the healer would do everything she could to make sure that Dawn lived.

After only a couple of seconds of examining the wound, Elsa said, "You need to help me get these blood-soaked garments off her."

Cree did not hesitate. He went to work with Elsa removing Dawn's garments, though it wasn't easy. The bloody areas refused to let go. Once they were done, Elsa had him slip a clean cloth underneath her wounded side, and then she set to cleaning the area.

Cree remained close by watching the healer and waiting for word that the woman he loved would live. He did not know what he would do without Dawn. She had become his life and he did not want to think of a day without her. She brought a smile to his face and made him laugh and he hadn't done both in a very long time. And besides, he simply could not sleep without her in bed beside him.

He pressed his hand to his chest the way she did when she would tell him she loved him. Damn, damn, damn if his heart didn't belong to her, every pounding beat of it and his soul was lost to her as well, for there wasn't anything he wouldn't do for her. This beautiful woman with no voice was his whole life, and he wouldn't have it any other way.

Elsa cleaned the injured area well and when she dropped the cloth in the second bucket of clean water, she looked up at Cree and smiled. "It doesn't even need a stitch. The weapon caught no vital area. It was more of a nick than anything, though the preponderance of blood made it appear much worse. Some wounds bleed more than others, though I cannot say why."

"Then why did she slip into darkness?" Cree asked relieved, though still concerned.

Elsa shook her head. "I cannot say, though carrying a babe can tire a woman and with all Dawn has been through, this last incident just may have been too much for her. And so she slipped into a much needed rest."

"The babe is well?" Again he asked with concern, not wanting Dawn to wake and find that she had lost their babe. She knew him well and knew that as soon as he learned of their child that he would protect them both, and he would not disappoint her.

"Dawn is strong and has kept your babe safe. Both mother and child do well as far as I can tell," Elsa assured him.

"You will tend her daily," Cree ordered.

Elsa smiled. "If that is your wish, my lord, though I do not think Dawn will agree with you. She has done well since she first realized that she carried your babe and I have no doubt she will continue to do so."

"You knew she was with child and never told me?" Cree said with a touch of anger.

"It was not my place, my lord, it was meant for Dawn to tell you, not me."

Cree was ready to argue when he held his tongue. Elsa was right. Dawn would have wanted to tell him and though he had concerns about such a possibility, he also had wondered what a child of theirs would be like. And with Old Mary telling him that he would have many sons and only one daughter, he knew that those children would be born of Dawn and him, for they made love so often that Dawn would be forever carrying a babe of his.

"You are a good healer, Elsa," Cree said.

"And you, my lord, will make an excellent father. Now I would suggest Dawn not be left alone until she finally wakes, and then she should rest, though I daresay she will be up and about quick enough. Nothing seems to keep her down. "

"Will she need rest?" Cree asked ready to decree it if he must.

"Dawn will not take a chance in harming the babe. She will do what she must without being ordered to."

"Dawn finds a way around such things and does more of what she wants than she most," Cree said with a sense of pride.

"Then let her be, for she knows best. I will return tomorrow morning and check on her, but I don't anticipate a problem. The wound will be tender, though it will heal fast enough and leave a small scar, nothing more."

"I bless the day I found you," Elsa," Cree said in way of appreciation.

"As do I, my lord," Elsa said with a bob and took her leave.

Sloan arrived shortly afterwards to let Cree know that they hadn't found the culprit yet, but they would continue searching. He wasn't' surprised when Cree informed him that he would not leave Dawn's side until he was certain that she would be all right.

As night settled in, Cree sat on the bed beside Dawn and watched her sleep. He wished she would wake. There was so much he wanted to say to her. But she needed her rest and even if she did wake, talk would have to wait.

He tended the fire and ate a little of the food Flanna had brought and assured the worried woman that Dawn would be fine. Flanna insisted on leaving some soup by the hearth to keep heated for when Dawn woke. After one last report from Sloan, Cree finally decided it was time for bed. He would crawl into bed with Dawn and be careful not to disturb her wound, but there was no way that he would sleep separate from her.

He was stripping off the last of his garments when he turned and saw that her eyes were open. He didn't go directly to her. He continued disrobing.

He was such a magnificent creature and no matter how many times she laid eyes on his naked form, she couldn't peel them away. She loved looking at him, though touching and tasting was definitely more to her liking. He was sculpted to perfection and she wondered if the babe, a boy if she were to believe Old Mary's prediction, would be as handsome as his father.

Once Cree finished, he eased himself down on the bed to rest stretched out, close against her. "How are you feeling? Are you hungry? Flanna left soup for you. Do you have pain? I can have Elsa bring you something for it."

She pressed her finger to his mouth to stop him from talking. Then she took his hand and pressed it to her stomach, anxious to know how he felt about the babe, for she recalled his surprised expression when he had realized what she had been trying to tell him.

"You have been injured. You need rest. We'll talk another time."

She shook her head adamantly and pointed her finger up and down emphasizing that they would talk here and now. She had to know. She couldn't wait. She had to know if he wanted their child as much as she did.

"It can wait," he said wanting her to rest.

She shook her head.

"You have been through enough. We'll talk tomorrow."

She shook her head more vigorously. She could not wait that long.

"Shake your head all you want. It will change nothing."

Anger bubbled up in Dawn and, to Cree's surprise, she scurried out of bed with a facial wince and quickly slowed her pace, which irritated Cree, and went to stand by the curtain that separated the two rooms. She pointed at it while she glared at Cree.

"Are you telling me to leave?"

Dawn tapped her lips and then pointed at the curtain.

"You're giving me a choice? Talk to you or leave?" he asked incredulously.

Dawn nodded, raised her chin, and crossed her arms over her chest.

Cree stretched out on the bed, crossing his arms beneath his head. "I'm not going anywhere and I'm not talking, so you may as well come back to bed."

It infuriated her that he gave her no choice, but then she didn't have to join him in bed. She went to the hearth and sat in front of it, bunching her legs up in front of her. Her mind had been so overwrought that she had forgotten about her wound and winced again from the catch in her side, though the only indication of it was a hunch of her shoulders and the pain-filled grimace she made when she stretched her arms to wrap around her raised legs.

Cree flew off the bed, and to her side, when he caught her reaction. "Damn it, woman, you're stubborn." He went to pick her up, and she shoved his hands away, then tapped at her lips. "All right," he relented. "We'll talk, but briefly."

She doubted that their talk would be brief, but if he wanted to believe otherwise that was fine with her.

He scooped her up gently and deposited her on the bed with the same tender care, then got under the blankets to sit beside her. He reached out to take her in his arms, and she brushed his hands away and tapped her lips.

He leaned over until the tip of his nose touched hers. "Don't push my hands away when I reach for you." She raised her hand to respond but he grabbed it. "Under any circumstances."

Then he did something completely unexpected.

He splayed his hand across her stomach. "You and the babe are well?"

She nodded.

"How long have you known?"

Her fingers counted off a month.

"You've known a month?"

She nodded, scowled, and pointed at him wanting to know if he was angry, needing to know.

When he didn't respond right away, she thought he didn't understand her and she went to gesture again, but he stopped her. He rested his hand on her stomach. "I heard you. I am not angry. I am overwhelmed with joy that you carry our child."

Our child. Dawn felt her breath catch. He was happy that she would have *their* babe. Her breath caught again, only this time with worry, and she patted his hand that continued to rest on her stomach and searched his face with troubled eyes. If he was happy, why didn't she see it in his eyes?

He leaned down and kissed her softly, then cupped her face in his hands. "I wish you would have told me sooner."

Dawn cocked a brow in question, confused by his mixture of joy and anger. Was he truly happy or...

He smiled and kissed her again. "Trust me, I am more pleased than you'll ever know. Quickly though, I realized that I have failed, and rarely do I fail, to protect you not only from being harmed, but from getting you pregnant while being my mistress and now failing to protect my unborn child as well. That is not acceptable to me." He paused a moment to softly caress her cheek with his finger. "Tell me. You knew you were already with child when I told you to take the potion to prevent such a situation, weren't you?"

There was no longer any point in hiding the truth from him, and so she nodded.

"You could have aborted the babe by taken the potion, but you didn't. You chose to defy me and protect our babe."

She nodded again.

He cupped her chin. "This is one time I am grateful for your defiance."

She patted her chest to let him know that she felt the same.

"While I wish to shout out the news for all to know, there is much to be settled first," he said letting go of her chin.

She let him know that she agreed.

"There are possibilities now that didn't exist before." He took her hand again and brought it to his mouth to kiss it. "I must ask you something very important."

She pressed her hand to her ear to let him know that she was listening.

"I need you to promise me that no matter what happens, no matter what you hear, no matter what transpires over the next few days or weeks that you will trust me, never doubt me and that you will remain by my side and not think it prudent to leave me."

She cringed inwardly, feeling guilty that she had already given it thought, though she was quick to cross her heart and give her promise. And to seal it, she told him that she loved him, her hand going from her heart to his.

He pressed his hand over hers. "I am fortunate that you love me."

She smiled, though it appeared more a gentle laugh as she nodded, as if she let him know that he was very fortunate to have her love him.

"You think it humorous that I should feel fortunate?" he said giving teasing pokes to her ribs.

She raised her hands to ward off his playful attack and cringed from the pain that shot through her.

"Damn," Cree mumbled. "I forgot about your wound."

And of course a yawn had to attack her just then, since she was feeling more relaxed than she had in hours.

Cree shook his head. "And you're tired and need rest. That's it. No more talk. It's time to sleep." Dawn had no intentions of arguing with him. He helped her stretch out and then eased her against him when he stretched out beside her, making certain that her wound was left undisturbed.

Another yawn hit Dawn and she was prepared for sleep to claim her fast. The problem started when she felt Cree harden against her backside. Fatigue never kept her body from responding to his and now wasn't any difference.

She wiggled against him as if adjusting her position, which she was, though it was to fit more snuggly against his growing hardness. After all, a quick joining would surely help her sleep soundly.

His hand pressed against her stomach, as if wanting to prevent her from moving, then he must have thought better of it, thinking he would disturb the tiny babe inside her, and he moved his hand down further.

A definite mistake.

She didn't wait. She placed her hand over his and guided it between her legs.

"You are too tired, and do you forget you were wounded?" he whispered, though she could hear desire thick in his voice.

She shook her head and encouraged his hand to delve and explore.

His growling groan in her ear fired her passion even more, and she pressed her backside hard against his bulging groin.

"Damn it," he mumbled and retaliated by slipping his finger inside her.

She pressed her finger against his arm, once, twice, three times.

"You like that do you?" he whispered in her ear.

She shivered, his warm breath tickling her ear and nodded vigorously.

"You will not lift a finger and disturb your wound. Tonight I do all the work." He chuckled and nuzzled her neck. "Though this work I thoroughly enjoy doing."

There were times Cree was gentle with her, but tonight he showed her a gentleness she hadn't known existed. He lavished her body with kisses, teased her with gentle touches and when he was ready to enter her, he slipped one arm beneath her back to easily lift her while he placed a pillow behind her head, and then carefully laid her down.

She silently sighed with his tender thoughtfulness. And then he moved down between her legs to ease them apart with his hands, taking his time to stroke her legs and tell her...

"You are so beautiful and so soft." And with that he leaned over her and entered her slowly as he braced both arms along the sides of her shoulders and lowered his head to capture her lips with his.

He moved then, picking up speed and rhythm, and she grabbed his arms without thinking of her wound and cringed, her eyes shutting tight against the pain.

He stopped abruptly and her eyes shot open, and she shook her head adamantly.

"Do not move," he ordered sharply.

She nodded, fearful he would not finish what he started and that she could not bear.

"I told you that I will do all the work."

And he did.

Dawn climaxed hard not once but twice, Cree joining her in the second one. And no soon as they finished and he wrapped her in his arms, then her eyes closed and she fell asleep.

Chapter Twenty-two

Cree woke at sunrise, though was quite content to remain abed with Dawn in his arms. She had fallen asleep instantly after he had made love to her and had slept peacefully. He had worried that her wound would wake her, but her fatigue had been more powerful than her pain and he was glad she had gotten to rest.

He was still a bit shocked over the news that he was to be a father. He was also shocked at the joy that had seized him when he had learned about the babe. He had never known such a wonderful feeling, though perhaps it was that he had never known such happiness. And since Dawn had entered his life he had known endless happiness along with a substantial amount of worry and fear.

That worry and fear had gripped him soon after learning of the babe, and the thought that he could lose them both, if he failed to protect her, had filled him with immense anger. Once he had left the cottage, he was more determined than ever to make certain that he made Dawn his wife. He would not let his child be born a bastard.

He also knew that once Kirk learned the news, he would insist that Dawn wed his friend and that would never happen. Besides, with what Kirk had told him, it had made it possible for him to petition the King to negate the present marriage agreement between him and Lucerne and arrange one between him and Dawn.

But first there were secrets to uncover and identities to be confirmed and, when he had all the proof he needed, he could contact the King. The only thing he feared was that the King would want concessions so that everyone would be appeased. And he wondered what they would be.

Dawn stirred, cuddling closer against him and he tucked the blanket over her shoulders. There was so much he wanted and needed to say to her, but the time wasn't right. Most importantly, though, the situation wasn't right. And he blamed much of that on himself. After his mother had died, he had had no choice but to put his sister in a convent, and he had sworn he would let no one dictate his life. He had worked, though mostly battled hard, to reach that point. Now it was only the King he answered to, and he found even that too restrictive.

What he had learned though was to manipulate those in power to get what he wanted, and he wanted Dawn and nothing would stop him from having her as his wife.

The soft tap to his chest had him glancing down at Dawn, her eyes not yet fully opened. She looked as if she peeked between her lashes, and yet she seemed to see him clearly, since she reached up to gently caress the scowl bunched between his eyes.

He shook his head. She needn't know his trouble thoughts.

Dawn thought otherwise.

She tapped her chest, then his and then crossed her heart, reminding him that he had asked her to promise to trust him. Then she tapped his chest again and crossed his heart and shrugged, asking if he promised to trust her. Then she took hold of his hand

and laced her fingers with his and squeezed tight, as if reaffirming their commitment to each other.

"You are asking of me, what I asked of you... to trust you. He squeezed their joined hand. "That we are one and nothing can separate us." He loved the way she talked with her hands, since most of the time to do so, she had to touch him. And he loved when she touched him, whether innocently or passionately, he loved the feel of her hands on him.

Dawn nodded with a smile.

"You would never think of leaving me, would you?" he asked needing her to reaffirm that they were inseparable. He did not like the soft scowl that disappeared as fast as it had appeared on her face. He grew angry, though truthfully it was more worry. "You have thought of leaving me?"

She was not good at hiding her thoughts from him. He could read and hear through her silence too well. She released his hand, patted her stomach, and shook her head.

"You thought I didn't want the babe?" he asked, though why wouldn't she? He had demanded she take something to prevent conception. What had he expected her to think? And then it hit him... she would have left him to protect their child. He silently cursed himself for being such a fool. "You would have left me to protect our child." His scowl deepened. "That means you would have accepted Kirk's offer of wedding his friend."

He turned such a fierce look on her that she felt a twinge of fear.

"I would have never let that happen." He grinned then and proudly. "I would have killed him before you ever got the chance to wed him."

Her twinge dissipated with his grin, and she shook her head and poked him in the ribs.

He grabbed her finger and kissed it, then he brought his lips to hers and before he kissed her said, "Never ever doubt that I want our child and never ever doubt that we are one."

She had no chance to respond, his lips settled on hers. She recalled the envy she had felt when Lila told her about her first kiss and how wonderful it had been and how she wouldn't mind kissing Paul over and over again. Dawn had hoped one day she would feel the same about someone. As time had passed, she had doubted that day would ever come, and then a miracle had happened... Cree kissed her.

She finally got to experience her own joy at being kissed and would have never thought it could be so utterly magical or that she would never want his kisses to stop. And she loved all the different ways he kissed her, like now with a fierce possessiveness that confirmed what he had said... they were one.

Her body began to respond to his deepening kiss, which was something that always happened, whether his kiss was filled with passion or tender caring. It didn't matter; her body quickened. And at that moment, besides feeling passionate, she was feeling playful, so she slipped her hand down to take hold of him.

She wasn't surprised to find him hard. It seemed to be a perpetual state with him when they were in bed together. Though she was surprised at his reaction, he stopped kissing her.

"Your wound?"

She hadn't even given thought to it and she didn't intend to, at least not now. She shook her head and, to prove her point, pushed him on his back and slowly climbed on top of him. Her passion surged with her actions and she found herself more than eager to have him inside her.

He grinned. "In a hurry?"

She halted her fumbling, not from the twinge of pain that caught at her wound, but from his grin. And with sharp gestures, she let him know that she needed him to be inside her right this very moment.

His grin faded and he took control, his hands taking hold of her hips and lowering her down on her back. It was a quick joining for them both, each building rapidly toward a powerful climax. And as they drew near... a heavy pounding sounded at the door.

"Ignore it," Cree commanded as he quickened his thrusts.

Dawn gripped his steel-hard arms tighter and did as he said, trying desperately to focus on nothing but his hard, continuous thrusts.

Both poundings continued and a voice was added to the one at the door.

"Cree," Sloan yelled in between his fist hitting the door. "Cree! It's important."

Dawn shook her head and shoved at Cree's shoulder to go see what Sloan wanted.

He growled like an angry bear. "Don't dare move. I'll be right back."

Cree stomped out of the room, swung open the door, grabbed Sloan by his shirt, jerked him inside and slammed the door shut.

"This better be important or I'm going to kill you," Cree warned.

"Not only is Gerwan's caravan about to enter the village, but the King's cleric is here to wed you and Lucerne."

Both men turned at the noise. Dawn stood in her nightdress, her hand at her mouth as she hurried to a nearby bucket to retch.

Cree flew to her side and called out to Sloan, "Get some snow."

Sloan flew out the door and Cree felt helpless as he kept an arm around Dawn and watched her suffer through dry heaves. When she finished, he scooped her up and carried her into the other room and laid her gently on the bed. He pulled the blanket over her, tucking it around her and sat beside her.

Sloan rushed in with a bucket filled with snow and stopped suddenly to say, "Dawn carries your child doesn't she?"

Cree held his hand out for the bucket. "If you breathe a word of it I will cut out—" he stopped himself from telling Sloan that he would cut out his tongue, not that he ever would, but it was a way of letting Sloan know he had gone too far. Not anymore though, not with the way such words hurt Dawn.

Sloan understood without Cree having to say anymore. "I give you my word that I will not breathe a word of it to anyone."

That was all Cree needed to hear, for Sloan was a man of his word.

Sloan handed the bucker to Cree and then stepped back.

Cree took some snow and placed a small amount by Dawn's mouth. "At least you won't dry heave if the babe protests again." He then turned to Sloan. "How long before everyone arrives?"

"The cleric is about an hour away and Gerwan about thirty minutes or more. Turbett and Flanna have everything in hand for their arrival."

"Go," Cree ordered. "I will be there shortly."

Sloan nodded and left.

Cree placed more snow by Dawn's lips. "Is this the first time the babe has made you ill in the morning?"

She shook her head, though held her hands apart to gesture a gap.

"It has been a while since you have felt this way?'

She nodded.

He tucked a strand of her hair behind her ear. "I am asking you to rest today, since ordering you to do anything doesn't seem to work. And it would be cruel of me to punish you for not obeying when you already suffer... in far too many ways. Though I remind you to trust me and believe me when I tell you that all will be well."

She had no trouble trusting him and, feeling poorly, she had no intentions of going anywhere... for now. So it was easy for her to nod and let him know that she would rest.

He stood and dressed, then leaned over her and kissed her. "Later I will make certain we finish what we never got a chance to."

She smiled and crossed her heart and shrugged.

He tweaked her nose and smiled. "I promise, though it isn't necessary. Nothing will stop me from making love to you." He gave her another quick kiss and left.

Dawn didn't care for the shiver that ran through her. She feared with Gerwan's arrival that Cree's visits would be fewer. But she trusted him, not that she wasn't going to still see what she could find out for herself. She yawned, feeling a bit tired and decided to do as he had asked, and rest. She snuggled beneath the warm blanket and before she knew it, she was sound asleep.

~~~

Cree had washed and dressed in fresh garments and then consulted with Sloan in his solar. Cree wasn't at all pleased to find out that the tracks left by Dawn's attacker had gone cold and the culprit had yet to be found.

"Someone helps this person," Cree said after hearing Sloan explain.

"My thoughts as well," Sloan agreed.

"You spent some time with Lucerne the other day. Do you think she is capable of such treachery?"

Sloan rubbed his chin. "She's an odd one. One minute she lashes out over just about everything and the next minute she collapses against me, as if everything is too much of an ordeal for her. And damn, if she never stops complaining about how her head aches. Then just when I can't take anymore, she suddenly calms and turns pleasant. She wears too many faces for my liking, which leaves me to think she cannot be trusted."

"What of Bree? Can she be trusted or do you fancy her too much to see her clearly?"

Sloan cocked a brow. "Fancy her or not, I won't let any woman blind me. She seems sincere enough and worried that she'll be made to return to Lucerne and serve her. Old Mary doesn't seem to have a bad word to say about her and since the old woman has an eye for seeing beyond, I figured she would know if the lass should not be trusted."

"A point I considered myself," Cree admitted. "What of Lucerne's other servant? Magda is it?"

Sloan nodded. "She spends all her time stitching Lucerne's garments and mostly keeps company with the servants that do the stitching for the keep."

"Keep a good watch on them all," Cree ordered. "There is something there that we are missing."

Sloan nodded, and then cleared his throat.

"Say what you will," Cree said knowing Sloan was preparing to say something that Cree might not want to hear.

"You're not going to let you're babe be born a bastard, are you?"

"No, never would I allow that."

"What about the agreement you made with the King? He'll take these lands from you if you don't wed Gerwan's daughter."

"But Lucerne is not Gerwan's daughter," Cree said and went on to explain what Kirk had told him about his affair with Gerwan's wife years ago. He then finished with, "And with McClusky land bordering Gerwan's land, it would give the King an even stronger hold on this area if he joined the two. Besides, he wants that port built and he knows I'm the only one capable of seeing it done. I can get this to work if I can prove without a doubt that Lucerne is not Gerwan's daughter and that Dawn is Kirk's daughter. I'm concerned though that the King will demand concessions. He'll want to appease everyone so that no one rants against him."

Sloan scratched his head. "Damn, this could work."

"Yes, it could and while I rued the day that Kirk McClusky arrived here, I am now grateful that he did. And until we can sort this all out, Dawn—and now my child—are not safe."

"The extra guards were added. She'll not be able to go anywhere without them. And Kirk's warriors also mull about her cottage. I don't see how anyone could get to her."

"How often have you known me to order her to stay put and she does otherwise? Add to that the many times you didn't hear me tell her, and you now know that Dawn does what she wants, when she wants."

Sloan grinned. "Damn, I haven't known anyone who dared not obey you."

"I should have cut out that ton—" Cree stopped abruptly and shook his head.

Sloan's grin grew. "Damn, can't say it anymore, can you? Guess my tongue is finally free of worry... thanks to Dawn."

"Don't tempt me," Cree snapped.

"Oh hell, we both know you would have never cut my tongue out. It was just a warning that I had gone too far." Sloan laughed. "Now I can go as far as I like."

Cree turned a murderous scowl on him.

"You're going to have to do better than that," Sloan said continuing to laugh.

"Keep it up, I'll find a way to make you pay."

"I don't know about that," Sloan teased.

Cree suddenly grinned. "I think you should remain by Lucerne's side throughout this whole ordeal."

Sloan's smile quickly faded. "You don't mean that."

"But I do mean it," he said and stood.

"I was only teasing you," Sloan said in the way of an apology.

"I'm not," Cree said and walked to the door. "Stay by her side every moment and see what you can find out."

"What about Bree? Wouldn't it be better if I became her shadow?"

"I'll assign someone else to her."

"Who?"

"Not your concern."

Sloan shook his head as he walked over to join him at the door. "Having my tongue cut out would have been less painful."

"But not as much fun for me," Cree said and slapped him on the back.

Chapter Twenty-three

Dawn woke with a start. She wasn't sure what woke her. It was as if someone yanked her out of her sleep. She didn't mind though, she felt rested and wanted out of bed. She hurried and dressed, all the while listening to her stomach rumble with hunger.

She combed the tangles out of her hair with a worn bone comb, then plaited it and let the braid fall down her back. Then she went in search of something to eat. She was disappointed when she found that no food had been left for her on the table and laughed silently. Had she gotten spoiled with having food brought to her? She certainly was capable of cooking for herself. It was just that right now, she was so hungry she wished that she didn't have to wait to eat.

With a quick glance at her cloak, she thought about walking to the kitchen and getting something that was already prepared. She went to grab her cloak and stopped suddenly, recalling that Gerwan had been due to arrive and not knowing how long she had slept meant that his troop could be arriving this very moment. She had no desire to watch his entrance into a village that no longer belonged to him.

A knock sounded and the door opened and in came Dorrie with a basket of food. Dawn smiled brightly and ushered her in with an eager wave.

"We were ordered to let you sleep, but being it's close to noon, Flanna insisted food be brought to you." Dorrie sat the basket on the table and began taking things out.

Dawn didn't wait. She reached for a piece of bread and began munching on it, her eyes growing wide with each delicious item Dorrie placed on the table. When she finished, Dawn handed her a tankard of hot cider.

Dorrie took it with a smile and sat. "I can't stay long. The kitchen is busy. The Gerwan party will be here any moment and though none wish to greet him, all have agreed that it would be a poor reflection on Cree if they didn't."

Dawn smiled and nodded, agreeing with the villagers and happy to know that they thought highly of Cree and chose to show respect for him.

Dorrie leaned in closer and lowered her voice. "Are you truly Kirk McClusky's bastard daughter?"

Dawn shrugged, for what proof was there?

"The villagers continue to worry that there will be a battle over this."

Dawn shook her head and tapped her chest, then waved her hand back and forth.

Dorrie smiled. "You won't let that happen."

Dawn nodded.

"I told everyone that. I told them that you would do what was best for the village just as you did when Colum sent you to tend Cree. You are an unselfish soul and your choice would be for the good of all or even one person." She smiled. "Just as you protected me, you would protect others." She jumped up then. "I must go or Turbett will get upset. He is so much more than he appears. He gives extra food to his workers and he teaches them. I have learned so much about food from him that when it came time for my punishment to end, I asked to stay on and Turbett was pleased to have me. Another thing I have you to thank for." Dorrie gave Dawn a quick hug and left the cottage.

Dawn ate with a cluttered mind. She certainly didn't think of herself as a selfless soul. She had done what she had to do to survive just like many of the villagers. Cree's capture of the village had heralded in a prosperous time for all, and no one wanted to see that change. Life was good and everyone wanted it to remain that way.

Another knock sounded and in walked Kirk. "I came to see how you were feeling."

Panic rose in Dawn. How did he know she had been ill this morning?

"Your wound does not cause you too much pain I hope," he said as he approached the table.

Dawn smiled, having again forgotten about her wound and waved for him to join her. He hurried to do so. She shook her head, pointing to her side that truly did not cause her as much discomfit as everyone assumed.

"I am glad you are feeling well."

Dawn pointed to the food and her mouth.

"You are hungry."

She nodded and handed him a piece of bread.

He shook his head. "I have eaten, though my appetite is not what it should be. I worry about you and your mother. I do not want to see her suffer after all these years, and I do not want any harm to befall you."

Dawn wondered what Ann Gerwan would do when she laid eyes on Kirk after all this time. And what would she do when she learned of Dawn? Would she want to meet her or would she want nothing to do with her? But more importantly, what did she herself want from her true mother?

~~~

"The King has sent a cleric?" Lucerne all but screamed at Cree when she learned the news. "But we are not to wed for at least a month's time yet. Does he expect us to wed sooner?"

Cree hadn't thought of that. Could that be why the cleric had arrived early? Did he have a message from the King for the wedding to proceed immediately? He had to solve the riddle of Dawn's birth soon or all could be lost. If he had been concerned for just himself, he would take Dawn and go off with her and to hell with everything. They could be happy together just the two of them. But it wasn't only about him. It was about all the men who had fought beside him and the women who had endured hardships with the promise that one day they would all have a home.

He could not disappoint them; he would not.

"There are preparations to consider and my wedding dress is not finished yet." Lucerne wrung her hands. "This is a nightmare. It cannot be; I will not stand for it."

For once Cree agreed with the distraught woman, though he had no response for her and was relieved when one of his warriors entered the Great Hall to inform Cree that Gerwan's caravan was near.

Lucerne jumped up and hurried to fetch her white fur-lined cloak from the nearby bench. "We must be waiting on the steps to greet them or my father will think you disrespectful." Her frown, which had seemed perpetual, suddenly disappeared and she smiled causing Cree to catch his breath at how stunningly beautiful she was. "Mother, on the other hand, would worry if I was not there to greet her. She has always worried over me."

Cree realized then how much Lucerne loved her mother, and it troubled him as to what would become of her when the truth was revealed. But if she was the one behind the plot to kill Dawn it wouldn't matter, she would get what she deserved. But if she wasn't, then she would be an innocent victim of this whole ruse just like Dawn.

"Hurry," Lucerne shouted when Cree hadn't moved and then realized her error and sought to correct it. "I am sorry, my lord, I am excited to see my mo—" She bit at her lower lip for a moment, squeezed her eyes shut, rubbed at her head, and then opened them slowly and calmly said, "I am eager to see my parents."

Cree stood. "Then we should not keep them waiting."

Lucerne smiled and nodded and waited for him to come and offer his arm. Reluctantly, he did and they walked out of the keep to wait on the steps, though not before he cast a glance to Sloan to follow.

Sloan, who had sat silently at the dais listening to their exchange, cringed and followed them out.

It wasn't long before the caravan approached and came to a halt in front of the keep steps. Cree couldn't help but notice that while the villagers had gathered to watch Gerwan's arrival, not one of them cheered his entrance.

That Gerwan was perturbed was obvious as he remained mounted on his horse with an arrogant tilt of his head and waited for Cree to approach him.

Lucerne went to step forward and Cree held her back. She shot him a disapproving glance.

"I am lord of this land and your father will pay me the respect due me."

Lucerne did not argue with him; she remained by his side.

Cree stood firm at the top of the steps and Roland Gerwan remained rooted on his horse. Then Cree saw Ann Gerwan alight from the wagon with the help of a young warrior who kept pace behind her. She was a tall, slender woman much like Dawn and with plain features as well, though there was an elegance about her that caught the eye and made one think to bow before her. She walked over to her husband and laid a gentle hand on his leg while she spoke with him.

Gerwan huffed and puffed and snapped at his wife, but in the end he dismounted his horse and held his arm out for her to take and with regal steps they climbed the keep stairs side by side.

Lucerne made a move to step forward and Cree held her in place once again. And as Gerwan reached the step beneath them, he waited for the man to bow and pay his respects. Cree wasn't surprised when Ann stepped forward, no doubt knowing her husband wouldn't.

Ann bowed her head gracefully. "We are pleased to finally have arrived at your home, Lord Carrick."

"The village appears to have prospered," Gerwan said with a nod. "It is good that you have worked the peasants hard. They can be a lazy lot if you don't have a heavy hand with them."

Lucerne jumped in before Cree could respond, which was good since Gerwan irritated the hell out of him, and he felt like squatting him as he would a pesky bug.

"Father," she said with a bow of her head and then turned to her mother, her smile growing. "And mother, I am so pleased that you are here. Please come in out of the cold. Food and drink await you."

"I hope you had chambers prepared, Lucerne," Gerwan said as if he scolded. "It has been an arduous journey and I will need to rest after I eat."

"Everything is ready for you, Father," Lucerne confirmed with a confident nod. "I'm sure you will enjoy the visit."

Not quite, Cree thought and wondered what the man would do when his world came crashing down around him.

~~~

The more Dawn talked with Kirk McClusky the more she liked him. He was a caring man and loved his children deeply. It was obvious by the way he talked with such pride about the daughter he had lost or the way he proudly boasted about his son. She had often wondered about her father, having been too young when he died to remember him, though now she wondered if perhaps the man her mum had told her about had ever existed. Or had he? Had her mum described her true dad? Had she known all along whom her true father had been?

"I hear that a cleric, sent by the King, will arrive soon to wed Cree and Lucerne," Kirk said and Dawn nodded. He reached out and took her hand. "I will not leave here until all of this is settled and I know that you are content with your decision. Though if you so choose to go home with me, then we can leave here whenever you want. The choice is yours."

Dawn smiled, nodded, and tapped her chest showing her appreciation.

Kirk squeezed her hand. "I am your father and I will always be there for you whenever you need me."

Comforting warmth ran through Dawn and her smile grew. It was nice to have a father after all these years and such a loving one. She suddenly recalled Old Mary's warning... *trust no one.* Was she wrong in believing Kirk to be a good man? The thought rattled her and she suddenly felt unnerved.

"Something upset you, I can see it on your face," he said concerned.

She shook her head, but he would not have it.

"Please, Dawn, trust me, I mean you no harm. I only want what is best for you."

He seemed sincere enough and it was probably Old Mary's warning that had doubts and fears suddenly nagging at her. And for some reason they poked hard at her, to the point that she abruptly stood and gestured that they should go for a walk.

"Splendid idea, a brisk walk can help clear a burdened mind."

Dawn nodded, hoping he was right, since at the moment her mind was overly burdened with worry.

Kirk retrieved her cloak off the peg and draped it over her shoulders and pulled the hood up over her head. "The weather has turned colder. Do you have gloves?"

Dawn reached for Cree's gloves on the table and slipped them on, his familiar scent drifting up to tickle not only her nose, but her senses. He wasn't even here and he could excite her. She chased the thought away, though it kept creeping back to remind her just how much she missed him when they were parted from each other. That made her think about just how much she loved him and how she wished she was free to go and find him and...

She shook her head. How could she be in a perpetual state of desire for him? It was wicked. She was wicked and what was even more wicked was that she didn't care.

Kirk explained to Elwin that they were going for a much needed walk. Elwin signaled two nearby warriors over and instructed them to follow the pair. She wondered why he and the other guard that had been added to her cottage hadn't followed, but she dismissed it soon enough.

Dawn was grateful that they walked along in silence. She had no desire for conversation. She much preferred to simply feel the cold air sting her cheeks and catch her breath. They meandered through the plowed paths and Dawn felt her mind easing. They walked all the way to the entrance of the village and stopped when they spotted a small caravan guarded by several warriors approaching. Neither of them had to say anything. They had both heard snippets of chatter about the uneventful arrival of Roland Gerwan as they had walked. That would leave this arrival to be only one person—the cleric.

Dawn's unease returned and a muscle tightened in Kirk's arm. It seemed that they both had grown anxious with his arrival. Kirk ushered her off the path and they both stood watching the enclosed wagon roll toward them.

Villagers began to gather, word having spread about the King's cleric being due to arrive and while some were eager to have a look, others hurried off. Many believed that clerics brought the wrath of God with them and wanted nothing to do with any supposed holy man.

The wagon rolled closer and everyone watched it approach until suddenly heads started turning the opposite way. Dawn and Kirk followed to see what had caught everyone's attention and Dawn's eyes turned wide.

There was Cree on his steed barreling down the path. He wore no cloak, though he did wear a deep scowl and the look in his eyes had believers, or not, crossing themselves in protection as he flew past them.

Dawn wondered why the cleric's arrival had elicited such anger in him until he stopped abruptly in front of her, his stallion pounding the ground, appearing as annoyed as his master.

He didn't say a word. He leaned down and snatched her up around the waist, which had her wincing and him cursing and readjusting his arm, and then he dropped her in front of him on the horse. He turned his steed around and with the same fast gait took off.

Dawn realized that his actions had shocked everyone silent. Though what troubled her was that she caught sight of the cleric, his neck stretched out the window watching the whole scene unfold with disapproving eyes.

Chapter Twenty-four

Cree no soon as closed the door to Dawn's cottage then he said, "I thought I told you to rest."

She slapped her chest, held her wrists together as if shackled, and shrugged.

"No, you are not a prisoner but—"

She prevented him from continuing by holding her hands up and then walking her fingers across her hand to demonstrate that she had gone for a walk.

"You were just attacked yesterday and you chance going out today?"

Her eyes narrowed in anger and she pointed to her wound, pounded her chest with her fisted hand and shook her head adamantly.

"You're not going to let that stop you?" he asked to make sure he understood her foolishness.

She snapped a definitive nod.

Cree ran his hand through his hair, growled like an angry bear, and then grabbed her by the shoulders. "Did you once stop to think how worried I would be when I learned that you went for a walk?"

So that was where Elwin had gone... to tell Cree. And he hadn't thought twice about leaving his new arrivals. He had come in search of her. Her heart fluttered and she couldn't help but smile.

Cree didn't smile, though his brows shot up as if confused.

She tapped his chest with one finger and then tapped her own, her smile growing.

He didn't seem to understand her at first and then suddenly it seemed to dawn on him. "Yes, I came for you. I was worried to death that something would happen to you and our babe. You seem to forget, or simply ignore the fact, that someone means to see you dead and that his time is running short."

In all honesty, she hadn't given it thought. Her only thought had been to get out of the cottage, breath some fresh air, and clear her troubled mind. He was right though, she should have been more diligent, but then she was with her father, who she had momentarily wondered if she could trust.

She sighed silently over her own foolishness, tapped his chest, and nodded.

"Did you just agree with me?"

She nodded and tapped her temple.

"Are you saying that you should have known better?"

She nodded again.

Cree stood there speechless, staring at her.

She waited a few moments and when he still hadn't spoken, she grinned, tapped his lips and shrugged.

"Yes, you have rendered me speechless."

She eased herself free of the grip he had on her shoulders and drifted forward to rest against him. His arms went around her instantly. And all she could think about was not how she had caused him to worry, but how he had come after her. And with no regard to what anyone thought, he had scooped her up and carried her away. And right in front of the cleric, though giving that thought, it might not have been the best thing for the cleric to see.

But right now she didn't care. He had been her champion, and he deserved a gift.

She brought her lips to his and kissed him lightly at first and felt his body relax. Then she turned the kiss a bit more demanding and his body relax some more. Then she took hold of his face and kissed him with such a fierce hunger that his body tensed and he grew hard against her.

"Damn, I don't have time for this," he said with regret after he pulled his mouth away from hers, a difficult task since she had refused to let him go, and damn if he hadn't enjoyed the struggle.

She shook her head, holding up two fingers.

"No, not even two minutes. I should have never left my guests in the first place and now the cleric has arrived."

She had taken hold of his wrist and was tugging him toward the other room, and he wasn't stopping her.

"But I had to make certain for myself that you were all right. Actually, I wanted to make certain you were safely sequestered in your cottage or I would not have a moment's peace."

As soon as Cree realized that he stood in the other room, he shook his head and glared at her. "You want me that badly?"

She let out a long silent sigh as she moved her hand slowly down between her legs.

Her hand never quite got there. Cree lifted her up with one arm around her waist, her feet dangling a few inches off the floor, as he walked her over to the bed and laid her down on it. Her skirts were hoisted, his leggings dropped, and he entered her knowing she was wet and ready for him just as he was hard and throbbing for her.

It was a quick joining, though no less explosive. They burst together in a sudden and stunning climax that left them both breathless.

A pounding sounded at the door, and they both laughed.

He kissed her quick. "At least this time we got to finish." He was off her in a flash and adjusted his garments as she did hers, and then they both hurried into the other room.

Elwin was at the door when Cree opened it. "Sloan says to hurry, my lord, the cleric has arrived and is questioning why you took the lass up on your horse."

"Is he now," Cree scowled and Elwin stepped back. "And how does he know it was me who did that and not simply a warrior?"

Elwin's brow went up and Dawn stepped around Cree and ran her hand up and down the front of him and cocked a brow.

"Are you saying that it's obvious who I am?" Cree snapped.

"That's what she's saying," Elwin said nodding in agreement.

Dawn nodded too.

"It's none of his—"

Dawn pressed her fingers to Cree's mouth to silence him and turned to Elwin and held up one finger and nodded for him to step away.

"A minute it is," a startled Elwin said not believing how easily Dawn had silenced the mighty Cree. He stepped away and closed the door leaving them alone.

Cree removed her fingers from his lips, though held on to them. "You dare stop me from speaking?"

Dawn smiled for it was said with a touch of humor, and she rubbed at the now barely noticeable scowl.

He released her hand and his arm snaked around her waist to yank her against him. "Warn me all you want not to be angry, but when it comes to you, no one better question me." He tugged playfully at her ear. "Now, listen well. I have enough to concern me. Promise me that you will stay in the cottage so that I need not worry about you."

It was her turn to scowl.

"Just for the rest of today while I get everyone settled. Besides, it grows colder and no doubt will snow and I want to know that you are safe and warm in your cottage. I will even send Flanna to visit with you."

Dawn brightened at that and nodded as she crossed her heart, promising him.

"Good." He gave her a quick kiss. "I may be late in returning to you tonight, so if you grow tired go to bed."

She shrugged and pretended to shake him.

He leaned down and nuzzled and nipped at her neck before whispering, "You have my word that I will wake you."

One last kiss and they parted.

Happiness wrapped around Dawn like a warm comforting blanket and she hugged herself. She should, at this moment, be worried. After all, the cleric was here to unite Cree and Lucerne, but with Cree sending Flanna to visit she would learn what was going on. And Kirk would visit with her again as would Dorrie and Lila would no doubt—

There was barely a knock on the door when it sprang open and Lila hurried in. And she hadn't even closed the door before she started talking. "Tongues are wagging in the village. It seems that the cleric thought Cree's actions with you inappropriate and he has made inquiries as to who you are."

Dawn's brow shot up.

"No one dared to tell the cleric that you were Cree's mistress, but your name was mentioned as was the fact that you could not speak. I don't think Cree is going to like what the cleric had to say about that."

Dawn waved for her to continue, impatient to hear it.

"He said that the lack of a voice was the devil's work."

Dawn stepped back as if slapped and shivered. It wasn't good when a cleric claimed that anyone was touched by the devil.

Lila put her arm around her and hugged her close. "The cleric will rue the day that he goes up against Cree."

Dawn smiled and nodded. There was much truth to her words. The man did not stand a chance against Cree no matter how much God protected him. Dawn gestured for Lila to visit a while and she did, baby Thomas being in Paul's care, which meant she had some time. In no time the two women were chatting away as was their way when they got together. And for a while Dawn's worries eased.

~~~

Cree walked into the Great Hall annoyed. He would have much rather have stayed with Dawn. He was growing ever tired of being separated from her.

"That was rude of you not being here to greet cleric Mathias," Gerwan said standing in front of his chair on the dais.

Cree stopped abruptly when he reached the dais. The cleric sat next to Gerwan. He was a man of medium height and slender form and garbed in costly garments.

Gerwan unwisely continued. "And to have blatantly insulted my daughter, your future wife, by leaving us to go to your mistress is inexcusable. She had to excuse herself and retreat to her chambers, suffering from an horrific headache you no doubt caused. You owe her, and everyone else here, an apology. But then I don't know why I waste my time explaining this to you. How could a barbarian know anything about civility?"

Cree reached across the table so fast that Gerwan had no chance to react. Cree's hand had him by the neck and slammed his head down on the table directly next to the cleric's hand. "You'd be wise to remember that I am a barbarian and that I would think nothing of cutting out your tongue for daring to reprimand me."

Gerwan tried to speak, but Cree only tightened his grip and the man choked for a breath.

"If you dare speak to me in such an insulting manner again, I will see you put in the stocks for all to see, and then I will show you what true barbarians do to their captives."

He released Gerwan who choked for a breath and when he finally got one, he continued to hungrily grasp for more. Ann stood to try and help her husband, but he shoved her away with such force that she stumbled, though luckily fell to sit in her chair.

"My son," the cleric Mathias said.

"I'm not your son," Cree said curtly. "Do you have a message from the King for me?"

"I do and—"

"Not another word," Cree ordered. "My solar now." He then turned to Flanna who was standing to the side. "Go tell Sloan I want him in my solar and assign a servant to look after Lucerne."

"Yes, my lord," Flanna said and hurried off to do his bidding.

Cree didn't wait for the cleric to stand and follow him, he proceeded to his solar. The cleric entered several minutes after Cree and took a seat by the hearth. Sloan entered a few moments later, closing the door behind him and latching it.

Cree took a seat by the cleric while Sloan stood to the side of the hearth.

"Tell me," Cree commanded.

The cleric didn't keep him waiting or attempt to chastise him. "The King wishes your wedding to proceed with haste. He wants to make certain that you secure this land."

Cree thought of telling him about the possibility that Lucerne wasn't Gerwan's daughter, but that would set things into motion that could prove more harmful than helpful. It was better that the cleric didn't know anything until he had some proof to show him. Otherwise, the man might think he was concocting a story to delay the wedding. How then did he actually delay the wedding?

"I will unite you and Lucerne on Sunday in five days' time," the cleric announced.

Sloan spoke up. "Lucerne will not be pleased. Her wedding dress is not yet done."

"Then put more women on the task or she will be wed in a different gown," the cleric said annoyed at such a petty excuse. "The King has spoken and so it shall be done." He turned to Cree. "Now, my son, you must cleanse yourself of this wicked woman. Tell me of the sinful things she has made you do so that you may cleanse yourself of such evil."

Cree was about to lurch out of the chair when he felt Sloan's hand clamp down on his shoulder. He tempered his anger as best he could and said with a coldness that had even Sloan shivering, "What I have done to this woman is nothing compared to other evil I have committed. You do not have enough time or the stomach to hear all the wicked things I have done. Keep your distance from me cleric Mathias or you too will be touched by unspeakable evil."

Though the cleric eased away from Cree, he said, "I can help save your soul, my son."

"The devil got my soul a long time ago and there's no getting it back." Though Cree couldn't help but wonder if, by some miracle, Dawn had latched onto his soul and was beginning to bring it out of the abyss.

Cleric Mathias stood and moved further away from Cree. "The King also requested that I stop at the abbey to see how your sister was doing."

Cree didn't care for this news. Why would the King concern himself with Wintra?

"The abbess was pleased that you had finally sent for your sister. It seems that Wintra is a spirited lass and is like her brother when it came to following rules. Though it had taken time, the abbess insisted that Wintra had learned the proper behavior for a young woman."

Wintra had had an independent nature since the day she had been born, and she had always been inquisitive wanting to know everything. Cree hoped they hadn't changed his sister that much. She also had been a loving and affectionate child. He had hated the day he had left her at the abbey and tried to explain that he had had no choice that at least there she would be kept safe. She had wanted none of it. She had wanted to go with Cree, had begged him to take her. His heart had broken completely that day when he rode off and left her crying and screaming his name.

"The nuns were busy packing her things and getting Wintra ready for her return home to her brother," the cleric said. "The abbess was thrilled when I told her what plans the King had for Wintra."

Cree's heart lurched in his chest and he felt every muscle in his body tense. "What plans?"

"The King feels that you have served him well and he is pleased with your beneficial marriage arrangement, and so that you do not have to worry over your sister's future he is preparing a similar marriage arrangement for her."

Cree sprang out of the chair. The King was looking to benefit himself and no one else. "To whom?"

"The King did not share that information with me. I am sure he will let you know in due time. But rest your mind. The abbess insisted that Wintra has acquired all the skills necessary to serve as an obedient wife."

Cree had hoped to arrange a marriage for his sister. One that she approved of, not one forced on her. He had also wanted to have some time with her before she wed and went off with her husband. He supposed he wanted to make amends for having been forced to leave her at the abbey. "Did you tell my sister the news?"

The cleric shook his head. "Of course not, it was not my place, though I cannot say whether the abbess spoke to her about it or not. Regardless, this would be exciting news for her. It isn't every day the King arranges a marriage for a peasant lass. Wintra is a lucky young woman."

There was some truth to his words, but Cree couldn't help but think that Wintra might not agree.

Chapter Twenty-five

No soon as Lila left Dawn, then a knock sounded and Elsa entered.

"I've come to see how your wound fairs," Elsa said placing her healing basket on the table.

Dawn smiled and nodded to let her know that the wound was doing well.

"It doesn't pain you?"

Dawn held up two fingers barely separated.

Elsa nodded. "A little, that is good, but I will have a look anyway."

Dawn removed her blouse and eased down her skirt to make it easy for Elsa to examine the wound. Elsa thoughtfully draped a shawl over her so that she would not take a chill. She talked as she unwound the bandage.

"All is well with you and Cree now that he knows of the babe?"

Dawn broke into a huge smile and nodded vigorously.

Elsa seemed to breathe a sigh of relief. "I am so happy and relieved to hear that. And I wouldn't doubt that he has a plan to see that you two wed."

Dawn's eyes popped wide.

Elsa patted Dawn's shoulder. "He would never let a child of his be born a bastard, though he had expressed concern over your affliction being passed on to a babe."

Dawn shrugged, her eyes questioning, and her finger counting off the fingers on her other hand wanting to know when Cree asked this of her.

"Not recently. It was when he talked to me about preventing conception."

Dawn, herself, had feared passing on her affliction to her child. She had also worried that Cree would not want a child with her for that very reason. But since he had learned of the babe, he had not mentioned the possibility and she wondered if it troubled him.

She certainly did not want her child to suffer as she had. But with Cree as her father, the lass would have a far better life than Dawn had had as a child. And if what Kirk McClusky said was true, it would mean that if Dawn gave birth to a daughter then she would surely be voiceless just like all the McClusky women before her. But then Old Mary had predicted she would have a son, but what would happen when she had a daughter?

"Do not worry yourself," Elsa said with another pat to her shoulder. "Your child will be who he is meant to be, and I have no doubt that Cree will love him with his whole heart just as he does you."

Love. Yes, Cree loved strongly, though he never spoke the words. She wondered what kept him from telling her.

"The wound looks good. No swelling and only a minimum of redness. You were lucky. It could have been much worse."

The subject was soon changed and after helping Dawn back on with her blouse, Elsa sat to talk with her about birthing. She wasn't surprised to learn that most women hadn't wanted Dawn to help in their births. Superstition ran rampant in the Highlands and naturally the women would worry that somehow Dawn's affliction would affect their babes.

Elsa told her about some births she attended, some stories making her laugh and others bringing a tear to her eye. If Elsa's intentions were to ease her mind about giving birth, she had. They parted with a hug and Dawn set to work placing what was left of the food in the basket to be collected later.

Dawn turned a chair to the fire and sat feeling a bit tired, though content, at least for the moment, and she would take each moment one at a time and enjoy those she could. She did wonder what was going on at the keep and was anxious for Flanna to visit and let her know. She also expected Cree to share any news with her. He had promised to trust her just as she trusted him. So there was no reason for him to keep anything from her.

A large yawn let her know just how tired she was actually feeling, and she decided a nap would do her and the babe good. She walked into the other room, got under the warm blankets, and fell asleep as soon as her head touched the pillow.

~~~

Cree was glad to see that by the time he returned to the Great Hall everyone had taken their leave and would not return until the evening meal was served. He sent one of his men to let Kirk McClusky and his son to know that it was safe for them to meet and that they were to come to his solar.

Sloan waited along with Cree, both men enjoying a tankard of ale.

"Anything to tell me about Lucerne?" Cree asked.

Sloan shook his head slowly. "That woman is crazy. One minute she's ranting, the next she's crying, and then all of a sudden she's nice, not that it lasts long, but the nice part of her, miniscule as it is, isn't bad. Her mother is with her now and it seems as if her presence has calmed her."

"You sound as if you feel sorry for her and perhaps that's exactly how she wants you to feel."

Sloan rubbed the back of his neck. "I thought about that and I've made sure to stay aware, but so far I haven't seen anything that would have me believing that she is somehow involved with wanting Dawn dead."

"Keep searching."

"Damn, how long are you going to punish me?"

Cree didn't answer, the door opened and Kirk and Torr entered. The two men joined Cree and Sloan and tankards were filled and talk began.

"I think the best thing for us to do is to have me approach Ann privately and confirm for certain that Dawn is my daughter," Kirk said.

Cree agreed. "Yes, we definitely need confirmation on that. And we need to move fast since the cleric intends to perform the wedding ceremony on Sunday. I'd like to have proof before then that Lucerne is not Gerwan's daughter."

"I worry that Lady Gerwan will deny it," Torr said. "She would be condemning herself and Lucerne if she did. She has lived with the lie all these years. Why tell the truth now and risk so much. And if she does do that, what is left for us to do?" He turned to his father. "Do you call her a liar in front of all?"

Kirk shook his head. "I could never do that."

"What then do we do?" Torr asked.

"We do what must be done," Cree said as if issuing an edict.

Torr looked to Cree. "Does that mean letting Dawn go with us, her family, where she will be safe?"

Cree stared at him for several silent moments and Torr held his gaze, not giving him the satisfaction of looking away.

Cree lunged forward in his seat and jabbed a finger in Torr's direction. "You must be deaf or aching for another punch. I've told you repeatedly that Dawn is mine. She belongs here with me and here is where she will stay. We will find a way to see this done."

No one said a word, but all wondered who would be the one to suffer in the end.

~~~

Dawn stretched herself awake. Her stomach grumbled, letting her know that she had slept longer than she had planned. She got out of bed with another stretch and then a rub to her lower back. She was still feeling the remnants of sleep when she entered the other room at the same time the door opened and Cree walked in.

She smiled and wondered if it was later than she had thought. Yet no supper had been left on the table for her, so what was Cree doing here? Not that it mattered. She was glad to see him and went straight into his arms. Her arms whipped around his neck and she kissed him with such passion that he instantly hardened against her.

"I love the way you greet me," he said nuzzling his face in her neck and then playfully nipping along her warm skin. "I missed you and wanted to see you since it will be several hours before I can return to you."

She poked him, letting him know that she felt the same... she missed him and was glad he was there with her.

"There isn't a time I don't want you," he whispered in her ear. "Though at the moment I must be content to simply hold you and that I don't mind doing at all. You were fashioned for my arms, a perfect fit."

She tapped his lips to let him know that their lips fit each other perfectly as well, and then proved it with a slow kiss that was filled with as much passion as the last and had him growing even harder.

Cree groaned and reluctantly eased her away from him, though it was a struggle. His mind was already stripping her of her garments and feeling himself slipping into her. He stepped back quickly and held her at arm's length with more resolve than he thought he had, though wished he didn't.

"Later tonight, I promise I will satisfy your need for me and mine for you. Until then be good and behave." He stepped away from her and she pouted, and damn if he didn't want to nip and suck on her lower lip that he was certain she had stuck out on purpose. "Flanna will bring your food soon," he snapped annoyed that their time together was always limited and turned away from her.

Cree flung the door open before he could change his mind and Elwin stood there as if he had just been about to knock. "Old Mary has requested to see Dawn at her cottage."

"Have you checked the area?" Cree asked.

"Every bit of the short distance from here to there and the surrounding area," Elwin assured him.

Cree turned to Dawn to find that she had already slipped on her cloak and was ready to go. He pointed his finger at her. "Then men will escort you there and back. You will go nowhere else. Understood?"

Dawn nodded as she waved him anxiously out the door.

"Now you want me gone?" he asked sounding disappointed.

She grinned and purposely allowed her hand to skim slowly and tauntingly across his hardened groin as she eased passed him out the door. She was tugged back against him after only taking two steps.

His arm rested snug around her waist and he planted his mouth next to her ear and whispered, "You will suffer the consequences for that little teasing taunt later."

He gave her a playful shove away from him and when she was out of arm's reach, she smiled sweetly, shrugged, and crossed her heart asking if that was a promise. He scowled, though smiled and before he could step forward, she turned and tugged at Elwin's arm to hurry him along.

Dawn found herself feeling lighthearted and happy, though God knew she shouldn't be feeling that way with all that was going on. But she was in love and it felt so deliciously wonderful that she couldn't help herself. And who knew what the morrow would bring. She would hold on to her happiness whenever it showed up.

When they arrived at Old Mary's cottage, Elwin made her wait outside with two warriors that had accompanied them while he went in and looked around. When he was satisfied it was safe, he bid her to enter.

"I will wait right outside the door," he said and closed it.

Dawn slipped her cloak off as she turned to smile a greeting at Old Mary seated at the table. She stopped in mid-stride of placing her cloak over the chair when she noticed the somber expression on the old woman's face. Her stomach clenched sensing that something was wrong and with a quick gesture voiced her concern.

Old Mary's attempt at a smile only heightened Dawn's worry and when she pointed to a chair and told Dawn to sit, she did so without hesitation, her limbs having grown weak with dread.

"You are a brave lass," Old Mary began and the dread spread clutching at Dawn's heart. "And it will take even more bravery to see this through, but in the end love wins... love always wins."

"No it doesn't," the soft voice came from the shadows.

Startled, Dawn turned and the shadows, in the corner by the bed, moved, though it was actually the cloak hanging on the peg there that moved, and out of the darkness stepped Lady Ann.

She laid eyes on Dawn and stared for several moments before speaking. "I must talk with you."

Dawn had wondered what the meeting between her and her true mother would be like, if ever the possibility presented itself. And here it was. Dawn hesitated, captured by the sight of her mother's regal baring and lovely garments. She was tall and slender, much like Dawn, and she wore the most beautiful deep green velvet gown beneath an even deeper green fur-lined wool cloak. Her long brown hair that held not a trace of gray was wound in an artful design at the crown of her head, and though her features were plain, they somehow caught the eye.

Dawn finally nodded, though worried that she was not going to like what the woman who gave birth to her had to say.

Old Mary got up and moved away from the table and Ann Gerwan sat.

"My daughter Lucerne told me about how a plain, voiceless woman had caught the heart of the mighty warrior Cree and that the crude McCluskys were here and Kirk McClusky claimed the voiceless woman to be his long lost daughter. Lucerne is praying that is so and that you will leave with the McCluskys and that Cree will see that your departure is for the best."

Dawn wondered if Ann felt the same and continued to stare at the woman, waiting for her to go on.

Ann wrung her hands nervously in front of her on the table. "By now I am sure that Kirk has told you about him and me."

Dawn confirmed that with a nod.

"I feel I owe you an explanation for the decision I made those many years ago. It was not an easy choice that I made, but a necessary one. I knew Roland would never accept a—damaged—child. He would see to it that you died before the day was through and I would not see harm come to you." Ann nodded to Old Mary. "She was the healer who attended me at your birth, and I begged her to take you away and keep you safe. The problem was I needed a babe to replace you. Mary found one and brought her to me..." A tear slipped down Ann's cheek. "The tiny babe settled comfortably in my arms, as if she knew it was where she belonged. Both your lives were miraculously saved that night and I believe it was the way it was meant to be. At least, it is what I have told myself these many years so that it made my difficult choice somewhat bearable."

Dawn rested a hand to her stomach, the fear of having to face such a horrifying choice roiling her stomach. And she couldn't help but feel sympathy for this woman who was her mother, and yet a stranger to her.

"I had no idea what Mary did with you and I did not want to know. I was glad that she disappeared that night and never returned. I thought she had taken you far away, and it would have been better if she had."

Her words stung, though Dawn did not show the pain they caused. She remained stoic and listened.

"Lucerne has been my daughter these many years and I loved her as I would have loved you, just as I am certain that the woman who raised you loved you as her own. I made a difficult choice then and I make another now." She took a deep breath, as if needing to fortify herself for what she was about to say. "I cannot and I will not acknowledge you as my daughter. It would mean death for not only you, but Lucerne and myself. Roland would never forgive my infidelity or my betrayal in passing off a peasant's child as his own." She clutched her hands together. "I am begging you to save not only your life, but Lucerne's and mine and leave with your father and never look back, never return to Cree."

Chapter Twenty-six

Dawn stared at her mother. She had sent Dawn away years ago to save her and herself and now she was asking Dawn to willingly go away this time. Her mother hadn't seemed the least bit interested in her. She hadn't even bothered to ask how Dawn felt about Cree. Her only thought was for Dawn to sacrifice as she once did and continued to do.

Dawn stood and tapped her chest, and then her head.

Ann stood flustered. "I don't understand."

Dawn shook her head. She was right about that. Ann Gerwan did not understand her daughter at all.

Old Mary stepped forward. "Dawn says she will think on it."

"What do you mean you will think on it?" Ann demanded. "You have no choice; you must go away."

Dawn bristled at her command and threw her shoulders back and her head up. She ran two fingers across the palm of her hand, jabbed toward Ann, then tapped her chest and shook her head.

Old Mary interpreted again. "You run; I don't."

"That's nonsense," Ann said, her face pinched in a frown. "I do what must be done. Your selfishness will see us all suffer."

Dawn glared at the woman, turned, and left the cottage, striding past Elwin shaking her head. He followed close on her heels and the other warriors flanked her sides, keeping pace with her. Her anger mounted with each forceful step. When she reached her cottage, she marched right in and shoved the door shut behind her. She paced in front of the table, her chest heaving, and her anger showing no signs of abating.

That woman certainly was no mother to her. Ann Gerwan cared not a whit for her. She had accepted Lucerne as her daughter and why not? The young woman was beautiful in all ways and she had a voice. What woman wouldn't want a daughter like her compared to Dawn.

Dawn sank down on a chair, her hand grabbing the table. Ann had talked about holding Lucerne in her arms and how she had been so content. Dawn wondered if Ann had even bothered to hold her or had a *damaged* daughter been too much not only for the father but the mother as well?

She was also growing ever more frustrated with everyone claiming that they were trying to protect her—keep her safe—when truly what they were doing were deciding her fate with no thought to her own desires. Her mother had taught her that survival sometimes meant finding the strength and courage to do the things you didn't think you could do. She had called on that courage the day Colum had informed her that she would please the prisoner Cree in whatever way he wanted. She needed to call on that courage again, but for what? Did she do what Ann Gerwan ask, what her father also wanted? Or did she do as the man she loved asked of her and trust him that all would work out well?

She knew the answer, had known it all along. It had never truly been a question in her mind. She would trust Cree; she would always trust Cree for from the moment they met he had never failed her.

He may be dictatorial and demanding but she was beginning to see that he acquiesced to her more than he realized. And that knowledge not only made her feel loved but made her feel powerful, something she had never felt before.

She jumped up and began pacing again. She was angry with Ann Gerwan all over again. The woman hadn't shown an ounce of endearment toward her or cared what she asked of her. It seemed to Dawn that her life did not matter to Ann. All that mattered was that Dawn obeyed her command and leave, no talk of any other possible solution.

Dawn heard a knock at the door and stopped pacing.

Flanna entered and stopped abruptly when she caught sight of Dawn. She hurried to close the door, set the basket down, and went straight to her reaching out to slip her cloak off before easing her down in a chair. "What's wrong? You look upset."

Flanna had become a good and trusted friend, but Dawn thought it would not be wise of her to talk of what just happened for various reasons. One being that she feared if anyone realized that Flanna knew something she could possibly be made to suffer for it. She did however intend to be honest, to a degree. She tapped her chest, pressed a finger to her closed lips, and shook her head.

"You cannot tell me?"

Dawn nodded.

"You don't have to, I think I know. It has something to do with Ann Gerwan."

Dawn looked puzzled. How could she know that?

Flanna grabbed the basket from by the door and placed it on the table. She was quick to take a jug from it and fill a tankard. "A special wine Cree is serving this evening in honor of the Gerwan's arrival, though Ann Gerwan arrived only a few moments ago and seemed quite agitated and flushed to the surprise of her husband and daughter who appeared rather pale. I tell you there is something wrong with that young woman... crazy if you ask me."

Dawn smiled and wondered if perhaps Flanna was right.

"So Lady Gerwan finally sits herself down, and then downs a whole goblet of wine as if she was parched beyond reason. Then she chugs down another quick one after that and starts blathering about how pleased she is that her beautiful daughter and Cree will soon wed."

Dawn's smile faltered some at the thought of them wedding, but then she recalled Cree's words to trust him and so her smile once again brightened.

"And poor Sloan," Flanna said with a chuckle. "Cree has assigned him, actually it's a punishment for not protecting you well enough, to guard Lucerne. At least that's the way she looks at it. Cree on the other hand wants to know what his intended is up to at all times." Flanna shook her head. "Sloan is not a happy man and I don't blame him. Who would want to be around that harpy all day?"

Dawn hadn't known Cree punished Sloan and a terrible punishment it was to be stuck with that woman.

"I also found out that a warrior has been assigned to report all Bree's movements and whereabouts to Cree, though I hear tell that she isn't up to much. When she's not tending Old Mary, she's helping Elsa. She's not one to sit around idle that one and she's a sweet thing and so grateful that Cree has offered her a home here."

Dawn felt a twinge of guilt for turning Bree away that day she had come to the cottage and asked to speak with her. It seemed that Bree was sincere and she hoped that her innocence would soon be proven.

"Tongues are stirring once again about the man who attacked you. It seems that the tracks just disappeared. They were there one minute and then suddenly they were gone, as if the person vanished into thin air. The villagers are claiming him a ghost or demon, depends on who you talk with and who has had the most to drink. But you have to admit that it is strange. I mean how do tracks just suddenly stop?"

That was a good question, especially with him having suffered a wound. Why wasn't there a blood trail? She wondered where the tracks were and if she could have a look for herself. Maybe Cree would take her in the morning.

Flanna joined Dawn in a glass of the fine wine and continued chatting. She caught Dawn unaware when she asked, "Did Ann Gerwan pay you a visit and advise you to go away and not darken her daughter's bright future?"

In a sense, Dawn supposed that was exactly what Ann had suggested and so she nodded.

"Don't pay her any heed, she's just trying to protect that crazy daughter of hers." She stood. "I better get back and see that things are running properly, but I'm glad Cree gave me permission to spend some time with you. I was eager to share with you what I had learned thus far."

Dawn tapped her chest.

"No need to thank me, I enjoy snooping and uncovering secrets," Flanna said with a whisper, then tilted her head to stare at Dawn with a raised brow. "You look upset again. Was it something I said?"

Dawn shook her head, not quite sure what was disturbing her, though she certainly had enough problems to choose from.

"Don't you go worrying yourself. All will go well, you'll see. Cree won't have it any other way." She gave Dawn's hand a reassuring squeeze, and then out the door she went.

Dawn found herself pacing again shortly after Flanna left and growing annoyed. *Secrets.* There were just too many secrets and Dawn appeared to be at the center of them all. And Lord forbid that one secret should be brought to light. It would be the ruin of lives, the death of some and yet freedom for her.

Dawn continued pacing, thinking, and growing more frustrated.

~~~

Cree sat in his chair at the dais ignoring the talk going on around him, his thoughts on how long and hard he had fought to get here. He had wanted a better life not just for himself but also his sister and the men and women who had fought along with him. He had known things would not prove easy but he had been determined, still was, to have what he wanted.

He had never expected to fall in love along the way. And listening to the inane chatter going on around him made him realize all the more how much he wanted Dawn as his wife. The thought of being straddled to Lucerne for the rest of his life made him think that he would much prefer death.

His eyes latched onto Flanna entering the Great Hall. She had to be returning from visiting Dawn and he almost bolted out of the chair to go ask her how

Dawn was. Damn but he missed her terribly and he couldn't wait until later when he would see her again.

His muscles grew taut and he inched his way up to sit straighter in his chair when he noticed that the lines on Flanna's face were drawn tight, as if in concern and he immediately wondered if it had anything to do with Dawn. He went to stand when Roland Gerwan directed a remark to him that silenced everyone at the table.

"I hear the McCluskys were trapped here by a snowstorm. You are wise not to have them in the keep, heathens the lot of them, especially the son Torr. I have heard tales of him that are not fit to be repeated."

Cree turned a scowl on the man. "Perhaps I should invite them to join us and we can ask them if the tales are true."

Ann Gerwan gasped. "If that is your wish, my lord, then Lucerne and I will take our leave."

So the lady does not wish to see her old lover. Did she fear he would reveal their secret tryst those many years ago? Cree also wondered if Ann Gerwan would seek out Kirk and speak with him privately now that she knew he was here. Perhaps he could manage to hasten that meeting.

"The McCluskys are fine warriors and are far from heathens. I will have them join us for a meal and you will see for yourself." He didn't give anyone a chance to debate the issue with him. He stood. "Now if you will excuse me there is a matter I must attend to."

"Is it that important that you must attend to it now?" Lucerne asked, as if insulted that he should even think of excusing himself.

"Yes, it is," Cree said and gave a nod to Sloan reminding him to remain close to Lucerne, and he rolled his eyes as if he was suffering the torments of hell. Cree ignored him and the disapproving glares and went to find Flanna.

Servants stopped to move aside and lower their heads as Cree headed along the narrow stone passageway that connected the kitchen to the keep, though kept it at a safe enough distance in case of a fire.

He knew he'd find Flanna in the kitchen. Turbett and she had been spending much time together. It seemed that the pair was attracted to each other, though no one would ever think them a fine match. Where he was broad and thick, Flanna was short and narrow and more than plain features. And yet the two wore the happiest expressions when around each other.

Cree stopped abruptly just before stepping into the kitchen. Is that how others viewed Dawn and him? Did most believe them odd fitting? He shook his head. He didn't care what others thought. How he and Dawn felt was the only thing that mattered.

Work stopped as soon as Cree walked into the kitchen.

"My lord, is there a problem with the food?" Turbett asked, as if he could not believe his own question.

"Rest easy, Turbett, nothing is ever wrong with the meals you prepare, I but wish to speak with Flanna."

Turbett nodded, though frowned and Cree got the feeling that Flanna may have shared her concern with him.

Flanna stepped forward and nodded toward the storage room. Cree followed her silent suggestion and she followed him into the small space.

Cree quickly asked, "Is Dawn all right?"

"She is upset?"

"Why?"

"It seems the reason Ann Gerwan was late was because she went to see Dawn and advised her to leave here and not darken her daughter's bright future. Of course those are my words but Dawn's nod confirmed that it went something like that."

Cree didn't waste a minute, he turned and left Flanna staring after him, though she wore a smile. The devil was going to protect his own.

It didn't take long before Cree was entering Dawn's cottage, not bothering to knock, but then he never did. He saw that his unannounced entrance had brought her pacing, in front of the hearth, to an abrupt stop. But what concerned him the most was the sadness in her eyes.

He was at her side in an instant and she fell into his embrace just as quickly. He felt her body shudder and begin to tremble and he knew that she was crying. And it ripped at his heart far worse than any knife ever could.

He held her tight and let her weep. He assumed that Ann Gerwan was the cause of her tears. He would find out for certain as soon as Dawn's tears were spent and she could explain. And then he would eventually see that the woman suffered for making Dawn cry.

Dawn didn't want to let go of Cree. She had never been more relieved to see him. Somehow her anger had turned to an overwhelming sadness and all she wanted, all she ached for was his arms around her. And now that he was here, she never wanted him to let her go.

Her arms went around his neck when he lifted her and carried her into the other room, and when he sat on the bed resting her in his lap, she laid her head on his shoulder. They sat that way until Dawn's tears faded and her heaving stopped.

Cree lifted her chin and wiped the last of her tears off her cheeks with his finger. "Now you will tell me who made you cry so badly, so that I may whip the person to shreds."

He was not teasing; he meant it and Dawn could never knowingly be the cause of someone's suffering. So she decided that instead of answering, she would kiss him. Besides she wanted to kiss him. His kisses were magical and at the moment she needed his magic.

She brushed her lips over his, though surprisingly he didn't respond. So she pressed her lips to his in a more assertive kiss and still he didn't respond. He always responded and that he didn't... troubled her.

"You'll not distract me with kisses; I'll have my answer."

He was determined to have his way; she heard it in the strength of his tone and Cree always got his way. Unless she could distract him with...

Slowly her hand crept down along his chest, over taut muscles, and images of him naked sprang into her mind. She loved tracing her fingers over every inch of him, the teasing not only would grow him hard but would turn her wet.

A tingle settled between her legs and turned quickly to a soft pulse. She was ready to take him inside her now and that was what she wanted to do...

make love with him and forget the pain her true mother had caused her.

She slipped her hand beneath his tunic and then down past the waistband of his leggings, her fingertips just grazing along his hairline. A short distance more and her fingers would wrap eagerly around his—

She startled when he grabbed tight hold of her wandering hand and yanked it out of his leggings.

"You'll not be distracting me. I want my answer."

She didn't want to talk about it right now; she wanted to make love and forget. And so she locked her lips firmly shut showing him that she had no intentions of telling him anything, at least until they made love.

"Going to be stubborn?" he asked, though didn't give her a chance to respond. He whispered near her ear, "I think not." And with that his hand disappeared beneath her skirt.

Chapter Twenty-seven

Dawn had no doubt that he intended to tease her unmercifully until she gave him what he wanted and while she expected her stubbornness to burst forward and deter his plan, she was shocked at her response. She burst into silent tears again.

"Damn," Cree mumbled and with haste he eased her down on the bed while keeping her cradled in his arms.

She turned her face into his chest and wept. She didn't know why she wept again. She had thought all her tears had been spent and her sadness washed away, but she had been wrong.

"I'm sorry, Dawn, I'm so sorry. Don't cry. Please don't cry," Cree whispered in her ear.

She cried even harder upon hearing the mighty and infamous Cree apologizing to her. She would have never expected it of him and yet he had said he was sorry and from the anguish in his voice, he meant it. And she cried some more.

He didn't know what to do; how to stop her tears. He only knew that he hated to see her cry. It was heart-wrenching to feel her body wracked with sobs while not a sound spewed past her lips. His anger grew as she continued to weep.

"I'm going to kill that bitch," he mumbled feeling more helpless than he had in a long time. When he finally felt her tearful heaving subside, he eased her away from him to wipe at her wet cheeks as he asked, "I would take your pain if I could. I hate seeing tears in your beautiful eyes. Talk to me, tell me what has brought you so much sorrow."

Dawn stared at him, her eyes round with astonishment. She felt as if he had just told her that he loved her. Why else would he offer to suffer in her steed if he didn't love her? And that he thought she had beautiful eyes? Beautiful wasn't a word that had ever been used in conjunction with her. Only someone who loved her dearly would think her beautiful and the only other person who had ever thought her beautiful had been her mother.

She sniffled back more tears, though a few escaped and his fingers quickly swiped them away.

"No more tears, I insist," he ordered curtly and she had to smile hearing the commanding Cree she was used to. "A smile—much better—now talk to me; I'm here for you."

He had been there for her since they had first met under odd circumstances. And this man that once caused her to shiver with fear now made her quiver with passion. And where once she trusted him not a whit; she now trusted him with her life.

She eased out of his arms and sat up. He did the same, shoving pillows behind his back to lean against, as if settling in and preparing to listen.

Dawn wasn't sure where to start; she wasn't even sure what was driving her sorrow. So she decided to start with her visit to Old Mary and finding Ann Gerwan there.

Her gestures were like words to Cree. He could hear them in his mind and he loved the sound of her soft yet strong voice. "Lady Ann was at Old Mary's waiting for you?"

Dawn nodded and continued, though the pangs in her heart made her realize that the meeting with Lady Ann had left her with more pain than she had anticipated. And the more she related the incident to Cree, the deeper the pangs to her heart. But the part that gave her pause, that made it difficult for her to tell Cree, gripped at her heart and she grew silent, unable to go on.

Cree leaned forward reaching for her hand and gave it a reassuring squeeze. "Tell me, Dawn."

She laced her fingers with his and attempted a brave smile, though she could not maintain the charade when she gestured to Cree that her mother had accused her of being selfish.

He scowled and glared at her a moment before saying, "Are you telling me that Lady Ann called you selfish?"

She cringed and nodded, the word striking her just as harshly now as it had then.

"Lady Ann has sealed her fate," Cree announced, as if condemning her and a chill ran through Dawn. "You are the most selfless person I have ever known. Far too often you have placed another's safety ahead of your own and without thought to the consequences. If anyone is selfish, it is Lady Ann and a fool is she as well."

Cree was without a doubt her champion. He let no one speak ill of her and though her actions may have upset him on occasion, he had never truly punished her. He kept her safe, protected her, and loved her. She was blessed the day he had entered her life, though she certainly would not have thought it. But then fate works in strange ways.

"How did this meeting end?" he asked.

Dawn tossed her head up and walked her fingers across her palm.

"You walked out on a titled woman?" He laughed and gave her hand another squeeze. "I would have loved to have seen her face when you did that. I am proud of you; you are a brave woman." He reached out and grabbed her around the waist and settled her in his lap. "And you are *my* woman." He kissed her then and the little sorrow that lingered was chased away by the loving magic of his kiss.

She thought his intentions were to make love, for her body had certainly stirred to attention, so she was surprised when he continued their conversation.

"Now I will tell you what took place in the Great Hall tonight."

Dawn was delighted that he intended to share news with her, but then they had agreed to trust each other and she was pleased to know that he intended to keep his word.

He hugged her against him wanting her as close as he could possibly get her. "Lady Ann has made it known that she is not interested in being in the same room as the heathen McCluskys."

Dawn wondered over her true mother's reasoning. Had she wanted to protect her daughters? Had she wanted to keep her secret safe? Had she ever loved Dawn's father? So many questions yet to be answered.

Cree voiced a similar concern. "It could be fear of discovery, of betrayal, even after all these years that has her not wanting to see Kirk McClusky again. Or she could be the selfish one wanting to protect her status. It will take some digging to uncover the truth."

Yes, it would take some digging, but there was a truth Dawn knew and intended to keep firm in her heart. It was with slow and heartfelt gestures that Dawn told Cree that she had been lucky to have been given to a woman who had been a wonderful mother and had loved her dearly.

"I wish I could have known your mother. She sounds like an extraordinary and courageous woman. You are such a woman and will be such a mother," Cree said with conviction and slipped his hand to rest upon her stomach.

She placed her hand over his and nestled her head in the crook of his neck.

"I will see the both of you safe," he said, as if making a promise.

She nodded and patted his hand letting him know that was something she already knew.

They remained snuggled in silence for a while, content for the moment to be as they were... together. Life would be good for the two of them once they were wed and he yearned for that time to be soon.

Dawn felt herself grow sleepy, the difficult day having caught up with her. She yawned and snuggled closer to Cree. The thought of making love lingered in the recesses of her mind, but for once the need for sleep overpowered it.

Cree felt her body grow limp against him and he was tempted to slip his hand beneath her skirt and stir her to passion. But she rested contentedly in his arms knowing that he would see her kept safe... even from him.

He almost laughed, though worried the sound would disturb her near slumber so he kept silent, much like she had been forced to do all her life. He rested his cheek on the top of her head and splayed his hand across her stomach. It was difficult to comprehend that his babe nestled safe and comfortable there, but as she rounded it would become apparent, and he would become even more protective.

By then she would be his wife and living in the keep and he could see her anytime he wished. It had to be so; he would not have it any other way. He continued to hold her until his own eyes grew heavy with sleep, then he slipped her off his lap onto the bed.

He went and added more logs to the fire before shedding his garments. Then he gently eased her boots off her feet and took care in slipping off her clothes. She barely stirred, though he did. How could he not? Each time his fingers grazed her soft flesh, he found his member popping to attention. He warned himself to behave; she was tired and so was he. He climbed in beside her, grateful sleep seemed heavy upon him. He eased her on her side so that he could settle himself around her, and then he pulled the warm blanket over them.

He closed his eyes expecting sleep to claim him, hoping it would, but his body had a different idea, especially since her backside nestled snugly against his groin. Not to mention that his hand had settled over her breast and he itched to play with her nipple.

"Damn," he muttered and wisely, though reluctantly moved away from her. The day and her tears had exhausted her and she needed sleep. He could not be so callous and think only of himself. He could wait until morning to make love to her.

She turned and wrapped herself around him, her leg hooking over his, her head resting on his chest and her hand...

"Damn!" he mumbled as her hand settled so close to his groin that he felt himself grow harder. He berated himself for not having left his and her clothes on. But it was too late now, the deed was done and he would suffer for his foolishness.

She rubbed against him, as if in need and he thought for a moment that she had woken but was disappointed when she settled peacefully against him after a few moments.

This was going to be a long night if he couldn't get to sleep and soon. He remained as still as he could, not wanting to lose the battle he was waging to wake her and plunge into her since his need was growing stronger by the minute.

He forced his eyes closed intending to force himself to sleep when suddenly her hand drifted over his hardness and took hold. His eyes sprang open and he waited, but nothing happened. Her hand remained still, her grip firm, and he lay in agony.

Wake her you fool, he argued with himself but he couldn't bring himself to do it. It would be selfish of him, and this was one time he certainly would enjoy being selfish.

His breath caught as her hand began to move and he remained still not wanting to disturb her, not wanting her to stop. And she didn't. He closed his eyes and enjoyed himself thinking any minute now she would stop and he would be left aching. She slowed some and he thought it the end, but a moment later she resumed a steady rhythm and he smiled at his good fortune.

He lay there enjoying himself when suddenly she stopped. He silently cursed the end of his good fortune, though what happened next nearly had him bolting off the bed.

Dawn eased herself down over him and took him in her mouth. His eyes popped open and he leaned up on his elbows. She lifted her head and gave him a wicked lick.

He grinned and shook his head. She had never been sleeping; she had been teasing him and damn if he hadn't enjoyed it. He dropped back and let her have her way with him.

She licked, nipped, and sucked until he thought he would go mad. Then the thought hit like a punch to the gut... she had complete power over him at this moment. He bolted up, his hands reaching for her waist, grabbing hold, and lifting her up and over to drop on the bed, and then he came down on top of her.

With a quick nudge of his knee to spread her legs apart, he sunk into her and he knew he would not last long. She had aroused him to the point of climax and there was no controlling it. He had to come; he couldn't stop it, and he wanted her to join him.

Dawn startled when he swiftly and all in one fluid motion swung her off him and beneath him and entered her like an avenging warrior. She grabbed his stiff forearms on either side of her and held on as he hovered over her repeatedly driving in and out of her.

"You'll climax with me," he ordered. "That's not a request."

She had no trouble obeying his command; she had wanted the same herself.

Their breathing turned as frantic as their movements and it wasn't long before Cree threw his head back and roared, his climax so powerful that it wracked his whole body with wave after wave of pleasure.

Dawn once again lay in the aftermath of a climax that she always found difficult to believe could be better than the last one. Making love with Cree was like finding happiness over and over and over. It was pure magic.

Cree dropped on his back beside Dawn to catch his breath. He reached for her hand and laced his fingers with hers, then brought it to his mouth to kiss a couple of her fingers before resting their joined hands on his chest.

In a moment, when he regained his breath he intended to finally tell her how much he loved her that nothing would stop him from loving her and that he would always love her. It was time she heard it from; she had to know how he truly felt about her. And he had to tell her; felt compelled to tell her, to pledge his love to her.

Sleep had a different idea and before their breathing completely calmed their eyes closed and sleep claimed them both.

Morning and a frantic pounding at the door brought an interruption of their peaceful sleep and had them both dressing quickly. A light snow flurry followed Elwin into the cottage when Cree opened the door.

He shook his head as he spoke. "Chaos reigns in the keep. Lord Gerwan is demanding the return of his daughter's servant. Lady Ann is driving Flanna crazy with her demands, insisting that extra servants help finish Lucerne's wedding attire even if it means working on it day and night. And Lucerne is insisting that she speak to Turbett directly concerning the food for the wedding celebration." Elwin stopped shaking his head. "And Kirk McClusky wants to speak with you."

"And I want to speak to him. Have him sent to my solar." Cree said and turned to Dawn. Last night came rushing back to him and he dismissed Elwin with a wave wanting to be alone with Dawn.

Elwin had barely closed the door when Cree had Dawn in his arms. "I had hoped for a leisurely morning before I had to take my leave." He caressed her cheek with the back of his hand. "I love the feel of you." He couldn't seem to come right out and tell her that he loved her. Last night had been the perfect time, this morning and his need to rush was not a good time. "Last night was... magic."

Dawn smiled and nodded feeling the same.

"There is much I must see to today. I will return when I can."

She nodded understanding, then remembered that she had hoped to convince him to take her to the spot where the tracks of her attacker had suddenly vanished. She wondered if he would allow her to go with her guards and so she asked.

"Absolutely not," he said empathically. "You will stay put in the safety of this cottage until we catch the culprit."

Dawn stepped away from him and planted her hands on her hips and sent him a wicked glare. She could not continue to be confined to the cottage, and she let him know it with quick, jabbing gestures.

Cree recalled how she had told him that she felt like a prisoner and though she wasn't, he could understand why she felt as she did. And so he relented... somewhat. "You may go out as long as you remain in the confines of the village. You are not, I repeat, you are not to go into the woods." He reached for the door latch. "I mean it, Dawn. Do not test me on this for you will suffer the consequences."

She jutted her chin out and kept her hands planted firmly on her hips.

"You'll not have your way in this; I'll make certain of it." With that he stormed out the door.

Her hands fell off her hips and her shoulders slumped. She didn't like that he left angry with her and without kissing her. They had had such a wonderful night together and it disturbed her that the very next morning could be so opposite.

The door suddenly flung open and Cree strode in kicking it closed behind him. He stood there a moment and then he began walking toward her as he did his hand went to his chest and tapped it, then he rested his hand over his heart and when stopped in front of her he pressed his hand over her heart.

He had just told her that he loved her and with gestures the way she did. Tears pooled in her eyes and before she could respond his arm caught her around the waist and he yanked her against him. "You're my woman and I love you. I love you more than I ever thought I could possibly love anyone. You're my breath, my heart, my very being and if anything should happen to you I could not bear it. I will make time later this morning and take you into the woods where you want to go, but for now I ask you to stay put so that I will not go out of my mind with worry."

He kissed her then with a passion that tickled her senseless. And when it ended, she tapped her chest, placed her hand to her heart and patted there several times then pressed it over his and patted there several times as well.

"You love me that much do you?" he asked teasingly.

She smiled and shook her head and stretched her hands out wide on either side of her flicking her fingers over and over.

He stared at her for a moment and she thought that he might not understand, and then he shook his head as if he didn't quite believe what he was about to say. "Your love for me is never-ending?"

She nodded, brought her hands to his face, cupped it, and kissed him.

They lingered in the kiss, parted reluctantly, and when the door closed Dawn pinched herself to make certain she wasn't dreaming. It was real, no dream, Cree had just told her that he loved her.

Chapter Twenty-eight

Cree walked to the keep anxious to be rid of the people who had brought such misery into his life. It was time to do what he did best... go into battle with only one thought in mind... victory. The moment he had told Dawn that he loved her changed everything. This farce of a marriage could not be allowed to take place. No good would come of it for him or his clan... or for the King, and Cree intended to make him understand that.

Once in the Great Hall, he stopped a moment to speak with Flanna. She gave a nod and hurried off to do as he requested, and then he proceeded to his solar. Unfortunately, Lucerne cornered him before he could escape her or before Sloan could stop her.

Cree noticed the dark half-circles beneath her usually vibrant eyes and the pallor of her skin. She looked as if she hadn't slept at all or hadn't slept well for days. And she appeared frantic, as if what she was to speak with him about was a matter of life or death.

Sloan was right behind her. He shook his head, rolled his eyes, and held up his hands as if in prayer shaking them at Cree, pleading to be freed of his punishment.

"My lord," Lucerne said rushing around in front of him to block his path. "It is imperative that I speak with Turbett concerning the wedding feast."

"Turbett has preparations for the feast well in hand," Cree said, though he didn't know that for certain. However Turbett had handled far greater challenges, so a wedding feast should prove no difficulty.

"But I have certain requests and concerns—"

"Talk with Flanna; she will see that Turbett is made aware of them." He went to step around her and she grabbed his arm. He glanced down at her hand and then turned a warning scowl on her. "I don't recall giving you permission to touch me."

She stepped away from him. "And I will *never* give you permission to touch me."

"I don't need your permission, as my wife, I may touch you whenever I wish."

"I am not your wife yet."

"And God willing you never will be."

"Believe me, my lord, I pray every day that He will spare me from the devil."

Cree leaned forward, his face not far from hers. "Perhaps you would be better off asking the devil himself."

"You are a cruel, cruel man," Lucerne said.

"And you will do well to remember that."

"I pray that the devil and his whore get their due," Lucerne cried out, her body trembling with anger.

Cree's hand shot out and grabbed her around the neck. He shoved her up against the stone wall, her eyes bulging and her hands slapping at his rock-hard arm. "Be careful of your words, for they will seal your fate." He released her and turned to Sloan. "Keep her out of my sight or I might do something that I will regret," —he shook his head— "and see that Elsa has a look at her." He walked off leaving Sloan to see to Lucerne.

Kirk McClusky was waiting in Cree's solar, the warrior who had accompanied him taking his leave as soon as Cree entered.

"I want this done and finished before week's end," Cree said walking over to Kirk. "I will not wed that shrew. I will wed your daughter and the King will approve it."

"You are sure of this?" Kirk asked hopeful.

"Once we have what we need to prove that Dawn is your daughter and that Lucerne is nothing more than a peasant's child, I'm sure he'll agree to the change in arrangements. We do have one problem though. It seems that Lady Ann does not intend to admit that Dawn is her daughter." Cree explained Dawn's meeting with Ann Gerwan.

Kirk was standing, though sunk slowly to a chair as the story unfolded. "I cannot blame her for wanting to save both daughters. And it was better that she didn't know where Dawn was all these years. Any mother would be tempted to see how her child was doing. And all of this must have come as a shock to her. She is doing what she feels best for both young women."

"You still have feelings for Ann Gerwan?" Cree asked wondering why.

"I never stopped loving her and I feel I am to blame for what she has suffered. And now she is about to suffer again. I would not want that to happen."

"What of Dawn? She is an innocent in all this and has been made to endure more than anyone. You and Ann have gone on to live your lives without interruption or care, while Dawn was left to toil as a peasant. She was lucky to have had the generous, kind, and loving mother that she did. Isn't it about time that Ann and you thought of her instead of yourselves?"

"I would agree with you, but there is more than one person to consider in this dilemma."

Cree shook his head. "Not to me. There is only one... the woman I love."

Kirk's face lit with a smile. "I knew you loved my daughter, though I wondered if you would ever admit it."

"I was looking for a good time to tell her when I realized—"

"The heart decides when it is time," Kirk finished.

Cree nodded. "My heart has been bursting with love for your daughter—I believe—from when we first met. She is the most courageous woman I have ever known. It is amazing how she has survived and thrived with her affliction, and now having gotten to know her so intimately, I realize that she never thinks of it that way. It is who she is and she never lets it stop her. That takes more fearlessness than a warrior entering battle, for battles come to an end for warriors, not so for Dawn."

"She is a remarkable lass," Kirk said with pride.

"No thanks to you or Ann," Cree snapped, "though you can now change that. You both can finally see that Dawn has a good future with a husband who will love and protect her."

"I agree, but I cannot do it at the cost of others," Kirk said adamantly. "Ann was right when she told Dawn that acknowledging her as her daughter could mean death for the three of them. You forget that Lucerne is also an innocent in this as well."

"And you forget that I care only for Dawn and what she has been made to endure all these years while you, Ann, and Lucerne have lived well."

"There must be a way," Kirk said, as if pleading with Cree.

"If there was time to plot and plan, but according to the King's command I am to wed Lucerne by week's end. The only thing that can prevent our union is the news that Lucerne is not Roland's Gerwan's daughter."

"Then it will not only be Dawn's life we need to worry about but Ann and Lucerne's as well."

"Not so for Dawn. Once the secret is revealed, a threat no longer exists."

"Doesn't it then become revenge?"

"There is that possibility, which is why this secret must be revealed and the culprit behind it caught."

"I fear there will be much suffering for all."

"And the alternative is what? For Dawn to be whisked away again and forced to live a life she doesn't want while everyone else continues on happily?" Cree laughed. "That is not going to happen. This time Dawn will have the life she chooses, not one forced upon her."

A knock sounded at the door.

"It is time for Ann Gerwan to realize that the devil wants his due."

~~~

Dawn used the private time she had to have a thorough washing. Elwin saw to it that she got a few buckets of snow, which she melted in the cauldron in the hearth. Then she had proceeded to scrub herself from head to toe and she felt more refreshed than she had in days. She had slipped into the dark red velvet gown she had been stitching to fit her, though she thought it too grand for her, but it was warm and so comfortable she couldn't resist. When she had dropped it over her head, she could not believe how nicely the soft velvet had fallen so perfectly along her curves. And while she would never dare wear such a grand garment for anyone to see, she was looking forward to seeing what Cree thought of it. She was now combing the last of the tangles out of her wet hair when she heard raised voices outside her door.

Her stomach clenched before she reminded herself that she was well protected. However she wasn't protected from her curiosity, and she drifted closer to the door to listen. A woman was screeching, her voice so frantic that it upset Dawn and she reacted without thinking... she yanked open the door.

All sound ceased and all eyes settled on her.

It was Lucerne who spoke up first and though her voice trembled with concern, or perhaps it was fear, she remained calm. "Please, I wish to speak with you."

Sloan stepped around her blocking the path between her and Dawn. "You need to see Elsa as Cree ordered, and then you need to return to the keep and rest."

"No," Lucerne shouted. "Elsa can wait. And as far as resting, I have done nothing but rest and I am tired of it. I wish to speak with this woman and if she is as brave as everyone claims she is, then she will speak with me."

Dawn stepped to the side so that she could see passed Sloan to Lucerne and extended her hand to her, curious as to what the woman had to say.

"Cree will not allow it," Sloan said.

Dawn tapped his arm to get his attention, then pointed to her cottage, tapped her chest and pointed to Lucerne and then her cottage.

"Everything in the village belongs to Cree, therefor it truly isn't your cottage and whether you invite her to enter or not doesn't matter. Cree would not permit it. Now we will be on our way and disturb you no more."

As soon as Sloan turned, Dawn reached out, grabbed Lucerne by the wrist, and rushed her into the cottage, quickly closing the door behind her and latching it. Why she had reacted without thought or consequence she couldn't say, though she blamed it on her curiosity. She was tired of secondhand information. She wanted to learn for herself about the woman—who in a way—had assumed her identity without even realizing it. And she had only so long before Cree arrived, since no doubt they would send for him, and he would pound down the door... not that Sloan didn't attempt to.

"Dawn, open this door right now," he demanded pounding on it until it sounded as if it would splinter. After several moments he stopped and issued a dire warning. "Lucerne if you hurt Dawn, Cree will kill you on the spot."

All turned quiet and Dawn was certain that they waited for Cree's arrival. She wasn't concerned that Lucerne had any intentions of harming her. She had sensed something in Lucerne that she had not seen the other times she had been in her company... fear. And she wondered what had changed.

"I have no want to hurt you," Lucerne said. "I simply want to talk with you."

Dawn pointed to a chair and Lucerne sat slipping her cloak off her shoulders. Dawn sat opposite her, closer to the hearth, and waited for Lucerne to speak.

Several minutes of silence passed and Dawn wondered if the distraught woman would ever speak. She sat staring, though not at Dawn, and wringing her hands until Dawn feared she would rub the skin right off them.

Finally, she leaned forward bracing her arms on the table and said, "My mother told me that I should tell you to leave and seek a good life with your father, Kirk McClusky. But I can't do that. You see I don't want to wed Cree, I never have. I am being forced to do so out of duty to my family.

"Upon my arrival here I put on a brave persona as my mother had advised. She had told me to demonstrate my strength and take charge so that Cree knew he could count on me." A tear ran down from the corner of her eye. "But on first glance I feared Cree, though I dared not let him see it." She wiped away the tear. "I can't keep up this ruse. My headaches grow worse, I cannot eat, and my own mind confuses me. I pray every day that I will not be forced to wed Cree, but if I do," —she shuddered— "at least with you here I will not have to bear him in my bed after I do my duty and he gets me with child."

Lucerne wiped away other tears that trickled down her cheek. "Do you love Cree?"

Dawn nodded and smiled.

"I was in love once."

Dawn's brow furrowed.

"Is it so hard to believe that anyone would love me?"

Dawn shook her head, though she continued to wonder how Lucerne could seem so different from all the other times they had seen each other. It was almost as if she was two people in one and it had Dawn wondering if she could believe anything she said. Was everything an act, even the fear?

"Did you wonder if anyone would ever love you?"

Her remark startled Dawn. Had they truly had something in common?

"Nothing is ever what it seems, is it?"

Dawn had to agree with her there. She wasn't sure of anything or anyone...except Cree. That reminded her that he should be there any minute and she wanted to make the most of the time that Lucerne and she had together.

Dawn pointed to Lucerne, then to herself and shrugged, hoping the woman would understand her.

"What do I want from you?"

Dawn nodded.

Lucerne leaned forward and began to whisper.

~~~

Cree stepped to the side as Ann Gerwan entered the room with a flourish, her eyes on him.

"I am glad you summoned me, my lord, there is much for us to discuss," she said with a respectful nod.

"You are right about that. There is much for us to discuss." He stretched his hand out. "And I've asked Kirk McClusky to join us."

Lady Ann turned, her eyes grew wide, and she looked ready to run, and she did... right into Kirk's arms. Tears followed as the two hugged.

"Enough," Cree bellowed as he walked toward them.

They broke apart but remained holding hands.

"Your reunion is heartfelt but I am more concerned with the product of your union...Dawn."

"I went to see her, my lord," Lady Ann confessed tearfully. "Perhaps I shouldn't have but I couldn't stop myself. I was curious about the daughter I gave away so that she might live, and I was concerned for her safety."

"Why?" Cree snapped.

Lady Ann blushed profusely. "She is your mistress and no good can come of that. I failed her once; I did not want to fail her again or the lass who took her place. They are both innocents and I do not want to see them suffer because of Kirk's and my indiscretion."

"Love," Kirk corrected. "This dilemma is all because we fell in love. You should have come to me, Ann."

She pressed a gentle hand to his cheek. "And what would you have done? Gone to war for me?" She shook her head. "I did what needed to be done. I protected our daughter."

"You should have told me," Kirk said. "You should have sent her to me."

Lady Ann placed her hand on his chest and he moved her closer to him. "I am sorry. I did what I thought best."

"It is I who should beg your forgiveness for not having taken you away from that fool."

"Enough," Cree bellowed again. "Reminisce later. Now we concentrate on Dawn." He looked to Ann. "I will not wed a peasant."

Lady Ann gasped and Kirk angrily said, "That wasn't necessary, Cree."

"I told you before and I will say it again so that Lady Ann is well aware of it. Dawn is my first and only concern. What becomes of anyone besides Dawn matters not to me. You both will do well to remember that."

"What of Lucerne?" Lady Ann asked. "She has been a good daughter and none of this is her fault."

"I will offer her a home here in Dowell," Cree said.

"As a peasant?" Lady Ann asked incredulously.

"Dawn is a peasant. I do not see you worrying about her status."

"She can go with Kirk and have a good life," Lady Ann said, as if it solved the problem.

"Dawn isn't going anywhere," Cree said adamantly. "She will remain here with me and I will wed here."

Lady Ann gasped again. "You cannot be serious."

"I am very serious; it will be done," Cree warned. "You will either cooperate or suffer the consequences."

"Is that a threat?" Lady Ann demanded.

"You are no fool, Lady Ann, you know full well it is a threat."

"Let's calm down and discuss this," Kirk said attempting to be the voice of reason.

"If there was time, we could discuss it," Cree said, "but thanks to the King there is no time. This is the way it will be and nothing is going to change that. Now we can work together to make this easier on everyone or I will handle it myself and let those suffer as they may."

Lady Ann clung to Kirk and he in turn glared at Cree. "Truly, Cree, can't you be a little more understanding of this delicate situation?"

Before Cree could respond, there was a pounding at the door and it flew open, and Sloan rushed in. Cree sent him a potent scowl.

Sorry, my lord," Sloan apologized, "but there is an emergency with Dawn."

Chapter Twenty-nine

Dawn stared wide-eyed at Lucerne.

"You don't believe me," Lucerne said disappointed. "I need someone to believe me, someone to help me, someone that doesn't think I'm crazy when I tell them that I am being poisoned."

Dawn didn't know what to think. The woman had been so irrational at times that it was difficult to believe anything she said. And to think that someone was poisoning her was a bit farfetched, yet she had to agree with Lucerne when she had said 'things are never what they seem.'

Dawn shrugged, though kept her shoulders up and cocked her head in question.

"Why?"

Dawn nodded.

"I wish I knew. I think that is why no one believes me. Why would anyone want to poison me? I had confided my fear to my mother but she has always thought that I was overwrought and paid me no heed. Roy believed me. He was one of my father's warriors, one of the better and more skillful ones." Lucerne wiped another tear away. "We fell in love and when I told Roy that I thought I was being poisoned, he began making plans for us to leave. And then the news came that I was to wed Cree," —she shivered—"we hurried our plans along and the day before we were to make our escape, Roy was killed in an accident or so my father says. I believe he discovered our plans and had Roy killed.

"I was numb with grief and had no time to grieve. I was packed up and began my journey here the very next day with my mother warning me not to be a foolish woman. She told me that a man like Cree would not tolerate simpering women. That I was to take charge upon meeting him and let him know that I would be a strong and capable wife."

Lucerne laughed and shook her head. "I feared Cree upon meeting him, but obeyed my mother and made my situation worse. I had also thought that the poisoning would stop but it didn't, it followed me here."

Dawn eyed her skeptically. Was the distraught woman imagining things or could her story be true? Dawn wanted to be sympathetic, especially if her story was true. To lose the man she loved was horrifying but to think that her father may have had him killed on purpose was abhorrent. It made Lucerne just as much a prisoner as Dawn, leaving neither of them choices, but rather chattel to be given away or sold at whim. But she also had to be cautious. There were so many secrets that it made Dawn wonder which ones held the truth.

"I hoped you would understand and help me, but I see in your eyes that you don't believe me," Lucerne said her shoulders slumping, as if the weight of her burden had just grown heavier.

Dawn reached out and took hold of her hand, her decision to throw caution aside an instinctive one. Why should she believe this woman? Perhaps it was the way tears filled her eyes, how her voice cracked, and how sorrow gripped her face when she spoke of losing the man she loved.

Dawn squeezed her hand, nodded her head, and then patted her chest and pointed to the woman.

"You do believe me and will help me?" Lucerne asked hopefully.

Dawn smiled and nodded vigorously.

Lucerne gripped Dawn's hand tightly. "I thought the stories about you were idle-tongue gossip, but the more I learned, the more I realized the truth behind them. You are a brave woman to not only defy Cree, but to help and protect others, and you have the strength to love and tame the devil."

The terrifying roar rattled the door and had both women jumping out of their seats and clinging to each other.

"My God, if that is Cree's battle cry no wonder he is so feared," Lucerne said trembling beside Dawn.

"DAWN!" The shout hit the walls of the cottage like a battling ram. "OPEN THE DOOR OR I'LL BREAK IT DOWN!"

Dawn trembled a bit herself worrying that perhaps this time she had pushed him too far. She left Lucerne, who reluctantly released the grip she had on Dawn, and went to open the door, though jumped back as she did to take a protective stance in front of Lucerne.

Cree stormed in the cottage, pushing the door open the remainder of the way so hard that Dawn thought she heard the wood crack. Sloan entered behind him and hurried to shut the door on the curious faces that had gathered outside.

Cree went to say something when he suddenly stopped, his dark eyes roaming over Dawn and she could have sworn that she saw a spark of pleasure and appreciation in them, and she realized it was the red velvet gown that had caused his unexpected reaction.

She almost smiled, though stopped herself. Now was not the time for grins.

"Explain yourself," Cree demanded though not quite as forcefully as Dawn had expected. The dress had worked magic and she would have to remember that.

She was more than happy to have the chance to do just that. She pointed over her shoulder at Lucerne, then tapped her chest, then her lips and rolled her finger over and over in front of her mouth.

"Lucerne wanted to talk with you?" he asked.

She nodded.

"About what?"

She puckered her lips and tapped her finger to them.

"A secret?"

Lucerne gasped.

Dawn turned to Lucerne and took her hand and gave it a reassuring squeeze before releasing it and stepping close to Cree. His arm instinctively circled her waist and her heart, as usual, melted to his touch. How she could have ever thought what they shared was sinful, she didn't know, and it mattered not to her now. Cree loved her and they trusted each other and that was the only thing that mattered.

She looked to Lucerne, pressed her hand to her chest, then to Cree's, and then back to her chest.

"Dawn is telling you that we trust each other explicitly and share all things with each other. What you shared with her, you can safely share with me."

Lucerne burst into tears and lowered her face into her cupped hands.

Cree shot Sloan a sharp nod and Sloan rolled his eyes, but before he could go to Lucerne, Dawn slipped away from Cree, to his annoyance, and went to Lucerne and wrapped her arms around her. The woman melted against Dawn and wept. When it didn't seem as if she would ever stop, Dawn eased her down to sit on a chair by the table. She then hunched down in front of her and tapped her finger at Lucerne's lips and pointed to Cree.

"He won't believe me."

"Do you believe her, Dawn?" Cree asked.

Dawn nodded without hesitation.

"I trust Dawn's judgment. If she believes you than so do I."

"But I've been such a shrew," Lucerne said.

"There you go," Cree said. "You have finally spoken the truth, so I now have reason to believe you." Dawn sent a scolding look his way and he ignored it. "Now tell me this secret that has obviously caused a problem so that I may see to resolving it."

Her wound giving her a bit of an ache, Dawn took the chair closest to Lucerne, the young woman refusing to let go of her hand.

Cree was quick to ask, "Are you all right?"

Dawn nodded and waved his concern off.

"You will not dismiss my concern that easily," he snapped.

Dawn felt Lucerne quiver and not wanting to make the situation any more difficult, she tapped her chest and bowed her head as if apologizing. Then tapped her chest again though slowly this time and gave him a gentle smile to let him know she was fine.

"That's better," he said with a wicked grin and Dawn narrowed her eyes at him. "That's even better, now I know for sure that you're all right." Cree turned to Lucerne and ordered, "Tell me."

With a voice that quivered now and then, Lucerne related the same story to Cree that she had to

Dawn. When she finished and Cree had remained silent, Dawn wondered if perhaps he didn't believe her after all. But she dismissed the thought as soon as it entered her mind. Cree had said that he trusted her judgment and he was a man of his word.

Cree finally spoke. "It wasn't you who tainted my food that night?"

Lucerne shook her head.

"Why did you beat Bree?" Cree asked.

Lucerne's eyes turned wide. "I never touched her. I thought perhaps she displeased you somehow and you took a hand to her or ordered another to do so."

"Have you always been so mean-spirited?"

Lucerne displayed no shock at his query, though her shoulders slumped, her burden weighing on her once more. She rubbed at her temple. "I do not believe I have been, but then lately it is as if I don't know myself, my headaches have worsened since my arrival here."

Cree looked to Sloan. "Find out what Bree has been up to." He turned back to Lucerne. "You're coming with me to see Elsa." He then settled a glare on Dawn. "And you're staying put here."

Dawn stood much too fast sending a sharp twinge to her side and caused her to involuntarily cringe.

Cree mumbled an oath and was beside her in an instant, his arm curling gently around her waist. "You will rest and I will not hear another word about it."

Dawn jabbed at her chest and then at his.

"You most certainly are not going with me."

Dawn did not want to argue with him, but she also did not want to be left in the cottage to pace and wonder what she was missing. She rested her head to his chest and patted it and then her own repeating the gesture several times.

"Pleading will do you no good," Cree said gently.

She thought of something that might do her some good. She held her wrists together as if shackled.

"I have told you time and again that you are not a prisoner"

"But she is... as am I," Lucerne said.

Dawn wasn't surprised to know Lucerne felt the same as she did, though she was surprised to hear her voice her opinion without sounding shrewish.

Cree looked from one woman to the other, though the only one that truly mattered to him was Dawn, he suddenly had a better understanding of Lucerne. And it surprised him to realize that her situation paralleled Dawn's. They each had been forced into circumstances that had allowed no choices.

He was growing more and more annoyed that this whole situation was taking twists and turns that outmaneuvered him too many times. Now he felt more than a sense of responsibility to Lucerne. The two women both were pawns in a deadly game... a game Cree intended to win. Until then he needed to keep them both safe.

Cree found an easy solution to his current problem, wishing everything else was so easily solved. He took hold of Dawn's chin. "You may come with us so that Elsa can have a look at your wound and assure me that all is well."

Dawn smiled and nodded happily.

He gave her a quick kiss before releasing her chin and turning to Lucerne. "And you will tell no one what was discussed here. You will let everyone think that you came here to confront Dawn as your mother had advised."

"What shall I say was Dawn's response?" Lucerne asked.

"Tell her that I intervened before you had time to speak with her."

Lucerne looked relieved and nodded.

"Sloan, take Lucerne outside and wait for us," Cree ordered.

Sloan nodded and the pair left, though not before Lucerne turned to Dawn and said, "Thank you."

As soon as the door closed, Cree eased her close against him, burying his face in her damp hair and inhaling gently, then he brought his lips to her ear and whispered, "You smell... inviting... and that dress... entices."

Dawn shivered, his warm breath tickling her ear and she instinctively turned her head to capture his lips in a much needed kiss. He was tender, she was hungry, and it didn't take long for him to feel the same. And before either of them lost control, Cree stepped away, his breath heavy and his groin throbbing.

"We need to go now," he demanded and she nodded agreeing.

He grabbed her cloak off the peg and draped it over her shoulders, though avoided touching her, and before he opened the door he turned to her and said, "Tonight I intend to feast on you."

Dawn nearly stumbled out the door, his words creating an image in her head that tingled her entire body senseless. He had done it on purpose, for he knew full well what his words would do to her. All she could think about was him licking and nipping every inch of her naked flesh.

Dawn stumbled again as they walked the snow-covered path.

His hand was quick to catch her arm and right her steps and the wicked look in his eyes told her that he knew exactly what he had done to her. She tried to yank her arm away from him, but he wouldn't have it.

"I'll keep a hold of you; I don't want you to fall."

Dawn had no choice but to comply, though she did turn her glance away. It was then she realized that it was snowing lightly and that more than the usual amount of villagers were out and about, and staring at the three of them.

Gossip was probably already spreading and why not? Cree was walking through the village with two women in tow, his intended and his mistress. And no doubt they believed that only a devil of a man would have the audacity to do such a thing. Or perhaps he was doing more than she realized, perhaps he was letting everyone know that he had the matter well in hand.

Elwin and two guards followed behind and to the sides of them, taking up sentry duties when they reached Elsa's cottage. Cree opened the door and held it for the two women to enter and then he followed them in.

Elsa bobbed her head. "My lord."

"Elsa, we have need of your help. Lucerne is being poisoned."

Lucerne's eyes filled with tears again, only this time a smile filled her face. "Thank you, my lord, for believing me."

"Dawn trusts you, so I trust you. Don't make me regret it."

"You have my word," Lucerne said.

"As for Dawn," Cree said turning to see her smiling at him. "Her wound pains her."

"I will have a look at Dawn first. Lucerne's problem will not have an easy or hasty solution."

Dawn was fine; there was nothing wrong with her. She was more interested in what was happening to Lucerne and what would need to be done to help her than a twinge to her small wound that was healing nicely. But Cree's concern had to be alleviated or they would never move on to Lucerne.

"Will you wait outside while I see to Dawn?" Elsa asked of Cree.

He looked ready to protest, then saw Dawn place a hand to her chest and gave a gentle nod and he knew she was saying *please*.

"Do not take long," he ordered and turned and walked out.

Elsa did not need much time to ascertain that all was fine with Dawn, and Dawn herself went to the door to let Cree know they were finished. She smiled and patted her chest.

"I'll let Elsa be the judge of how you are," Cree said, though looked relieved.

After Elsa reaffirmed what Dawn had told him, the healer asked them all to take a seat at the table. She filled tankards with hot cider, and then sat herself.

"Healing plants are wonderful but they can also be deadly if not used properly," Elsa explained. "And it takes a knowledgeable healer to know the difference. With the few questions I had asked you once before I began to suspect that you were ingesting something that was disrupting your nature and causing confused and erratic behavior. The headaches could be an effect of such ingestion."

"Are you saying that someone wants Lucerne confused and unstable?" Cree asked.

"It is a possibility," Elsa confirmed. "Depending on the poison used and the amount, it either can be deadly quite fast or make a person very ill until finally he is confined to bed and dies. That is not so with Lucerne."

"When did your problem start, Lucerne?" Cree asked.

Lucerne rubbed at her temple. "I think about three or four months ago, though the headaches are more constant since my arrival here."

"Was there any change in your servants or who prepared your food or drinks at that time?" Elsa asked.

Lucerne gave it thought and shook her head. "None that I recall."

"My suggestion to you is to make certain you know who handles your food and drink and see how you feel over the next few days. I would prefer not to give you anything, not even for the headaches since I do not know what you are already being given. My potion could make it worse rather than help it, so it is best you take nothing until we see what happens."

"You will eat only food that Flanna brings to you," Cree ordered.

Lucerne shook her head. "I forgot about something. I have a small pouch that contains a mixture that I use to make a nightly brew."

"Have it brought to me," Elsa said.

"Where did you get the mixture?" Cree asked.

Dawn listened to the exchange wishing she could join in. She almost did once or twice, when Cree asked the questions she was about to ask.

"It's a mixture my mother's family has brewed for years. The servants keep it available to us."

"That means many were aware of it and anyone could have tainted it," Cree said.

A knock sounded at the door and Cree called out for the person to enter knowing it was someone Elwin knew that Cree would wish to see.

Sloan entered. "I found Bree; she's dead and it appears that someone has murdered her."

Chapter Thirty

Cree had Lucerne escorted back to the keep and a guard assigned to her until Sloan could resume his duty and watch over her. Elwin was to take Dawn back to her cottage, but there was a problem, she refused to go. She wanted to go with Cree and find out what had happened to Bree.

"You are not coming with me," Cree said adamantly, draping Dawn's cloak over her shoulders. "You will return to the cottage and wait there for me."

Dawn shook her head vehemently.

"Do you truly believe you will win this argument?"

"She might," Sloan said and Cree turned a murderous scowl on him. "Bree's body was found in the woods behind Dawn's cottage."

Cree fisted his hands at his sides, furious that the young woman had been murdered so close to Dawn's home.

"It's also not far from where those tracks came to a dead stop," Sloan said. "Yet no one has been spotted there."

"Let's have a look," Cree relented and took hold of Dawn's hand. "You will not leave my side."

She nodded and gripped his hand.

Cree looked to Elsa who had stood silently by the hearth during the exchange. "Get Lucerne's pouch of herbs and see what you can find out. I'll have Neil sent to accompany you."

She nodded. "Aye, my lord."

They left the cottage and Dawn had to keep a swift pace to keep up with Cree's angry strides. With such a venomous scowl villagers were quick to move away from him, though she heard their whispers. And so did he.

Once they rounded her cottage Cree came to an abrupt stop and turned to Sloan. "The people are already questioning my ability to keep them safe. First with the attempts on Dawn's life that are yet to be solved and now with this murder of a young woman they had befriended. I will not have my leadership questioned, and I certainly will not have my clan at risk. No one rests until the murderer is found."

"I already have Henry seeing if there are any tracks to be found and I have men scouring the surrounding area to see if they can find anything," Sloan said.

"Good," Cree said and looked to Dawn. "Are you certain you wish to see this?"

She nodded without hesitation.

"If you should change your mind—"

She shook her head, this involved her, and Cree needed help. There was no way she was going to be left out of it.

"You're a stubborn one," Cree said, though with a hint of admiration.

Dawn smiled and slowly shook her head, patted his chest, and then her own and held up two fingers snug against each other.

Cree leaned down, brushed his lips over hers and whispered, "You're right about that, we stick together always."

Sloan led them to where Bree's body was found and while Dawn thought she was prepared for what she would see, she wasn't. The pretty young lass had been beaten about the face so badly that she was barely recognizable and blood pooled forming a pillow beneath her head while the snow flurries had deposited a light blanket over her. The fingers on her one hand looked to have been broken and her ankle appeared to have been stomped on.

Dawn had to look away for a moment, her stomach protesting the gruesome sight.

"Are you all right?" Cree was quick to ask.

She nodded and took a deep breath before turning to once again glance upon the horrid scene.

"We've both seen beatings like this before," Sloan said. "Ones delivered in fits of anger."

Cree agreed with a nod. "But what brought on that anger is the question."

Dawn felt her stomach roil once again and felt the need to look away.

"Dawn?" Cree questioned with concern.

She did not intend to leave until he was finished and so she gestured that she was wondering about the area where her attacker had suddenly vanished.

Cree raised a skeptical brow but relented and walked her to the spot. Sloan followed along.

No tracks remained, the snow that had fallen since then having covered the area. Dawn glanced around and noticed a group of rocks, the last and largest rock not far from a pine tree, the lowest branch drooping from the weighted snow.

She went to walk away from Cree and was yanked to a sharp stop.

"By my side, remember?" Cree said with a tilt of his head.

She nodded and pointed to the group of rocks two steps away, and then to the low tree branch. Cree looked to Sloan who had followed Dawn's gesture and gave a glance at the tree.

Sloan nodded at the silent command and with careful steps jumped from rock to rock, almost slipping once, then leaped for the low hanging branch and pulled himself up onto it.

"So that's how the tracks vanished so suddenly," Sloan said dropping down from the branch.

"I'm surprised that Henry didn't realize that," Cree said.

Sloan scratched his head. "I think I recall seeing a warrior sitting on one of the rocks when I arrived at the scene."

"He was sitting?" Cree asked annoyed. "We'll discuss his punishment later. Right now make Henry aware of what we have discovered." He pointed at Bree's body. "And I want to know why the sentries assigned to this area saw or heard nothing. And where was the guard assigned to Bree? Get me answers, Sloan, and see that her body is stored until the ground is soft enough to accept her. Also, I'm moving Dawn to the keep."

Sloan was too shocked to speak, not so Dawn. She quickly darted in front of him and shook her head vigorously along with a finger she held up in front of him.

"You will put that finger down and we will discuss this in private," Cree ordered.

Dawn dropped her hand to her side, realizing it was not at all proper for his warriors to see her arguing with him. She tugged at his hand, anxious to settle this with him, for there was no possible way that she was moving to the keep.

"I have a few more things to discuss with Sloan, then we'll take our leave."

Dawn held up their joined hands and nodded at them.

"I will release you as long as you promise to stay in sight."

Dawn crossed her heart and he released her hand. "I will not be long."

She gave him a curt nod and wandered toward the body. She wondered over the rage that had caused such a horrific beating. Then she recalled the beating Colum, the former liege lord had given to Timmins, the smithy for questioning him. What she recalled most about it was that Colum seemed to enjoy every blow he had inflicted on the defenseless Timmins. It had served as a warning to others that Colum was not to be questioned. It had taken weeks for Timmins to recover. Bree hadn't been so lucky, and Dawn couldn't help but wonder if the man who did this to her had intended to beat her to death or had he been unable to stop.

She drifted closer to the body and gazed at the smashed ankle. Had he stomped on the slender ankle after he had realized she was dead? Was he angry at himself or at her? Had Bree been his accomplice or an innocent in it all? And if he could do this to Bree, what would he do to her if he caught her?

The thought caused her stomach to roil once again and that caused her to think of the babe. Even if she were to survive a bad beating like Timmins had done, would the babe? Knowing she was with child changed everything. She had to be more cautious and sensible in the choices she made. And she had to be careful of who she trusted. The killer could be lurking among them, a smile on his face, and a pleasant nature just waiting for the right time to strike.

Her glance went to Bree's face and it was as if she suddenly felt the blows the young woman had suffered and the fear that had to have churned inside her. This time her stomach did more than roil, it rushed up into her mouth and she hurried behind thickened bushes to heave.

Cree was there in an instant, his one hand pulling her hair back away from her face and his other hand going around her waist to support her. She felt better with him being there with her, though her retching didn't stop and when it did, she leaned back against him spent.

He held her firm as he leaned down to scoop up a handful of clean snow and held it in front of her. She took some and ran it across her mouth, but she was simply too worn out to do any more than that.

He tossed the remainder of the snow aside and lifted her up into his arms. She didn't have to look at him to know he was scowling; it was his way after all. So when she did look at him, his scowl wasn't a surprise or the concern she saw in his eyes and while she did not wish to cause him worry, she was pleased to know how much he cared. It was one time that his scowl made her happy.

Relief flooded her when he carried her to her cottage. She feared he would take her to the keep and she did not want to go there. And no doubt it would cause a disagreement between them, but she was determined to stay in her home.

Funny that she now felt that way about her cottage. At first it had felt strange to her and now it was where she enjoyed being the most, but then perhaps Cree had something to do with that. She doubted she would feel so comfortable in the cottage if Cree did not share it as much as he did with her.

One of the guards on duty opened the cottage door when he saw them approach and closed it as soon as they entered. Cree walked into the other room keeping her tucked close against him. And she was fine with that. She loved being in his arms. She knew that she was safe there and loved... loved so much more than she ever thought possible.

He stood her beside the bed and slipped off her cloak flinging it to land at the bottom of the bed. Then he eased her to sit and with quick yanks took her boots off and flung them across the room as if in warning that she dare not put them back on.

"You are to rest," he ordered.

She patted the spot beside the bed.

"Don't think to try and coerce me into getting your own way. It will not work."

She patted her lips and pointed back and forth between them, letting him know she wished to talk and once again patted the spot beside her.

Cree sat, though not close to her, a disappointment, but one she could remedy as they spoke.

"By evening you will be residing in the keep and there is no changing my mind."

He was emphatic about it, but then so was she... she would not reside in the keep. She raised her hands and he quickly captured them in one hand.

"Listen to me well, Dawn. Somehow you found a way into my heart. I do not know how you managed it, but you did. I do not believe you fully grasp the depth of my love for you and what it would mean losing you and our babe. I have survived pain in my life but I could not survive losing you. I love you so much more than I ever thought I could possibly love anyone."

He was right, she had known he loved her but she had never realized the depths of his love for her, and her heart soared with the newfound knowledge, as did her smile.

"The person who wishes you dead is here among us. I assume he expected to find you dead upon his arrival and when he didn't, he grew furious that his plans had failed. The vicious attack on Bree proves that he will stop at nothing to see you dead. I believed you well protected, but somehow this person has evaded all attempts at capture. My only recourse now is to keep you by my side at all times, where I know without a doubt you will be safe. And when he strikes next, I will be there to finish him."

Dawn wrinkled her brow. He was placing his own life in jeopardy by constantly keeping her close. He could very well suffer an arrow or dagger meant for her. Then what would she do without him? She felt as he did; she could not survive losing him. She yanked her hands free and began gesturing.

He let her go on and on and on until her hands began to slow and finally came to a rest. He then took both of her hands in his again and kissed her softly, though would have much preferred to kiss her with a hunger that was gnawing at his groin. Regrettably, now wasn't the time to satisfy that hunger.

"We want the same thing. What better way for us to achieve it than to remain by each other's side. Then we can protect each other."

Dawn shook her head, perplexed. Did he truly feel that she could protect him? She asked him directly, her hands moving much slower than before.

"You have proven several times to me just how brave a warrior you are. I have no doubt that you are capable of protecting me."

The seriousness of his tone made her realize that he spoke the truth. She had never thought herself brave, but she had been forced to be courageous upon meeting Cree. And she had grown braver, gaining a strength she had never thought herself capable of.

"You make me proud," Cree said and kissed her again briefly, though not quite so softly.

Dawn stared at him stunned by his words. He was proud of her. The only other person who ever told her that had been her mother. Dawn had never thought to hear those sentiments again. And her love for Cree grew threefold. The thought, however, of residing in the keep still did not sit well with her. She liked their time alone together here and besides, she felt as if she was surrendering to the culprit by leaving her home. Then there was the matter of what her presence in the keep would create.

She didn't know how she could convince him that taking her to reside at the keep right now would only make the situation worse.

"I know you are wondering how you can change my mind," Cree said causing her brow to quirk. "But it seems no matter how many guards I post—"

Her hand shot up and began gesturing, not giving him a chance to finish.

It pleased Cree that he was getting to understand her quick gestures more easily and so he listened to her tell him that all the guards he had posted had kept her safe. And that she would need to be diligent about making certain she did not go anywhere without them. And that his warriors would continue to inform him of her every move, and of course he could also spend more time with her. Her wicked smile and her hand moving along his leg left no doubt to what she meant. And while he wanted nothing more than her warm hand wrapped around his stiff rod, now was not the time or so he kept telling himself.

He grabbed her hand and smiled. "Later I will satisfy that insatiable lust of yours."

Her smile faded and she shook her head. Her hands moved slowly between them, now and again touching him, telling him that the slightest touch of his hand tingled her senseless and that at first she thought she was a sinful woman for having such wanton feelings until she finally realized that it was love that made her feel that way. And she wanted to love him as much and as often as she could for nothing felt more wonderful and satisfying than having him inside her, loving her.

That did it, he was lost. It took barely any time to get them both naked and him inside her where he proceeded to take his time loving her.

Chapter Thirty-one

An uneasy stomach woke Dawn the next morning and she slipped out of bed leaving Cree to sleep. She worked as silently as she could, preparing a brew for herself that she hoped would ease her nausea. She had been relieved when Cree had relented and agreed to allow her to remain in her cottage, though more guards had been posted.

She sat at the table, her mind filled with thoughts of poor Bree. Last night when Cree returned to the cottage he had been annoyed that none of the sentries had seen anything unusual take place in the area where Bree had been found, though the warriors had reminded that their duties were to patrol sections so there were times when areas were not being watched.

Dawn was so caught up in her thoughts that she startled when Cree's arm slipped around her waist, his hand settling over hers where it rested on her stomach.

He leaned over and pressed his cheek to hers. "Your thoughts are so deep that you forget I am here?"

She turned just enough for her lips to brush his, then shook her head and brushed her lips over his again, reminding him that that wasn't possible.

"I am glad to know that you do not forget or else I would have to return you to bed and remind you."

Dawn scrunched her brow and tapped her finger to the side of her mouth.

Cree grinned. "So you're not sure after all?"

Dawn was about to shake her head when a bout of nausea hit her so quickly that her eyes clamped shut and her hand pressed harder against her stomach.

Cree was quick to scoop her up and settle her in his lap, his large hand brushing hers away to gentle caress her stomach.

"He will learn to listen to me and not trouble his mother," Cree said as if issuing an order and as if the babe heard his da, the nausea calmed.

Dawn nestled against Cree quite comfortable to sit on his lap until she realized he was naked and she could feel him swelling against her. Of course it had her growing wet in an instant and she had no doubt that they would return to bed as soon as she felt well enough, which she did not mind at all.

"If you keep fidgeting against me like that you know what's going to happen."

She hadn't realized she had been doing that but now that she did know... she continued doing so.

A low groan rumbled in Cree's throat. "You're not feeling well."

Dawn squirmed even more.

"I'm warning you—"

She silenced him, rubbing her bottom slowly across his growing hardness.

"That's it," he said with a determination that thrilled Dawn.

Before Cree could get to his feet a knock sounded at the door.

"Damn, but I'm tired of these interruptions."

"Cree!" Sloan shouted and pounded the door at the same time.

"Enter," Cree yelled and when Sloan walked in Cree shot him a murderous glare. "This better be important."

"The fellow who attacked Dawn is at Elsa's cottage. He was seeking her help to heal the wound he suffered when he attacked Dawn. Elsa says he waited too long and he doesn't have much time left."

"I'll be dressed in a minute," Cree said and stood placing Dawn on the chair.

She was out of it in a flash and rushing past him into the other room to slip out of her nightdress and into her clothes. She sent him a look that warned that she would not be left behind.

Cree didn't want to waste time arguing with her, and besides he could see if Elsa had anything that would help ease Dawn's stomach. He hated seeing her suffer even if it was the natural course of things.

Dawn had her cloak on and was waiting at the door beside Sloan when Cree entered the room. He stretched his hand out to her as he approached reminding her that she was to stay near him. She took it and nodded and out the door they went.

Elsa didn't stand out of respect as she normally would do when Cree entered a room and it was easy to see why. A young man lay on the bed babbling incoherently. Elsa was busy bathing his face with a cool cloth and talking softly to him.

Cree released Dawn's hand and nodded to Sloan who stepped closer to her side as Cree walked over to the young man.

Elsa looked up at Cree and shook her head.

"Can he hear and understand me?" Cree asked.

"The fever has a hold of him so I cannot say for sure."

"Help," the young man cried out. "Please... help me."

The last of his plea could barely be heard.

His hand shot out and Elsa took hold of it. "It's all right, lad. It's all right."

"Noooo," he cried. "Help... have to help."

Cree had seen many a young warrior beg for help as he faced death. There was never anything he could do for them but sit with them so they wouldn't die alone. Something no one wanted to do alone.

But this young man had answers that could help save Dawn's life and he wanted those answers before the lad died.

He nodded to Elsa to move and once she did he sat. "Who hired you to kill the voiceless woman?"

The young man's eyes turned wide and he shook his head and was barely able to spit out, "Help."

"I'll help you but you must answer me. Who hired you?"

"Me good," the young man mumbled his eyes drifting closed. "Me good. Help."

"Answer me," Cree shouted.

Dawn rushed over to Cree and plunked herself down on his lap. Before he could move her off, she reached out and took hold of the young man's hand.

His eyes popped wide again and he barely got out 'love' when he started choking. His hand stayed clamped around Dawn's and when he was finally able to catch a breath he pleaded once more, "Help me."

One last cough and catch of a breath and he was gone.

Dawn held his limp hand for a moment before resting it on his chest. Then she stood and walked away from Cree, only half listening to the many questions he bombarded Elsa with. There was something about the young man's barely audible pleas that bothered Dawn. Something was missing from them and she couldn't quite grasp what it was.

"He was no warrior, begging for help to the very end," Sloan said joining Cree and Elsa.

"No, he was hired for a job that he failed to complete and in the end wanted nothing more than to be saved from death," Cree said.

Dawn braced her hand on the mantel and stared into the flames concentrating on the young man's pleas for help. What was it about them that disturbed her so? She shut her eyes and heard them over and over and over in her head.

"The question is who hired him and was he the one who beat Bree to death." Sloan said.

"And do the attempts on Dawn's life end here with him?" Elsa asked.

Cree shook his head. "Someone with too much to lose is behind this. The question is who."

The young man's words resonated in Dawn's head blocking out everything else. Over and over and over she heard, "Help me. Help Me. Help me." Until suddenly it became, "Help Bree. Help Bree. Help Bree."

Could that have been what the young man meant? "Help Bree." Had he been trying to protect her? Had he meant, "Bree good?" Had Bree been a pawn in this endless ruse? Had his dying breath been a plea to help save the innocent woman he loved? If so then who was it that had been using her?

Her stomach gurgled, reminding her that she had yet to eat breakfast. Her hand went to rest at her stomach and no soon as she did then Cree was at her side, his arm going around her waist.

"Are you all right?" he asked.

She turned around in his arms nodding, more concerned with what her thoughts had deduced than with her hunger pains. She began to gesture wanting to share what she thought the dying young man might have meant, and Sloan and Elsa drew nearer to listen.

"Bree?" Sloan asked perplexed as she spoke with her hands. "You think he meant Bree, not me?"

"He mentioned love, didn't he?" Elsa asked. "Could he have been in love with Bree and was trying to protect her?"

"From who?" Sloan asked.

"From whoever wanted Dawn dead," Cree said. "Bree could have been caught up in this mess by pure accident."

"Or on purpose," Sloan said. "She could have used the poor sap to do her biding."

"Either way," Cree said, "they were involved and someone was giving them orders."

Dawn spoke up, her hand tapping her chest before she threw both hands up, along with her shoulders, in a shrug.

Cree nodded. "You're right. With Bree and this young man dead, who is left to do you harm?"

Sloan answered that one. "The person who wants her dead."

Dawn grew lightheaded and for a moment she thought she would faint. She should have eaten by now. As of late she realized she was more hungry than usual in the morning and always felt good after eating. She needed to get food and quickly or she feared the consequences.

She went to take a step when a wave of dizziness attacked and she reached out frantically trying to grab something that would steady her. She was relieved when Cree scooped her up in his arms.

"What's wrong?" he demanded with more concern than anger.

Elsa answered for her. "You haven't eaten yet this morning have you?"

Cree turned to Sloan. "See that one of the men checks the cottage, if no food has been brought have him go to the kitchen and see that the morning meal is brought immediately. Then see that this body is stored with Bree's. When you are done meet me in my solar. There are things that need to be discussed."

Cree wouldn't put Dawn down so she could walk. No matter how much she insisted that she was all right, he wouldn't listen. He continued carrying her through the village, once again drawing attention to them, but that seemed to be a given. They received attention wherever they went in the village. She should be used to it by now, but she wasn't.

Flanna and Dorrie arrived with two baskets a few minutes after Cree and Dawn arrived at the cottage. He had lowered her feet to the ground, though kept his arms around her. The two women hurriedly arranged the food on the table and Flanna filled two tankards with hot cider before Cree dismissed them.

"I must go," he said turning Dawn around in his arms.

She gestured that he should eat.

"I don't have time. I must see to things."

She frowned, having hoped he was going to join her and they could make some sense of who wanted her dead.

He ran his finger over her pouting lips. "I will return later and let you know if I uncover anything."

That made her feel somewhat better and so she nodded, though didn't smile.

He leaned down and gave her a lingering kiss that neither of them made any move to end and it might have gone further if a knock didn't sound at the door.

Cree mumbled and then shouted angrily, "Enter."

No one entered.

Cree shouted again. "If I come to the door, you'll regret it."

The door opened slowly and Lila poked her head in, her face pale and her eyes wide.

Dawn was pleased to see her and urged her in with a wave of her hand.

Lila hesitated, her head downcast and her eyes darting from Dawn to Cree. "I am sorry for interrupting, my lord, I thought to visit with Dawn for a while if she was free to do so."

Dawn nodded vigorously, eager to talk with her friend and see if anyone in the village had heard anything about the murder. But Lila remained where she was, just inside the door, waiting for Cree's consent to enter.

Dawn poked Cree with her elbow since the scowl on his face was frightening her half to death.

He cocked a brow at Dawn and then looked to Lila. "It seems that Dawn favors a visit with you rather than me."

Lila's eyes turned wide and she looked as if she didn't know what to do or say.

Dawn shook her finger at Cree, who grinned, and she hurried over to her friend, her hands gesturing rapidly.

Lila leaned close to Dawn when she reached her side and said, "But he doesn't look like he's teasing."

Cree laughed and Lila appeared even more startled. Laughter was rarely if ever heard from Cree.

Dawn shook her finger at Cree again and Lila finally smiled recognizing the banter for what it was, playful teasing, much like she and Paul would do with each other.

Cree walked over to give Dawn a quick kiss and then turned to Lila. "I am glad you are here. Dawn needs to eat, the babe protests."

"I will see that she does, my lord," Lila said with a bob of her head and a smile.

"I am pleased that you are such a good friend to Dawn," Cree said.

More at ease, Lila said, "As she is to me, my lord, and I do have stories to tell about when we were young and reckless, if you would like to hear them sometime."

Dawn shook her head, though she appeared to laugh.

Cree's smile grew. "I very much do want to hear them." He gave Dawn another quick kiss and was out the door.

Lila immediately threw her arms around Dawn and hugged her. "I am so happy for you. It is so easy to see how much you both love each other." She then stepped away and gently shoved Dawn to the table. "Sit and eat and we'll talk.

Dawn was only too eager to talk with her friend. She had missed their daily talks and there was so much to tell her.

As usual Lila started talking and Dawn smiled, glad her friend was there.

"Has he told you he loves you?" Lila asked.

Dawn smiled and nodded.

"There is talk," Lila said lowering her voice, "that he is going to make you his wife. That once it is proven that you are Kirk McClusky's daughter the

King will grant him permission or at least the people are hoping the King will." Her eyes suddenly turned wide. "Talk of love has made me forget why I came here in the first place." She shivered. "Everyone is talking about the murder of that poor lass Bree. When I heard that she was found in the woods behind your cottage..." she shivered again.

Dawn patted her arm to comfort her.

"Did you really see the body?"

Dawn nodded and explained what she had seen.

Lila paled. "How horrible."

Dawn then explained about the young man who had just died in Elsa's cottage and her thoughts on how he may have been connected to Bree.

"You know Bree spent a lot of time in the woods. She told people that she wanted to learn all about the plants and be a healer like Elsa. But it's winter and with the snow there aren't many plants to be found. So what was she really doing in the woods?"

Dawn asked if Lila knew anything else about Bree.

"The villagers seemed to like her. She was a pleasant lass; no one had a bad word to say about her. And she must have been a good person or Old Mary would have never wanted her to stay in her cottage."

Dawn hadn't thought about that. Old Mary certainly wouldn't have wanted Bree around if she thought the young lass could prove harmful.

"There was something I saw I had thought odd but dismissed it. Now though with everything that is going on perhaps there was something to it."

Dawn was anxious to hear it and let Lila know with a quick gesture.

"I had forgotten something at the work cottage one night and was on my way back from there when I saw Lucerne's other servant, the one who spends her days stitching Lucerne's garments, leaving Old Mary's cottage. And the odd thing was that the two women hugged in the doorway before Lucerne's servant took her leave. What would she be doing visiting Old Mary? And why did it appear as if they knew each other?"

Chapter Thirty-two

After Lila left, Dawn paced in front of the hearth. Old Mary knew more than she was saying. What secret was she keeping and why? She wished she could talk with the old woman, though she wondered if Old Mary would be as evasive as she usually was.

Dawn finally sat down, turning a chair to face the hearth. A cold crept into her even though she was warmed by the fire's heat. Was it a portent of what was to come? She shivered at the thought and shivered again, the image of Bree lying dead in the woods suddenly invading her mind. Had she been an innocent or an accomplice? And if the latter, then who was her accomplice?

Lucerne certainly painted a picture of a confused and troubled woman or was it a ruse? And what of Lady Ann, her true mother? Was she truly trying to protect the daughter she had given birth to and the one she raised or was she more concerned with her own interests? And what of Roland Gerwan? Was he oblivious to it all or was he the master pulling the strings?

There was so much deceit involved that Old Mary had been right about warning her to 'trust no one.' But now with the two murders of possibly innocent people, something had to be done. The lies had to finally stop and the truth be told.

A sudden thought had her jumping to her feet. Old Mary knew more than she was saying. Did someone else know that as well and did that mean that Old Mary's life was in just as much danger as her own?"

Dawn didn't take time to think. She grabbed her cloak and swung the door open.

~~~

Roland Gerwan entered the Great Hall in hurried strides, stopping a few feet away from where Cree stood speaking to Sloan. "Good Lord, Cree, my daughter's servant murdered?" he said shocked, as if he didn't believe what he was saying. "I thought you a more competent leader. I daresay the King needs to know of this turn of events. Perhaps you are not as capable and worthy of a title as you believe."

Cree turned away from Sloan, who was shaking his head at the stupidity of the man, and turned a murderous glare on Gerwan. "There are many things the King is going to be made aware of and one of them is the duplicity of those involved and," —he grabbed the broom near the hearth and approached Gerwan—"how easily I snapped," —he swung the broom up and in one quick jerk snapped it in two— "the necks of the persons responsible for this heinous crime."

Gerwan paled and took several steps back away from Cree.

Cree threw the broom pieces to the floor. "Justice will be swift, though not painless."

Gerwan attempted to appear brave raising his chin a notch. "Titled men leave such dreadful tasks to lesser men."

"It is a lesser man who leaves a necessary, though often times repugnant task to others."

Gerwan tossed his chin up again. "I want to make certain that my daughter is in no danger."

"Is there a reason she should be?"

Gerwan stared at Cree, as if at a loss for words until finally he said, "You have a murderer running about."

"The spineless fool runs about thinking he will avoid me. I will find him soon enough. But tell me, why would you think that this coward would be interested in your daughter?"

Gerwan was once again at a loss for words and fumbled to find an answer. "Bree... was Lucerne's servant."

"How did Bree get that position?"

"I have no idea," Gerwan said with a wave of his hand. "That matters not."

"We'll see if it does," Cree warned.

"What do you mean?"

Cree moved toward the man so fast that Gerwan stumbled trying to back away from him. "It means that I am going to be asking endless questions of you, your wife, and Lucerne."

"Why?"

"You said it yourself... Bree was Lucerne's servant." Cree marched past the man and straight for his solar.

Sloan followed shaking his head at Gerwan as he passed him.

Kirk McClusky came around the corner just as Cree was about to enter his solar.

"May I have a word with you?" he asked and Cree waved him in.

Kirk McClusky didn't wait to speak. "Ann is terribly upset. She feels that the decision she made all those years ago has now returned to haunt the innocent. She believed she was doing the right thing for all concerned. And now she just wants to make amends for a deed she regrets."

"And how does she intend to do that?" Cree asked.

Kirk smiled. "She says that she will leave that to you, though she does request permission to talk with Dawn. She regrets the way they recently parted."

"Until I am certain that Lady Ann poses no threat to Dawn, I will grant no such permission."

Kirk appeared stunned. "Ann would never hurt our daughter."

"I don't know that for sure."

"Ann is repentant."

"You're certain of that?"

"Ann is a good woman and I blame myself for the terrible choice she had to make years ago. But it was a necessary one and one made to protect our daughter," Kirk said.

"The wiser choice would have been to send Dawn to you, but instead Ann gave the child away and cared not a whit as to what happened to her."

"And suffered every day because of that unselfish decision," Kirk said in defense of the woman he loved.

"Suffered?" Cree snapped. "She orders her helpless newborn daughter, who cannot utter a sound, given away to God knows who and she suffered? She was lucky that a good woman took Dawn and loved her as only a mother—" Cree turned away a moment and then turned back. "I have no more time to discuss this. We'll talk later and Lady Ann is not to visit with Dawn until I give permission. Is that clear, McClusky?"

The sharp warning in Cree's voice had Kirk drawing his head back, as if he'd been taken to task. "Perfectly clear." He gave a respectful nod and left without saying another word.

Sloan stepped forward. "What is it?"

"The woman who raised Dawn was a loving mother. Dawn has nothing but praise for her and loves her more than I think she could ever possibly love Lady Ann. For a stranger to give such love and have such patience with a child who is not her own takes a damn good reason."

"She was a good, unselfish woman."

"That she was. She unselfishly gave up the daughter she just had so that she would have a better life and took the babe, who had no voice, and loved her as she would have loved her own daughter."

Sloan's brow scrunched and he shook his head. "Are you saying that the woman who raised Dawn was Lucerne's mother?"

"I would wager a bet on it and I know someone who could confirm this."

"Old Mary," Sloan said with a grin, though it faded fast.

"You're thinking what I should have realized long before," Cree said heading for the door. "Old Mary's life could be in just as much danger as Dawn's."

~~~

Dawn almost collided with Torr if it wasn't for his hand grabbing hold of her arm and steadying her.

"Where are you off to in such a hurry?" he asked releasing her arm once her feet found firm footing.

"She'll not be going anywhere without Cree's permission," Elwin said stepping forward.

Dawn rolled her eyes at Torr and held her hands up in prayer pleading with him for help.

He smiled and winked at her, then turned to Elwin. "I'm sure Cree wouldn't mind if I accompanied Dawn to her destination."

Dawn sent Elwin a hopeful look.

"Send one of the guards to let Cree know where we'll be," Torr said and turned to Dawn.

Dawn hunched over and gnarled her fingers to let them know she wanted to go see Old Mary.

"Old Mary's," Torr confirmed with a nod. "That's not far and I'm sure Cree would not object."

Elwin sent one of the guards off to the keep to notify Cree, and then ordered two guards to follow behind Dawn while he took the lead. Torr walked alongside Dawn.

Torr lowered his voice. "My father had hoped to talk with you away from your cottage and prying eyes, but I see that may be impossible."

She nodded. She would not slip off and give Cree reason to worry, though she did wonder if he would be perturbed with her for not waiting for him to take her to Old Mary's. He had wanted her to keep close to him, but this was so important. What if Old Mary was in danger at this minute and she had waited. She would never forgive herself. Besides, she intended to pay heed to the old woman's words and 'trust no one' until all the secrets were brought to light and she could determine for herself who was friend or foe. Therefore, she would make certain not to go anywhere with guards she was unfamiliar with.

Old Mary was at the door as if expecting them, but then she probably knew they were coming. Her knowing frightened some in the village, but those who were friends accepted her uncanny knowledge.

Dawn was relieved to see her standing there well and safe.

"Come in, come in," Old Mary said with a smile. "The others will be here shortly."

"Others," Torr asked what Dawn was about to.

"Cree and Sloan are on their way," she said. "Sit and enjoy the hot cider Flanna just brought. It will help warm against the cold."

Dawn had been so intent on getting to Old Mary's that she hadn't realize how bitter the air had turned, but she felt it now in her ice cold hands.

"Another storm I daresay," Old Mary said. "It's a bitter winter we'll be having this year. It is a good thing Cree stored well for the winter. Not a one of us will starve."

Old Mary went on about the weather and recalled a few harsh winter storms she had survived, some barely when finally she stopped and looked at the door.

It opened a moment later and in strode Cree, Sloan behind him.

Dawn smiled having wondered while Old Mary chatted if Cree had come to the same conclusion as she had... that Old Mary could be in danger. After all they did think much alike and so she was pleased when he confirmed her suspicions, though he sent her a sharp scowl as he walked over to her. A warning that he was not pleased that she had left the cottage.

"You realized the same that I have," Cree said and bent down to whisper in her ear while giving her shoulder a squeeze. "And of course you had to come and make certain the old woman was all right, though next time you will notify me and wait until I come for you."

Dawn kept her smile and nodded.

"What realization?" Torr asked.

"That my life might be in danger," Old Mary answered and had them all staring at her. She grinned and shook her head. "You need not worry. I was wise enough to keep secrets myself."

"It's time to share them," Cree said and it wasn't a request. "Let me get you started. The woman, who loving raised Dawn, is Lucerne's birth mother, isn't she?"

Old Mary nodded slowly and curled her gnarled fingers around her tankard as best she could. "Yes, Lizbeth is Lucerne's birth mother."

Dawn was stunned by the news and glanced up at Cree wondering how long he had known.

He seemed to understand her unanswered question. "I only just realized it myself and came here to confirm it and to make certain that Old Mary was safe." He looked to Old Mary and commanded, "Tell us what happened."

Old Mary looked to Dawn and spoke to her as if she was the only one in the room. "Do you recall when I told you that it took a strong heart and much love to do what your mother did that night you were born?"

Dawn nodded.

"It was your mother Lizbeth I was speaking of, for she was the one true mother that night. She had barely given birth to Lucerne when I arrived with you in my arms. Lizbeth had lost her husband two months earlier. He had gone off to battle and never returned and she was barely surviving on her own. She had worried how she would manage once the babe was born.

"Lady Ann had ordered food and items that could be bartered, those combs she gave you being one of them, offered to a woman who would take you and surrender their newborn babe. Lizbeth saw this as a way for her daughter to have a good life and in return she swore to give the precious, voiceless babe, her new daughter, a good life as well. I had no doubts about handing you over to Lizbeth. I knew she would love you as her own and she did."

Dawn smiled and nodded, a single tear slipping down her cheek.

"What aren't you telling us?" Cree demanded.

"You have a knowing of your own, Lord Cree," Old Mary said with a grin.

"No, I know people and it's obvious there is more to your story, so tell us... what caused you to follow Lizbeth?"

Old Mary nodded as if confirming for herself that Cree's astuteness bordered on the intuitive. "Once a peasant knows a secret, her life is never safe. I made sure that Lucerne was settled safely with Lady Ann who was overjoyed with the blond-haired babe and then I took my leave, meeting up with Lizbeth. It wasn't easy for her to find a village or clan where she and Dawn would be accepted, which is why they moved around so much. There were times I wondered how she managed. I kept a close eye on them, but never became involved until I settled here in Dowell to make sure it was safe and then I got in touch with Lizbeth and had her join me."

"Why take the chance of settling in a village that belonged to Gerwan?" Cree asked. "You took a chance of Dawn being discovered."

"I knew it was inevitable that Dawn's identity would be discovered."

"Why?"

"A secret is no secret when more than one person knows it," Old Mary said and Cree nodded in agreement. "And I knew that fate had great plans for Dawn and nothing I did could stop it, but I could help."

"So you settled here and waited for fate to show the way," Cree said.

Old Mary nodded.

"How is Magda involved in this?" Cree asked.

Old Mary looked to Dawn. "Someone saw us."

Dawn nodded and waited, curious to know the answer.

"As I said Lizbeth was the truest of mothers and she wanted to make certain that her daughter was protected against any harm. She had a dear friend, much like Lila and Dawn are friends, whose husband was near to death and when he died she would not be able to work the croft on her own and would soon be homeless."

"Magda," Cree said.

Old Mary nodded. "Magda jumped at the chance not only to help her friend but herself as well. I took her to Lady Ann and convinced Lady Ann that she would make an excellent servant to tend the babe. She agreed without hesitation. A few years ago Lady Ann decided to replace Magda with a younger servant. Lucerne had grown very attached to Magda and made a fuss insisting that she be kept on to see to the care and stitching of her garments. Magda is brilliant when it comes to stitching garments. Lady Ann agreed."

"So her visit was nothing more than wanting to see an old friend?"

"It hadn't been her first visit to me," Old Mary admitted and Cree cocked a brow at her. "It seems that Lucerne was not her usual self and either was Bree. When she learned that Bree had accused Lucerne of taking a heavy hand to her, she was shocked. Lucerne had never touched Bree and she asked me to keep an eye on the young lass and see what she was up to."

"So that was the reason you requested Bree to remain with you," Cree said.

"I sensed the lass was troubled and with her staying close, I could better understand her problem. But Bree could be a sly one and was gone more often than here, especially at night when she thought I was sleeping. She would sneak out and not return until morning."

"And you never thought to share this with me?" Cree demanded.

"Magda asked me to give my word that I would say nothing. She feared being taken away from Lucerne and leaving her unprotected. She saw that you had no patience with Lucerne and did not believe that she suffered headaches. She felt she had no choice but to remain silent. It is the way of things with a servant's lot. Punishment can often be swift and unfair and so silence is often the best resort and—" Old Mary gasped and stood as the door flung open and Elwin rushed in.

"Kirk McClusky confronted Gerwan. Kirk lies injured and Gerwan lies dead."

Chapter Thirty-three

Torr jumped up. "How bad is my father?"

"A head wound with much bleeding; he lies unconscious," Elwin explained. "Elsa is on her way to him now. She ordered that he not be moved until she can have a look at him."

Torr flew out the door.

"What of Gerwan?" Cree asked as Dawn stood. He took her hand and gave it a tug letting her know that she was to go nowhere without him.

"Stabbed in the chest," Elwin said. "Lady Ann is there. She is the one who discovered them. She was to meet McClusky there. She's hysterical, blaming herself. A servant ran to get Lucerne to help her mother."

Cree gave Sloan a quick nod and he returned one in kind and hurried out the door. He then turned to Dawn. "You will remain by my side and if you don't I will see us shackled together. And it will be done if you do not obey me on this. Do you understand?"

Dawn nodded seeing an uncertainty in his eyes that frightened her.

"You know," Old Mary said as the two walked to the door.

Cree turned. "That more blood will be spilled before this day ends?"

She nodded.

"Whose blood will it be?"

"That I do not know. I only know that fate has finally revealed her hand."

Dawn realized that Cree worried that it would be her blood that would be spilled and she worried that it would be his. She squeezed his hand and moved closer to him as they hurried through the village.

He looked to her and gave a nod. "I am glad you comprehend the importance of staying by my side."

She nodded, knowing her concern showed as clearly in her eyes as it did in his. And then she tapped his arm and held her hand up keeping two fingers close together.

"You are telling me that I must do the same, stay close to you?"

She nodded, her fear of losing him growing and the babe must have felt the same for her stomach roiled with the dreadful thought. Her hand went to her stomach causing Cree to stop abruptly.

"You are not feeling well?"

She shook her head and rested her head to his chest, laying her hand on his chest over his heart.

He slipped his finger beneath her chin and lifted her face to look at him. "Do not worry yourself over me. Trust that I will keep you, our babe, and me safe."

She nodded, glad that the infamous Cree was by her side. They once again hurried along. They could hear Lady Ann's wrenching cries as they approached the stables where the incident had taken place. At the same time Lucerne rushed past them, Sloan right behind her.

Cree shook his head at Sloan as he passed them and Sloan hurried his pace catching up with Lucerne and stopping her before she could enter the stable.

"Let me go," she screeched at Sloan, holding her firmly in his arms.

"It is better you wait here," Sloan said.

Cree and Dawn reached them. "Your mother will join you shortly."

"I want to see my father," Lucerne demanded through tears.

"No," Cree said, as if issuing a final decree and turned away to enter the stable.

"How dare you let your whore see my father and not me," Lucerne screamed.

Cree swung his head around. "Your grief affords you some latitude and you have just used it all. Another disparaging remark about the woman I love and you will regret it."

Cree turned, though Dawn caught Sloan's hand rushing to clamp tightly over Lucerne's mouth.

As soon as Lady Ann saw Cree, she rushed away from the warrior, who she had been clinging to for support, and dropped before him. "Forgive me, my lord, I could not stop him. Kirk insisted that no one was safe and the truth had to be made known. It was the only way to end all the madness. I begged him not to confront Roland, to let you handle it as you saw fit, but he refused."

Cree nodded to the warrior who had followed behind Lady Ann. "Your daughter waits outside. We will talk later." He then motioned for two more warriors to join the other and issued orders. "Escort Lady Ann and her daughter to the Great Hall and remain with them. And tell Sloan to join me."

"Dawn should not see her father like this. She should join Lucerne and me, so that I may finally tell Lucerne the truth," Lady Ann said.

"Now is not the time," Cree said and nodded to his warriors. One took Lady Ann's arm and hurried her out of the stable. The other two followed.

Cree silently berated himself. He hadn't given thought as to how Dawn felt about her father being injured. Cree looked to Dawn. "Are you certain you are up to this? Kirk is your father and it could cause you quite an upset."

Kirk had only entered her life and while he seemed a good man, Dawn still had difficulty thinking of him as her father. It had been her and her mother for so long that a father wasn't easy to accept. Dawn patted her chest and nodded, and though her stomach was a bit queasy she had no intention of letting Cree know that. And she had every intention of seeing the scene for herself. Her silence allowed her to look and see while others talked and missed things.

"If you are sure and should you feel the slightest discomfit—"

Dawn finished for him, tapping her lips and pointing to him, letting him know that she would tell him.

He didn't seem convinced but there was little he could do, for he knew she would have her way. He turned and they went to stand opposite from Torr, kneeling next to his father, as Elsa worked on the unconscious man.

"How is he?" Cree asked.

Elsa answered without looking up. "A substantial head wound. It needs to be cleaned and possibly stitched and as with any head wound, I do not know when or if he will wake." She looked at Torr. "Though I will do all I can to see that he does."

"Did you know your father's intention?" Cree asked.

Torr shook his head, though remained kneeling next to his father. "No, though I could see that he had grown impatient with the whole ordeal. And when he found out about Bree's death today he was even more adamant about everything being brought to light. He felt Dawn would be safer that way."

"You didn't agree?" Cree asked.

"No, having heard Bree had been beaten to death made me think that whoever is responsible for it all has reached the point of desperation and that is a dangerous place to be."

"Do you believe Gerwan responsible and that your father somehow found out?"

Torr stood as two warriors approached with a pallet to place his father on and carry him to Elsa's cottage. He moved out of their way, though kept an eye on them. "I'll be along shortly," he said to Elsa and she nodded. He turned to Cree and finally answered him. "I can't say for sure. I know my father not only wanted to keep Dawn safe and see her happy, he also didn't want to fail Ann again. He never stopped loving her and I'm sure he hoped that somehow they could make things work for them. Perhaps he decided to confront Gerwan about his love for Ann. I know how angry I would get if another man dared to tell me he loved my wife; I'd want to kill him. Gerwan could have struck my father and perhaps he had enough time to deliver a lethal blow to Gerwan before he collapsed unconscious. This incident may have nothing to do at all with Dawn or again it may. I do not know. I only hope that my father wakes and is able to settle the mystery for us. Now I must go see to my father."

Cree nodded and Dawn tugged at his hand. He turned to her and she pointed to Gerwan's body. He scrunched his brow appearing as if he was about to deny her request to take a look at the body, so she didn't wait for him to reply. She walked over to it tugging him along behind her.

Once there Cree seemed as interested as she was. He released her hand, though issued no warning for her to remain near. He didn't need to; he trusted her to keep her word.

"I suppose Torr could be right. Kirk could have expressed his love for Gerwan's wife, it enraged him, and he struck out at Kirk. But instinct takes hold and before Kirk lost consciousness he pulled out his dagger and stabbed Gerwan." Cree rubbed his chin giving the scenario thought. "Torr is right about one thing." He looked at Dawn. "I wouldn't think twice about killing a man who claimed he loved you. Then I'd throw his carcass in the woods for the animals to feast on."

The gruesome thought turned her stomach and she shook her head.

"You don't know men, Dawn, they can be a lowly lot and unless a man stands in honor of the woman he loves; he is no man."

Her heart gave a patter and her stomach calmed. Cree was more of an honorable man than anyone would ever realize and he belonged to her. She turned her attention back to the body and ignored the urge to run and kiss Cree. It would not be proper action to take with a man lying dead near her feet. She studied the prone body and as with Bree's body something disturbed her about it.

After a few silent minutes Cree asked, "What is it that you see that I don't?"

Dawn pointed to the dagger that appeared to have directly punctured the heart. She then gestured as if Gerwan and Kirk were arguing, suddenly throwing her head back as if struck and stumbling as she reached for an imaginary dagger at her waist and lunged with stumbling steps at her foe. She then straightened and pointed at the dagger again and at her own chest where it would have hit and scrunched her brow and shrugged.

"I never thought of that," Cree admitted. "Your observation is a wise one. How could Kirk deliver such a precise blow after having suffered a severe head wound?"

Dawn held up two fingers, added one and then another.

"One or two others could have been here and delivered the deadly blow and near deadly one, or they could have thought they had killed Kirk."

Dawn raised her chin as if haughty and held up her skirt and pretended to walk as if she was in a rush.

"You think perhaps Lady Ann was heard approaching and the culprits ran?"

She shrugged, suggesting it a possibility.

"Torr is right. The person or persons behind this have grown desperate and are now more dangerous than ever. It seems that they will stop at nothing now to see their plan succeed. But what plan?" Cree said shaking his head and rubbing the back of his neck. "With Gerwan dead what stands in their way? Lady Ann can openly admit that you are her daughter and that Lucerne is the daughter of a peasant which frees me to wed you."

Dawn stared at him, her eyes wide her mouth open. He truly wished to wed her?

Cree thought there was something wrong when he glanced her way and then he realized what he had said. He went immediately to her side and took her in his arms. "I didn't mean to spew it out that way. It had been my plan all along to wed you."

Her eyes turned wider and her mouth feel open another notch.

"I'm making a mess of this," he said more to himself than Dawn. "I intended to marry you all along. There was no way I would spend my life without you." He turned away for a moment to gather his thoughts and his eyes took note of the dead body. "This is not the place for this."

He hurried Dawn out of the stable and to her cottage, the guards following close behind them. He latched the door once inside and wasted no time in yanking Dawn's cloak off her and taking her in his arms.

"I sometimes think of the moment that I knew that I loved you and I'm always drawn to our time in the hut together. You were fearful, yet brave, and your courage grew as I got to know you." He grinned. "You intrigued me more and more each day. And I found my hands eager to explore you." He shook his head. "If I were honest with myself I'd admit that I fell in love with you upon sight, which has been difficult for me to accept since I never thought that would be possible and yet..." he shook his head. "You claimed my heart long before I even realized I had opened it to you."

A tear slipped down Dawn's cheek as she threw her arms around Cree's neck and kissed him with a joy she had never experienced in her life.

He returned her enthusiasm deepening the kiss and the next thing they knew they were striping each

357

other bare and falling down on the bed together. Their passion could not be contained; they were hungry for each other and nothing could stop them from feeding it. And feeding it they did. His hands explored her with a startling eagerness that had her body bowing at his every touch. And when his mouth followed suit she thought she would leap off the bed, it felt so deliciously and wonderfully wicked.

"I want to linger and enjoy," he whispered harshly in her ear but my need is too great."

She pressed one finger to his arm agreeing and he quickly grabbed her legs and flung them over his shoulders as he positioned himself between them and drove into her with a forceful thrust that had her arching up to meet his demand.

He continued driving into her hard and she enjoyed every blessed minute of it. It didn't take long for their passion to build to an explosive climax, and Cree made certain it was one she would never forget. His hand reached out and teased the tiny pulsating nub and she nearly bolted off the bed, but his strong body and solid thrusts held her firm.

She came so hard that she didn't stop tapping his arm over and over and over and finally when she climaxed for a second time he joined her and exploded in a blinding fury that left him so spent that he collapsed on top of her.

Dawn soon realized that his weight did not allow her to breath and she pushed at his solid muscle. Her attempts grew a bit more frantic when he didn't respond until he finally rose up off her. She caught a quick breath followed by several more.

"Are you all right?" he asked anxiously.

She took a few more deep breaths and nodded.

"Damn, I came so hard I spent all my strength."

Dawn smiled wide.

"Pleased with that are you?" he asked tweaking her nose as he moved off her, though grabbed her around the waist to lie and placed her alongside him.

She nodded vigorously.

"So am I," he admitted though in a whisper, as if he didn't want anyone to hear. "From this moment on I refuse to do without you in my bed. You will be moved to my room in the keep. And as soon as all the documents are signed we will be wed." He tweaked her nose again. "That is if you'll have me."

She bolted up beside him. Was he truly giving her a choice? It was the very question she gestured him.

"Yes, I am asking you if you wish to wed me. I want you as my willing wife, not a prisoner or mistress forced to submit to me but as a woman who loves me and wants to wed me, bear my children and grow old with me."

She nodded vigorously before he even finished.

"That eager are you?"

She smiled softly, shaking her head and pressed her hand to her heart and then pressed it to his heart holding it there.

He rested his hand over hers. "Love me that much do you?"

She slipped her hand from beneath his and stretched her hands wide demonstrating that her love for him was endless.

He grabbed her around the waist and lifted her up and brought her down to rest over the length of him. His hands went to squeeze her buttocks playfully and his kiss teased. "Damn it, woman, I love you more than I ever thought possible." He growled low after nuzzling her neck. "You're mine, you belong to me, and I'll never let you go."

His words sent a tingle to her for the words spoke of his love just as deeply as if he had said I love you and she gestured the same to him. She jabbed his chest, poked her own, and grabbed his hand to lock her fingers with him letting him know that he belonged to her and she would never let him go.

He laughed softly. "Looks as if we're stuck with each other."

She nodded and kissed him gently, though he responded with more fervor.

After a few minutes of a kiss that titillated them both senseless he pulled away and said through bated breath, "Damn, I'm hard for you already and we've only finished making love."

She reached down and discovered just how hard he was and with a grin she rose up over him and with a silent sigh of pleasure lowered herself onto him. He groaned with anticipation and in no time they were lost in passion that neither of them hurried to abate.

Chapter Thirty-four

Dawn didn't want to move to the keep but Cree was adamant and she finally surrendered knowing he would not change his mind. All her things were placed in Cree's bed chamber, a sizeable room. Flanna fussed making sure everything was to Dawn's liking.

Dawn allowed Flanna to do as she wished. She was more concerned with finding out how her father was doing and preparing herself for Lucerne's reaction when the woman found out the truth about her birth. In a way she felt sorry for her. Dawn was now a noble while Lucerne was now a peasant. And she did not think that Lucerne could survive a peasant's life. And she fretted over how she would survive being a noble.

One thing she was happy about was that she had free reign of the keep. Cree had posted guards throughout the entire keep and while he had insisted that Dawn remain by his side, he soon found it a difficult order to maintain, thus the guards being posted throughout the keep and Elwin following her wherever she went.

She had been at the keep only a couple of hours and was already missing the solitude of her cottage. Everywhere she ventured someone was there. She was not used to so many people being around and it unnerved her. She much preferred her solitude or a cozy chat with her best friend Lila. That was how she had spent most of her time, and she favored it that way. How she would adapt, she didn't know.

Dawn was pleased when Flanna finally finished settling her things and after giving her friend an appreciative hug and seeing her out the door, Dawn found that she was tired. It had been an eventful day and it was only a couple of hours after noon. And though she was a bit fatigued, she wanted to see how her father was doing. She grabbed her cloak and went to the door, hoping she would not meet resistance to her plan.

Elwin, as usual, was outside the door and when he saw that she wore her cloak, he shook his head. "Cree says you are to stay in the keep."

Dawn gestured that she wished to see how Kirk was doing.

Elwin smiled. "In that case we don't have a problem. Kirk was moved here to the keep. Cree and Torr thought it best that way."

She was pleased that she'd face no resistance, though she did wonder over the true reason why Kirk had been moved here. Did Cree and Torr believe his life was in danger? She tossed her cloak on the bed and followed Elwin down one floor. With each step her mind churned wondering over different possibilities as to why with Gerwan's death, her life should still be in danger. What was it this person or persons were after? What value did her identity hold now with Gerwan dead?

Elwin opened the door to the room and stepped in. She was surprised to see him acknowledge someone with a bow of his head and was more surprised to see that it was the cleric who the King had sent to wed Lucerne and Cree.

"I came to pray for the lord's servant Kirk in his hour of need," the cleric said, his eyes narrowing as he spoke until his expression turned to a scowl. "You are Cree's harlot."

Dawn sent him such a scathing look that the cleric actually took a step back.

"It is not too late to redeem your soul," he urged. "We can pray together and cleanse you of the devil."

Dawn let him rattle on, her attention caught by the small vial in his hand. She pointed to it.

"I was anointing him," the cleric snapped and you should wait outside until I finish and then I will hear your confession."

She didn't move, she continued to stare at his hands that looked weathered and worn from toiling in the field. But if he was one of the King's cleric's what would he be doing toiling in the field?

He stepped toward her and before she could move he grabbed hold of her arm, his other hand held a dagger, the point pressed to her stomach. The vial he had held had fallen to the floor beside the bed.

"Unless you want me to cut your guard's throat, you better agree when I tell him that we are going to Cree's bedchamber where I will hear your confession."

She nodded, not wishing any harm to come to Elwin.

The long sleeve of his robe covered the dagger as they walked out of the room. "She wishes to confess her sins and cleanse her soul," the cleric announced and Elwin looked at him oddly.

Dawn nodded and placed her hand on Elwin tapping his arm twice, though the cleric could not see it.

Elwin returned with them to Cree's bedchamber passing Lady Ann on the way. She seemed in a hurry, claiming Lucerne was upset and needed her. When Elwin opened the door to the bedchamber, the cleric blocked him from entering the room.

"Confession is private, my son," he said.

Elwin looked conflicted and Dawn hoped he would remain outside the door and attempt to find out what she had been trying to tell him. She had grown fond of Elwin and didn't want to see him hurt and Dorrie would be devastated if she lost him, the pair having grown to love each other.

As soon as the door closed, he shoved Dawn toward a section of the wall and pushed on it, revealing a boarded up opening. He couldn't rip the boards down without calling attention to the noise and that's when the scream sounded. As soon as it did, the cleric kicked at the boards and shoved Dawn through the opening.

Dawn slipped as she descended on the narrow stone stairs a few times receiving some bumps to her elbows and knees. It did not take long to reach the bottom and once there the cleric, though by now Dawn realized the man was no cleric, kicked the boards until a sufficient opening was made and he forced her through it, following behind her and not letting go of her. His grip was so strong it stung her skin.

He shoved her toward the woods and Dawn already shivered from the bitter cold and prayed that Cree would be close on her trail.

~~~

Cree hurried along the hall with Torr and Sloan following behind, having been informed that Lucerne was carrying on uncontrollably. He stopped abruptly in front of Elwin wanting to make certain Dawn was all right.

"She rests?" he asked.

"The cleric is hearing her confession. Dawn seemed agreeable having nodded," Elwin said. "What does two taps to the arm mean?"

Cree kicked the door open and rushed into his bedchamber, Torr, Sloan, and Elwin following. His heart pounding wildly in his chest, he turned to Elwin. "When did she tap your arm?"

"When the cleric said they were going to your bedchamber so he could hear her confession, she reached out and tapped my arm twice."

"She was letting you know that wasn't so," Cree said, his fear escalating like never before. "Alert the men. Have them search the woods near where this secret passageway ends."

Elwin nodded and hurried off to see it done.

Cree didn't waste a minute; he entered the secret passageway, Torr, and Sloan following.

"He isn't a cleric is he?" Torr asked as they maneuvered the narrow staircase.

"No, he isn't," Cree said more determined than ever to find the bastard cleric and kill him.

"But he spoke about seeing your sister," Sloan said.

"I have no doubt he tortured the real cleric to get what information he could out of him so that he would be able to play the role well. I should have realized that something was wrong when he didn't refer to the abbey or Abbess by name."

"But who is he?" Torr said.

"That's what I intend to find out before I kill him," Cree said as they emerged out into the cold.

~~~

The man shoved and dragged Dawn when he didn't feel that she walked fast enough and his detailed threats of what he intended to do to her made her shiver more with fear than from the cold.

"I think tying you to a tree and cutting you good so that your blood attracts hungry animals is a fitting end for someone who has caused me endless trouble." He shook his head. "I forget that you cannot utter a sound. That is good, for then you cannot scream when the animals feast on you."

No matter what happened, she could not let him tie her to a tree. She had to get away from him and back to the keep. Cree would come for her. He was probably already on the way.

"I will be glad when this chore is done and I can be on my way. You've been more trouble than you are worth. No matter how many men I hired to see you finished, not a one could see the chore done."

Dawn didn't try to communicate with him, she let him talk wanting to learn all she could.

"Have to admit though that if it wasn't for my precious, darling wife who took on the chore of raising the dumb daughter of a noblewoman, I wouldn't have had the opportunity to make myself some wealth."

That stopped Dawn, and she turned to face the man claiming to be Lucerne's father.

"The stupid bitch thought I was dead. She never realized that I didn't want to come home to her and a whining babe. When I finally had no place to go, I returned home figuring my dependable wife would be there and what a surprise it was to find out that she was gone with who I thought was my daughter until I saw Lucerne. She was the image of my wife when I first met her." He gave her a shove and she fell to her knees and winced, a snow-covered rock jabbing into one knee. He hoisted her up with a roughness that jarred her. "Get moving. I'm tired of acting the pious man. I want this done so I can be gone."

The pain in her knee caused Dawn to stumble before she righted her steps. She could feel the blood running down her leg and she prayed that it would leave a trail for Cree to follow, though she did need to slow their pace.

She stumbled a few more times hoping that would help but it didn't matter. He suddenly yelled for her to stop.

"No doubt the infamous Cree is already on our trail and I'll not have him catch me. So your time to die has finally come." He took a drink from a flask he had retrieved from beneath his cleric robe and took several swigs, wiping his mouth on his sleeve. "I'm going to prick you enough after I tie you to a tree so that the mighty Cree gets here just in time to watch helplessly as you die."

Dawn held her hands up silently begging him not to do it, tears rushed from her eyes and he stared at her and laughed.

"Damn, but you're a sight to see begging and crying and not a sound coming from you."

Dawn collapsed to the ground, her chin near touching her chest and her shoulders heaving.

He walked over to her laughing and when he was near enough; she fisted her hand and swung it up hard to catch him right between his legs. He grasped from the pain and dropped like a dead weight.

She didn't hesitate; she ran.

"I'm going to kill you, you dumb bitch!" His scream echoed through the woods and Dawn prayed that Cree heard him.

She spotted droplets of blood on the snow—her blood—and followed them knowing they would take her back home, back to Cree. She had no doubt that as soon as the cleric recovered he would be on her trail, so she ran as fast as she could.

It wasn't long before she heard footfalls behind her. They pounded the earth so hard that she thought she felt the ground tremble. He was furious and when he caught her, he would make her suffer. Fear mingled with determination. She wouldn't let him catch her, she wouldn't.

Her knee pained her with every step she took but she refused to give up. She had the babe to think about and Cree and a future waiting for her that she had never thought possible. She would not let a man who cared for naught but himself to rob her of that.

"I see you, bitch, I see you and I'm going to make you suffer."

Dawn kept going and when she rounded a slight bend an arm snagged her hard around the waist and she found herself slammed against Cree's hard body. He quickly sequestered them behind a grouping of trees and bushes. She dropped her brow to his shoulder and rested her hand to his chest loving the feel of the leather stretched across his hard muscles. He had come for her and she had not a single doubt that he would. She looked up at him and smiled.

He pressed a finger to his lips warning her to be quiet. He treated her as if she had a voice and she loved him even more for making her feel that she was no different. She listened as the imposter cleric approached, his threats growing more vicious.

"Now I'm really going to cut you and make you suffer, bitch."

Dawn felt Cree tense and his scowl not only deepened; it grew dangerous. He eased Dawn to the side, once again warning silence and then turned and waited. When the cleric was near upon them Cree stepped out in his path and slammed his fist into the man's face. The crunch of bone echoed through the woods and before the man dropped to the ground for the second time Cree hit him again.

Cree's warriors had the culprit tied with rope and alert in no time.

"Are you all right?" Cree asked approaching her.

She nodded and hobbled toward him.

He scowled and she had to smile happy to see his usual scowl and not the murderous one. He wasted no time in hoisting her skirt to have a look at leg. As soon as he saw her wounded knee, he scooped her up in his arms.

"I'm carrying you back to the keep and don't waste your breath protesting. It is the way it will be."

She didn't protest; she enjoyed the comfort and safety of his arms, the beat of his steady heart and listened joyfully to his tirade of how he was going to keep her chained to him forever.

He didn't have to worry about that; their love already had them chained.

It didn't take them long to get back to the keep and it was a good thing since it had started snowing. They were just about to step into the keep when the cleric began convulsing and collapsed to the ground, his body writhing. He died before Elsa could be summoned.

Cree's shouts had his warriors scrambling as he rushed into the keep, holding her tight against him. Once in the Great Hall, he placed her on her feet. "Did he say anything to you?"

Dawn gestured slowly hoping Cree would understand her and as if he was interpreting, he repeated her words as she told him what the cleric, supposedly Lucerne's father, had told her.

Cree shook his head.

Sloan and Torr joined them halfway through and Sloan was quick to say when she finished, "So the other culprit is..."

"One of two women or both of them and I believe that your father has the answer," Cree said turning to Torr.

That had Dawn recalling the vial in the cleric's hand and with no time to explain, and ignoring the stinging pain in her knee, she ran for the stairs.

Chapter Thirty-five

An arm snaked around her waist before her foot hit the first step. Cree swung her up and around, planting her on her feet in front of him. "Nothing is more important than seeing to your wound."

She shook her head, pointed toward Torr who approached them along with Sloan, and then she pointed upstairs and tugged at his arm.

Torr rushed forward. "Is she saying that my father is in danger?"

Dawn nodded.

Torr flew up the stairs, Sloan behind him and Cree once again scooped her up, though this time he flung her over his shoulder, the staircase too narrow for him to carry her in his arms.

Once in the hall he set her down and as soon as he did she ran to catch up with Torr and Sloan. Cree shook his head as he chased after her.

Dawn entered the room to find Torr staring down at his still unconscious father and Sloan glancing about, though no one else was there. Dawn pushed Torr out of the way and dropped down to her knees, though winced when her wounded knee hit the floor.

Cree mumbled and reached down for her, but she brushed his hands away and dropped her head down to search under the bed, having last seen the vial on the floor by the bed. She didn't find it and she feared the culprit may have already given the poison to Kirk.

She looked up at Cree with worried eyes and he slipped his hands beneath her arms and eased her up on her feet.

"What do you look for?" he asked.

She held two fingers not far from each other and with two more fingers from her other hand, she demonstrated the width.

"A vial?" Torr asked.

She nodded and gestured how she saw it in the cleric's hand and how he dropped it when he held a dagger to her stomach.

Cree's face turned red with fury. "He held a dagger to your stomach?"

Dawn nodded and also gestured how the cleric threatened to slice Elwin's throat.

Several oaths slipped from Cree's mouth before he said, "The bastard is lucky he's dead or he would have been begging for mercy that I would have never granted him."

Torr bent over his father and felt his lips. "They are dry, but it has been some time since Dawn was here."

"Look around," Cree ordered. "A servant may have come in since then, and perhaps didn't see it and accidentally hit it with her foot or placed it somewhere. Not you," Cree commanded sharply when Dawn turned to help. You have been through enough and you have suffered an injury that needs tending."

Dawn tried to protest, wanting to help.

"Don't bother arguing. Sit and rest until Elsa gets here to tend your wound."

Dawn raised her hand but the warning look Cree shot her made her think twice and so she sat on the chair near the hearth while the men searched. She turned to the side for privacy to raise her skirt and have a look at her wound, since a twinge of pain had remained with her, when something sparkled from where the stone met the wood plank floor. She peered down and there snug in the groove was the vial. She picked it up and held it high as she turned around.

Cree took it from her. "We're going to use this as bait."

And they all listened as Cree laid out his plan.

~~~

Lady Ann patted Lucerne's hand offering comfort as they sat beside each other on the dais, the Great Hall filling for supper. "Do not worry, my dear, all will be well."

Lucerne did not respond; she rubbed at her aching temples.

Cree and Sloan joined them as did Torr.

"Has Kirk improved?" Lady Ann asked of Torr.

Torr smiled. "He has stirred and his eyes have fluttered, as if he fights to open them. Elsa feels he will wake soon."

Cree reached out and placed the vial next to his tankard. "Kirk was lucky. We found this poison the imposter cleric intended for him."

Lady Ann gasped. "How awful. Thank God Kirk is safe."

Lucerne stared wide-eyed at the vial and shook her head, then turned away.

"Yes," Torr kept his smile firm. "Father should wake soon and will tell us exactly what happened in the stable."

Color drained from Lady Ann's face and her shoulders slumped. "If only I had arrived at the stables a bit sooner. I may have been able to prevent the fatal incident from taking place."

"You cannot blame yourself and at least the culprit has been caught," Torr said.

"Nothing makes sense," Lucerne said. "Father is dead and why? What made him and Kirk McClusky fight? And a cleric who is no cleric? And why were there attempts on Dawn's life?" She shook her head. "It is all madness." She rubbed at her temples. "I must excuse myself, my head aches unbearably."

Lucerne stood, not waiting for Cree's permission, though she swayed a moment, as if she was about to faint and her hand reached out to the table near Cree to steady herself. Cree grabbed hold of her and signaled with a nod to Sloan. He reached her side and with a gentle arm around her waist helped her from the room.

"It is good that this nasty ordeal is finally at an end. Now Kirk's daughter will get what is rightly due her."

"Yes, Dawn will finally get what she so richly deserves... a titled husband. She and I will wed as soon as I contact the King and settle the details."

"And Lucerne?"

"I'm sure some kind of arrangement can be made for her, and then you and Kirk can finally be together."

Lady Ann lowered her head. "After an appropriate time of mourning, I cannot sully Roland's good name, though the wait will be difficult. I had thought I had successfully put Kirk from my mind, but when I saw him again after all this time, I knew my love for him had never died."

"Of course, when the time is right," Cree agreed.

Lady Ann dabbed at her tear-filled eyes. "This day has been too much for me. I beg that you excuse me."

"By all means, Lady Ann," Cree said, "you truly have yet to grieve."

She stood and stopped beside Cree. "Thank you, my lord, you have been most gracious."

Cree watched her slowly leave the room and when he glanced back at the table he saw that the vial was gone. "Damn." He turned to Torr. "Did you see which one took the vial?"

Torr shook his head.

"Well it shouldn't be long before we find out which one is behind it all."

~~~

Dawn was safely tucked in Cree's solar without a guard outside the door. Cree hadn't wanted anyone to know where she was and a guard outside the door would certainly give her presence away. She couldn't wait in his chambers since men were busy repairing the secret passageway, boarding it up until a more permanent fix could be made.

She wondered who the culprit would be, Lady Ann, her true mother, or Lucerne or perhaps the two women had worked together and partnered with Lucerne's father to see Dawn dead. She could not wait to learn the truth and for all of it to be over.

With a silent sigh she took a seat in front of the hearth to wait. The day had been long and filled with so much pain and sorrow for so many. She had made certain that word had been sent to Lila to let her know that she was all right or else as soon as Lila had heard of her abduction she would have been pounding at the keep doors.

It was so very nice to have such a good friend and to have added friends along the way. Even though it had been an ordeal since meeting Cree, she was blessed and grateful that he had entered her life, and she was ever so grateful that love had brought them together.

Her eyes drifted closed and her head lolled to the side. The fire's warmth, a soothing brew, her knee tended to and the troubled day behind her all served to relax her enough for sleep to claim her.

The rap at the door startled her awake and she hadn't been sure how long she had slept. She hurried out of the chair with a stretch of her sore neck, which lead her to believe she had slept for a while in the uncomfortable position. The culprit had surely shown herself by now. She hurried to the door eager to find out and lifted the latch. She was more than surprised to see Lady Ann standing there.

"I am so sorry for everything," she said and rushed into the room shutting the door behind her.

Dawn shook her head, shaking away the last of the sleep that muddled her mind.

She reached out to take Dawn's arm but instinct had Dawn backing away from her.

"Good lord, it's been a dreadful day, but it's over and done now." Lady Ann smiled. "And life can finally go on as it should... after you're dead." She raised her hand that had been hidden in the folds of her gown and grasped tightly in it was a dagger.

Dawn stared at her mother. She hadn't wanted her when she was born, she had hired men to see her dead and now with no one left to help her, she planned to kill her daughter herself.

"If only you had been born a lad," Lady Ann all but spit out the words like a snake spewing venom.

Dawn took another step away from her, her mind quickly calculating different ways to protect herself against the crazy woman, and hopefully biding time. Cree would check on her to make sure she was all right or at least he would have someone check on her. Either way she needed time.

She raised her hands, palms up, and shrugged wanting to know why.

"I suppose I should at least give you an explanation. That fool husband of mine could not sire a child so I had no choice but to find someone to do it for him. I could not believe my bad luck in choosing a man who had an affliction that ran through his family. I prayed that you would be a boy, but luck was not with me that day. I would have seen you dead, but that fool Mary is a loving soul and protected you as soon as you were out of me. So like an *unselfish* mother I sent you away, never expecting to hear from you again. Imagine my surprise when Colum informed me of a dumb lass residing in Dowell, on Gerwan land.

"Don't think because I waste my time explaining it all to you that you will be rescued. Cree and his cohorts hide in wait for someone to poison Kirk. The fool doesn't realize that it is you I want dead; I could care less about Kirk, though I will see to his demise in time."

Dawn had to keep her talking while she tried to see if there was anything in the room that she could use as a weapon to defend herself. But she needn't worry about keeping her talking. It seemed that Lady Ann had much to say."

"I did not wed a fool, work, and sacrifice all these years to have my wealth and lands striped away. Roland could not forgive the King for turning his lands over to Cree. His constant talk of gathering clans and reclaiming his land from Cree would have left us with nothing. The fool couldn't see that Lucerne's marriage to Cree would be a great benefit to us. The King favors Cree and the clans respect his strength. And Cree would have easily squashed any attempt to take his newly acquired lands. Roland had to go. Unfortunately, Kirk entered the stables at the wrong time and like an idiot tried to help Roland. When I came upon the scene I was quite pleased with Philip, Lucerne's father. He had not only carried out our plan of killing my husband, but he also saved me the trouble of having to deal with Kirk."

She shook her head. "How stupid of us it had been to assume him dead. One more good whack to the head and then there would have been only you to deal with. I had already laid plans to do away with Philip. I wisely learned about plants. Poison being an easy way to rid oneself of difficult people. Once we fashioned the plan to abduct you from the keep, it was easy to make certain that his flask was filled with a lethal poison. I knew when Philip first made himself known to me, demanding things in return for his silence, that I could not let him live, though I could use him to my advantage. I explained that all wealth would be lost if you were left to live. And so I sent him to hire men to see to the task, which proved a complete failure."

Dawn could not believe that this woman who could kill and deceive so easily had given her birth. She thanked the heavens that Lady Ann had sent her away and that a loving and caring woman had raised her. And if she thought it was going to be easy to kill her than she was even crazier than Dawn had thought.

"I can see in your eyes that you think to best me," Lady Ann said with a smug grin. "Others have thought the same, Bree for one and that fool man of hers. All the lass had to do was keep giving Lucerne the potion that kept her confused until I arrived, and of course try to poison you, and what does she do? Almost kill Cree with the poison meant for you. Philip taught her a good lesson for that mistake and the beating was easy to blame on Lucerne. But then I discovered that that stupid man of hers had showed up to help her and had broken in through the secret passageway so that Bree could give him shelter from the storm. I had Philip make it perfectly clear what would happen to the two of them if they did not do as they were told."

Lady Ann shook her head in disgust. "But what does the stupid lad do, he wounds himself while attempting to kill you, in hopes of saving the woman he loves. Unfortunately, Philip completely lost his temper with the lass when he found out and beat her to death." Lady Ann shook her head again. "I knew then and there he had to be done away with or I would live to regret it."

Dawn's heart ached for Bree who had little choice but to obey or suffer the consequences. And how hard for the man she loved to stand by and not be able to save her. What was it that Cree had said to her? *A man who does not stand for the woman he loves is no man at all.* Bree's young man had stood for her even as he lay dying and a tear slipped from Dawn's eye for the young couple that never got to live and love.

"I've wasted enough time, though now you understand the lengths I would go to, to keep what is mine. With you gone there is nothing preventing Cree from wedding Lucerne. The King will command it. The land will then be secured and I will retain my title and home and I will finally be free of a husband's dictate. Now I've said enough; it's time for you to die."

Dawn raised her hand gesturing, though Lady Ann shook her head.

"I do not understand you," Lady Ann snapped.

Dawn pointed to her, the dagger, and then herself and shrugged.

Lady Ann scrunched her brow. "You wonder who will be blamed for your death?"

Dawn nodded.

"That's easy. Another culprit who has yet to be caught and of course I will have seen him run off and give a good description."

Dawn shook her head.

"Of course everyone will believe me. I will play the part well of a grieving mother."

Dawn laughed silently and Lady Ann grew furious.

"Enough," she said through gritted teeth. "It is time for you to finally die. Something you should have done at birth."

●   ~~~

Cree waited with Torr just inside the room next to where Kirk rested. Sloan and Elwin were positioned across the hall in another room. The doors stood slightly ajar as they waited for either Lucerne or Lady Ann to appear.

There was complete silence. No one uttered a sound or made a move and Cree took the time to think about all that had happened. He had yet to hear from Elsa as to whether Lucerne was being poisoned. It would be easy to slip something into the brew that had been given to her time and again.

Cree startled, jarring Torr.

"What is it?" Torr asked anxiously.

"The brew," Cree said, though Torr did not understand. "It had been something that had used before Lucerne was born. That means..."

Cree raced from the room.

~~~

"I'll make it quick," Lady Ann said. "After all you have suffered enough being voiceless."

Anger was a good deterrent to fear and propelled Dawn into action as Lady Ann ran at her, she grabbed for a tankard that had been left on the arm of one of the chairs and swung it at the dagger that was about to pierce her stomach. It flew out of her hand to the floor.

Dawn wasn't surprised that her mother didn't cry out in pain or that her face raged red with anger. The woman was demented and she wasn't about to let anything stop her from killing Dawn.

Dawn thought otherwise and lunged for the dagger.

Lady Ann did the same.

They both dropped to the floor, their hands reaching out in unison for the dagger. It skidded out of their reach as they tried to prevent each other from getting it. Lady Ann pounced on Dawn and lashed out at her face with clawing hands.

Dawn blocked her wildly flaying hands with her arms and rolled to her side forcing Lady Ann off her. She jumped, with a stumble, to her feet and her eyes turned wide when she saw that Lady Ann had retrieved the dagger.

"Damn you, die!" she hissed and rushed at Dawn.

Instinct took over and Dawn side-stepped the frantic woman, grabbed her wrist and held the dagger at bay. Lady Ann twisted with such strength that it knocked them both to the floor, the dagger pointed at Dawn's stomach. Dawn didn't hesitate, she twisted her mother's wrist and sent the dagger into her throat. Blood spewed all over Dawn's face and she watched the woman's eyes spread wide in shock, and then collapse on top of her.

Her breath caught and she closed her eyes; she had just killed her mother.

The door swung open but Dawn didn't turn her head. She was too numb to move.

Cree roared out Dawn's name and she was sure that this time he had splintered some of the rafters.

All Cree could see was blood and Dawn not moving. He flew to her side, dropping down on his knees. "I forbid you to die. I forbid it," he yelled grabbing her hand.

She opened her eyes and smiled. That was her Cree, demanding she obey him even when he thought her dead.

Relief flooded him and he quickly shoved Lady Ann's body off her before asking, "Are you hurt?"

She shook her head and he scooped her up in his arms.

Sloan rushed into the room and after a quick glance asked, "Dawn is all right?"

"She is a brave warrior who fought a good battle and won. See to this," Cree said with a nod to the body.

Sloan nodded and stepped out of the solar.

Cree walked to the door and stopped. "It is a good thing you obeyed me and didn't die, for I would have had to wage war with death itself to get you back. You're mine, you belong to me, and I'll never let you go."

Chapter Thirty-six

Two weeks later

"Why aren't you naked and in our bed?" Cree said walking over to where Dawn stood by the hearth in their bedchamber.

She didn't wait for him to reach her; she hurried to him and threw her arms around him.

"What's wrong?" he demanded holding her tight.

She shook her head against his chest.

Cree scooped her up in his arms and walked to the bed to sit down with her in his lap. "I know it troubles you to see how Lucerne suffers when she was innocent in this matter, but only time will heal her. Elsa said that the potion Lady Ann had been feeding Lucerne, to keep her confused and doubtful, had been so potent that she must take another potion to help with the problems it caused. That was why she was having such bad headaches and her emotions were so erratic. Bree had changed the potion hoping to help Lucerne regain her old self, though I wonder if she will ever be herself again after finding out about her true identity and the circumstances surrounding it."

Dawn nodded, though couldn't help but recall how Lucerne had clung to Sloan when she had been informed of Lady Ann's death and the circumstances surrounding it. She hadn't cry, hadn't say a word, she had simply clung tightly to Sloan.

"From what Sloan tells me you and Lila have been a great help to Lucerne. He told me that she looks forward to spending time with you two and hearing all about her true mother. Magda has also been a great help to her," he said and nuzzled playfully at her neck.

She scrunched her shoulders against the titillating tickle that ran through her and gestured that he helped as well.

"At your insistence," he said kissing along her neck, "I allowed her to reside in the keep, though I would have preferred her in a cottage, until we see what can be done with her. An answer to the message I sent to the King informing him of everything should be here soon and I'm sure he'll have some suggestions concerning Lucerne's future."

Dawn grabbed hold of his face, stopping him from feasting at her neck, though she would have much preferred to let him continue. She pointed to him and then to her and then gestured a crown on her head and shrugged, her brow already scrunched in question.

"I have no doubt that the King will grant us permission to wed. Roland has sent a message along with mine claiming you as his daughter so it would be a good and satisfying union to the King. Besides, I informed the King that I would wed no other but you."

Her eyes turned wide in fright.

Cree laughed. "Do not look so fearful, I have demanded things from the King before and have gotten them. He knows I serve him well and so he tolerates me or perhaps he's fearful of the infamous Cree as so many are."

Dawn laughed, though it was silent, it was obviously a hardy one.

Cree scowled. "You are not fearful of me, lass?"

It wasn't the scowl that made her shiver but the burning passion that suddenly ignited in his dark eyes and ignited her own budding passion.

He brushed his lips over hers. "You are right to fear me, love, for I intend to stripe you bare and make endless love to you tonight."

She smiled and crossed her heart with one finger.

"Yes, I promise that tonight we will love like never before."

Dawn shivered and laid her hand over heart, and then placed it on his heart holding it there so that he knew how very much she loved him. It didn't surprise her when he did the same, their gestures speaking louder than words.

He stood and eased her to her feet, his hands going to the ties of her blouse and as he untied each one he followed it with a kiss to her chest until the last one exposed her breasts and he nuzzled his face in between the two, soft mounds, then kissed the tops of each before bringing his mouth to hers to kiss and whispered, "I'm going to feast on every inch of you tonight."

Dawn shivered in anticipation and licked her lips to let him know she intended to do the same to him.

"Damn, you grow me hard so fast that it hurts," he said and his hands moved to hurry to get her out of her clothes so that they could begin their feast.

A knock pounded at the door.

"Damn, I thought once out of that cottage I'd never suffer another interfering knock again."

Another rapid knock sounded.

"This better be important or whoever stands outside my door will suffer my never-ending wrath," Cree yelled out.

The door opened and Sloan walked in. He stood staring at Cree speechless.

Dawn grabbed hold of Cree's hand and squeezed.

"Tell me," Cree ordered grateful that the woman he loved was standing next to him.

Sloan hesitated obviously reluctant.

"Tell me, Sloan," Cree snapped sharply.

"Your sister has been abducted."

~~~~~~~~~~~~~~~

Coming soon, book three in the Highlander trilogy... Highlander's Captive.

Titles by Donna Fletcher

Single Titles

San Francisco Surrender
Untamed Fire
Rebellious Bride
The Buccaneer
Tame My Wild Touch
Playing Cupid
Whispers on the Wind

Series Books

The Wedding Spell (Wyrrd witch series)
Magical Moments
Magical Memories
Remember the Magic

The Irish Devil
Irish Hope

Isle of Lies
Love Me Forever

Dark Warrior
Legendary Warrior

The Daring Twin
The Bewitching Twin

Taken By Storm
The Highlander's Bride

Return of the Rogue (Sinclare brothers' series)
Under the Highlander's Spell
The Angel & The Highlander
Highlander's Forbidden Bride

Bound To A Warrior (Warrior King series)
Loved By A Warrior
A Warrior's Promise
To Wed A Highland Warrior

Highlander Unchained
Forbidden Highlander

About the Author

Donna Fletcher is a *USA Today* bestselling romance author. Her books are sold worldwide. She started her career selling short stories and winning reader contests. She soon expanded her writing to her love of romance novels and sold her first book SAN FRANCISCO SURRENDER the year she became president of New Jersey Romance Writers. Donna is also a past President of Novelists, Inc.

Drop by Donna's website www.donnafletcher.com where you can learn more about her, read Book News, find a printable Book List, and read her blog.

Want to be alerted to Donna's book releases? Sign up for Book Alert. Send Donna an e-mail at donna@donnafletcher.com with Book Alert in the message box and you're all set.

Made in the USA
San Bernardino, CA
12 December 2015